Harry Bowling was born in Bermondsey, London, and left school at fourteen to supplement the family income as an office boy in a riverside provisions' merchant. He was called up for National Service in the 1950s. Before becoming a writer, he was variously employed as a lorry driver, milkman, meat cutter, carpenter and decorator, and community worker. He lived with his wife and family, dividing his time between Lancashire and Deptford before his death in 1999.

HARRY BOWLING

When the Pedlar Called

headline

First published in 1998 by
HEADLINE BOOK PUBLISHING PLC

This edition published in paperback in 2016 by
HEADLINE PUBLISHING GROUP

2

Cataloguing in Publication Data is available from the British Library

ISBN 978 0 7553 4047 7

Typeset in Times by Palimpsest Book Production Limited,
Falkirk, Stirlingshire

Printed and bound by CPI Group (UK) Ltd, Croydon, CR0 4YY

MIX
Paper from
responsible sources
FSC
www.fsc.org   FSC® C104740

Headline's policy is to use papers that are natural, renewable and
recyclable products and made from wood grown in sustainable forests.
The logging and manufacturing processes are expected to conform to
the environmental regulations of the country of origin.

HEADLINE PUBLISHING GROUP
An Hachette UK Company
Carmelite House
50 Victoria Embankment
London EC4Y 0DZ

www.headline.co.uk
www.hachette.co.uk

To my wife Edna
with my love.

Prologue

The warm summer sun was climbing into a clear sky as the people of Quay Street went off to work on Friday morning. Mrs Simms was busy sweeping the dust and grime from her doorstep and Mrs Metcalf set out for the shops, while one or two women stood at their front doors chatting to their neighbours, and Iris Meadows delayed the milkman as usual with her latest piece of gossip. It was the usual scene in a normal, nondescript Bermondsey backstreet which had survived the Blitz and was now in the front line once more, since the first flying bomb had roared over and dived into the Thames less than four weeks ago. Hidden by a large wharf at the end of the turning, the river betrayed its presence with a subtly pervasive smell of sour mud, and the tall arms of the quayside cranes rose up beyond the closed gates of the wharf yard.

'I wouldn't 'ave believed it if someone 'ad told me,' Iris was going on, 'but I saw it wiv me own eyes. I really don't know what this street's comin' to.'

George Price had his eyes fixed on the gently swaying crane

1

hawser and he shook his head slowly to let the widow Meadows know he was paying attention to what she was saying. 'Must 'ave bin quite a shock,' he ventured.

'Shock? I'll say it was a shock,' Iris retorted with a formidable look on her face. 'I just 'appened ter go ter the winder ter straighten the curtains when I saw 'er staggerin' past. Pissed out of her brains she was. She could 'ardly stand. I thought she was gonna end up in the gutter. 'Ow she reached 'er front door wivout fallin' arse over tit I'll never know. That was bad enough, but standin' there outside 'er door doin' a striptease was disgustin'. Mind you, I always knew Bel Fiddler was a brazen 'ussy, but that was shockin' be'aviour, even by 'er standards.'

George Price hid a grin. 'Didn't anyone try ter stop 'er?' he asked.

'Not till she was down to 'er knickers,' Iris replied, 'then 'er sister Chloe came out and dragged 'er in the 'ouse. What was she finkin' about? Gawd knows who else saw 'er. People must 'ave bin lookin' frew their curtains, what wiv the noise she was creatin'.'

The dairyman made to move on by rattling the crate of empty bottles he was holding. 'Oh well, I'd better be settin' off,' he said. 'I don't want the sun warmin' the milk or I'll be for it when I get ter Sumner Buildin's.'

The widow Meadows had a few more pieces of gossip for the kindly, patient milkman but she desisted with a little sigh. It'll keep for another day, she thought as she watched him lift the shafts of his barrow and lean his weight against the load.

It had started off a normal morning in Quay Street for most, but it didn't seem like a regular workday for Nell Bailey as she came down the stairs at number 6 and slumped into her easy chair. Usually hale and hearty, Nell felt decidedly under the weather and gratefully took the mug of steaming tea from

Josie, her eldest daughter. 'Me froat's like sandpaper,' she groaned, 'an' I feel like I've bin kicked from piller ter post.'

'Sounds like the 'flu,' Josie said with concern. 'Why don't yer take the day off an' go back ter bed? I'll look in at dinnertime an' get yer some soup or somefing.'

'Nah, I'll be all right once I rouse meself,' Nell replied. 'Pass me down those Aspros from the mantelpiece, luv.'

'I shouldn't take them on an empty stomach,' Josie warned. 'Why don't yer 'ave a slice o' toast first?'

Nell nodded unenthusiastically and cursed her luck. What a time to get sick, she thought. It was Friday and all week she and her machinist workmates at Rayburn's had been going flat out on a new clothing contract, which meant that their bonus earnings could break all records. Missing work today would put a large dent in her paypacket, which was bad enough, but having to spend the day in bed was unthinkable. Even after the birth of each of her children she had been up and about the next day. 'It's standin' talkin' ter that silly old bitch Dot Simms,' she growled. 'She was full o' cold, coughin' an' bloody splutterin' all the time she was talkin'. It was all a load o' nonsense anyway – as if I was interested in 'er personal life. I got troubles o' me own.'

Josie smiled as she went out into the scullery to put some bread under the gas-stove grill. Her mother was a soft touch for everyone and always willing to listen to their troubles. It was just the way she was feeling that made her talk so. 'Want some more tea, Mum?' she called out.

'Nah, I'll get dressed while yer do that toast,' Nell told her.

By seven thirty Nell was feeling a little better. 'I'll be all right,' she declared. 'At least I'm sittin' down all day. I'll take some more Aspros wiv me.'

As Nell made to leave Kathy came down the stairs with a gaping yawn. 'I wish it was Saturday,' she groaned, pulling her cotton dressing gown more snugly around her slim figure.

'Work's fer fools an' 'orses.'

'Well, yer better put yer nosebag on then,' Josie said, grinning at her.

'Why are yer always so cheerful in the mornin's?' Kathy moaned.

'It's anuvver day an' the sun's shinin,' Josie said with a flourish.

'Get 'er,' Kathy growled. 'Are yer seein' that Johnny Francis again ternight?'

'Yep.'

'I thought yer would.'

'What's it ter you?'

'Its nuffink ter me,' Kathy said sharply. 'I never fancied 'im anyway. Too much of a show-off fer my likin'.'

'Not now 'e's not,' Josie countered, glaring at her younger sister.

'Look, I'm off now, an' I don't want you two arguin', understand?' Nell scolded them.

As she left the house on that sunny morning Nell could hardly be expected to know what the day had in store for her and, as she made her way out into Jamaica Road to catch the tram to work, her thoughts centred on the absent member of her family, her husband Frank.

Easing back the joystick and levelling out his Spitfire, Squadron Leader Miller smiled to himself as he saw the white cliffs of Dover gleaming in the bright sun up ahead. About time, he thought. The fuel was getting dangerously low and he didn't want to be forced to land on some farmer's patch. It wouldn't exactly be the perfect ending to the day he was hoping for. The Messerschmitt he had downed during the sortie had taken his total to ten kills and Miller sighed contentedly as he glanced around the blue sky.

'Christ Almighty!' he said aloud as he saw the three flying bombs moving in a V formation at ten o'clock.

Without thinking he banked sharply and pulled back on the yardstick, climbing level and moving in close. There was no time to waste. Soon the bombs would cross the coast at Dover and be fired on by the shore batteries. 'Come on, Miller old son,' he mumbled through clenched teeth. 'You've heard the stories about tipping the bombs. Let's see if you're up to it. God, what a story for the mess. Might even get a bar to the DFC into the bargain.'

The fighter pilot neared the rear bomb and inched closer, resolutely forcing doubt out of his mind. He was flying at over three hundred miles an hour and to tamper with a contraption containing a large amount of high explosive at that speed was 'tantamount to committing *hara kiri*', the station commander had told them.

As he gently eased the stick over, Squadron Leader Miller felt sweat breaking out on his forehead. It would be a gamble, but he had to try. At least it would lengthen the odds of survival for those poor bastards in London, if he was successful.

'Steady, Miller. Good man, Miller,' he said, imitating Tubby Wilcox, his flying instructor.

The coast was coming ever closer and it had to be now or never. The Spitfire's wingtip was just beneath the flying bomb's and with a sharp jab at the stick he rolled his aircraft, glancing metal against metal. 'You did it, you beauty!' Miller shouted out in sheer exultation as he saw the flying bomb tip over and spiral down towards the Channel.

As he banked away from the coastal batteries Miller saw the puffs of white smoke mushrooming out around the two remaining flying bombs, then the ball of fire as one of the shells hit its target. The blast rocked his Spitfire but it did not worry the pilot. 'Just wait till I get back to the mess,' he chuckled, and burst into song. "'They'll never believe me, they'll never believe me.'"

Ralph Hennessey walked across the sun-baked tarmac at Lisbon airport and climbed the steps of the Londonbound clipper. Strapped to his wrist was a diplomatic bag, and tucked under his arm was an English translation from the Portuguese of *Dead Day in the Afternoon* by Emilio Scanchos, a famed writer who had shot himself soon after the novel was finished.

Hennessey was feeling nervous. He had never worried about flying, otherwise he would not have become a courier for the British Consulate in Portugal, but a country's neutrality did not seem to count for much where the Germans were concerned. Last year, he recalled, while Winston Churchill was meeting up with the army brass based in North Africa, a fat man smoking a large cigar was seen to board a plane at Lisbon. A secret agent relayed the information to his contacts and the plane was subsequently shot down over the Bay of Biscay by German fighters. Thirteen civilians perished, including the film star and matinee idol Leslie Howard, but the real target was in Gibraltar at the time, enjoying an aperitif at the British Embassy.

The clipper took off on time and climbed high and fast out to sea before adopting a wide looping trajectory designed to keep it outside the range of any hostile aircraft. Hennessey ate the disgusting meal and drank the insipid coffee then settled back to sleep with the bag resting at his feet and the novel in his lap. Later that afternoon the clipper landed safely at the RAF airstrip at Croydon and the courier walked unconcernedly through the customs shed, gripping the handle of the bag and his personal bag, with the novel under his arm.

'Good book?' the customs officer inquired with a cheery grin.

'This novel contains the last thoughts of a madman actually,' Hennessey replied, smiling briefly at his private joke.

'How so?'

'The blighter who wrote it shot himself soon after. Stark raving mad apparently.'

'Intriguing.'

'I'll let you have it when I've finished with it,' Hennessey said flippantly, imagining what the man's face would look like if he had chanced to read it. There were certainly crazy thoughts within the covers of the book, but they had not all been penned by the author.

The customs officer turned his attention to the other passengers as the courier walked out into the balmy evening air and climbed into the waiting car. So far so good, Hennessey sighed; now came the important business, once he had signed over the diplomatic bag.

Dust had settled over the carnage and the rescuers were still digging for the remaining victims. Ten women had still to be accounted for and Rayburn's owner stood weeping unashamedly nearby as yet another call went out, 'Bring up a stretcher!'

The women had worked through the air raid, as was the custom during the flying-bomb attacks. Usually the raids were short lived, and the explosions were greeted with a shaking of heads, a few filthy epithets directed at the perpetrators, and words of sympathy for the victims. This afternoon however the victims were the machinists of Rayburn's themselves. Nell Bailey had felt a sudden shock of falling, a deafening noise in her ears and then blackness. Now, as she regained consciousness, she could see faces looking down at her and felt a soothing hand on her brow. Pain came suddenly, like a wave that pulsed through her and she groaned.

'We're going to give you something for the pain, so that you'll be able to sleep,' the surgeon informed her.

Sleep was the last thing Nell wanted at that moment. She wanted to know what she was doing there, and why she hurt so much? What had happened to her?

Soon after the surgeon had jabbed the needle into her arm her thoughts grew as heavy as her body and Nell's eyelids fluttered and dropped as the pain started to subside. 'We copped it, didn't we?' she managed.

'Sleep now, Mrs Bailey,' the nurse said quietly as she leaned over the bed, but Nell's eyes were already closed.

Chapter One

Josie Bailey set off to work at ten minutes to nine, after first rousing Tommy with a cup of tea and reminding Kathy that the hands of company clocks did not stand still. Tommy wasn't much trouble in the mornings, usually waking up as bright as a button, as Nell often remarked, but sixteen-year-old Kathy was quite different. She had found a job in the office of an engineering firm at Dockhead, a five-minute walk from the house, but she invariably left it till the last possible second before she left, despite any amount of coaxing and cajoling.

Josie walked out of Quay Street into the traffic noise of Jamaica Road and turned left towards Rotherhithe Tunnel. She had been with J. Wilkins and Sons for two years now and was happy in her job as a sales assistant at the paint firm, handling phone orders from builders and decorators. It was an old-established concern that had remained in Bermondsey during the Blitz and there was a distinct family atmosphere about the place.

'Mornin', luv. You're lookin' very bright an' breezy,' Tom Clary the warehouse foreman remarked.

Josie gave him a sweet smile and raised her eyes in reply.

Tom was acceptable in small doses, she felt, but not one to give any sort of encouragement to.

Two other girls shared the small sales office and they were both at their desks when she walked in.

'Mornin', Josie. Anuvver day, anuvver dollar,' Gwen Simpson sighed as she filed away at her fingernails.

'Mornin', Gwen, mornin', Mary,' the young woman said cheerfully as she slipped in behind the desk and adjusted her summer dress over her knees.

Mary looked up with her large dark eyes and mumbled a reply, which elicited a wry smile from Gwen. 'I don't fink our Mary's very 'appy this mornin',' she remarked. 'They've 'ad a row.'

'You an' Bert?' Josie said, trying to look surprised.

Mary's round face was full of misery and she lowered her eyes again to the telephone at her elbow as though willing it to ring. 'Selfish git, that's what 'e is,' she complained. 'Wants everyfing 'is way. I don't seem ter count any more where 'e's concerned. I told 'im straight . . .'

Mary's words tailed off as Oliver Wilkins walked into the room. The eldest son of John Wilkins the owner, he was working hard to become as dynamic as his father, but still had some way to go. 'Morning, ladies,' he blustered. 'Very good figures last week and we topped the target last month, so let's see if we can do the double this month.'

'I had a call from Galbraith's as soon as I walked in this morning, Mr Wilkins,' Gwen said in her telephone voice, fluttering her eyes at the podgy, sandy-haired young man. 'They're ringing back later with an order.'

'Well done, Gwen, keep it up,' Oliver said brightly as he turned on his heel.

'Stupid prick,' Gwen growled. 'Just imagine goin' out on a date wiv 'im.'

'I wouldn't turn 'im down,' Mary said.

'No, I don't s'pose you would,' Gwen said out of the corner of her mouth. 'Trouble wiv you, Mary, is yer not particular enough.'

'Yes, I am.'

'No, you're not. Look at Bert.'

'An' what's the matter wiv Bert?'

'You tell me. You're the one always slaggin' 'im off.'

'Come on, ladies, let's stop this bickering and get some ordering done,' Josie bellowed, mimicking Oliver Wilkins.

The morning passed quickly enough, and after lunch at a local cafe the three young women walked back to the office through the bright sunshine.

''As anyone realised there's bin no air-raid warnin's this mornin',' Gwen remarked.

'Yeah, I was just finkin' that but I didn't wanna put the mockers on us,' Mary replied.

As they reached the firm the siren blared out.

'I wish you'd kept yer thoughts ter yerself,' Mary grumbled.

They hurried under cover and for the next few minutes the ominous roar of a flying bomb grew louder as it arrived low in the sky above. The young women looked at each other in a frightened silence and as the throaty roar spluttered and died they held their breath. The muffled explosion rattled windows and Mary brought a hand up to her mouth.

'More lives lost,' Gwen groaned. 'When's it all gonna end?'

The all-clear sounded a few minutes later and the sales team went back to work, fielding constant telephone calls. At three o'clock the canteen assistant brought in cups of tea and Josie leaned back in her chair and hunched her shoulders. 'I don't fink we're gonna 'ave any trouble toppin' last month's figures,' she remarked. 'These phones 'aven't stopped ringin'.'

Suddenly the air-raid siren wailed out once more and Mary

11

looked from one to the other. Nothing was said as the three waited for the usual roar, each tormented by their own thoughts and fears for their loved ones. The flying bombs were indiscriminate, falling in a fatal dive once the engine cut. Hospitals, schools, dwellings: none were exempt from destruction.

''Ere it comes,' Gwen said fearfully. The roar grew louder and then they heard the inevitable cough as the last of the fuel was burned up. The following silence seemed to last for ages, then a loud explosion rattled the windows once more and shook the floor beneath the three young women.

'That one was even nearer,' Mary said. 'I'm scared.'

'Ain't we all, luv,' Gwen replied calmly as she took out her nail file and set about tidying up her long talons.

Josie had to admire the brassy blonde. Nothing seemed to fluster her and she was the perfect foil to the nervous, grumpy Mary.

'Try an' relax,' Gwen told her, and a grin appeared on her face. 'Pull yer shoulders back an' sit up straight in that chair or you'll end up lookin' like Quasimodo.'

'Who's Quasimodo?' Mary asked.

'Don't you know anyfing?' Gwen berated her. ''E was the 'unchback o' Notre Dame.'

'I remember,' Mary said, brightening up a little. 'Robert Newton played the part, didn't 'e?'

'Charles Laughton,' Gwen said with a resigned sigh.

Being an astute and forward-looking businessman, John Wilkins had installed three separate lines in the office so that the callers could contact their regular salesgirl direct, and Josie had given her number to Kathy and Tommy as well as her mother in case of emergencies. If anything terrible was to happen during the air raids, at least she would get to know sooner rather than later. She had heard some horrendous stories of people going home from work to find their house in ruins and their loved ones killed.

'As I was sayin',' Gwen remarked sarcastically to Josie.

'Sorry, luv, I was miles away,' Josie replied quickly.

'Don't tell me. There you was, on the balcony starin' up at the moon an' the stars,' Gwen sighed. 'All of a sudden Paul Henreid strolls up an' lights two fags an' passes one over. "I love nights like this," 'e ses in that silky, sexy voice of 'is. "Nights like this are made for love."'

'Go on then,' Josie said smiling.

Gwen's face grew serious with concentration. ''E comes up close an' takes you in 'is arms an' you can feel the passion risin'.'

'Yeah.'

'Then 'e whispers, "Let me make love to you, my darling," an' you say, "Take yer lecherous 'ands off me, yer dirty ole git."'

'Trust you ter spoil it,' Mary said amid the laughter.

Suddenly the all-clear sounded and it was quickly followed by the phones ringing once more.

'Good afternoon, J. Wilkins here. How can I help you?' Josie said as she clasped the receiver to her ear.

'Josie, it's me, Tommy,' the tearful voice croaked. 'Somefing terrible's 'appened. It's Mum. Rayburn's got a direct 'it.'

'Oh my God!' Josie cried out in anguish. 'What's'appened to 'er?'

Tommy fought back his tears. 'I 'eard a big bang as me an' Denny Taylor were goin' fer a walk down ter the market an' then we 'eard people talkin' as they got off a tram so we run up ter the factory ter make sure. Some o' the ladies 'ave bin taken to 'ospital an' they're still diggin' fer ovvers.'

'What about Mum?' Josie almost screeched into the phone.

'I couldn't get any news,' Tommy told her. 'They wouldn't let me anywhere near the place.'

'Go 'ome an' wait there for me,' Josie ordered him. 'I won't be two minutes.'

Rayburn's lay in ruins, with rubble still being cleared from the road as the slow convoy of traffic inched by. Ambulances, stretcher vehicles and two police cars stood nearby while rescue workers tore away at the debris with bare hands. Two bodies lay on stretchers at the kerbside and another stretcher supporting an unconscious young woman was being gently eased down into willing hands as Josie and Tommy arrived at the scene. Charles Rayburn stood beside one of the ambulances and next to him a dust-caked policeman was poring over a list.

'Excuse me but my mum works 'ere,' Josie told the constable breathlessly. 'Mrs Bailey. Nell Bailey.'

The policeman gave her a sympathetic smile and quickly scanned the list. 'She was taken out alive,' he announced. 'She's at Guy's Hospital.'

'Was she badly 'urt?' Josie asked fearfully.

'I can't give you any details of injuries,' he replied. 'I'm sorry, luv.'

'Come on, Tommy,' Josie said quickly, putting her arm round the weeping lad's shoulders.

Guy's casualty department was a scene of frenzied activity when the Baileys arrived and Josie drummed her fingers impatiently on the counter of the reception as she waited for the nurse in charge to finish talking to another anxious inquirer. 'My mum – Mrs Bailey. Nell Bailey,' she almost shouted out nervously as the nurse turned to her.

Once again the terrifying seconds seemed to slow down and stop, then finally the nurse looked up from the register and smiled at her reassuringly. 'Your mother's in Blake Ward, second floor,' she said.

Josie could feel her heart pounding as she led Tommy up

the marble stairs to the second floor. 'We've come about Mrs Bailey,' she told the ward sister. 'She's our mum.'

'Come into the office, dear,' the sister said kindly. 'Your mother's been through a terrifying experience but her injuries are not as bad as could have been expected. She has a back injury and a lot of bruising but at the moment she's sleeping peacefully. It would be better if you could wait until visiting time tomorrow before seeing her, but if you'll take a seat I'll see if the doctor can have a word with you.'

As soon as the sister left Tommy looked up at Josie. 'I'm gonna go in the army an' fight the Germans, soon as I'm old enough,' he growled. 'It's not right ter bomb innocent people. We don't do it.'

Josie placed her hand on his head. 'Don't you worry, Tommy,' she said quietly. 'By the time you're old enough ter go in the army the war'll be over, an' yer gotta remember that lots of innocent people get killed an' maimed in war. When we bomb Germany some o' the bombs fall on schools an' 'ospitals; it's unavoidable.'

'But we don't send over flyin' bombs just ter kill civilians,' the lad persisted.

Before Josie could answer, the door opened and a red-eyed young doctor walked into the sister's office and smiled at them. 'So you two are Nell Bailey's children,' he said, sitting down on the edge of the desk. 'I'm Doctor Lewis, and I'm in charge of looking after your mother. Actually she was very lucky: there were no broken bones, though she has badly twisted her back and she was in a lot of pain. There's extensive bruising and contusions as well and she'll have to remain here until her back mends, which could take a couple of weeks. There is also the shock to consider. We'll have to keep an eye on her but we're giving her something for the pain and trauma and we don't think there'll be any other problems. Do you understand?'

They both nodded. 'Thank you, doctor,' Josie said smiling. 'Can we just take a peep before we leave?'

'Just a peek but don't wake her,' the doctor warned. 'The sleep will do her good.'

Tommy stood back from the bed, feeling awkward as Josie bent over the coverlet and looked down at the pale, peaceful face of her mother. 'We all love yer, Mum,' she whispered as she kissed her forehead with a feather-light touch of her lips. 'Kiss 'er goodnight, Tommy,' she urged her brother. 'Gently though. On 'er forehead.'

The young lad stepped forward and leaned over the bed-clothes. 'Night, Mum,' he murmured as he kissed the sleeping figure's cool forehead.

Nell Bailey's lips moved slightly and Josie pulled Tommy back from the bed. 'I 'ope we ain't disturbed 'er,' she whispered. 'Come on, Tommy, let's go before she wakes up an' sees us.'

Outside in the balmy evening air the sound of starlings resting from their labours in the tall plane trees chorused across the hospital square. Above, the sky was a patchwork of colour and a purple hue was beginning to herald the dark.

'She'll be all right, won't she?' Tommy said suddenly, his voice cracking.

Josie put her arm over his shoulders and pulled him to her as they walked home to Quay Street. 'Course she will. Our mum's tough. We're all tough, us Baileys.'

Tommy smiled up at her and then his face took on a serious look. 'We're gonna 'ave ter let Dad know,' he said.

'I'm gonna go an' see 'im later,' Josie reassured him. 'First though there's the tea ter get, an' we'll 'ave ter be careful what we say ter Kathy. You know 'ow hysterical she can get.'

As the two walked into Quay Street the neighbours were waiting.

'What's the news, luv?'

"'Ow is she, Josie?'

'We 'eard about Rayburn's gettin' bombed from the copper.' Charlie Fiddler came up to the inquiring knot of women. "'Ow is she, luv?' he asked.

Josie gave them all a brief account of her mother's injuries and Charlie smiled. 'Sounds like she's gonna be fine,' he said encouragingly. 'By the way, your Kathy's wiv our Sandra. I'll tell 'er yer 'ome. Better still, come on over an' 'ave a cuppa. I bet yer ready fer one. You can tell Kathy yerself then.'

Ralph Hennessey strolled out of the Foreign Office, made his way to a nearby pub named the Grapes and ordered a large brandy. So far so good. The diplomatic bag had been safely delivered and his own small bag containing personal belongings had been taken to the hotel by the chauffeur, who had been instructed to book the usual room for seven days this time. Normally Hennessey would return to Lisbon the following day, but he had taken some leave to attend to urgent matters quite different to his usual diplomatic business.

He stood at the bar counter with one arm leaning on the polished wood as he listened vaguely to the hubbub around him.

Two well-dressed men looking slightly the worse for drink leaned on the bar a few yards along. 'I tell you, Toby, the man's a lush. You can tell by listening to him. Every word's slurred and it sounds as if he's reading from a script.'

'They'll catch the blighter, mark my word,' Toby replied firmly. 'Lord Haw Haw be damned. I'd put the man up against the wall and shoot him dead without losing a minute's sleep, I really would, Cyril. He doesn't even rate a trial in my book.'

'Oh come on now, old man,' Cyril said, burping loudly before going on. 'That's where we excel. Good old British justice. Envy of the world, what.'

'Well, I still say it's too good for the likes of that treacherous rat,' Toby persisted. 'They should deal with him the way they do with the German agents. A trial *in camera* and then the firing squad.'

'Well, have it your own way,' Cyril conceded. 'Same again, Norman.'

Hennessey smiled cynically to himself. He had been lucky, it was true, but he had also refused to take any unnecessary risks. Every move he made was carefully calculated and planned beforehand, and this time extra care would need to be taken. He was going to meet with representatives of a powerful group whose influence was far-reaching, and the nature of their aims and objectives was such that he could quite easily be erased if it suited their purpose. For that reason Hennessey, or Werner Reismann as he was known in his native land, had well-laid plans for every eventuality.

Another double brandy, which he consumed quickly, then Hennessey strolled out into the warm night to hail a taxi. 'Stepney Reach,' he told the driver, and to dispel any questions as to why anyone would want to go to that part of London at night he added, 'I'm meeting an old friend at the Lighterman.'

'I know it, sir,' the driver replied. 'Nice pub. One of yer old river ones. Got a lot o' character. Yer should be careful though, what wiv you lookin' respectable like. There's some that might fink yer well-'eeled, if yer know what I mean.'

'Yes, I understand, and thanks for the tip,' Hennessey said. 'If you pull up outside the pub I won't be in any danger of getting robbed.'

'Stayin' the night, sir?'

'If I'm invited, but if not I'll ring for a cab.'

'It'll be the sensible fing ter do,' the friendly taxi driver remarked.

The agent leaned back in his seat. This meeting was merely

to test the water and he was not intending to move too fast too soon. The details of the plan he had brought from Lisbon remained inside the novel back at his hotel, and he would only divulge the full contents when he was sure of a committed response. One thing troubled him, and he tapped his fingertips together as he pondered. His contact had warned him that the group was in conflict over the question of collaborating with organisations professing other political and philosophical doctrines, and the way things stood at the moment they might well not accept the plan no matter how tasty the monetary carrot.

Hennessey thought about the information he had been given. The League of White Knights had been infiltrated by one of his countrymen and was indeed all it professed to be, a clandestine organisation, run on similar lines to the masonic orders but with total discretion on the part of the chairman and his cabinet, or cadre as they preferred to be called. The organisation's name was an allusion to their main aspiration: white supremacy in the British Isles. Anti-semitism was a central tenet of their Fascist ideology, and the group expressed a kinship with Franco and Mussolini in preference to Adolf Hitler and his henchmen. They dreamed of a utopia, of one day taking their seats in a Fascist government with a strong mandate from the citizens of the United Kingdom to make the country pure and virile once more, in a way that had not been possible since the slaughter of so many of the finest young men with the purest bloodlines during the Great War.

The taxi pulled up outside the Lighterman and Hennessey paid the driver, adding a fair-sized tip. It was going to be a very enlightening meeting, he thought as he pushed open the saloon-bar door and walked into the smoke-filled interior.

Chapter Two

It was dark outside as Nell Bailey's three children sat together in the neat and tidy parlour. Still shocked by what had happened to their mother, Tommy and Kathy listened quietly while Josie spoke.

'Mum's gonna be all right, but we've gotta make sure that she doesn't lay in that 'ospital worryin' over us,' she reminded them. 'That means we've gotta do all we can ter carry on as normal. Kathy and I'll go ter work as usual an' you, Tommy, 'ave gotta keep out o' mischief while yer on school 'olidays. No playin' on the barges, an' no lettin' that Taylor boy get yer inter trouble. I know what a darin' little sod 'e is from talkin' to 'is muvver. So be warned.'

Tommy nodded dutifully and Josie went on. 'Now we've gotta remember ter do all the fings Mum would do like payin' the rent, gettin' the shoppin' in an' keepin' the place nice an' tidy. We've all gotta muck in an' you, Kathy, will 'ave ter take your turn wiv the 'ousework. I can't be expected ter do it all.'

Kathy pouted. 'I do me share already.'

'Sometimes,' Josie corrected her.

'I can 'elp,' Tommy volunteered.

'You can 'elp by keepin' that bedroom of yours nice an'

tidy,' Josie told him. 'An' no leavin' yer fings lyin' around all over the place like you always do.'

Tommy nodded. 'What about Dad?' he asked.

'We'll talk about that later,' Josie replied. 'First we've gotta make sure that we all agree ter do what we can ter stop Mum worryin', an' that means all of us pullin' tergevver, instead o' bickerin' over every little fing.'

'We don't bicker all that much,' Kathy said quickly. 'It's only when yer keep on at me in the mornin's about the time. I always get ter work on time, an' anyway nobody bovvers if I'm a few minutes late.'

Josie smiled at her younger sister. 'Well, let's 'ave a truce. You promise me that yer'll get up in the mornin' a little more cheerful an' I'll promise not ter nag at yer.'

'Are yer gonna go an' see Dad termorrer?' Tommy asked.

Josie nodded and fidgeted in the armchair. 'Look, Tommy, why don't yer start by makin' us all a nice cuppa an' then when we're finished talkin' I'll do us some supper. An' mind 'ow yer go wiv that gas, it keeps poppin'.'

As soon as Tommy left the room Kathy fixed her sister with a hard look. 'I don't fink you should bower ter go over an' see 'im,' she said sharply. ''E's ended up makin' Mum's life a misery wiv 'is drinkin' an' 'e ain't doin' nuffink about it, that's fer sure.'

Josie knew it was pointless trying to justify their father's behaviour to Kathy. She did not know how his drinking problem had started, but perhaps it was high time she found out. 'Now listen ter me, an' don't interrupt,' she said firmly, shifting forward in her chair and clasping her hands together. 'When the war started Dad tried ter join up. Like most farvvers 'e was worried about 'is family an' what'd 'appen to us if the Germans got 'ere, but in Dad's case they wouldn't take 'im because o' the chest wound 'e got in the Great War, so 'e joined the rescue squad. I know from over'earin' 'im talkin' ter Mum that 'e went frew some terrible times diggin' people out from bombed buses, an' worst of all was the time the Rovver'ive Children's 'ospital got bombed. Dad's squad was the first on the scene an' they 'ad ter dig out all the little babies an' young children, a lot of 'em dead or terribly injured. Can you imagine what it must 'ave bin like fer 'im an' those men? Mum told me 'erself that Dad was ill fer months afterwards. 'E used ter wake up in the night screamin' out, covered in sweat. That's when 'e started drinkin'.'

'Yeah, but . . .'

'Kathy, just listen fer a minute, will yer?' Josie urged her. 'At first it wasn't a problem. Dad just went up the pub fer a couple o' pints in the evenin's. 'E said it 'elped 'im sleep better, but it slowly got ter be three or four pints, an' then durin' the day an' all weekends 'e'd be in the pub, tryin' ter blot out the memory o' those poor kids. All right, I know that Dad wasn't the only one who went frew that experience an' p'raps most o' the ovver men didn't take ter the bottle, but people are different, we all are. Everyone 'as a different way o' copin' wiv such fings, an' in Dad's case it was drink. I don't fink you know this, but one o' the men in Dad's rescue squad 'ung 'imself from 'is banisters a few weeks after.'

'I can understand what yer sayin',' Kathy cut in, 'but when 'e saw what effect 'is drinkin' was 'avin' on Mum, surely that was the time 'e should've pulled 'imself tergevver.'

Josie nodded. 'Yeah, it should 'ave bin, but the booze 'ad too much of an 'old on 'im by then. Dad did try. Mum told me 'e really made an effort, an' fer a week or two fings seemed ter get better, but 'e slipped back into it again an' then it went from bad ter worse.'

'All right, I know Dad never 'armed Mum or even laid a finger on 'er, but I can't fergive 'im fer the shame an' un'appiness 'e brought down on all of us,' Kathy said quietly. "'E was the laughin'-stock o' the street. Even the kids used ter foller 'im along the turnin' callin' out to 'im, "Pissy Frank" an' "drunken ole bastard". I cried when I 'eard 'em. It was terrible.'

Josie reached out and touched her sister's knee. 'It was a terrible time fer all of us an' Mum 'ad ter tell 'im ter go, ter save us any more pain, Kathy, but I 'appen ter believe that she could 'ave done more. We all could 'ave done more ter support 'im an' protect 'im from 'imself.'

'Well, I don't fink we could 'ave done any more,' Kathy replied quickly.

'Yes, we could,' Josie told her, 'but that's all water under the bridge now. Dad's gotta know about what's 'appened ter Mum an' first fing termorrer I'm gonna go over Stepney an' sort 'im out. Maybe this is just the fing. Maybe it'll turn out ter be a blessin' in disguise.'

Tommy came in carrying three mugs of tea on a small tin tray. 'I 'eard what yer said about Dad,' he remarked. 'I was listenin' outside the door. Can I come wiv yer, Josie?'

'Not termorrer,' she answered, smiling despite herself, 'but yer'll get ter see 'im soon, I promise.'

At number 24, Annie Francis sat knitting in the parlour, occasionally glancing over at her son John, who was slumped in the armchair facing her with his chin resting on his chest and his hands clasped as he snored gently. He had made quite a bit of progress since he'd got home and it was largely due to the Bailey girl, she had to admit. Josie was a nice kid and the only one to stay around after his return. Where were all those pretty girls who used to swarm around him before he'd been injured? They had no time for him now. Pity he hadn't taken more notice of Josie Bailey then. Still he was back from the beach at Normandy alive, and for that she had to be thankful, even if he had come home a physical and mental wreck, with chest wounds, a broken shoulder and shell shock.

Johnny Francis roused himself and glanced up at the clock on the mantelshelf. 'She's late,' he remarked, yawning. 'She said she was gonna fetch me that book from the library.'

'I don't fink Josie'll be callin' ternight after what's 'appened,' Annie replied.

'What's 'appened?' John asked.

'I told yer earlier.'

'Told me what?'

'About Josie's mum bein' caught up in that bombin' at Rayburn's,' Annie said puffing in exasperation.

'I don't remember.'

'Well, I did.'

'If yer did yer did,' John growled, 'but I don't remember.'

Annie shrugged her shoulders. 'You'd better rouse yerself an' get a shave before yer farvver gets in,' she warned him. 'Yer know 'ow 'e's bin gettin' on at yer ter tidy yerself up a bit.'

The young man got out of the armchair reluctantly. Shaving had been a problem since he'd got back home. His hands shook so much he was surprised he hadn't cut his throat before now. 'Yeah, all right, Muvver,' he sighed.

At number 18 the Fiddlers were having their supper and Charlie was complaining to his three daughters about the food. 'This cheese don't look too good,' he said with a frown.

'I only bought it last week,' Chloe told him.

'Well, it's goin' mouldy already,' he growled. 'Look at this.'

'I cut all the mouldy bits off,' Chloe replied.

'Well, 'ere's a bit yer missed,' he retorted. 'I dunno, I work 'ard all day an' what's me fanks: mouldy cheese an' stale bread fer supper. I'm beginnin' ter feel like Oliver Twist.'

''E don't taste very nice eivver, but at least there'd be no fat on 'im,' Bel said with a grin.

Charlie looked round the table at his three plump daughters as they sat there chuckling. 'D'you know what,' he said. 'I 'ave this dream: I'll come 'ome an' the 'ouse'll be all peaceful an' quiet, an' I'll pour meself a brown ale an' make meself a nice crusty bread sandwich wiv fresh cheese an' pickles, then I'll lean back in the armchair wiv me feet up an' listen ter some music wivout any interruption.'

'An' where are we in yer dream?' Sandra asked him.

'All married off,' Charlie laughed.

'We ain't in no 'urry ter piss off, Farvver,' Chloe told him indignantly. 'We like it 'ere, don't we, gels?'

'Too bloody true,' Bel replied.

Charlie pulled a face. 'You know what I'm gonna do?' he said.

'Do tell us, Farvver, we're all ears,' Sandra said quickly.

'Yeah, I bin meanin' ter talk ter yer about that,' he replied. 'Anyway I'm gonna call ole Stymie Smith in next time 'e comes round the street an' ask 'im ter make me an offer fer you three.'

''E ain't so old,' Bel cut in. 'A gel could do worse. At least 'e knows 'ow ter treat a woman.'

''Ow would you know?' Charlie asked.

''Cos I 'ad a drink wiv 'im the ovver night.'

'Yer never.'

'I did.'

'Not that night yer came 'ome pissed an' did that bloody striptease outside the front door?'

'Yup.'

'Well, you should be ashamed o' yerself,' Charlie growled. 'There's me tryin' ter bring yer up respectable an' yer just rub me nose in the dirt.'

Bel studied her long fingernails. 'Stymie wants me ter go fer a ride on 'is 'orse-an'-cart termorrer,' she told him.

'Oh my good Gawd,' Charlie groaned. 'You wouldn't, would yer?'

'What's wrong wiv that?' Chloe wanted to know. 'She'd be doin' no 'arm.'

'Let 'er, Dad,' Sandra piped up. 'She'd look the part on that cart, an' besides, Stymie might give 'er some tips on 'ow ter become a totter.'

'A totter!' Charlie roared. 'Women don't do tottin'.'

'There's a first time fer everyfing,' Chloe reminded him.

'Well, from now on I wash me 'ands o' the three o' yer,' the harassed father growled. 'You just do as yer like, but don't come cryin' ter me when yer drop yerself in the shite.'

'As if we would,' Bel said grinning.

Charlie had had enough, and as he climbed the stairs to the sanctity of his bedroom he realised only too well that he had lost the battle long ago. You're a silly old fool, he thought. What chance have you got to bring a nice lady home and impress her while those three harridans rule the roost. Start thinking, Charlie, or you'll have them under your feet for ever. And with that threat in mind he sat down on the edge of the bed and started to scheme.

Ralph Hennessey attracted little attention as he walked to the counter and ordered a pint of beer. The riverside pub was always full of strange faces; city workers took their ladyfriends there for a drink and rivermen rubbed shoulders with well-dressed customers, while the locals tended to shun the pub, feeling that it had not got a family atmosphere. It suited Hennessey and it suited the tall, distinguished-looking man with a white rose in his lapel who stood a few yards away.

'It's a nice night,' Hennessey remarked as he turned casually towards him.

'Ralph Hennessey?'

'The one and only.'

The man drained his glass and put it down on the counter. 'I'm going for a leak,' he said. 'Give me a few seconds then slip out. The lavatory's to the right but you'll want the stairs to the left.'

A few minutes later formal introductions were being made in the small sparsely furnished room above the saloon bar.

'My name is Anderson, Victor Anderson, and this is Sidney Holman and Ben Thorburn. Take a seat, won't you, Mr Hennessey.'

The courier did as he was bid and faced the others across the small bare wooden table. 'I'm honoured,' he answered, inclining his head. 'Finally, the chance to meet members of the League of White Knights.'

'I hope the information you have on our movement is favourable,' Anderson said.

'Yes, of course,' Hennessey replied. 'Obviously you guard the integrity of your organisation jealously and I respect that, but your past contacts with my people have led to some . . . mutual distrust. Since the beginning of hostilities things have changed, it's true, but nevertheless I trust your aims and objectives remain the same as those of the people I represent: a Fascist, nationalist government immune to the clamours of the international Jewish conspiracy.'

The grey-haired Anderson nodded, and his mouth curled in a brief smile. 'Only the methods are different, and such differences have led our countries into war.'

It was Hennessey's turn to smile. '*Lebensraum*, living-space.'

'Not forgetting your policy of incarcerating all undesirables, as opposed to our plans for compulsory repatriation,' the stocky Sidney Holman interjected. 'We have need of *Lebensraum* too, if you compare the size of our country to yours.'

Anderson raised his hand. 'We could quite easily get into a lengthy discussion about our differences, but time is a commodity we can't afford to waste, gentlemen,' he said with authority. 'As I understand it our motive in being here tonight is to listen to what you, Mr Hennessey, have to say concerning your plan and how it might be of mutual benefit to both our sides.'

Hennessey nodded. 'Back in my hotel I have a plan which was drawn up by the Fuehrer himself and countersigned by the chiefs of staff,' he began. 'Within a few weeks London will be targeted by the latest and most advanced weapon in our armoury, a weapon against which there is no defence, namely a ballistic rocket missile; and coming on the heels of the flying bombs the new weapon will be bound to spread panic. Also in the autumn, our forces under the new commander Von Rundstedt will begin a counter-offensive which will halt the Allied advance towards Germany. The objective of the Fuehrer's radical plan is to ensure that, at that moment, your country will sue for peace.'

The three men facing the agent stared at him intently and Ben Thorburn's dark eyes narrowed as he leaned his heavy bulk on the table.

'I'm just the courier,' Hennessey continued, 'a very small cog in the machine. All I need is for you to request to see the full details of the plan. That is my brief. What I can tell you, is that ample funds will be made available for your organis-ation. At this very moment half a million pounds in gold is lying in the vaults of a bank in Zurich, ready to be credited to an account named by you, after the successful implement-ation of our plan. There will of course be additional funds immediately available should you agree to go ahead. Twenty-five thousand pounds will be paid into a separate account in Switzerland for the pre-planning and acquisition of the requisite personnel. I myself will arrange to get it to you, via a transfer to an account in Dublin. Transfers between two neutral countries will pose no problem. And now, gentlemen, since I can see you are becoming a little impatient to learn where all this is leading, allow me to explain the crux of the plan. Essentially it is this . . .'

In the heavy silence that followed Anderson exchanged quick glances with his two companions and then his eyes fixed on Hennessey. 'Like you, we are just part players in all this,' he said quietly. 'We'll have to report back with all you've told us to a full League membership meeting, Mr Hennessey. If you'll let me know at what hotel you're staying we'll send a messenger with details of where and when we can next meet.'

'I'd prefer it if you notified the contact, bearing in mind that I do have to return to Lisbon on Sunday week,' the courier replied. 'I'm sure you understand my reasons for extreme caution. What I have would be damning to me, and to you too, once you became involved.'

Anderson looked at his two colleagues in turn and then nodded. 'All right. Perhaps in the light of these . . . er, proposals, it's a wise course of action. We'll be in touch within a couple of days, which only leaves me to say that the monthly meeting of the Stepney Green Bowling Club is now adjourned.'

Hennessey left Stepney for his hotel after last orders at the Lighterman, and as he leaned back against the leather cushion of the taxi he smiled to himself. The details of the plan contained between the pages of the novel were certainly damning, but until the strand of thin wire inside the spine was removed the book itself was lethal. Acid would destroy not only the incriminating pages, but also the hands and face of anyone meddling with them.

Chapter Three

The Quay Street folk were up and about early on Saturday morning. The widow Meadows was already cleaning the outside of her parlour windows with a belligerent look on her thin face and Bel Fiddler was standing opposite by her front door talking to Dot Simms, her next-door neighbour. 'The poor kid was frantic wiv worry an' she was cryin' 'er eyes out but me an' Chloe managed ter calm 'er down a bit,' Bel was going on. 'It was a good job me an' Chloe wasn't at work yesterday.'

'Was you off sick then?' Dot Simms asked, already knowing what Bel was about to say.

'Nah, we took the day off ter go after anuwer job.'

'Did yer? Ain't you 'appy where you are then?'

Bel pulled a face. 'Me an' Chloe got the sack, but don't put it around,' she replied.

'Whatever for?' Dot asked, looking suitably shocked.

The whole street already knew about the incident at the jam factory through Freda Baines at number 7. She worked at the same factory and had seen what happened herself, but each person she had told, which was almost everyone in the street, had been sworn to secrecy.

'The foreman on the boilin' floor's a pig an' 'e's always

sortin' me an' Chloe out fer all the dirty jobs,' Bel explained. 'Anyway we'd 'ad enough of it an' when 'e told us ter scrub out one o' the boilers we told 'im ter get somebody else ter do it. It ain't a woman's job anyway. There's fellers there ter do that sort o' fing.'

'So yer told 'im ter stick the job.'

'You bet we did,' Bel said throwing her ample shoulders back. 'You should 'ave 'eard Chloe go off at 'im. Did she give 'im a mouthful. "Clean the poxy boiler yerself, you dozy git," she said. "Yer takin' us fer a couple o' prats."'

Dot Simms already knew the full story but feigned ignorance. 'Good fer you,' she told her.

Charlie Fiddler shouted out something from inside the house and Bel pulled a face. 'I'd better go in,' she said quickly. 'I promised to iron 'im a shirt fer this mornin' an' I ain't done it yet.'

Dot grinned and crossed the street, only to be pulled up by Iris Meadows.

'Did you see 'er performin' the ovver night?' the widow asked.

'No,' Dot said with her usual innocent look.

'Pissed as a puddin' she was,' Iris muttered, nodding across the street.

'Who, Bel Fiddler?'

'Who else.'

'What 'appened?'

Iris Meadows folded her arms. 'It was gettin' late an' I 'eard this commotion outside, an' when I looked frew me winders I saw that prat strippin' off. In the street, would yer believe.'

'Good Gawd!' Dot gasped, knowing full well from living next door to the Fiddlers for the past ten years that anything was possible where they were concerned.

'She was down to 'er underwear before Chloe pulled 'er

in,' Iris went on. 'I blame Charlie Fiddler meself. 'E should
'ave given those gels of 'is a good 'idin'. I'd do it if they were
mine. They ain't too old fer a good wallopin'.'

Dot Simms felt that she was never going to reach the
market that morning, and when she saw Freda Baines coming
along the turning she took evasive action. 'I gotta run,' she said
quickly, thinking up a lie. 'My Albert's waitin' fer the mornin'
paper.'

'Can't 'e get it 'imself?' Iris said, still looking belligerent.

'Yeah, but I told 'im I'd get it fer 'im,' Dot replied. 'I let 'im
'ave a lie-in this mornin'. 'E's bin doin' a lot of overtime this
week an' 'e's played out.'

'Poor fing,' Iris mumbled to herself sarcastically as Dot
hurried away. 'A bit of extra work an' they're knocked out. Lazy
gits the lot of 'em.'

At number 6 Josie was getting things organised. 'Now look,
you two,' she announced. 'I'm gonna get down the market
before all the stuff goes. Kathy, you wash up the breakfast fings
an' Tommy, you go up an' tidy that bedroom of yours. It looks
like an 'erd of elephants trampled frew it. An' make yer bed
while yer at it. I'll change the sheets termorrer.'

'When yer gonna go an' see Dad?' Tommy asked her.

'As soon as the shoppin's done,' Josie told him.

'Why can't I come wiv yer?'

''Cos yer can't,' his sister said firmly. 'Look, when I come
back from shoppin' I'll give yer the money ter go ter the pie
shop fer yer dinner.'

Tommy seemed pacified but Kathy pouted. 'I don't wanna
'ave pie an' mash fer me dinner,' she said quickly.

'No one's sayin' you've gotta 'ave pie an' mash,' Josie
countered. 'I'll get me an' you somefing else.'

Kathy felt a little sorry for her surly attitude towards

her sister and she gave her a smile. 'You'd make a good mum,' she said.

Josie smiled back at her. 'We'll cope till Mum gets better,' she replied. 'It's just a question of us all pullin' tergevver, an' I know yer'll do your share.'

Kathy took the hint and started to tidy up the parlour while Josie went into the scullery to fetch her coat.

'I might be some time,' Josie remarked as she reached for the shopping bag. 'I promised ter get that book from the library fer Johnny.'

Kathy bit back on a sharp retort. 'Don't worry, I'll make sure Tommy does 'is room out,' she said.

Josie gave her a quick look. 'Don't wind 'im up, though,' she urged her. 'Try a little encouragement.'

The neighbours were quick to show their support as the young girl walked along the turning.

'I got some nice grapes fer yer mum,' Freda Baines told her.

'Give 'er our best when yer see 'er,' Gladys Metcalf said.

'Chin up, luv, she'll be right as rain soon, you'll see,' another called out.

Josie hurried out into Jamaica Road, and on her way to the market she called in at the library. Inside it was cool and quiet, with one or two old men scanning the newspaper boards and another elderly man sitting at a table, seemingly engrossed in a large volume.

'I've come fer the copy of *White Fang*,' Josie said smiling. 'You told me you'd 'ave it ready for me if I called in yesterday.'

The bespectacled library assistant touched her chin and looked bemused. 'Er, I'm sorry, what was the name?'

'Bailey. Josie Bailey.'

'Oh yes. I remember. *White Fang*. Now let me see, was it returned or not?'

Josie waited impatiently while the assistant flipped through a pile of books on the shelf behind her.

'I'm sorry, I'm afraid it's still not been returned,' she said finally. 'It should have been, it's overdue. Some people are so thoughtless. They seem to forget that other people might like to read the novel too.'

Josie looked undecided. 'In that case I'd better try an' pick anuvver one,' she sighed.

'I know we have one or two more by Jack London. Perhaps Ronald can help you.'

Josie saw the young man approaching and he looked a little flustered as the assistant beckoned to him.

'Can you help this young lady find something by Jack London?' she told him.

Ronald pushed his spectacles up on to the bridge of his nose and ran a hand through his thick sandy hair. 'I know we've got *Call of the Wild*,' he said. 'Then there's *The Sea Wolf*. If you'd like to follow me.'

Josie felt self-conscious with her high heels sounding loudly on the polished floor as she trailed in the wake of the enthusiastic young man.

'It's unusual for a young lady to go much on Jack London,' he remarked as he reached an aisle and put his hand on a shelf. 'What with all the blood and fur and guts flying about.'

'Actually it's not for me,' Josie explained. 'It's fer a neighbour who can't get 'ere 'imself.'

'Oh I see,' the young assistant replied smiling as he walked slowly along the aisle, his forefinger brushing the novels. 'Ah, here we are. *The Sea Wolf*. A grand story. A bit scary though, but then you won't be reading it, will you?'

'That'll 'ave ter do,' Josie told him. 'Fanks fer takin' the time.'

'It's a pleasure, Miss, er . . .'

'Bailey. Josie Bailey.'

'Do you come here often, for your neighbour I mean?' the young man asked, immediately regretting the cliche.

'About once a week,' she replied.

'This neighbour of yours must be an avid reader,' he said. 'It usually takes me a fortnight to get through a book, sometimes much longer, depending how exciting it is. I like Westerns myself, but unfortunately Western novels aren't exactly spilling off our shelves, as you can see.'

Josie hadn't noticed but she nodded. 'Well, fanks again,' she said smiling.

The young man wasn't finished. 'If you'll follow me I'll get it checked out quickly,' he told her.

Josie watched while he stamped the book, slipping the ticket into a small folder which he placed in a tray, and when he handed it to her he gave her one of his best smiles. 'I look forward to seeing you next week, Miss Bailey. That's if I'm still here,' he added.

'Oh?'

'Call-up,' he said importantly. 'I'm on tenterhooks waiting. Navy, as a matter of fact.'

'You'd better make the most o' civilian life then,' Josie said smiling.

'I'm sick and tired of it, to be perfectly honest,' he replied quietly with a conspiratorial wink. 'This job is the only one I've ever had since I left school. I really want to see some of the world, even if it is in the forces. Anything's better than this mundane, boring existence.'

Josie studied the fresh-faced lad with blue eyes which seemed full of gentleness and good humour and she felt suddenly sad. Johnny Francis had once had the same zest for life glowing in his eyes, and now he was a physical and mental wreck, struggling to remember the person he had once been.

What terrors and atrocities would be waiting for this pleasant young man once he was away from the normality he so eagerly wanted to escape, she wondered. 'Well, in case I don't see you again, good luck,' she told him.

'I don't think it'll be that quick,' he replied. 'I can see me still being here at Christmas, the way things are going.'

Josie gave him a parting smile and stepped out from the cool of the library into the sunlit Jamaica Road. Albion market was situated alongside the Rotherhithe Tunnel and by the time she arrived it was packed. News of her mother's injury had preceded her and she was obliged to tell several stallholders how things were, but she found it upsetting and was glad when she finally finished her shopping and set off home. She had to get over to Stepney before visiting the hospital and timing was going to be tight, she fretted. There was no point in doing things the other way round. By the time she reached her father he would most likely be sleeping off the effects of a lunchtime drinking session.

The St James's Church clock showed ten thirty and Josie bit on her lip as she turned into Quay Street. There wouldn't be much time to spend with him, she thought. None at all if her father wasn't at one of his usual haunts.

As she approached her front door she had to sidestep the tools which Billy Emmerson had strewn across the pavement while he serviced his motorcycle. 'I'm sorry, Josie,' he said quickly. 'By the way, I was sorry to 'ear about yer mum.'

The young woman gave him a warm smile. Billy was a nice lad who was forever tinkering with his beloved motorbike and she felt sure that any young lady with whom Billy got involved would surely have to take second place in his affections. 'I'm goin' in ter see 'er later,' she told him as she put the heavy shopping bag down by her feet and massaged her numb fingers.

'I could give yer a lift up the 'ospital if yer like,' Billy offered.

'It's nice of yer, Billy, but Kathy an' Tommy are comin' wiv me,' she replied, 'once I'm back from Stepney.'

'Yer dad?'

Josie nodded. The Emmersons were friends as well as neighbours and knew that Frank Bailey was now living across the water.

'I could run yer over there,' Billy suggested. 'It'd save time. Those eighty-twos ain't very reliable on Saturdays.'

She knew that he was right, but the thought of riding pillion on that sorry-looking contraption of his daunted her. 'No, it's all right, it won't take long,' she replied. 'Fanks anyway.'

'I've only bin mendin' a kinked fuel pipe,' he went on. 'The bike's runnin' like a dream really. Why don't yer fink about it? You could get cattled wiv those buses.'

'If I change me mind I'll let yer know,' Josie said with a smile as she picked up her shopping bag.

'I'll be 'ere,' he replied grinning.

Quay Street could not boast a corner shop but it did have what had once been a smithy, and was now the home of Stymie Smith and his noble steed, as the street's wag Wilco Johnson described it. At forty years of age Seth Smith, or Stymie as he was called, felt that he had inherited nothing but trouble when he bought the horse-and-cart from one of his uncle Broomhead's pals. Broomhead had had a good round and made a fair living totting around the Bermondsey backstreets and Stymie had got it into his head that he could emulate his uncle and do as well for himself, providing the old nag stayed the distance, but things had not turned out that way. Stymie lacked his uncle's craftiness and left it to providence whether the day was going to be a good one or a bad one, whereas Broomhead pushed his luck to the limit. 'If they ain't got nuffink ter get rid of I can't do anyfing about it,' Stymie often told his tired old horse as they plodded through the backstreets on bad days. He didn't know that when Broomhead wasn't doing too well he would resort to doorknocking instead of merely calling out for old lumber.

On Saturday morning Stymie had to pop back to the yard at the end of the turning to get another bag of chaff for his nag, who seemed to be reluctant to pull the cart more than a few yards without stopping for a breather. 'Get that down yer, yer lazy ole git,' the totter growled as he slipped the nosebag over the animal's head. 'When I've 'ad a cuppa an' a couple o' slices o' drippin' I'm gonna collect that ole scrap from the builder's yard in Weston Street an' yer better be more enthusiastic this time or I'll consider sellin' yer ter that cat's-meat man in Tower Bridge Road.'

The truth was that Stymie loved his old horse and fretted over him like a mother would her child. He considered the nag to be quite good-looking when he was currycombed, his mane plaited and hooves painted black, which admittedly wasn't very often, but it was going to be done this afternoon all ready for the jaunt up to Blackheath with Bel Fiddler.

As he climbed up into the seat and took up the reins Stymie was almost dislodged by the horse rearing up as Billy Emmerson kick-started his motorbike. The nag flailed his front legs and set off at a reasonable trot before Stymie managed to rein him in. ''Old up, yer scatty git,' he growled. 'Surely yer used ter that bloody idiot kickin' up a racket by now.'

The horse blew hard and shook his head and then Stymie raised his eyebrows in surprise as he saw Josie Bailey come out of her house and straddle the machine, holding the young man round the waist as they rode out of the turning.

'I fink I'll get rid o' you an' buy meself a motorbike,' the totter muttered, dreaming of roaring off with the buxom Bel Fiddler's warm body pressed snugly against his.

Chapter Four

When Josie walked into the house after her shopping trip she put the bag down on the parlour table expecting both Kathy and Tommy to come fussing like they always did when their mother returned from the market. Josie had not forgotten that they both liked apples and plums and she had made a point of getting some for them. It was quiet, however, and the young woman called out, 'Kathy? Are you there?'

A mumbled reply came from the scullery and when she went through she was surprised to see her younger sister sitting at the small table looking very sorry for herself. 'What's 'appened?' Josie said quickly.

Kathy looked up at her with tears in her eyes. 'It's Mum's best pot,' she answered in a choked voice. 'I couldn't 'elp it, honest, Josie. I was just cleanin' the dresser an' as I was dustin' the pot it fell out of me 'ands on the floor. It just 'appened.'

Josie gave her an encouraging smile. 'Look, it's only a little china pot. It's no big fing.'

'But it's Mum's favourite,' Kathy went on as the tears started to fall. 'She loved that pot. She said it was one o' the first bits o' china she got.'

Josie slipped her arm round her sister's shoulders. 'Now

you listen ter me,' she told her. 'Mum's not gonna be worried about that silly little ornament. She's got ovver fings ter worry about. Besides, if we'd 'ave moved it around somewhere Mum would never 'ave missed it, I bet yer.'

'Tommy made me feel worse,' Kathy said, wiping her eyes with the back of her hand. ''E told me I was a stupid, clumsy cow an' yer'd give me a good tellin'-off when yer found out.'

'Oh 'e did, did 'e?' Josie growled. 'Well, I'll 'ave somefing ter say when I see 'im. Where is 'e by the way?'

'The Taylor boy called fer 'im.'

'I 'ope 'e made the bed an' cleaned that room up first,' Josie said quickly.

'Nah, 'e said 'e'll do it later.'

'Oh right. Well Tommy's in fer a shock when 'e gets 'ome.'

'Could we buy Mum anuvver pot like that one?' Kathy asked.

'Look, just ferget it,' Josie urged her. 'Mum breaks fings. We all do. None of us are perfect. Now put yer face under the cold tap an' stop bein' so silly. By the way, there's some fruit in the bag. Come on, 'elp me unpack it.'

Time seemed to be racing and Josie became more and more agitated. Apart from the traipse over to Stepney, Johnny Francis would be expecting her to take his book in, especially as she hadn't called the previous evening. And there was Kathy. She seemed to be trailing behind her from room to room seeking more reassurance. 'Kathy, can yer pass me those ovver shoes from under the bed,' she asked as she sat brushing out her hair at the dressing table.

'Yer won't 'ave a lot o' time,' Kathy pointed out.

'I know,' Josie sighed. 'Look if I'm late gettin' back you an' Tommy go straight ter the 'ospital. I'll get a bus from the Tunnel an' see yer there.'

'When shall we wait till?' Kathy asked her.

'No later than twenty ter two,' Josie replied. 'I expect Mum ter be a lot better terday an' she'll be waitin' impatiently fer the visit. I don't want us ter be late.'

'If we do get there first shall we tell Mum where you are?' Kathy asked.

'Of course. Mum'll expect me ter let Dad know what's 'appened.'

Kathy watched her elder sister put on her shoes and straighten her stockings on her slim shapely legs. 'I wish I was as pretty as you,' she said suddenly.

Josie laughed aloud. 'You are. An' remember you're still growin'. When you fill out yer'll 'ave a lovely figure. I can see it comin' already.'

'Do you really fink so?' Kathy said, looking pleased with the compliment.

'Of course I do,' Josie said smiling. 'By the time you're eighteen yer'll be the prettiest gel round 'ere. An' then watch all the boys come callin'. Oh dear, look at the clock. I'd better get goin' or I'll never be back in time.'

As she hurried down the stairs Josie hoped Billy Emmerson was still outside, and when she opened the front door she was relieved to see him sitting on his motorcycle with his goggles up on his forehead chatting to a friend. 'Billy, is yer offer still on?' she called out.

'You betcha,' he said grinning.

'I'll just change me coat then,' she told him.

Billy slipped his goggles down over his eyes and kicked the machine into life, and when Josie clambered on he leaned round. ''Ave you ever bin on one o' these before?' he asked, and she shook her head. 'Well, there's nuffink ter be scared of. Just lean wiv me when we corner an' 'old on tight. Okay?'

Josie's reply was lost on the wind as they roared out of the street. She found the experience exhilarating after the first few nervous moments and soon they were travelling through the quiet Rotherhithe Tunnel which led out into Stepney.

'Where now?'

'Turn left, then second right.'

Billy steered the motorcycle into the side street and Josie pointed up ahead. 'Those buildin's,' she said, shouting to be heard.

The young man pulled into the kerb and cut the engine as Josie clambered off. 'Don't worry, I got all day,' he said grinning.

'I wish I 'ad,' she remarked with a quick smile.

As she hurried up the dusty wooden stairs to the first floor Josie could still feel the stinging sensation of wind on her face from the ride and imagined that her hair must look a mess. There was no answer to her first knock and she banged louder. The door opposite opened and a grey-haired old lady peeked out. ''E ain't in, luv,' she croaked. 'Went out early 'e did. I dunno where though. It ain't my place ter pry.'

Josie thanked the old woman and hurried back down the stairs. The next stop would be the Grapes, a little public house by Stepney Green, and Billy started the engine as soon as she emerged from the block. When they arrived Josie peered in through the door of the public bar but could not see her father. By now she was getting a little concerned. Where could he be?

'We could do a tour o' the local pubs if yer like,' Billy suggested.

Josie shook her head. 'No, I can't ask yer ter wait any longer,' she told him. 'I'm more than grateful fer the ride.'

Billy leaned back on his machine and folded his arms. 'I dunno what yer worried about,' he said, showing his strong white teeth as he grinned at her. 'I told yer already I got all day, an' I can't fink of a better way o' spendin' it than wiv you.'

'You are nice, Billy,' she replied, returning the smile. 'Can we try a couple more?'

'As many as yer like. Come on, jump on.'

At the third pub they found him, and Josie's heart sank as she caught sight of her errant father. He was sitting alone at a table looking very unkempt. His large hand was clasped round the pint glass on the table in front of him as though he was protecting it and there was a vacant glaze in his dark eyes.

Leaving Billy outside the young woman walked through to her father and touched his shoulder. 'Dad, it's me, Josie,' she said quietly, aware that people were staring over at them.

'Good Gawd! So it is,' he slurred. ''Ow are yer, luv?'

'More ter the point, 'ow are you?' she replied.

'I'm okay. A bit boracic at the moment but I got some work lined up,' he said.

Josie studied his unshaven face and noticed the pallor beneath the stubble. 'Yer gotta leave that alone, Dad,' she said kindly. 'You're lookin' ill.'

'Yeah, I know,' he replied. 'I'm gonna do it, once I pull meself tergevver.'

Josie sat down beside him. 'Dad, I've got somefing ter tell yer. Mum's in 'ospital.'

''Ospital?' Frank echoed.

'She was caught up in a flyin' bomb attack,' Josie explained. ''Er factory got a direct 'it. Mum was dug out o' the rubble. She's got a twisted back an' lots o' cuts an' bruises.' Frank was struggling to take it all in and he nodded. 'Did you 'ear a word of what I just said?' Josie asked angrily.

'Yeah I did, gel,' he replied quickly. Then to her amazement he burst into tears. She had never seen him cry before and it cut into her like a knife. 'Pull yerself tergevver, Dad, people's lookin',' she muttered.

'I can't 'elp it,' he said, turning his head away from her in embarrassment as he stood up.

'Let's get outside,' she said.

They stepped out into the morning sunshine and Frank Bailey screwed his eyes up as Josie took his arm. 'It's a fine day,' he said sniffing. 'Yer say yer mum's in 'ospital. Which one?'

'Guy's.'

'I'll come an' see 'er soon as I get cleaned up,' he declared, seeming unsure of which way to go.

'Dad, yer need a shave an' a good bath,' Josie said quietly.

He turned away and walked unsteadily towards some wooden fencing beside the pub, and before Josie could stop him he crashed his clenched fist against the planking. Billy saw it happen and he hurried over to steady the older man as he staggered backwards. 'Yer've split yer knuckles, Mr Bailey,' he said, reaching into his trouser pocket for a handkerchief to stem the bleeding.

Josie took her father's other arm and stood watching while Billy tied the makeshift bandage. 'Was that really necessary, Dad?' she asked anxiously.

'I'm all right,' he replied calmly. 'I'll go an' get a shave an' then I'll go up the baths. Yer muvver won't reco'nise me when I get there. Guy's, yer say?'

'Visitin's two till three, an' seven till eight ternight,' she told him.

Frank stood up straight and pushed out his chest. 'Right then. I'll be on me way.'

The two young people watched him walk unsteadily along the turning and disappear around a corner. 'This is madness,' Josie said with sadness in her voice, 'but I love 'im, Billy, I want 'im back 'ome. We all do.'

'I know,' he said quietly. 'This could be the fing what does it.'

'I 'ope yer right. I pray ter God yer right,' she replied.

'Come on, it's turned one o'clock, if yer wanna make the 'ospital on time,' he reminded her.

'Billy, I really appreciate what yer done.'

'I ain't done nuffink, 'cept give yer a lift on me bike.'

'You done much more,' she said firmly. 'You was there when I needed yer, an' yer bandaged up me dad's 'and as well.'

'I 'ope I can always be there for yer,' he said seriously.

'You're a good mate, Billy.'

He wanted to say more but stifled a reply. Josie was all he had ever wanted but she was Johnny Francis's girlfriend, and he would have to bide his time. He was sure that she would end up getting hurt and he hoped he would still be around to pick up the pieces. It was unlikely though. His electrical apprenticeship had just ended and he was now due for call-up.

As she made to get on the bike Josie suddenly kissed him on the cheek. 'Just ter say fank you,' she smiled.

Billy's face lit up. 'Cor! What a day,' he said loudly.

The journey back took just ten minutes and Josie had time to change and wash the grime from her face before the three of them left for the hospital. Tommy looked nervous and Kathy was very subdued as they stepped down from the tram and made their way into the grounds. Josie had resisted the urge to take her brother to task for his outburst towards Kathy, thinking that it wasn't such a good idea before the visit, but he would be sure to get the sharp edge of her tongue once they got back home, she vowed.

Nell Bailey was lying flat but she managed a warm smile as her children bent over to kiss her. 'I gotta lie like this fer a whole week,' she moaned. 'I s'pose I'll survive though. Pull up some chairs. 'Ow are you all? 'Ow yer copin'?'

'Mrs Baines sent yer some grapes,' Josie said, taking them out of the shopping bag.

'That was nice of 'er.'

'Wait till Polly Seagram 'ears about what's 'appened,' Josie said smiling.

Nell pulled a face. 'I'm dreadin' it, much as I love the woman,' she replied. 'There'll be no keepin' 'er away. She'll take over the bloody 'ospital, I can just picture it.'

Josie could too. Polly and Bernie Seagram had been next-door neighbours at number 8 for as long as she could remember and Polly was one of those people who always seemed to be on hand, involving herself with a troubled neighbour or helping out in an emergency. Polly was her mother's best friend and Josie knew that when she and Bernie got back from their extended visit to Polly's sister in Reading the sparks would fly. 'Oh by the way,' she said, 'we've got yer some jam tarts to 'ave wiv yer cuppa as well.'

'Josie's a right little mum,' Kathy remarked quickly as the three made themselves comfortable beside the bed.

'Yeah, she makes me clean me room,' Tommy added smiling.

Josie gave him a blinding look. 'Yeah, they're bein' really good,' she said. 'I bet yer feel really sore, don't yer, Mum?'

'I'm black an' blue all over,' Nell replied, 'but I was very lucky, so they told me. There was a beam come ter rest above me body an' it stopped the rubble from crushin' me. Ovvers weren't so lucky though.'

Josie saw the tears forming in her mother's eyes and she reached out and touched her arm. 'You're tough, Ma, you always were. Yer just gotta get all the rest yer can. Yer'll soon be up an' about. But yer not gonna do anyfing when yer do get out, not fer a long while. Me an' Kathy an' Tommy are gonna look after yer.'

'Does yer farvver know about me?' Nell asked her.

'Yeah, I saw 'im this mornin',' Josie told her.

''Ow is 'e?'

''E looks very well,' Josie lied.

'Is 'e workin'?'

'I fink so. I never asked 'im.'

'Did 'e say 'e'll come in ter see me?'

''E said 'e'll be in this evenin'.'

Nell nodded, and her face suddenly took on a sad look. 'Mrs Baker an' the Kelly sisters are dead,' she said. 'So's poor ole Betsy Goodwin. There was twenty died in all, an' there's some still on the danger list.'

'Try not ter fink about it, Mum,' Josie begged her. 'You've gotta concentrate on gettin' well.'

''Ow can I just ferget it,' her mother replied disconsolately. 'Those people who got killed were good friends o' mine, friends fer years. I'm not gonna ferget it ever. I can 'ardly believe I'm still alive meself.'

Josie tried to draw her on to lighter subjects to cheer her up a little, and Kathy bided her time, waiting for the right moment to break the news. 'Mum, I got a confession ter make,' she said after a while. 'I broke yer china pot. The one yer like so much.'

'It was a pure accident,' Josie added quickly. 'Kathy was busy cleanin' the dresser an' it just dropped out of 'er 'ands.'

Nell smiled. 'Kath, I'm gonna let yer into a little secret. I couldn't stand the bloody pot.'

'But yer said it was yer favourite.'

'I know I said it was, but I was gettin' really fed up wiv it,' Nell told her. 'I used ter put the sprigs of 'eavver in it that the gypsies brought round, saying it'd bring yer good luck. Well, it didn't bring me good luck, did it, so I'm glad the pot got broken. Next time the gypsies call I'll tell 'em there's no use in me buyin' any 'eavver 'cos I've got no pot ter put it in!'

Everyone laughed and Nell suddenly winced. 'I wish they'd let me sit up. It's so uncomfortable 'avin' ter lay on me back.'

'By the way, I didn't pay the tallyman this week, Mum,' Josie said.

'Sod the tallyman,' Nell growled, but then she said, 'Yer paid the rent though?'

'Course I did.'

'What about the milkman, an' the money on the slate at Kellerman's?'

'All took care of.'

'Are yer sure yer farvver's all right?'

Josie nodded. 'I told yer already. 'E's lookin' well. But 'e ses 'e's missin' yer.'

Nell's eyes hardened. 'I miss 'im, but I couldn't live wiv 'im, not the way 'e is. Maybe when 'e proves ter me 'e's kicked the 'abit I'll consider takin' 'im back.'

'Yer'll see the difference in 'im when 'e comes this evenin',' Josie told her, crossing her fingers. ''E's really tryin' ter change, I can tell.'

'Go on, pull the ovver leg,' Nell said smiling. 'You always took 'is side. It goes wiv the breedin' I 'spect. Yer've got 'is colourin' an' determination. I just 'ope 'e's determined enough ter give up the drink. If 'e is then 'e'll beat it.'

'Billy Emmerson took Josie over ter see Dad on 'is motor-bike,' Kathy said suddenly.

Josie pulled a face at her and Nell looked anxious. 'Yer gotta promise me yer won't go on that bike of 'is any more,' she said sharply. 'I've always worried about you goin' on motor-bikes. They're dangerous fings. Lots o' young men 'ave bin killed on 'em.'

Josie had no chance to reply before a nurse came up to the bed to announce that it was time for a blood pressure and temperature check. Later though, when it was time to leave, Nell reached out and touched her arm. 'Remember what I said,' she urged her. 'I've got enough on me plate wivout 'avin' ter worry about you ridin' round on that bloody bike.'

The visiting bell sounded and Josie stood up. 'I'll pop in

ternight, Mum,' she said. 'Come on, kids, kiss Mum an' let's leave 'er ter get a bit o' shut-eye.'

As they walked out of the hospital Tommy shaped up and kicked a stone along the street. 'Can I play out ternight, Josie?' he asked her.

'No, you can't,' she said sharply, 'an' what's more I'll be wantin' an explanation fer why yer didn't do as you was told terday.'

'I was gonna . . .' Tommy faltered, 'but . . .'

'Wait till we get 'ome fer yer excuse,' Josie told him. 'An' it better be good or yer'll stop in fer a week.'

Tommy lapsed into a sulky silence. Josie was getting too bossy, he thought to himself. If she carried on too much he'd clear off and go and live with his father. At least he wouldn't go on the way Josie did. Make beds, clean the bedroom. That wasn't boys' work, it was girls' work. Why didn't she get Kathy to do it?

The afternoon sun was still hot as the Baileys walked into Quay Street and Tommy prepared to defend himself. Bloody sisters. Why couldn't he have had some brothers instead, he moaned to himself.

'Tommy.'

'Yeah?'

'Come 'ere.'

The young lad sauntered over.

'Now what excuse 'ave yer got fer not tidyin' that bedroom up?'

'Well, I was just about to when . . .'

Chapter Five

Stymie Smith had collected a cart full of scrap iron plus a few bits of lead and copper from the builder's yard and he felt happy at the haul. The iron wouldn't bring in much but the lead and copper alone were worth the trip. Now there was a lot to do if he was going to be ready by three o'clock, he thought as he opened up the gate and backed the horse and cart into his yard. First the cart. It would have to be unloaded on the quick and then given a hose down. The nag was ready for a nosebag and then he would give him a good combing. There was some black stain somewhere to tart up the hooves and the harness needed a quick rub over with Bluebell to take the tarnish off. What else? Oh yes, the dicky seat. Bel Fiddler couldn't be expected to sit on that tatty old cushion with the straw poking out. Better get one of the cushions from the armchair, not that they were much better, but at least they weren't spilling their innards all over the place.

Stymie set to work, and by two thirty he was almost finished. 'Now where's that paint tin?' he mumbled to himself as he rummaged through the shed.

The nag stood compliantly while the black stain was applied to his hooves, and when the totter finally straightened his long angular frame and grunted the horse stamped, as though pleased with the results.

'Right then, you can 'ave a few minutes more while I go fer a quick pint,' Stymie said, tweaking the animal's ear, 'then yer gonna pull this cart up ter Blackheath. That's if it ain't too much trouble for yer.'

At the Fiddler household Bel was putting on lipstick in her bedroom while downstairs Charlie Fiddler sat back in his armchair with a black look on his face. 'Gawd knows what the bloody neighbours are gonna say when they see 'er up on that cart,' he growled to Sandra.

'Sod 'em,' the youngest of his brood replied without looking up from the paper.

'Yeah, but we 'ave ter live round 'ere an' I don't want us ter be the talk o' the street,' he told her sharply.

'We already are, an' it don't worry us, so why should it worry you?' Sandra said, folding the paper up. 'They started talkin' when Muvver pissed off an' they ain't stopped since.'

'Wiv the strokes you three pull I don't wonder,' Charlie retorted. 'Look at the ovver night. If Chloe 'adn't pulled Bel in she would 'ave showed 'em everyfing.'

Sandra smiled sympathetically at her harassed father. She realised that it hadn't been easy for him after their mother had run off with the insurance man. He was only forty-five but he looked older, though he still had all his own teeth and most of his hair, even if it was greying at the temples. He had taken his wife's desertion well, all things considered, but then her parents had been at each other's throats for as long as she could remember. It was a wonder that they stopped arguing long enough to conceive any children. 'Look, Dad,' she said soothingly, 'Bel's not doin' any 'arm goin' fer a ride. Stymie's all right, an' 'e ain't the sort ter take advantage.'

'I ain't worried about Stymie takin' advantage,' Charlie said quickly. 'Once Bel gets 'er 'ooks into 'im 'e's gonna wonder what's 'it 'im.'

Chloe came into the parlour and threw herself down into a vacant armchair. She was big, the largest of the three girls, with a flat open face and a broad smile that seemed to light up a room. 'What's Crosse an' Blackwell's like, Dad?' she asked.

'What d'yer mean, what's it like?' he replied.

'Me an' Bel are finkin' o' goin' there fer a job on Monday.'

'Well, as far as I know it's all right,' he told her. 'There's a lot round 'ere works there, though I don't know about you two.'

'What d'yer mean?'

'Well, yer so unpredictable.'

'Fanks fer the vote o' confidence.'

'Well, you are,' he growled. 'Look at the last job. One day yer come 'ome singin' the firm's praises an' the next yer slaggin' it off.'

'Factories are all the same,' Chloe said, tucking her legs under her in the armchair. 'It's all donkey work an' they end up treatin' yer like shit.'

'If yer go slaggin' off the foreman yer can't really expect anyfing else, can yer?' Charlie reminded her. 'As far as I can see, yer won't improve yerself till yer start lookin' fer a different job, away from factories I mean.'

'Such as what?'

'Well, there's office jobs.'

'I couldn't stick workin' in an office,' Chloe replied quickly. 'I'd really like an outside job.'

'Yeah, you could work on a broom, or drive an 'orse-an'-cart,' Charlie said with a lopsided grin.

'You're a fat lot o' use wiv yer suggestions,' Chloe said dismissively. ''Orse-an'-cart indeed.'

'Well, Bel's gettin' some practice in,' Charlie rejoined.

Just then they heard the cart on the cobblestones and Chloe hurried out to the foot of the stairs. 'Stymie's 'ere, Bel,' she called out.

Bel sashayed down wearing her best summer dress and a big straw hat.

'You look very nice,' Chloe remarked.

'Very smart,' Sandra added.

Charlie thought otherwise. 'What made yer put that stupid 'at on?' he growled. 'That's yer muvver's old 'at an' I couldn't stand the bloody fing on 'er.'

Bel gave her father a look of contempt as she strolled past him to the front door. 'I might be late, so don't wait up,' she said airily.

'Where yer goin', Brighton?' Charlie countered.

'Black'eath if yer must know,' Bel told him quickly.

'That bloody nag won't manage it,' he said grinning. 'It's all up 'ill, remember.'

'He's a lovely animal,' Chloe said as she followed Bel out of the house. 'Dad,' she called back, 'fetch some sugar lumps or an apple for him.'

'We ain't got no sugar lumps, nor apples,' Charlie hollered back.

'Well get him some celery then.'

People stood at their front doors watching as Charlie fed the horse with a stick of celery and Stymie ruffled up the cushion before helping Bel Fiddler up into the seat.

'Get a load o' that, will yer?' someone sneered.

'Don't it make yer sick.'

'What a carry-on.'

'I fink she's got pluck.'

The widow Meadows rounded on Wilco Johnson. 'Pluck?' she growled. 'She looks like a gypsy's woman perched up there on that cart. She'll be knockin' on the doors sellin' clothes-pegs next.'

Bel waved cheerily to the bystanders as Stymie flicked the reins and got the nag moving, and Charlie Fiddler shook his head in resignation as he went back inside the house. 'Sandra, what yer done wiv that newspaper?' he asked.

'Bel took it wiv 'er ter sit on, Dad, in case the cushion was dirty,' she told him.

'Well, in that case I'm gonna see if Wilco wants ter go up the Star an' Garter fer a pint, an' in case I'm late don't wait up,' he mimicked.

'Make sure you're in by midnight or I'll put the bolts on,' Sandra said with a straight face.

Stymie was feeling a little shy as he sat next to Bel on the cart. The horse was trotting along merrily towards the Tunnel and Bel looked as though she was enjoying herself, but he wanted to create a good impression from the start and he was racking his brains for something sensible to say.

'Nice day.'

'Yeah, it's lovely,' Bel said smiling.

'The nag's doin' well.'

'Umm.'

'I combed 'im at dinnertime.'

'All of 'im?'

'Dusted 'im wiv flea powder as well.'

''E's not cooty, is 'e?' Bel asked quickly.

'Nah, I don't fink so, but it don't do ter lean all over 'im, just in case 'e 'as got a couple.'

Bel had no intention of leaning over the nag but she started to worry a little in case something did make its way up on to her.

'I've seen 'em the size o' yer fingernail,' Stymie went on.

'Not on my nag but on some ovvers. When yer stamp on'em they crack. Suck yer blood they do. Yer can always tell when a nag's got fleas, they keep twitchin' their ears.'

Bel stared forward at Stymie's horse as he plodded along and a look of horror suddenly appeared on her face. "E's just twitched 'em!' she said loudly.

Stymie smiled. 'Nah, not that sort o' twitch. That's a different twitch.'

Bel lapsed into silence, beginning to wonder if she had made a mistake in agreeing to an afternoon jaunt on the cart, while Stymie covered his embarrassment by whistling a little too enthusiastically. When he saw Blackheath Hill loom into view, the nag abruptly slowed down in despair, but the totter had anticipated the animal's reaction and he flicked the reins. 'Come on, my ole beauty. You can do it,' he said encouragingly.

The horse did well but was blowing loudly when the cart topped the rise. Ahead was a sea of green on both sides of the road, with kites flying and children playing and adults picnicking on the lush grass.

'There's a little pub by the village,' Stymie told Bel. 'Fancy a stop?' When she nodded he grinned. 'Good. There's a trough across the road. The nag can get a drink too.'

'Stymie, will yer tell me somefing?' Bel asked as they turned into the side lane towards the village.

'What's that?'

'Why ain't that 'orse got a name? You always call 'im yer nag.'

"E 'as got a name but I rarely use it.'

'Why?'

'Let me tell yer,' he said with a sage look. "Orses are as crafty as us, more so in many cases, an' if yer get too familiar wiv 'em they tend ter get as temperamental as their cousins the mules.'

'What is 'is name?'

'Benny.'

'Benny? That's a funny name fer a nag.'

'It was a funny bloke who I bought 'im off,' Stymie said chuckling.

They reached the village pub and the totter pulled back on the reins, letting his horse dip his head into the trough. 'Right then, I'll just stick the brake on,' he said, wrapping a chain round a rear wheel spoke and fixing it with a hook.

As they walked up to the door of the pub they were confronted by a huge man in an apron who had been collecting glasses from a wooden bench. 'Sorry but we don't admit gypsies or travellers,' he told them in a firm voice.

'We ain't no bleedin' gypsies,' Stymie spluttered. 'I'm a respectable totter what can pay fer 'is beer.'

'That's as maybe, but we don't entertain totters eivver,' the man affirmed.

Stymie looked up at the sign which boldly announced 'The Traveller's Rest' and puffed loudly. 'Come on, Bel, let's find a pub where we're welcome,' he growled.

'Yeah, we'll do that, an' you can stick yer poxy pub right up where the monkeys stick their nuts,' Bel told the potman.

'Ne'er mind, Bel, I know anuvver pub where they're not so fussy,' Stymie said as she climbed up on to the seat.

As they made their way through the village Bel noticed a smile playing on the totter's lips. 'An' who's frew you a bun?' she inquired.

'It was that sign over the pub,' he replied with an artful look.

'So?'

'It was only 'angin' on 'ooks.'

'So?'

'Well, I was finkin' o' makin' an early start on Monday,' he remarked blithely. 'I'm gonna come up 'ere an' replace that sign before anyone's up.'

'What wiv?'

'I collected a load o' junk from a builder's yard terday an' amongst it there was an ole lavatory seat. It'll be just the sign fer that shit-'ouse of a pub,' he said grinning.

At number 6 Quay Street, Tommy Bailey worked hard at cleaning his bedroom. Josie had had words with him, but he felt he had got off pretty lightly as it went. She could have kept him in, but with Dennis Taylor sitting outside on the kerb she had relented. With the words, 'Next time yer don't do as yer told I'll keep yer in fer a week,' ringing in his ears he had hurried up the stairs and set to work with a vengeance.

Josie busied herself in the scullery preparing the evening meal and Kathy sat watching her with a smile on her small oval face.

'What you grinnin' at?' Josie asked her.

'The way you cut those potatoes,' Kathy replied. 'Mum cuts 'em in 'er 'and.'

'Yeah, well I'm not as used ter peelin' spuds as Mum.'

'It seems strange wiv Mum not bein' 'ere,' Kathy said sadly.

'Yeah it does, but we gotta soldier on, as Dad would say.'

'When yer saw 'im was 'e drunk?' Kathy asked.

'Nah, course not,' Josie said quickly.

'Was 'e really upset about Mum?'

'Well o' course. Dad still loves Mum very much, despite all that's 'appened,' Josie said reassuringly.

'I wish I could believe it,' Kathy remarked.

'You believe it, Kath, 'cos it's true.'

The younger sister watched as Josie sliced the last of the potatoes on the edge of the draining-board. 'I want to, Josie.'

'Well just do. Now I want yer ter watch those spuds, an' when they come ter the boil turn the gas down low so they're still simmerin'. Okay?'

'Why? Where are you goin'?'

'I told yer. I gotta take that book over ter Johnny. I won't be long though.'

'What about the greens?'

'Don't touch the greens, I'll put 'em on when I get back,' Josie told her as she picked up the book from the dresser.

She left the house and crossed the street, knocking on number 24, and Jack Francis answered the door with a welcoming smile. 'Come on in, luv,' he said cheerfully. 'Our John'll be glad yer called. I fink 'e's lookin' forward ter readin' 'is book.'

'It's not the one 'e wanted,' Josie replied. 'That was still out, but I got anuvver one by the same bloke. I fink 'e'll like it.'

'I'm sure 'e will,' Jack smiled.

When she walked into the parlour she saw Annie Francis sitting alone. 'Where's Johnny?' she asked.

''E's gone upstairs fer a lie-down,' Annie told her. 'It's 'is 'ead. 'E's bin gettin' a lot of 'eadaches lately.'

Jack Francis gave his wife an irritated look. 'I'm sure they come on from bein' in the 'ouse all the time,' he remarked.

'I fink it's more than that,' Annie replied. 'Gawd knows what 'e's bin frew.'

Josie tended to agree with Jack but she kept her own counsel. 'Look, I'll leave the book 'ere,' she said. 'I'll pop over again after I get back from the 'ospital this evenin'.'

''Ow is yer muvver?' Jack asked quickly. 'I bet you fink we're a right couple not askin' before, but yer know 'ow it is. That lad's worryin' the life out of us.'

'I shouldn't worry too much,' Josie replied encouragingly. 'Johnny's makin' good progress. 'E reads a lot now an' 'e'll soon get 'is confidence back fer goin' out.'

'It's not just the goin' out that worries 'im,' Annie answered. 'It's meetin' people an' bein' expected ter talk about what 'appened to 'im at Normandy.'

'It's understandable,' Josie said. 'It must 'ave bin a terrifyin' experience.'

'Yeah, 'e was wounded soon as 'e landed,' Annie said quickly.

'All right, Muvver, don't torture yerself wiv the details,' Jack urged her, turning to the young woman. 'She goes on about it over an' over again. She's even got ter talkin' about it in 'er sleep.'

'Well, I'd better get back,' Josie said. 'Visitin's seven till eight this evenin'.'

'Is there anyfing we can do?' Jack asked.

'No, it's okay, but fanks anyway,' Josie said smiling as he walked her to the door.

When he returned his wife gave him a hard look. 'There was no need ter tell the gel I talked in me sleep about it,' she said sharply. 'She'll fink I'm goin' dolally or somefing.'

'An' so yer will if yer don't try an' put it all out o' yer mind fer a while,' Jack countered. 'At least our John's come'ome, which is more than can be said fer a lot of ovver poor sods.'

Annie looked up at her husband and nodded. 'Yer right, luv,' she said. 'I s'pose I've gotta stop dwellin' on fings. 'Ere, d'yer reckon our John an' Josie'll get serious?'

Jack shook his head slowly. 'I'd like ter fink so,' he replied. 'That Bailey gel's bin an absolute brick since 'e come back 'ome. Most of 'is improvement's down to 'er, but I can't honestly see 'em gettin' tergevver properly. I fink she would, but once our John finds 'is feet again 'e'll be swannin' off like 'e always did. None o' the gels could take 'im seriously. 'Ow could they? 'E didn't even take 'imself seriously.'

'Well, I 'ope yer wrong,' Annie told him. 'Josie Bailey's the best fing that's 'appened to 'im an' I 'ope 'e remembers it.'

When the visitors' bell sounded at eight o'clock that evening Nell smiled at her three children as they prepared to leave.

'Don't worry, somefing might 'ave come up. 'E'll be in termorrer, you'll see.'

'Well I 'ope 'e is, or I'll 'ave somefing ter say to 'im,' Kathy said sharply.

Josie gave her mother a sad smile as she ushered Tommy and Kathy out of the ward, and when they had left Nell turned her head to one side and felt the tear run down her cheek. She had got the nurse to brush her hair before the visit and put a little powder on her face and a touch of lipstick as well, and she had been looking forward to seeing Frank again. It seemed that Josie had been covering for him. He wouldn't change now, he couldn't. It was too late.

Chapter Six

Sidney Holman settled back in the carriage and opened the evening paper as the train pulled out of Liverpool Street Station bound for Cambridge. It was a warm Saturday evening and ahead of him was the special meeting of the League of White Knights, which should have given him something to look forward to, but Holman was feeling decidedly worried.

A stocky, dark-haired and handsome man in his early fifties with a successful career as an insurance broker, he had developed strong feelings before the war about the way the country was moving, and subsequently found that he was not alone. There were others, successful men in various fields, with whom he came into contact and they too shared his misgivings. As they perceived things, the country was effectively being run by Jewish businessmen who were rapidly corrupting a weak Government and, as if that was not bad enough, Communism, having already possessed Russia, was gaining support in Britain and tending to generate unrest amongst the working classes. Another worry Holman shared was the future demise of the British Empire. Early signs from the colonies and protectorates were disconcerting. They were beginning to assert the right to independence and activists were attempting to stir up unrest.

India and Africa might conceivably slip from the imperial embrace, and Holman and his new-found associates felt that something should be done. The feelings of the silent majority should be heard in the right places.

In his prime, single and energetic, Holman had thought that the answer lay in a movement which was quickly gaining ground, the British Union of Fascists, led by the charismatic Sir Oswald Mosley. Fascism had already taken root in Spain and Italy and was coming to a strange and sinister fruition in Adolf Hitler's Germany. It had been exhilarating to don the black uniform and march through the East End streets with strong, like-minded men, taking on the Jewish saboteurs of the state and heralding the coming purification of Britain.

Sidney Holman was older now and wiser, and as he folded his newspaper and put it down beside him he thought about the changes which had led to him becoming a member of the League of White Knights. At first the violence aimed at the Jewish population during the thirties' marches had been limited to skirmishes en route but it steadily grew more brutal, with serious injuries and deaths, and finally in 1936 the Government was forced to ban all uniformed political marches throughout the country. The movement continued to grow regardless, and immediately prior to the war there were more than twenty thousand members, but in the dark days of 1940 when Oswald Mosley and over seven hundred of his major supporters were interned, the movement began to break up. The following year a few businessmen who had been in the forefront of the violence on the streets banded together to form the League of White Knights; Fascism was their enduring creed and a Fascist government their prime aim. The new movement was a limited fraternity, fiercely guarding its cloak of secrecy, but although violence had given way to subversion and infiltration, the old fight still went on.

Sidney Holman smiled to himself when he recalled his euphoria in those early, heady days, and later his feeling of importance at receiving the invitation to become a member of the League of White Knights. Now though he tried to suppress his fear, dreading the thought of the League accepting the plan which Hennessey had brought over, and he felt obliged to argue against it at the meeting, regardless of the consequences.

When the evening train pulled into Cambridge Station a car was waiting, and the broker sat quietly in the back seat watching the university town give way to flat open country. Soon the driver turned into a narrow lane and then entered a tree-lined drive that led up to a white-stone mansion set in extensive and well-kept gardens. Inside the members were chatting together over glasses of sherry and wine and Holman caught sight of Anderson talking earnestly with Sir Barry Freeman, the current First Knight, as the elected chairman was known.

'Ah, good evening, Holman,' the tall lean Freeman said, extending his hand. 'Anderson has just been giving me an off-the-cuff briefing, but I'll look forward to your conclusions with pleasure. By the way, Wilson's over there, and Ryder too. Go along and lessen their darkness, why don't you, old chap.'

Eric Wilson and Horace Ryder were country landowners who were at that moment vehemently deprecating the evils of Communism, and in particular the nightmare threat of public ownership of land. They turned to Holman as he approached.

'Hello, old chap, how the devil are you?' asked Eric Wilson.

'I'm fine, Eric, and you two?'

Horace nodded his reply as he brought a glass of sherry up to his lips and Eric smiled. 'In the pink, Sidney, and eagerly awaiting your report. I say, what an honour for you, eh, old boy?'

'I was just part of the team, Eric,' Holman replied. 'It was merely a case of listening carefully to what was proposed and reporting back on it.'

'You're far too modest,' the ruddy-complexioned squire told him. 'Play your cards right and who knows, it might mean a shortlisting for the next First Knight.'

'If I'm too modest then you're far too kind,' Holman answered with a smile. 'My money would be on Anderson.'

Both the squires nodded. 'Good man,' Horace remarked. 'Certainly the short-odds candidate.'

Sir Barry Freeman tapped a spoon against his wine glass to attract attention. 'If you would all be so kind as to make your way into the sanctum, then we'll convene.'

The meeting took place in a large, oak-panelled study warmed by a large log fire, and it began with the swearing of the ritual oath by the Knight-in-Realm to use right and proper judgement and to oversee the impending discussion with impartiality and good faith.

The ceremony had always seemed contrived and disingenuous to Holman. Sir Barry Freeman, installed at the centre of the cadre table, would listen to the views of the members then recommend the way ahead, like a field marshal assessing a campaign, and the voting would invariably reflect his view.

'And now the report,' Freeman said, waving a hand in Anderson's direction.

The tall, distinguished-looking man rose up from his armchair, one of the many which faced the long, purple velvet table of the cadre, and gave a dry cough. 'Yesterday evening Holman, Thorburn and I, on instructions from the cadre, met with a certain Ralph Hennessey, who was representing his Reich masters. At that meeting we were given the outline of a plan which has been drawn up by Adolf Hitler himself and counter-signed by his chiefs of staff. As Hennessey described it, the plan is progressive in nature, with two basic aims: an armistice, and the facilitation of a British Fascist administration.'

The sudden mumble around him died quickly as Anderson cleared his throat. 'If we agree to the central premise, the whole plan will be made available for us to study in detail, and should we accept its proposals the following financial arrangements will be put in place: immediately after the execution of events half a million pounds in gold will be transferred into a numbered account in Zurich. Furthermore, twenty-five thousand pounds will be made available to us for use in planning and implementation.'

'Good Lord!' Horace Ryder gasped as the muttering of voices rose once more.

Anderson looked slowly around the floor and then turned to the front table. 'While outlining the plan Hennessey revealed that in a few weeks' time London will be attacked with a new weapon, namely a rocket missile, against which there is no defence, and that later in the autumn the German high command will order their forces to begin a counter-offensive over a wide front which will halt the Allied advance. Coming closely together the two developments will certainly hit the British people as a disheartening setback to the long-awaited ending of the war. Of course Adolf Hitler appreciated that the resolve would almost certainly still be there to battle on, unless of course the country was already reeling and in disarray from a lack of leadership. The adoption of the plan therefore hinges on our decision whether or not to liaise with Nazi Germany, and whether or not we agree to organise and carry out the assassination of the Prime Minister Winston Churchill.'

An astonished clamour of voices greeted this disclosure and Freeman raised his hand for silence as Anderson took his seat. 'Thank you, Victor. Maybe you would care to begin the discussion by furnishing us with your views on the matter.'

Anderson remained seated. 'My feelings are that the country would certainly be thrown into turmoil if the assassination was carried out,' he said thoughtfully, 'but I'm not convinced that there would be a national desire for an armistice, not at this stage of the war. With the Russians closing in on the German frontier and the British and American forces making progress from the west it would seem to be only a matter of time before Germany capitulates.'

Ben Thorburn raised his hand and was given the floor. 'My feelings are that the plan would have every chance of working,' he began. 'Recent polls indicate that the coalition government is unpopular, while Churchill is seen as the one man, the only man, with the charisma and resolve to lead the country to victory. His removal would, as Anderson said, throw the country into turmoil. The polls also demonstrate that the British people are split over their choice of the first peacetime government, and there's room for a vibrant and progressive party to gain considerable ground. I feel that with energetic campaigning to get our message over and the right choice of candidates, we could be in the forefront.'

Another member offered his support. 'I feel that Thorburn is right,' he began. 'In my estimation the principal future threat to this country and the Western Allies is posed by the spread of Communism, infecting hearts and minds and then engulfing whole nations. An armistice between Britain and Germany would engender some resentment in Washington but it would release the American forces and allow them to concentrate their efforts on the Pacific war, while making possible an alignment by us and the Germans against the threat from the east. With all military aid to Russia suspended and their forces facing a major logistical problem of supplies their advance would grind to a halt.'

Holman could see the direction the meeting was taking and

he held up his hand. His contribution was made with a passion that took the assembly by surprise. 'I have been a member of the League since its inauguration and I have been proud to be a part of it, but the arguments I have listened to tonight fill me with dread,' he declared plainly. 'The adoption of this proposal would place our organisation in an invidious position. We would be inextricably tied to an alien power whether we liked it or not. A Fascist power yes, but one which has by its very methods alienated the world and brought about a war that could have been avoided.'

The other members maintained their stony silence as Holman drew breath and glanced briefly from one to another of them before addressing the cadre once more. 'My personal feelings are that the plan was drawn up out of desperation,' he continued, 'and desperation can be a bad bedfellow. Adolf Hitler has nothing to lose and everything to gain, let us not forget that. Furthermore, for us to believe that Winston Churchill's assassination will bring about an armistice is like reaching for the stars with a ladder. I believe Churchill's words, "We will accept nothing but total surrender", are not mere rhetoric, but rather a true reflection of the British people's resolve. Too many lives have been sacrificed on the altar of war, both military and civilian, for a negotiated armistice now. I am therefore stating my position as clearly as I can: I am against even studying the plan.'

'That's finished him as a candidate,' Horace Ryder muttered to Eric Wilson who was holding up his hand to speak.

When the squire stood up he smiled briefly. 'I have vivid memories of the days before the war, when we, the British Union of Fascists, marched through the streets of East London and fought hand to hand against the Jewish troublemakers. I was proud to be part of that action and I know you were too. All of us have shed blood for the cause and now, when we are that much older and unable by law to assert ourselves in the way that we would wish, should we shy away from the drastic but effective measures that would finally bring about the Fascist government for which we have strived so long? No, we should not. Instead we should have no compunction about removing the main obstacle to our future success, no more than we would about swatting a fly or stepping on an insect. I happen to believe that one day in the not-too-distant future Germany and this country will become allies to rid themselves of the overriding danger of our times, the scourge of Communism.'

Holman sighed as he let his shoulders sag in the chair. The vote of the cadre still had to be taken but he knew instinctively which way it would go. History had seemingly not taught them anything. From the Gunpowder Plot to the Siege of Sidney Street, the past was littered with the discovery or betrayal of subversives at work, caught redhanded and forced to face the torture chamber, the axe or the rope, or else summarily and ingloriously despatched.

'Are there any more comments from the floor?' the First Knight asked.

The members remained silent and rose from their seats as one when the cadre stood up to leave the study.

'I was sorry to hear that you felt that way,' Anderson said to Holman as he came up to him. 'I have my own reservations, of course, but I'm sure that the end will justify the means.'

'I wish I had your conviction,' Holman remarked as he got up. 'We could all end up being rowed through Traitor's Gate.'

'I don't think so,' the tall man replied with a disarming smile. 'Our invisibility has always been assiduously preserved, especially since the Millington affair. All of us understand the paramount importance of secrecy and any negotiations, monetary or otherwise, have been and will continue in future to be carried out through the usual third party.'

'Ah yes. The mysterious Mr X,' Holman said with a sardonic expression. 'I wonder if he'll be a party to the choice of assassin, should the vote go as we expect and the plan be accepted.'

Anderson sat down in a vacant chair and motioned Holman back into his seat. 'Look, old man,' he said with a sigh, 'we've been good friends for a long time now and I do understand your reservations about this whole affair, but I'm prompted to offer you some advice. Don't talk about your misgivings outside the meeting. Remember Millington?'

Holman smiled. 'I drink very little these days and I tend to keep my own counsel. If Millington had done likewise, he wouldn't have ended up being scraped out from under the wheels of a tube train. Besides, I tend not to stand too near the edge of the platform when I do use the underground.'

'Good man,' Anderson replied, returning the smile. 'Come on, let's get a drink. I think the cadre will be some time yet with their deliberations.'

The members were making themselves comfortable in the large room next to the study and Holman noticed the two country squires standing together in earnest conversation beneath a portrait of one of Sir Barry Freeman's illustrious ancestors. He could see Crutchley and Williamson, both merchant bankers, chatting with Julian Robins of Robins and Buckley, marine engineers, and he spotted Charles Pelham standing alone and looking decidedly worried as he self-consciously sipped a glass of Bordeaux. 'Catch you later,' Holman said to Anderson, and made his way over to Pelham, 'Hello, Charles. Not had a chance to chat to you yet.'

'Good evening, Sidney,' the bank manager replied in a quiet, quick voice, barely suppressing his nervousness. 'Listened to your comments with interest. Have to say I share your qualms. Didn't feel able to elaborate though. You seemed to have said it all.'

Holman felt touched by his sentiments. Pelham had been a good friend of the unfortunate Herbert Millington and he knew that his demise had hurt Pelham more than he cared to admit. He was not one to express his feelings to all and sundry, wisely preferring to confide only in those he trusted implicitly. 'I fear the worst, Charles,' he said quietly. 'This is not Ridley Road, Dalston where we used to gather to march on Bethnal Green, and we're not just a group of young bucks planning to break a few heads. This is a grand old country mansion and we're all respectable businessmen who should be enjoying the fruits of the labours of our youth. I find the extreme measures of this plan quite simply abhorrent.'

'So do I, old man,' Pelham said quickly. 'There's still the vote, though I think we all know what the outcome will be.'

Holman watched as the bank manager ran a hand over his bald head and wondered whether it was alcohol or anxiety that made his blue eyes look even paler. 'How did we all get into this, Charles,' he remarked wearily.

The banker smiled stiffly and dropped his voice to a whisper. 'We've believed in the dreams of our youth for too long, Sidney. We still take ourselves seriously, while the real world out there makes clowns of us. Good God, man, where do you think that promised half a million in gold is coming from? That money has been looted from occupied countries, from churches, cathedrals and mansions like this one, and from the ghettos whose inhabitants were stripped of their possessions before being taken away for forced labour or worse.'

'I never realised that you felt so strongly about this,' Holman said quietly. 'You sound very disillusioned.'

'Make no mistake,' Pelham replied. 'I still believe in the ideal of Fascism as an alternative government, but the time when that ideal could be implemented in this country is long past, and I can't equate repatriation with extermination.'

'That's rather a strong comparison,' Holman remarked.

'Yes, but an apt one,' Pelham said, putting down his glass. 'I'll tell you something. I recently authorised and set up a large loan to a Jewish businessman from the Mile End Road. Imagine his outrage if he ever found out that his bank manager was once a Mosleyite Blackshirt and is now a member of a Fascist organisation. Anyway, the Jew wanted to make it plain that a portion of the money he planned to borrow would be given to an organisation which was active in helping to ease the plight of Jewish people wherever possible. He had enough collateral to back the loan but I think he needed to tell me what was on his mind. We chatted a bit and he explained that the organisation he was intending to support was smuggling information out from occupied countries. His parting shot was this: "Be prepared, for when the Allies cross the Rhine and the Russians come in from the east they will uncover unspeakable evil. They will bear witness to things that will haunt them until their dying day." I heard those words, Sidney, and I saw the look on his face. The writing's on the wall, old man, and I curse my cowardice. Why didn't I have the courage to stand up in that study and add my fears to yours? Why didn't I say that even agreeing to look at the plan would be tantamount to collusion in exterminating millions of men, women and children? Was it because I feared being pushed under the wheels of a train? Perhaps. Or perhaps it was because I've believed too long in a dream that has slowly turned into a nightmare, and I don't even have the strength to believe in myself any more.'

Holman stared at the distressed banker, inwardly shocked by his words. 'You have just made the case against this proposal, Charles, and if I may say so, much more eloquently than I,' he murmured. 'There's hope for you yet, and I pray to God that there's still hope for me too.'

'The cadre's returning,' someone called out.

The First Knight's voice sounded solemn in the silent study as he read out the verdict. 'We the cadre have decided to look at the plan which has been outlined to us, and we will convene at a time to be arranged for our recommendations to be put to you. Thank you for your indulgence, gentlemen.'

'And may the Lord forgive us,' Pelham mumbled to Holman as they left the study.

Chapter Seven

After the sporadic flying-bomb attacks on Saturday, when four of the weapons flew over and fell north of the river, Sunday morning started quietly, and the people of Quay Street were hoping that even the Nazis had come to respect the sabbath. Charlie Fiddler strolled into Jamaica Road to get his newspaper and Stymie sorted out the lavatory seat and threw it on to the back of his cart ready for an early start on Monday. The widow Meadows was expecting a visit from her eldest daughter Rose and the two grandchildren and she had called at the sweet shop for two bars of white chocolate and a couple of Golly bars. She knew that Rose didn't like the children having the toffees, complaining about the damage they inflicted on their teeth, but Iris got them anyway.

At number 23, the last house on the left from Jamaica Road, Wilco Johnson was using the egg water to have a shave. He had been meaning to call at the Baileys' house to find out how Frank was, having already offered his condolences to Josie on her mother's injuries. Frank Bailey had once been Wilco's drinking partner and the two had often threatened to drink the Star and Garter dry.

Wilco was a tall, thin man in his early fifties with a mop

of unruly grey hair and a bulbous nose with blue veins which gave away his liking for alcohol. He was a confirmed bachelor and had got his nickname from his old friend, who said he reminded him of a wing commander because of his handlebar moustache and his refined way of speaking. This morning however Wilco looked anything but an RAF officer as he tried to steady the hand that held the razor. He was used to living in a shambles, but even he wondered what exactly had happened after the pubs turned out on Saturday night. The parlour looked like it had been spun round by a hurricane and there was a strange coat crumpled up by the scullery door.

The groaning from the upstairs landing startled Wilco and he dabbed at the nick on his chin as he hurried out of the scullery. 'Oi! What you doin' up there?' he called out as he saw Jumbo Watson balanced precariously at the top of the stairs.

'Got a cuppa 'andy, Wilco?' Jumbo asked him as he gripped the banister rail with both hands.

'No, I haven't, but you can make one for the two of us, if you can manage it down those stairs.'

'I appreciate yer kindness,' Jumbo said hoarsely as he slouched into the scullery and picked up the empty kettle.

'What kindness?'

'Lettin' me stay the night.'

'Did I?'

'Yeah, don't yer remember?'

'Hang on a second, it's all coming back to me now,' Wilco said, stroking his forehead. 'Wasn't it something about your missus cutting your throat if you went home drunk again?'

'Yeah, that's right, an' I found a friend in need,' Jumbo replied. 'My Adeline promised me all sorts o' terrible fings so I 'ad ter stay out. Ter be honest, I expected ter kip on a park bench but you offered me a spare bed. It was really nice of yer, Wilco, an' one day I 'ope ter repay yer kindness.'

'Never mind about that now, just make the tea, and I like mine strong so make sure you put enough tea in the pot,' Wilco told him.

Jumbo Watson did as he was bid and produced a presentable cup of tea which went some way in pacifying Wilco, who was always irritable after a drinking session.

'I'll give yer an 'and wiv the washin' up if yer like,' Jumbo said, glancing over at the pile of dirty crockery and pots and pans on the draining-board.

'Thanks, but I'll leave 'em till later,' Wilco replied. 'I've got to call at the Baileys' this morning.'

'Shame about Nell Bailey,' Jumbo remarked. 'She always passed the time o' day whenever she saw me. She was lucky though, by all accounts. Quite a few o' the women died in the blast. It just shows yer, none of us know what's round the corner.'

Wilco sipped his tea. 'I wonder if anybody's told Frank about it,' he said.

'Gawd knows,' Jumbo replied. 'I ain't seen anyfing of 'im since 'e moved out.'

'He's living over Stepney,' Wilco said. 'Frank's got some pals over there.'

Jumbo drained his cup and hauled himself to his feet. 'Well fanks again, mate, I'd better get goin' an' face the music.'

Fifteen minutes later Wilco knocked at number 6. 'Hello, my dear, I've just called to find out if you can let me have your dad's address,' he said. 'I was thinking of looking him up, find out how he's coping.'

''E's copin' very well,' Josie told him with a hint of sarcasm in her voice.

'I take it he knows about what happened to your mum.'

'Yes, I told 'im,' Josie replied.

'So can you let me have his address?' Wilco went on.

'I'm sorry, I don't know it,' she lied. 'I met me dad in a pub.'

'Well, next time you see him tell him Wilco was asking after him, will you?'

Josie went back into the scullery to finish washing up the breakfast things. Giving Wilco her father's address would be a pretty brainless thing to do, she thought. Her father was bad enough already and she felt very let down. He had promised faithfully to get to the hospital for the evening visit and she remembered the look on her mother's face when the bell went and he still hadn't made an appearance. Well he was going to get the sharp end of her tongue, that was for sure, she promised herself. In fact it might be a good idea to go over and confront him again. God only knew what excuse he would offer this time.

As she was drying the last of the crockery Josie heard Ellie Woodley calling to her over the backyard fence. Ellie and Larry Woodley had been the Baileys' next-door neighbours for years and the two women were in the habit of dropping in on each other for a chat and a cuppa.

'D'yer need any washin' done, luv?' Ellie asked her as Josie opened the scullery door. 'I got a nightdress she can borrer an' a dressin' gown if she ain't got one. Those 'ospital ones ain't much good. I know from when I was in there last year.'

'No, it's all right, Ellie, but fanks anyway,' Josie answered. 'I took a spare nightdress in yesterday, an' 'er dressin' gown.'

'Well, yer know where ter come if yer need anyfing,' Ellie reminded her. 'My Lal said that goes fer 'im too, in case yer need 'im ter help.'

As soon as Josie stepped back into the scullery Tommy came in and slouched down at the table. 'Josie, are yer goin' over ter see Dad again this mornin'?' he asked.

'As soon as I've finished 'ere,' she told him.

'Can I come too?'

'No, I've got to 'urry.'

'But I won't 'old yer up.'

'Tommy, I said no.'

'But why?'

'Look, it's not good that yer see Dad while 'e's the way 'e is.'

'Why not?'

'Just because.'

'That's no answer,' Tommy said quickly, his pale-blue eyes opening wide.

Josie sighed heavily as she sat down facing her younger brother. 'No it's not, Tommy,' she agreed. 'Dad's let 'imself go an' 'e looks scruffy an' dirty. In fact every time I go ter see 'im I 'ave a go at 'im an' tell 'im ter try an' smarten 'imself up a bit an' get a shave. 'E'll change fer the better I know, an' that's the time fer you ter see 'im. Less bad memories the better, an' one day yer'll fank me for it.'

'The trouble is yer treat me like a child,' Tommy said, lowering his eyes. 'I wouldn't be upset if I saw 'im the way 'e is now. P'raps if I did it might shock 'im inter doin' somefing about it.'

Josie looked at him with love in her eyes and wanted to put her arms around him, but instead she tapped him on the arm. 'Maybe yer right. Maybe it might make 'im pull 'imself tergevver seein' you,' she said smiling. 'Come on, let's get ready.'

At Number 24 Annie Francis was busy ironing in the scullery when her son John walked in. 'This is a good book,' he remarked as he placed it down on the dresser.

Annie took comfort from his appearance and general manner. He had had a shave and changed his shirt and had even taken the trouble to comb back his tight wavy hair. What was more he had managed to raise a smile. 'Josie Bailey certainly looks after you,' she remarked. 'There's not many men can say they get their library books changed for 'em. She's a nice kid an' you should appreciate what she does.'

'I do, Ma, really I do,' John assured her. 'In fact I was gonna ask if she'd like ter come ter the pictures wiv me ternight.'

Annie felt her heart leap. Since her son had come home from the war he had only gone out of the house when he had to. Most of his time was spent reading or dozing in the armchair. 'I'm sure she'll jump at the chance. Mind you it'll 'ave ter be after visitin' time,' she reminded him.

'I was fergettin' that,' John said, looking a little disappointed. 'It'll be too late fer the pictures by the time she gets out o' the 'ospital.'

'Ask 'er if she'd like ter go fer a walk,' Annie suggested.

John shook his head. 'I'm not up ter walkin' very far just yet,' he replied.

'Well you know best,' Annie sighed.

'Yeah, so don't push me, Muvver,' John told her curtly, his brief animation now gone.

At Field Operations Headquarters, Berlin, General Von Mannheim sat back at his desk, impatiently drumming his fingers on the smooth surface as he waited for the decoding to be completed, then abruptly stood up and walked stiffly to the window. Across the wide square he could see the dome of the university building glistening in the sun, standing out in sharp relief against the ruins of the once proud city. Von Mannheim stood for a moment, thinking of the meeting of generals the previous day, and he smiled bitterly to himself. They were like-minded he knew, each and every one of them angry at his own powerlessness to make any military decisions without the authority of the leader Adolf Hitler. The Fuehrer was now masterminding the campaigns on both fronts and his edict had gone out to all commands. 'Not an inch must be given and every soldier must be prepared to stand and die for the Fatherland.'

Von Mannheim sat down at his desk once more and pulled

the gold-framed photo towards him. Claus was barely twenty when he died on the Eastern front, and now Lotte had gone into a clinic diagnosed with acute depression. Claus had been her only son and she had idolised him. She had wanted him to go into the family banking business, and she had never forgiven her husband for persuading their son that the army was the way ahead for him. At least he would rest at peace now while his country tore itself to pieces under an increasingly unbalanced leader, who despite everything it appeared was yet planning and plotting the next ten years when the British and German peoples would unite to wipe the scourge of Communism from the face of the earth. The Fuehrer hardly ever left his bunker now, and along with Bormann and Goebbels he spent much of his time poring over campaign maps and issuing directives to the weary field commanders who were loath to pass them on to their exhausted troops.

The sharp rat-tat before the door opened made Von Mannheim sit up straight in his seat; a clerk entered, placed the sheet of paper down on the desk and gave the Nazi salute, only to be dismissed with a cursory wave of the hand. In a side room the two senior officers were waiting, and when their chief walked in they clicked their heels in a Prussian salute.

'Relax,' Mannheim bade them. 'I hope you liked the cognac, it's becoming harder to get these days. Pour yourselves another, and one for me if you will.'

When the three were comfortably seated with full glasses he imparted the information transmitted that day from a field operative in Bermondsey, England. 'Gentlemen, it would appear that the fish has taken the bait. We await a firm decision but it does seem positive. I will be seeing the Fuehrer this evening to tell him the news, but in the meantime we have work to do. Hoess, you will set the wheels moving at the Treasury and have them on standby. Lindsdorf, I want you to deal with another matter that was brought up in the message just received. It would appear that many of our flying bombs are over-running the centre of London and dropping in less populated areas to the north of the city. The necessary adjustments will have to be made if we are effectively to carry out the first stage of the Blitzkrieg. We want the Londoners to be stretched to the limit by the time the first rocket missile is launched. Follow it through the chain of command and do not accept anything other than a cast-iron guarantee of future success. You'll have my personal signed letter and that will be enough.'

The air-raid siren sounded and Mannheim cursed. 'The city's in ruins and still they come, the Americans by day and the British by night. What are they targeting, the rubble?'

Chapter Eight

Josie and Tommy stepped down from the number 82 bus, walked through into the shabby backstreet and entered the rundown buildings.

'Cor, this is a real dump,' Tommy remarked.

They hurried up the creaky wooden stairs to the first floor and knocked on the third door. There was no answer but the old lady opposite came out and peered shortsightedly at the two youngsters. 'You was 'ere yesterday,' she croaked.

'We're Frank Bailey's children an' we're lookin' for 'im,' Josie said quickly.

'Well, 'e's in there but yer better knock loudly, 'e's most likely in bed,' the old woman told her.

Josie hammered loudly on the door but still there was no answer.

''Ang on a minute, I got a key,' the woman said. 'Frank gave me a key ter mind fer 'im, in case 'e mislaid 'is.' She disappeared back into her flat and re-emerged puffing loudly. ''E was in a state when 'e got 'ome late yesterday afternoon an' I ain't seen 'im since. 'E didn't go out last night. 'E couldn't 'ave managed it, bearin' in mind 'ow 'e was.'

'Are you sure 'e never went out last night?' Josie asked with a puzzled frown.

The old woman was having trouble getting the key into the lock and she paused to give the young girl a hard look. 'I might 'ave dodgy eyes, luv, but there's nuffink wrong wiv me 'earin'. If 'e'd 'ave gone out last night I would 'ave 'eard the door go.'

She finally managed to turn the key and then stood back while Josie went in with Tommy following behind. 'Dad, are yer there?' she called out.

The living room was in a squalid state and getting no answer Josie pushed open the bedroom door and gasped. Her father was lying on his back in the bed, snoring lightly, his face resembling a raw piece of meat. There was a plaster covering one of his eyebrows and dried blood along both cheekbones. His lips were blue and swollen, and as the children stared down in horror at him he stirred and groaned.

'Dad, it's me, Josie. Tommy's 'ere too. Dad, are you awake?'

He opened his eyes and winced as he tried to sit up. 'Josie. Tommy. Why d'yer come? I didn't want yer ter see me in this state.'

'We came ter find out why yer didn't go in ter see Mum, that's why,' Josie replied sharply. 'Just look at yer. You're a disgrace. After promisin' me yer'd go in ter see 'er.'

Frank eased himself up against the iron handrail with an agonised expression on his face as he clutched at his lower ribs. 'It ain't what yer fink, luv,' he gasped. 'It wasn't the drink.'

'Don't gimme that, Dad,' she retorted. 'I'm not gonna take any more o' your excuses. Mum wanted so much fer you ter go in an' see 'er an' she was really upset when yer never showed last night.'

'Yer farvver's tellin' the trufe, gel,' the old lady said from the doorway. ''E wasn't pissed when 'e came back 'ere yesterday. There was no smell o' drink on 'im whatsoever. I should know, me an' Mrs Brody from upstairs 'ad ter get 'im in the flat an' inter bed. 'E'd collapsed on the stairs.'

'Whatever 'appened, then?' Josie asked.

Frank Bailey took a painful breath. 'After yer left yesterday I went straight round ter the baths, an' then I went ter the barber's an' got an 'aircut an' shave,' he began. 'I was determined ter get in ter the 'ospital last night. I was on me way back from the barber's an' I saw these blokes givin' ole Barney Pierce a good goin'-over on a bombsite. Yer see, Barney 'ad 'ad a stroke o' luck on the dogs on Friday night an' it came ter quite a few bob. 'E was tellin' everyone about it in the pub yesterday before you came in, an' then 'e went off ter the bookies ter collect it. Trouble was the Makin boys were in the ovver bar an' they must 'ave got to 'ear about it an' follered 'im out. They were the ones I spotted kickin' the daylights out o' Barney. I couldn't stand by, I 'ad ter do somefing to 'elp 'im. I shouted out at 'em ter leave 'im alone but they didn't take no notice, so I ran over an' managed ter pull one of 'em off the poor sod. I could see then that Barney was out cold. Then the Makins turned on me. I did what I could but they're an 'andful, believe me, an' I got a good kickin' fer me troubles. I must 'ave passed out fer a while an' when I come round I saw Barney sittin' on some bricks. The silly ole sod was grinnin' like a Cheshire cat. 'E still 'ad 'is winnin's. 'E'd put 'em in 'is sock.'

'Trust you ter get yerself involved,' Josie said with an old-fashioned look.

'What else could I do, luv, walk away?' Frank replied appealingly.

'Well, I'll tell yer what yer can't do,' Josie growled. 'Yer can't go in an' see Mum in that state.'

Frank nodded. 'I know I look a mess, but it'll 'eal up in a couple o' days. I'll come in an' see 'er then. The worst of it was they broke me pocketwatch.'

'It don't matter about yer watch,' Josie said quickly.

'Oh yes it does,' Frank replied, wincing as he reached for the timepiece on the chair beside his bed. 'Just look at it. It's the watch yer mum bought fer me on our weddin' anniversary back in thirty-eight.'

'Don't worry, I'll get it fixed at the watchmender's in Jamaica Road,' she told him.

'I dunno. I s'pose they could replace the glass, but just look at the 'ands, they're all bent.'

'I can but try,' Josie replied. 'But what about you? You should get those ribs sorted out. They could be busted.'

'Yeah, I'll get cleaned up soon as yer gone an' then I'll go an' see ole Doctor Samuels. 'E's the local sawbones. 'E'll fix me up.'

Tommy stepped up beside Josie and put his hand on the bed. 'When yer comin' 'ome, Dad?' he asked. 'We all miss yer. Mum does too, I know she does.'

Frank put his hand on the lad's head and ruffled his hair. 'I got fings ter do first, Tommy lad,' he said quietly. 'Soon I'll be ready, an' then I'll come back over the water an' ask yer all if yer'll take me back.'

'Yer don't 'ave to ask,' Tommy replied.

'Oh yes I do,' Frank told him. 'After the misery I've inflicted on you all I gotta let yer see that I'm ready fer anuvver chance.'

'I'll get yer a cup o' tea an' then I'll clean the place up a bit,' Josie offered. 'I got time.'

'Don't worry yerself, gel, me an' Mrs Brody are gonna clean it up,' the old lady cut in. 'We'll make 'im a cuppa.'

'Well, let's 'ave that watch,' Josie said.

Frank handed it to her and pulled the bedclothes up around him. 'I'll get in the 'ospital in a couple o' days, yer got my word on it. If I went in now I'd scare yer muvver 'alf ter death.'

Josie kissed him gently on his bloodstained cheek and Tommy held out his hand.

'Look after 'em all, son,' Frank told him as he pumped his arm.

★

The claws were out at number 18 Quay Street but Charlie Fiddler was adamant. 'Oh no, you bloody won't,' he said loudly. 'That woman's in enough pain wivout 'avin' ter suffer you two.'

'That's nice, ain't it,' Bel growled. 'We'd be out ter cheer 'er up, we wouldn't upset 'er for anyfing. Besides, Nell Bailey was good to us when you went down wiv the quinsies. She got the shoppin' in fer us while we was at work, then she showed us 'ow ter do yer poultices.'

'I don't fink the poor woman 'ad much choice,' Charlie said quickly. 'The first one you put on made me eyes pop. Then yer nearly pierced me windpipe wiv that safety pin yer stuck in the bandage. You was bloody useless, the three of yer. Gawd knows 'ow yer'd get on if I snuffed it.'

'We'd manage,' Chloe deadpanned. 'Anyway, I fink we should go over an' see Josie Bailey. I bet she'd be over the moon about us goin' in ter see 'er mum.'

'I wouldn't bet on it,' Charlie said sarcastically.

'I bet we'd make Nell laugh about Bel doin' the striptease,' Sandra said grinning.

'And what about our Bel goin' out fer a ride on Stymie's cart?' Chloe added. 'I bet Nell would roll up about what Stymie's plannin' ter do.'

'I despair o' you lot, really I do,' Charlie growled. 'Come back, Mabel, all is forgiven.'

'We don't want 'er back 'ere,' Sandra said quickly. 'She made all our lives a misery.'

'An' now you three are takin' up where she left off, but the number o' victims 'as bin whittled down ter one,' Charlie pointed out.

'You don't really mean that, Dad,' Bel said, putting him in a head lock and planting a wet kiss on his forehead.

'Get off me, yer silly cow,' Charlie yelled. 'Yer'll break me bloody neck.'

Bel released him and looked at Chloe. 'Gonna make a cuppa?'

'Nope.'

'Why not? Me an' Sandra always seem ter be makin' the tea. I fink it's about time you started pullin' yer weight.'

'Yeah, all fifteen stone of it,' Sandra muttered.

'I ain't that 'eavy, yer saucy cow,' Chloe shot back. 'Look at you. At least I got a bit o' shape. You look like a tub o' lard.'

'I fink I've got quite a nice figure, considerin',' Bel told them self-importantly. 'Stymie reckoned I reminded 'im of Mae West.'

''E would do,' Sandra replied. ''E's as blind as a bloody bat.'

'It's all right, yer only jealous,' Bel said haughtily.

'Jealous? Of that scruffy-lookin' totter?' Sandra snorted. 'Talk sense.'

'Now are you lot gonna shut up fer five minutes?' Charlie implored them in a raised voice. '*Two Way Family Favourites*'ll be on soon an' I wanna listen to it, if yer don't mind that is.'

'We don't mind,' Bel said casually. 'We're goin' out anyway. We're gonna pop in the Star an' Garter fer a drink.'

'Gawd knows what the customers must fink when you three walk in,' Charlie replied. 'In my day a woman on 'er own daren't go in a pub unescorted.'

'Yeah, but fings 'ave changed since the Romans,' Bel reminded him with a wry smile. 'There's a war on, in case yer've forgot. A lot o' men are in the services an' there's a lot o' young women left on their own. What are they s'posed ter do if they fancy a drink, go in the side wiv their jugs? That's all right fer the ole biddies, but not fer young women.'

'Anyway we're known in the Star an' Garter,' Chloe told him.

'Yeah, I bet you are,' Charlie growled.

'An' what's that s'posed ter mean?'

'Look I ain't gonna carry on wiv this conversation,' Charlie concluded. 'Now will one of yer, an' I don't care which one, go an' put that bloody kettle on, an' let's 'ave a nice cuppa before I die o' thirst.'

It had been a makeshift Sunday lunch at the Baileys' and just as Josie was putting on her coat ready to leave for the hospital Johnny Francis knocked at the door.

'This is a surprise,' she said smiling. 'You just caught us, we're goin' in ter see our mum.'

The young man nodded. 'I fergot you was goin' ter the 'ospital. I came over ter see if yer'd fancy the pictures ternight.'

'I'd love to but I can't,' Josie told him. 'It's seven till eight visitin' in the evenin' an' it'd be too late.'

Johnny looked disappointed. 'Maybe some ovver time. By the way, 'ow is yer mum?'

'She's mendin' well but she's grumblin' about bein' made ter lay flat all the time,' Josie replied.

Tommy and Kathy were standing behind their elder sister and becoming impatient. 'It's nearly ten ter two,' Kathy reminded her testily.

'Yeah, I know,' Josie said quickly, then turned back to John. 'I'll call in soon as I get back.'

'You told me Johnny Francis wouldn't go out o' the 'ouse,' Kathy said as they hurried towards the tram stop.

'Only if 'e really 'as to, but terday was a first,' Josie conceded.

'I fink yer wastin' yer time wiv 'im,' Kathy remarked.

'Oh yer do, do yer?'

'Yeah, I do. Ginny Allen reckons 'e'll ferget all about you an' what yer've done fer 'im when 'e gets out an' about again.'

'Oh, does she? Well what does Ginny Allen know?'

A number 68 tram rumbled up to the stop and the Baileys clambered aboard. 'I wanna go upstairs,' Tommy said quickly.

'Get in there,' Josie told him firmly, motioning towards the lower deck. 'It's only a couple o' stops.'

Tommy puffed loudly and gave the conductor a pained look. 'Yer can see more from upstairs,' he complained.

'Yeah, the sights o' London,' the conductor replied, holding out his hand for the fare.

Tommy ignored him and glared out of the window while Josie fished into her purse for change.

'I 'ope Farvver means what 'e said about visitin' Mum,' Kathy frowned.

'Dad'll be there in a few days,' Josie replied. ''E gave us 'is word.'

'A fat lot o' good that is.'

'Whatever 'e is or whatever 'e ain't, Dad's never broken is word yet,' Josie told her sharply.

'You're always defendin' 'im,' Kathy growled, 'but if 'e don't go in soon an' I see 'im I'll really tell 'im off.'

'Don't you worry, I'll be doin' the same.'

They hurried down from the tram and made their way under the railway arch which led out into St Thomas Street opposite the hospital.

'Now look, you two, I don't want eivver o' yer mentionin' anyfing ter Mum about what's 'appened ter Dad,' Josie warned them. 'I'll tell 'er 'e's in bed wiv the 'flu an' 'e promises ter come in soon as 'e's up an' about again. An' brighten up yer faces, you look as miserable as sin both o' yer.'

Tommy spread his lips wide to show his large white teeth in a comical grimace and Kathy offered a brief smile that turned into a large puff. 'These places give me the 'orrers,' she remarked. 'Especially that ward Mum's in. They've all got plaster on their legs an' arms, an' there's that woman wiv the water stuff drippin' into 'er.'

'Well what else d'yer expect?' Josie sighed. 'It's a surgical ward.'

They found their mother looking a little miserable but she tried to put a brave face on it. 'I'm sorry I ain't much company, but yer get bored bloody stupid layin' around like this all the time,' she sighed.

'Never mind, it won't be fer much longer,' Josie said with a smile. 'Anyway I've seen Dad. 'E's bin laid up in bed wiv the 'flu but 'e's gettin' over it an' 'e said 'e'll be well enough ter get in an' see yer in a few days.'

Josie tried to keep the conversation light and humorous as they chatted together, but after a while Nell Bailey seemed to have grown distracted, and there was a faraway look in her eyes. Josie wanted to reassure her about Frank's intentions but she held back, feeling that it might make things worse.

Tommy was getting fidgety and he stood up quickly as the visiting bell sounded. Kathy stayed where she was and looked towards the sister's office. 'She don't give yer any leeway, does she?' she moaned. 'There's still a minute ter go by that clock.'

Josie told her and Tommy to wait outside for her and when they had left the bedside she took her mother's hand in hers. 'I'm sure Dad will come in soon,' she said quietly. ''E gave me 'is word.'

'Yeah, 'e'll come when 'e's ready,' Nell told her. 'If I looked miserable it wasn't frew finkin' about yer farvver. As a matter o' fact, I was finkin' about Lucy Briars. They dug 'er out about the same time as they got ter me but she was in a really bad way. They put 'er on the open order, an' I 'eard she died this mornin'.'

Josie shook her head sadly as she saw the lone tear escape

from the corner of her mother's eye and run down the side of her face. Her own eyes filled and she blinked quickly. 'I know Lucy was a good friend o' yours, Mum, but yer gotta concentrate on gettin' well. You was lucky an' yer gotta be fankful for it.'

'I know,' Nell said, giving her daughter a brave smile. 'Don't you worry about me, I'm doin' fine.'

The stockily built man in his early forties pulled back on the lead as his dog picked up a scent. 'All right, boy. Let's sit down here for a bit,' he said as they approached a wooden bench.

Down below the bends of the river looked serene in the low afternoon sun, and even from that distance, high above on the promontory at Greenwich Park where General Wolfe surveyed the scene, the agent could see the sway of the crane hawsers. The place was alive with families and children on that summer Sunday and an ideal place for the rendezvous, he felt.

The dog squatted on its haunches, its tongue hanging out after its exertions off the lead, and the man sat deep in thought. Things were moving swiftly. Early on Saturday evening he had received a phone call from Sir Barry Freeman, who told him that the anglers were going fishing, and later on he had received another cryptic phone message, reporting that the fish were jumping. It told him all he wanted to know, and early that Sunday morning he had transmitted a coded message to Berlin.

While he waited the agent absent-mindedly stroked the dog's ear, focusing his thoughts on the task in hand. For over a year now he had been virtually inactive professionally speaking, until four weeks ago when he received a coded message from Berlin, instructing him to contact the League of White Knights through Sir Barry Freeman and inform him that his organisation could benefit greatly if they agreed to meet a representative of a sympathetic group at a date to be set in the very near future.

The League had been selected by the High Command in Berlin after careful analysis of the information received through one of their field agents, whose persistence and cunning had subsequently brought about the death of the very man who had been the source of his information, League member Herbert Millington.

It had transpired that Millington's liking for the bottle caused him to be a little loose-tongued at his club and at City bars. Names had been dropped, and with some liquid encouragement he had openly bragged about his involvement with the Fascist League of White Knights. Had he taken more notice of the Government posters which reminded everyone that 'Careless Talk Costs Lives' he would no doubt still be here today, but unfortunately for Herbert Millington he chose not to, and the life his careless talk cost was his own. His disclosures had not only been relayed to the Field Headquarters in Berlin by the generous gentleman who had been a willing listener, they had reached the ear of Sir Barry himself, and as he viewed it he had little choice but to protect the integrity of the movement.

The agent waited patiently, enjoying the warmth of the afternoon sun. After he had sent the transmission off that morning he had phoned Hennessey's hotel, asking the receptionist to pass a message on to the courier that his mother would be arriving home at midday. It was the signal for him to be at a certain public call-box at that time, and when he answered the call Hennessey was made aware of what had taken place. The League of White Knights had met on Saturday evening and had agreed to study the plan in detail before making a firm decision. They had asked for the plan to be forwarded to them, and to that end the man and his dog were here.

It was almost four o'clock when the tall slim man with the fair wavy hair approached the bench carrying a book under his arm. 'He looks a nice little fellow,' he said, bending to pat the dog.

'Man's best friend,' the agent replied, with a brief smile.

Hennessey straightened up and returned the smile before walking off with his hands in his pockets.

The agent waited for a few minutes, then he got up and walked slowly down the steep pathway which led to the park gates. Under his arm was the novel, made safe as far as the acid was concerned, containing the plotting and planning of a desperate tyrant who had brought most of the world to arms, the German Fuehrer Adolf Hitler.

Chapter Nine

On Monday lunchtime Josie Bailey called in to George Stephens' Watch and Clock Repairs with her father's battered pocketwatch. It was a tiny shop wedged between a greengrocer's and a butcher's, with a side door that led up to a flat above. It smelled of oil and linseed, and when the bell over the entrance sounded the proprietor walked out from a back room wiping his hands on a piece of cotton waste. 'What can I do for you, my dear?' he asked with a smile which revealed large, tobacco-stained teeth.

Josie laid her father's watch down on the counter and looked up at the watchmender with concern. 'Can you fix this?' she asked.

'Excuse me a moment,' he replied as he reached under the counter for a clean cloth. 'I've just been oiling the casing of a grandfather clock. It's a very messy business. Umm. This is in a state, isn't it? Has it been dropped from a height?'

Josie shook her head. 'I don't fink so. It's my dad's, an' I fink it just got trampled on.'

The watchmaker smiled. 'The reason I asked was because the cogs usually come adrift in a heavy fall, which often causes more damage. Anyway let's take a look inside.'

Josie watched intrigued as the thick-set man prised open the back cover and examined the works through an eye glass. 'Well, there doesn't appear to be any internal damage,' he remarked, 'but the hands and glass will need to be replaced as you can see. I'm afraid it'll cost twelve and six. Will you leave it now or go away and think about it?'

Josie bit on her lip. 'I know it's not an expensive watch but it's got sentimental value. I'll leave it wiv you,' she decided.

'Give me a few days,' the watchmender replied. 'I may have to order the hands from Clerkenwell Road but I have a replacement glass.'

Josie looked around the shop while the owner wrote her out a receipt. The walls were covered with clocks. Small cuckoo clocks and modern wall clocks of every shape and size were on display, and she marvelled at the variety. ''Ow much is that alarm clock?' she asked. 'The blue one next ter the cuckoo clock.'

'Twenty-five shillings,' he told her. 'It's got a double alarm. Twice as loud, my dear.'

'I'll fink about that,' she said as she picked up the receipt.

As she reached for the door handle the watchmaker leaned his elbows on the counter. 'Tell me, are you Frank Bailey's daughter?' he asked.

Josie was taken aback. 'Yes I am, as a matter o' fact,' she replied. 'You know my dad?'

'I tend to know people through their possessions,' he replied. 'I saw the identification markings inside the cover of the watch and I've just remembered seeing the same numbers and letters before. You see the makers usually put their mark on a watch, next to the craftsman's. It gives an indication of origin to any watchmender who might want to contact them. Purely technical, my dear, but sometimes certain numbers stick in the mind and I recalled talking to your father about this particular watch some few months ago. He brought it in saying that it was losing time and it just needed a slight adjustment on the spring balance. Then after I'd fixed it he asked me if he could pawn it. I had to say no. I'm not a pawnbroker and to be frank the watch is only a cheap one. A lot of pawnbrokers wouldn't take it anyway.'

'Me dad was out o' work at the time,' Josie told him.

'Yes, I think he must have been,' the watchmender said, smiling kindly.

The Traveller's Rest at Blackheath was not one of the draymen's favourite deliveries. For a start the cellar was small, with a very low ceiling, but what really made it worse was the reluctance of the landlord to offer the deliverymen a drink after they had sweated to stow the beer properly.

''E's an ungrateful, tight-fisted sod, why should we tell 'im about the water seepin' in the cellar,' the driver said disgustedly as they finished the job. ''E should 'ave bin down there 'elpin' instead o' standin' at the cellar flap countin' every crate. Let the tight bastard find out fer 'imself.'

The brewerymen sheeted up the dray and walked round to the front of the pub to get their delivery note signed. The Traveller's Rest was not yet open for business, but as the three took their places at the bar in the vain hope of a charitable drink they were all grinning.

'Right then, guv. There wasn't any breakages, was there?'

The drayman's intonation was ignored by the landlord. He knew that if he offered the men a pint each they would cover the expense for him by deducting a few breakages from his tally, but he was damned if he was going to encourage them. They were never satisfied. One pint would soon become two and in the end the brewery would query what was going on. 'No. No breakages.'

'It's a shit-'ole of a cellar, that one, guv,' one of the draymen remarked. 'It does yer back in.'

The landlord nodded, wondering why the smiles on the men's faces had grown larger. 'Right, there we are,' he said, quickly signing the delivery note and passing it back over the counter.

'I've always thought it was a nice name fer a pub, the Traveller's Rest,' the drayman said as he pocketed the note and climbed down from the bar stool. 'Somewhere ter rest yer arse when yer burdened.'

'Some names are crap,' the driver replied as the three walked out of the bar. 'I like "The Throne Room" meself.'

The landlord shook his head as he heard the crew's laughing voices. 'They're getting worse,' he sighed to his wife who had just come into the bar. 'Bloody morons, that's what they are. It's hard to get a sensible word out of any of them. That's why I won't offer them a drink.'

'Quite right, dear,' the wife said. 'Once you start you have to carry on, and just think of it, if they're late delivering for some reason we'll have them sitting at the bar upsetting our clientele.'

'Exactly,' the landlord replied. 'Twenty years at the same public house and not a single blemish against us. Next year when the Blaydons retire we should be favourites to get the big one.'

'I do hope so,' his dutiful wife nodded. 'The Clarendon is top-notch and the turnover there is excellent, according to Mr Morris. Wouldn't it be lovely if we were successful.'

'Never you fear, dear, we'll be the new tenants of the Clarendon, mark my words.'

Later that morning, just before opening time, Mr Morris the area manager stormed into the public bar, his face flushed. 'Gordon!' he called out loudly. 'Where are you?'

'Just in the back, old chap,' the landlord replied, slipping through into the bar.

'Is this still the Traveller's Rest, or have you taken it on yourself to change the name off your own back?' Morris fulminated. 'I mean you've not decided to change the name to "Public Urinal" have you?'

'I say, old man, steady on.'

'Steady nothing. Go outside and tell me what the hell is going on.'

The landlord walked out of the bar and came back in with his head in his hand, shocked at the sight of a dirty old lavatory seat hanging over the door. 'Oh my God!' he groaned. 'Who would have done such a thing? I'll fetch the ladder and get it down before we open.'

The landlord's tribulations were not over, for when the area manager went down to the cellar to check the stock he found himself standing ankle-deep in cold, evil-smelling water. 'Gordon!' he screamed out, then muttered to himself, 'And they want the Clarendon. They've got about as much chance of taking that over as I have of shagging Betty Grable.'

Sir Barry Freeman was a big man, broad-shouldered and with a determined step that belied his age. Now coming up to his fifty-fifth birthday, he was still enjoying a healthy and virile existence. Once, as a section leader with the Blackshirts, he had been in the thick of the troubles, and his prowess had become a byword. Little wonder that he was chosen as the First Knight from the beginning, and now after two terms of office the League members did not quite take him seriously when he indicated that it was time for someone else to carry the torch.

Victor Anderson realised that he was in the frame to don the mantle of office, but he knew that too confident an attitude could well create resentment amongst some members. The First Knight carried much on his shoulders and the membership had to be sure that their leader could be relied upon to fulfil the duties of office with confidence and discretion. To that end he had deliberately showed caution at the meeting when he stated that in his opinion the assassination of Churchill would not necessarily bring down the Government. Now, as he waited for Sir Barry to arrive at the Savoy Grill, he smoked his cigar and sipped his coffee with relish.

'Ah there you are,' the First Knight said with a smile as he approached the table, partially concealed by the large frond of a parlour palm growing in a clay pot. 'Nice we could meet. I had to excuse myself from a directors' lunch but I'm sure they'll get on famously without my input.'

The attentive waiter approached and gave the spotless table a quick brush with a napkin. 'Can I bring you the menu, gentlemen?' he inquired.

Sir Barry nodded and felt inside his coat for his cigar case.

'Here, try one of these,' Anderson offered.

'Good Lord! Havana. Rolled and shaped on the thigh if we're to believe the Cubans.'

Anderson smiled. 'They were a present actually, for services rendered.'

'Don't tell me any more, it could be incriminating,' Sir Barry said as he drew on the cigar.

The waiter came over with the menus and Anderson selected the sole while Freeman chose the sea bass.

'I thought you were a little reticent at the meeting, old man,' the First Knight remarked as the waiter went away with their order.

'I didn't want to encourage too much expectation,' Anderson replied. 'We are asking a lot.'

'Have you ever sat round the table with trade unionists?' Sir Barry wanted to know.

'Never had the pleasure.'

'Well, I have. They usually ask for the moon and settle for much less.'

'The first rule of negotiation, I believe,' Anderson smiled.

'Correct,' Sir Barry replied, studying his glowing cigar. 'Now if we apply that criterion to our situation where does it leave us?'

'If I may be so bold, I would say it leaves us with half a million in gold and a war raging on until 1945.'

Sir Barry nodded. 'The promised new weapon they are setting against us will be marginalised as the Allies' advance overruns the launch sites, and providing the German counter-offensive doesn't totally succeed I can't envisage a mass call for an armistice. Of course there will be loud cries from various quarters for that very thing, but generally speaking the populace will honour their murdered leader by voting to fight on until the Nazis capitulate unconditionally.'

Victor Anderson drained his coffee cup and set it down on the table. 'I have to be honest . . .'

'Please do.'

'When I first met Hennessey and heard the outline I felt that it was the ravings of a madman, and I haven't changed my mind.'

Sir Barry Freeman looked thoughtful as he gently eased the inch or so of ash from the head of his cigar. 'Yes, but there is a certain merit in it,' he pointed out. 'I think we all share the belief that the war is as good as won. What is unsure is the final settlement. How will the victors divide the spoils? What will happen to the vanquished? Churchill's position on this is well documented. He will settle for nothing less than a war crimes trial. With him out of the way and with an ailing American president, the door will be ajar for new leadership with less inflexibility, which is important when you consider that we'll have to contend with a Communist threat rolling in from the east. As I see it, the League of White Knights should go along with the plan and utilise the money made available to us in shrewd investments, biding our time until the country is ready for an alternative Government. We have to bear in mind of course that the funds will need to be transferred in their entirety before the end of the war. After the cessation of hostilities pressure will be brought to bear by both this country and America for neutrals to freeze all Germany's assets wherever they are.'

Victor Anderson nodded. 'Dublin comes to mind.'

'It would be a good choice, don't you think?'

'I do.'

'The food's on its way,' Sir Barry said smiling. 'Do I take it then that I can count on your support and backing at the discussion on Wednesday evening.'

'Of course.'

'Good man.'

As they tucked into the fish a waiter hurried over and leaned down to whisper a few words in Sir Barry's ear.

'Splendid,' he replied, smiling over at the curious Anderson. 'I left instructions with my secretary to telephone as soon as the package arrived. Never was a great reader, but this is one novel I'm going to enjoy.'

On Monday evening the stockily built man made his way by bus and tube to Willesden Green. In that part of north-west London there was a large Irish community, and he was hoping to find one Irishman in particular. It had been some time now since they had last met but as he pushed open the public-bar door of the Napier Arms he was confident of finding him, assuming of course that he was still alive.

The traveller from Bermondsey and agent for the Third Reich walked casually to the counter and ordered a Guinness. 'Do you ever see anything of that son of a bishop Sean Feeney these days?' he asked with a smile as the drink was placed in front of him.

The barman looked at him suspiciously. It was unheard of for a stranger to walk into a pub in that particular area and immediately inquire about a member of the IRA. 'And why would you be asking?' the barman quizzed him.

'Sean Feeney owes me and I've come to collect,' the agent told him. 'Alternatively I can put some good business his way. If you do lay eyes on yer man tell him Kelly was asking after his welfare.'

The barman nodded and as soon as the customer took his seat by the entrance he called another barman over. A few quick words were exchanged then the second man slipped out from behind the counter and hurried out into the busy thoroughfare.

The agent had taken a newspaper from his pocket and appeared to be engrossed in the racing page, but out of the corner of his eye he had seen what went on and knew that he would not have long to wait before things started moving. He drank his Guinness and, aware that the barman was eyeing him, he walked up to the bar once more and ordered another drink to put the poor fellow's mind at rest. Just then the door opened and two well-built men sauntered up to the counter and stood one on each side of him. 'Mr Kelly?'

'Yes, that's me.'

'You were asking after Sean Feeney.'

'That I was.'

'He owes you a favour, you said.'

'Yes, and I'm sure he'll remember it.'

The man to the agent's right spoke for the first time and his tone was much more menacing. 'A stranger coming into a pub predominantly used by Republicans and bandying names about is acting rather stupid, wouldn't you say?'

The agent smiled. 'Not if he knows it will get an effective response,' he replied. 'Let's face it, a less blunt approach would have achieved nothing. As it is, you are going to find out just what I'm up to, one way or another, so I suggest you let me buy you both a drink and we can sit down and discuss things civilly.'

The man in the grey suit on his left nodded. 'That sounds reasonable,' he said. 'We'll have the usual, Brendan.'

The agent put down a note to cover the cost of the drinks then he walked over to his table flanked by the two men.

'Actually Sean Feeney owes me an explanation, nothing more,' the agent began after they had made themselves comfortable. 'We worked together in the Republic before the war. We were assembling machinery at a factory in Cork, and when we were paid off we agreed to meet the following week to go out on a night of revelry. Two hours I waited for that son of a bishop, as he liked to be called, but he never showed up. He had given me his London address previously and told me that he used this pub when he was in the area. Anyway I came here to look him up just after the war broke out and there he was, large as life and drunk as a prelate. I gathered that he was active in the cause, and we arranged to meet here again the following week but true to form he didn't show up. I could only assume he was back in the Republic, or wherever.'

'And what is this proposition you have for him?' the man in the grey suit asked.

'That's for Sean's ears alone,' the agent replied.

'We could quite easily hammer it out of you,' the man told him calmly.

'Of course you could, but I don't think Sean Feeney would appreciate it.'

'Come with us,' the other man said, getting up.

The agent walked between them along the High Street and soon they directed him into a backstreet. One of the men knocked on the door of a run-down house and Sean Feeney himself answered the knock. 'Why if it's not yer man himself,' he said smiling broadly, his eyes wide with surprise as he stepped forward to embrace the agent warmly.

The large shabby room was lit by a single naked bulb hanging from flex and there was very little in the way of furniture apart from a table, two chairs and a tattered sideboard. The floor was partially covered with a straw mat and here and there the wallpaper hung down amid patches of damp.

'Sorry for the state of the place but I'm obliged to keep out of sight for the time being, Danny boy. You understand.'

Danny Kelly nodded and smiled. 'Still active then?'

'We'll all die for the cause one day, Danny,' he replied. 'But why the visit? I heard you were in the war, wearing the King's uniform.'

'We all serve in our own way,' Kelly remarked. 'Which brings me to the reason I came over. I need your help.'

'Fire away.'

'Word has it that the Pedlar is active again, or might be persuaded, if the price was right.'

Sean Feeney's face suddenly darkened. 'We don't mention that name any more around here,' he replied in a sober voice. 'The man's a law unto himself. We won't touch him after that nasty business in Belfast. You remember it. He was contracted to take out the Loyalist leader Burke and he succeeded in wiping the whole family out as well. His excuse was that the man's brothers were armed and were turning their weapons on him, but it wasn't true. The area commander ordered a contract on him but he fled to America. It should have been followed up. It could have been, quite easily, but there were other matters pressing at the time and so the bastard was lucky enough to survive. He's back in this country now, as you seem to know, but I can't help you locate him. It would put me in a bad light and I need that like I need a hole in the head.'

'You owe me one, Sean.'

'I owe you nothing.'

'Remember the time you stood me up in Dublin? You left me roasting when I needed your help.'

'It was unavoidable.'

'Yes maybe, but you never told me the reason why.'

'I couldn't.'

'Well anyway, it's all water down the Liffey. You can still help an old friend.'

'Don't ask me, Danny boy. You're taking advantage of our friendship,' Sean Feeney said darkly.

'All I need is a place to start looking, Sean. Surely that's not too much to ask?' Kelly said, staring hard at him.

Sean Feeney leaned across the table, clasping his hands together tightly till his knuckles whitened. 'Okay so I give you the lead and you make contact. Then what?' he asked. 'The people who are looking after the Pedlar would want to know who led you to him. What would you tell them?'

'Oh, I'd never mention your name,' Danny Kelly said quickly.

'They'd check it out, and if they realised you'd lied to them they'd dump you somewhere with a bullet in your head. Have you not considered that?'

It was the agent's turn to press his point and he drew himself up, his fists tight knots on the table. 'I'd remain anonymous, Sean,' he replied. 'My job is to make the contact. I'd just be the middle man. It would all be done over the phone. No danger for either of us, and no comebacks. If the Pedlar wants the job he can make his own arrangements with the hirer.'

Sean Feeney stared down at his clenched hands for a few moments, then he looked up, his pale blue eyes searching those of his old friend. 'I'm going to take a chance with you, Danny boy,' he replied. 'This is for old time's sake, but don't let me down, or you'll be mumbling your apologies to my headstone.'

'God forbid, Sean.'

'Tell me, would you recognise him?' the Republican asked.

'No, I've never seen his face.'

'Well, it's of no consequence if you're not going to meet him personally. The publican at the Fellowship Inn in Neasden is family. Word has it the Pedlar's staying there, but for God's sake be careful when you speak to him. The first thing he'll want to know is who put you on to him. You have to understand his position. There's many who'd happily put a bullet in his brain without losing a second's sleep, and if you're not on your guard I could end up like a slice of ham between two hunks of bread. Dead meat, Danny boy. Just remember, I'm a marked man already in the Loyalist books and I don't need my own to mark me up.'

'May I rot in hell screaming if I let you down, Sean,' the agent said with a passion that touched the other man.

The tension suddenly lifted in the room as Sean Feeney reached for the bottle. They drank to each other and then the agent made his excuses to leave.

'One last drink before you go, my old friend,' Sean Feeney said with some emotion, 'and a toast.'

They raised the refilled glasses and Sean smiled. 'May the good Lord carry you in the palm of his hand, and may you be safe in heaven half an hour before the devil knows you're dead.'

'May the road rise for you, and may you live to write your memoirs in a peaceful, united Ireland,' the agent replied with a smile.

Chapter Ten

As they had during the Blitz, the people of London began to accept the new uncertainty in their lives, the threat by day and night of sudden death from the skies, but unlike the earlier time there was a general feeling that it wouldn't last much longer. Soon the Allied armies would overrun the launching sites and press on into Germany and the war would be won. Morale was high, and for the first time since the war started people could begin to plan for a future, even if their hopes and dreams were guarded. Had they known however that there was another, much more advanced, weapon of terror in the Nazi armoury which was being quickly prepared for delivery, they would have been much less optimistic.

Like everyone else the folk of Quay Street went about their daily business with one eye to the future. For the Bailey family things were looking up. Nell Bailey was slowly recovering in hospital, Frank was beginning the fight to win back the respect of his family and Josie felt happy with the way she was handling things. Kathy and Tommy had accepted that she was in charge for the time being and were doing their best to help out in the house. Johnny Francis seemed to be making good progress in his rehabilitation and was gaining in confidence, and Josie had experienced the selfish pleasure of being desired. Billy Emmerson was showing his interest and she wanted to savour it, albeit in a careful way that would not give him any false hopes. Billy would always be a friend, a good, close friend, she hoped.

On Wednesday morning Polly Seagram stepped down from the taxi and looked up and down the street while her husband Bernie paid off the driver. She was a buxom woman, with a round face and a ready smile that seemed to radiate happiness. A mass of tight blonde curls framed her large hazel eyes, and her shapely, slim-ankled legs ended in tiny feet which were invariably clad in high-heeled patent shoes.

'It's nice ter be 'ome, luv,' she remarked as she put the key into the lock at number 8.

'Yeah, that sister o' yours 'as bin drivin' me right round the twist,' Bernie growled as he picked up the large suitcases and followed her into the house.

'She ain't so bad, luv,' Polly replied as she went into the scullery to put the kettle on.

'She's as good as gold, but she does go on, don't she?' Bernie puffed.

'Never mind! We're 'ome now, an' you can go up the pub ternight an' tell all yer mates what a poxy week yer've 'ad,' Polly told him with a crooked smile.

'As if I would.'

'Nah, I know yer wouldn't.'

Bernie was a crane driver at the Surrey Docks, and had been involved in the building of the Mulberry Harbour which had been towed across the Channel to facilitate the landing of men and supplies for the invasion. He was a slight, dapper man of fifty-two with thick dark hair, just two years older than Polly, who told everyone that she was forty-five. The Seagrams' marriage was a happy one, nourished by a constant exchange of repartee, sometimes praising, sometimes the reverse, but never insulting enough to initiate serious hostilities.

'Shall I take this case upstairs?' Bernie asked.

'Well, it won't walk up there by itself, now will it?' Polly replied.

Bernie came back into the scullery puffing and flopped down at the table, reaching for his tobacco tin. 'Ain't that tea ready yet?' he asked.

'Bloody 'ell, give us a chance, man,' Polly growled.

'It's that gas. It's 'alf pressure,' Bernie remarked. 'I 'ope they ain't 'it the gasworks again since we've bin away.'

''Ere, keep yer eye on the kettle,' Polly told him. 'I wanna see if Nell's in.' After getting no reply at number 6 Polly knocked at the Woodleys.'

''Ello, gel. When d'yer get 'ome?' Ellie Woodley asked her.

'Ten minutes ago.'

'Yer look very well.'

'Yeah, it was a nice rest, though Bernie didn't fink so,' Polly replied smiling. ''E got a bit fed up wiv me sister goin' off about this an' that. Mind you, 'e ain't got much room ter complain. 'Im an' Vi's ole man were pubbin' it every night. The pair of 'em were pissed as puddin's 'alf the time.'

'Is there anyfing yer need, save yer goin' ter the shops?' Ellie asked.

'Nah, I just knocked ter say 'ello an' ter find out if Nell's in.'

Ellie's face changed. 'Course you wouldn't 'ave known, would yer?' she said quickly.

'Known? Known what?'

'Rayburn's got a direct 'it last Friday. Nell's in 'ospital.'

'Oh my good Gawd!' Polly gasped. ''Ow bad is she?'

'She's in no danger but she's gotta lay flat fer a couple o' weeks,' Ellie told her. 'She's got a twisted back an' she's covered in cuts an' bruises.'

''Ave yer bin ter see 'er yet?'

'Nah, not yet.'

''Ow's the kids taken it?'

'Josie's copin' well but yer can see by their little faces 'ow worried they are.'

'I'll pop in this afternoon. No I won't, I'll go in this mornin',' Polly said positively.

'They won't let yer in, 'less there's an open order out,' Ellie reminded her.

'We'll see,' Polly growled. 'Well, I'd better get back indoors. I've left Bernie makin' the tea. It'll be like gnat's piss if I don't black it.'

Across the river in Stepney, Frank Bailey sat sipping a pint of bitter at the Lighterman. The riverside pub was also the haunt of Nobby Swan, an old friend of his who eked out a living with his small boat, ferrying and hiring it out. The craft was old and like its owner more than slightly weatherbeaten, but it had a forward cabin and a powerful engine that Nobby maintained in good order. In a weak moment he had named his boat *Marie*, after his long-suffering wife, who decided to leave him soon after. Undaunted, Nobby blacked out the last letter and added a few more. *Marie* became *Marigold*, and on that Wednesday morning as the riverman recounted the story to Frank he chuckled. 'Uppin' an' leavin' was the best fing that she ever did fer me,' he went on. 'I knew it 'ad ter be the boat or 'er. I asked 'er what she expected me ter do if I sold the bloody fing, work in a factory? She thought it'd be a damned sight better than scratchin' a livin' on the water. No idea, yer see. This life's in me blood but she couldn't understand it. Me farvver an' 'is farvver before 'im were rivermen, an' I done me stint as a lighterman before I bought the *Marigold*. Wouldn't 'ave it any ovver way. I can get pissed an' then roll inter the bunk I've installed in the cabin an' let the swell rock me ter sleep. Next mornin' a few sniffs o' the river blows all the cobwebs away an' I'm ready fer business.'

Frank smiled. 'Yer got it made, Nobby,' he told him. 'It was the same wiv my ole man. A lighterman all 'is life an"e fully expected me ter foller 'im. I 'ad ovver ideas though. I went in the cooperin' game as yer know. It was a good business ter be in, still is as a matter o' fact. They'll always want barrels. At one time I was gonna set up on me own but it wasn't ter be. The war an' all that.'

Nobby took out a clasp knife and flipped out a blade with which he scraped round inside the bowl of his clay pipe. 'I remember 'ow upset yer ole man was when yer decided ter go inter cooperin',' he said. 'Nice bloke was Jacko. Me an' 'im 'ad a few bevvies tergevver right 'ere in this pub.'

Frank made to pick up his glass but stopped himself. 'I'm goin' in ter see Nell this evenin',' he announced.

'She'll be pleased ter see yer,' Nobby remarked, knowing the history.

'Yeah, I 'ope so.'

'Course she will. Yer look quite spruce as it 'appens,' Nobby said smiling.

'I miss 'er, Nobby, an' I miss those kids too,' Frank told him. 'It cut me ter the quick when I saw the look in young Tommy's eyes last Sunday. Pleadin' they was. Anyway I told 'im it wouldn't be long. What else could I say?'

Nobby pointed to Frank's half-empty glass. 'Come on, son, drink up.'

Frank shook his head. 'I've 'ad that one an' I'm gonna make it do till after the visit,' he explained. 'I don't want me breath smellin' o' booze.'

'Well, I wish yer luck. It's a few hours till visitin' time, Frank.'

'Time'll pass quick enough,' Frank replied. 'Don's givin' me some work at 'is cooperage this afternoon. It's only a bit o' clearin' up an' doin' the fires, but it's work an' 'e pays a decent wage.'

''Ave you ever thought o' goin' back full time?' Nobby asked.

'Don's promised me a regular spot as soon as I sort meself out,' he answered. 'Yer can't do cooperin' if yer 'alf pissed.'

'Nah, I s'pose not,' Nobby agreed. 'Anyway you'll soon sort yerself out, an' there's always a berth on the ole *Marigold* when yer need it.'

'Yer a good pal,' Frank said smiling. 'I'll bear that in mind.'

It was nearing midday when Polly Seagram stepped down from the tram and hurried through the long arch towards Guy's Hospital. It might work if I pretend to be a Government inspector needing information, she considered. No that won't wash, you stupid cow. They'd want identification and you wouldn't be able to keep up the plummy accent long enough. Perhaps it'd be better if I just told the truth. I've just got back from holiday and Mrs Bailey's my closest friend. No, they'd just tell me to come back during visiting hours. Cobblers.

As she crossed St Thomas Street and walked into the hospital forecourt Polly's face broke into a wide grin.

'Good morning, sister. Lovely day isn't it?'

'Very nice,' the sister replied with a slightly suspicious look.

'Mrs Greene's under the weather so she's asked me to stand in for her.'

'Mrs Greene?'

'The hair lady.'

'The tall woman who does the patients' hair?'

'The same.'

'I thought her name was Rogers.'

'That's right, but Rogers is her professional name, the name over her shop. She's really Mrs Greene.'

'Oh I see.'

'Mrs Greene asked me to get any orders and to tell the patients she'll be in next week as normal. Will that be all right, sister?'

'As long as you're not too long. I'm awaiting matron's visit and the doctors are due round soon.' Polly gave the sister a friendly smile. 'Five minutes or so, that's all I need.'

Nell Bailey was snoozing lightly and when she felt the cool hand on her forehead she opened her eyes. 'Gawd 'elp us if it ain't Polly,' she said grinning.

'Who else d'yer fink it'd be, John Barrymore?' Polly grinned back.

'When d'yer get back?'

'About an hour ago.'

'Yer didn't lose much time gettin' in.'

'Didn't 'ave much ter do anyway, an' anyfing's better than sittin' lookin' at Bernie all day,' Polly joked.

Nell studied her fingernails for a few moments while Polly glanced down the ward to see if she was being observed.

''Ow did yer manage ter get in?' Nell asked her.

'I'm takin' orders,' Polly told her with a big smile.

'Takin' orders? What orders?'

'Perms an' sets.'

'There's a woman already comes in,' Nell said looking puzzled.

'A Mrs Rogers I believe,' Polly replied. 'That's who I'm takin' orders for. She's off sick, yer see.'

'Oh I see,' Nell realised, shaking her head slowly. 'Polly, yer gettin' worse. It's a wonder the sister fell fer it.'

'Well she's not come after me.'

'Give it time.'

Polly looked back along the ward again but could see no

sign of her. 'I fink she's got too much on 'er plate ter worry about me,' she remarked.

'Frank's promised ter come in soon,' Nell said suddenly.

'That'll be nice, gel. 'Ow is 'e?'

'Josie's seen 'im. 'E's bin down wiv the 'flu but 'e's gettin' over it. That's why 'e's not bin in before.'

'Is 'e still drinkin'?'

'I'd say so,' Nell replied. 'Josie tries ter cover it up, makes excuses fer 'im, but I can see the trufe in the gel's eyes. A muvver can always tell.'

'I'm sure Frank's fightin' the demons, Nell, an' 'e'll come out trumps,' Polly told her firmly. 'The man's got guts. 'E won't go under, not your Frank.'

Nell reached under her pillow for her handkerchief and dabbed at her eyes. 'I'm worried about young Tommy,' she said sniffing. ''E really misses 'is dad.'

''E'll be fine,' Polly said reassuringly. ''Ere by the way, I gotta tell yer this little story . . .'

Twenty minutes later the sound of voices in the corridor made Polly get up quickly. 'I'd better go, it sounds like the matron's visit,' she muttered.

As she hurried out of the ward she was confronted by the huge, starched figure of the matron. 'And who might this be?' she boomed.

'The hair lady,' the sister said quickly.

The matron waved her entourage into the ward and marched forward, but the sister held back. 'Did you get all your orders?' she asked in a sarcastic tone of voice.

'Yes thank you, sister,' Polly replied.

'How did you do it, by telepathy?' the sister retorted.

Polly realised she had been rumbled. Try flattery, she thought. She gave the woman one of her best smiles and flashed her eyes. 'You're a good sport, sister,' she said amiably.

The stern face of the ward sister relaxed slightly. 'Get out of here,' she growled.

On Wednesday the League of White Knights held their second meeting within a week and the panelled study was silent as the cadre took their places at the head table. Sir Barry Freeman stood up slowly and eyed the members. 'We have discussed the bones of the plan with you and taken your observations on board,' he began. 'They have been given every consideration and it is our decision that we will accept the plan and put it into effect with prudence and forethought. We shall not fail. In fact the opportunity it presents us with is absolutely unprecedented – the promise of final victory. A nationwide united movement of like-minded souls with the same aims and objectives as ours has always been an exciting but unlikely prospect, but with ample funds to project our message into the workplaces, the clubs, the pubs and social and sporting gatherings, it will become a vast and overwhelming reality. We will send our message on to the streets, and stamp on any opposition, and I give you my pledge: from this day on I will lead you unceasingly in our glorious quest, the individual purification of mind and body and the collective purification of our sceptred isle. To England and Saint George!'

'To England and Saint George,' the cry went up.

'And God forgive us all,' Sidney Holman growled to Anderson as they filed out of the study.

Remembering his promise to Sir Barry earlier that week Victor Anderson smiled calmly. 'Treat it as a boardroom decision, Sidney, and try not to lose any sleep,' he said dismissively. 'We agree a strategy and it takes place. It's not our job to smash heads and throw our enemies through plate-glass windows: nowadays a phone call is made and a deal is done. We're administrators now, not enforcers. A boardroom decision is made and a factory closes. A worker goes home that night with the news. Bills are pressing, the rent is due and the children need new clothes, new shoes. In desperation the man sweeps the streets or joins the dole queue. There's no let-up and one night, when the house is quiet and the children sleep, he steps off the landing with a rope around his neck. A board-room decision and a man hangs himself. Are we to accept his death as our responsibility? Should we refrain from decision-making? How many deaths would we have on our conscience if we abrogated our responsibilities in the boardroom? How many lives would be lost in the anarchy and chaos that followed?'

'I need a drink, Victor,' Holman said wearily.

'Stirring stuff. Admirable,' Charles Pelham declared loudly as the two friends came up to the drinks table.

Anderson looked closely at the banker and saw something in the man's eyes which troubled him. He was drunk admittedly, but he was also afraid. Had he talked too much to the wrong person, and received a warning? From his demeanour and the fear in his eyes it would appear so.

'You have no reservations then, Charles?' Holman queried casually.

'Good Lord, none at all. Definitely one hundred per cent in favour,' Pelham almost spat out. 'No reservations whatsoever.'

'Good to hear it,' Holman replied with a cynical smile.

Sir Barry Freeman approached the table and took Pelham by the arm. 'Someone I'd like you to meet, old chap,' he said.

The wine goblet nearly fell out of the banker's hands on to the table as he looked in the direction Freeman was indicating. Anderson watched the two move away and shook his head sadly. 'Our First Knight has just turned the screw a little more,' he remarked, and seeing the puzzled look on Holman's face added, 'Freeman's introducing Pelham to one of the new men – Winsley-Adams. Sworn in after the Millington affair.'

'I don't follow,' Holman replied.

'It's quite simple, old chap. Winsley-Adams was the last man to see Millington alive. As a matter of fact, he was standing right behind him when the train pulled into the station. His testimony was crucial at the inquest. He stated that Millington suddenly just dived under the train. Strange that, don't you think?'

'You mean . . .'

'Have another drink, old man,' Anderson said urbanely. 'It doesn't do to speculate too much.'

'You're right, I suppose,' Holman sighed heavily. 'The die was cast long ago, in the callowness of our youth. To England and Saint George.'

'There's no middle path for the likes of us, Sidney,' Anderson replied, then he lowered his voice. 'However, we can always consider other options which may well present themselves in the near future. A half million in gold that requires dividing up to avoid detection. The devil's loaves and fishes, one might say. And it's only natural to eat when you're hungry.'

'Rather difficult, wouldn't you say, if our friend Charles Pelham gets to control the purse strings?'

'I've a strange feeling Pelham won't be elected after all,' Anderson said quietly.

'Any ideas who might be?' Holman asked.

'Not for me to say, old boy, but if you wanted me to place a bet for you I'd put your pennies on Thorburn.'

'Short odds too, I've no doubt,' Sidney Holman conceded. 'City-trained, shrewd and totally committed.'

'Ruthless,' Anderson added.

'Victor, I think I'll have another drink,' Holman remarked roguishly.

'Me too. This conversation has made me thirsty,' Anderson told him. 'And given me something of an appetite.'

Holman smiled. 'One last toast. To loaves and fishes. May there always be more than enough, and may they taste as nice as they look . . .'

Chapter Eleven

Charlie Fiddler was trying to calculate how much he had won on the shilling-each-way double which he had placed with the street bookmaker that day, but the three girls were in a boisterous mood as usual and his accounting was suffering. 'Fer goodness sake keep yer noise down,' he shouted out. 'I'm tryin' ter work somefing out.'

'Give us it 'ere, I'll sort it out for yer,' Chloe offered.

'You don't understand bettin',' Charlie told her. 'It's a bit complicated.'

'What d'yer mean, I don't understand?' Chloe replied quickly. 'We used ter put bets on at the jam factory an' it was always me the gels got ter sort the winnin's out.'

Charlie puffed loudly. 'I bet that bloody factory was a den of iniquity,' he growled.

'We're better off out of it, Dad,' Bel remarked. 'Me an' Chloe 'ave got an interview at Sarson's termorrer.'

'Bloody 'ell!' Charlie said quickly. 'I thought you two were never gonna work in a factory again.'

'Yeah, but this is different,' Chloe told him. 'They pay good bonuses there an' we were talkin' ter . . .'

'That's it, take notice o' what ovver people say,' he cut in.

'What I was gonna say, before you rudely interrupted me, was we were talkin' ter Mag Smith whose dad runs the greengrocer's in Abbey Street. She works at Sarson's an' she said they're earnin' very good wages fer a forty-hour week. What's more, she said they're takin' people on soon an' we should get our names down quick as possible.'

'Yeah, well that's all very well, but it might be weeks before they give yer a start,' Charlie reminded her. 'What yer gonna do in the meantime, sit around the 'ouse drivin' me ter distraction?'

'Nope,' Chloe said mysteriously. 'Me an' Bel are gonna get some 'ome work.'

'What sort of 'ome work?'

Chloe dropped down heavily in the easy chair facing her father. 'There's this place in Long Lane what sends out work,' she started to explain. 'It's card sewin'. Yer get good rates an' it's clean work . . .'

'Now 'old yer 'orses,' Charlie said quickly. 'You've never done any o' that work before. It takes time ter get used to it, an' take it from me, yer gotta do a lot before you earn anyfing.'

'Well we're gonna try it,' Chloe insisted.

Charlie went back to his calculations only to be interrupted again by Sandra calling out to Bel who had gone into the scullery to make a pot of tea. 'I saw Polly Seagram at the chemist on me way 'ome from work. She was tellin' me she went in ter see Nell Bailey this mornin'.'

Bel came back into the parlour. 'I dunno what the Baileys must fink of us,' she sighed. 'There's Polly just got 'ome an' she's bin in already. We said we'd go over an' see Josie about us goin' in, but we never did.'

'Yeah, that's you lot all over,' Charlie growled. 'All talk.'

'Let's go over there now an' see if it's all right ter go in ternight,' Sandra suggested.

'Come on then,' Bel said getting up quickly. 'No time like the present.'

'Give me strength,' Charlie mumbled as his brood tumbled out of the house.

Frank Bailey walked up to the flower seller outside the hospital and bought a spray of mixed flowers, then as he climbed the wide stairs to the first-floor ward he popped a peppermint into his mouth. He had done well that day, he thought. Only one drink and an afternoon spent working at the cooperage. His suit was pressed and he had managed to persuade Mrs Brody to wash and iron his best shirt for the occasion. His brown brogues were polished but they squeaked as he walked along the ward and he felt uncomfortable holding the flowers. ''Ello, luv. 'Ow are yer?' he said smiling as he looked down on Nell from the foot of her bed.

'Mustn't grumble. 'Ow are you, Frank?'

'I'm keepin' well. Bin workin' terday.'

'That's good.'

'Done a full afternoon.'

'Did yer?'

'Time went quick.'

'I s'pose it did.'

'Can't yer sit up?'

'I wouldn't be layin' down like this if I could,' Nell said irritably.

Frank laid the flowers down on the foot of the bed and clasped his hands behind his back. 'Are the kids comin' in ternight?' he asked.

'They've bin in every visitin' time,' Nell replied. 'Our Josie's doin' a good job. Very sensible kid. Always 'as bin.'

'Yeah. Never any trouble.' Frank looked around the ward. 'Nice an' bright in 'ere.'

'Yeah.'

'I s'pose the kids'll be comin' in ternight then.'

'You already asked me that,' Nell said, becoming more and more uncomfortable.

'Yeah, so I did.'

'Frank, fer goodness' sake pull up a chair,' she puffed. 'You look stupid standin' there.'

He sat himself down by Nell's side and his hand went out to close over hers. 'I bin worried sick over yer,' he said quietly, gazing closely at her.

Nell forced a brief smile, aware of the heat of his hand. ''Ow yer bin, Frank?' she asked. 'Josie told me you 'ad the 'flu.'

He nodded. 'I'm okay now though. Will they be lettin' yer sit up soon?'

'Next week,' she told him. 'It's somefing ter do wiv the discs in me spine.'

'Are yer in much pain?' he asked, gently squeezing her hand.

She shook her head slowly. 'I was at first, but not now, providin' I don't move too quickly.'

Frank suddenly smiled and lowered his head.

'What's the matter wiv you?' Nell asked.

'I was just lookin' at yer an' I thought 'ow nice yer look, an' I was gonna say yer look a picture layin' there.'

Nell turned her face away shyly, feeling her cheeks flushing up. It was long ago now but it still seemed like yesterday. She remembered that morning had been breaking and the dawn light filtering into the tiny bedroom as she had stirred and turned onto her back. Frank had come into the room, wiping the smears of lather from his wide chin, his eyes fixed on her. The cotton nightdress had ruffled up around her waist so he could see the beauty of her shapely legs and smooth thighs. 'Yer look a picture layin' there, Nell,' he had said.

In response she had sat up quickly and grabbed the bedclothes by her feet, only to give up as his strong arms encircled her slim body.

'Two weeks,' she said almost to herself.

'Two weeks?'

'Yeah, that's 'ow long we'd bin married when yer saw me like that.'

'If I remember rightly I was late fer work that mornin',' Frank said smiling.

'If I remember rightly I 'ad our Josie nine months later,' Nell replied, returning his smile.

Frank was nodding, and as he looked away down the ward Nell studied him. He had only just shaved judging by the nicks on his chin, and he had taken some trouble to make himself presentable, but never would she have let him leave the house with fluff on the shoulders of his jacket. His shirt too was not ironed the way she would have done it. The collar was creased and his tie was a poor choice with that particular brown suit.

'Who does yer clothes?' she asked suddenly.

'Me usually, unless I'm in need o' somefing quick, then the woman upstairs does 'em. She's a good ironer.'

'Yeah, I can see,' Nell said drily. ''Ow old is this woman?'

'Knockin' on seventy I should fink,' Frank replied.

'Well, that's all right then.'

'Does Bill Watson know I'm not livin' at 'ome?' he ventured to ask.

'Yeah, someone must 'ave told 'im. 'E was askin' after yer.'

'Bill Watson was always strong on you,' Frank reminded her. 'Remember when 'e tried ter take liberties wiv yer when he was in the pub that night?'

'Yeah an' you floored 'im.'

'I'd do so again if 'e tried it on wiv yer while I was there.'

'There's no need fer you ter worry,' Nell replied. 'Bill Watson's found 'imself a nice little blonde.'

Frank moved his hand away from Nell's and nervously adjusted the knot of his garish tie. 'I got somefing ter say ter yer, Nell,' he began. 'Excuses don't mean much so I won't waste yer time wiv 'em. I just want yer ter know that I'm more determined than ever ter stop drinkin'. I've made a start already. Don Brady gives me a bit o' casual work at the cooperage now an' then an' 'e's promised me a regular spot soon as there's a vacancy. I'll be ready for it, Nell, I won't let 'im down, not after what 'e's done fer me. When I'm settled I'm comin' back ter see you an' the kids. I won't ask fer yer ter take me back. It may be too late. The feelin's you 'ad fer me might 'ave flown out the winder, but whatever, I'm gonna pay a visit an' you can be the judge. Eivver way I'd understand, but I'm not givin' up 'ope, not till yer look me square in the eye an' tell me ter get out o' yer life.'

'Fine words, Frank, but yer know what they say about words,' Nell answered with a sad look on her face. 'I wouldn't try ter stop yer visitin' us when yer feel it's time, just make sure yer've left all this be'ind yer once an' fer all. I wanna see the Frank I married, upright, shoulders back and always a smile on yer face, an' wiv that softness in yer eyes that used ter make me go all weak at the knees.'

'I can do it, Nell, I know I can,' he said with a break in his voice.

Visitors were arriving at other beds and Frank glanced along the ward to see Josie standing by the doors with Kathy and Tommy. 'I can see the kids. I'd better make room for 'em,' he said.

'Fanks fer comin' in, Frank,' Nell said softly.

'You just get well soon, luv,' he replied. 'I'll come in again soon as I can, if it's all right wiv you.'

'Just try stayin' away,' she growled.

He leant over the bed and let his lips brush her hot forehead. 'I love you, Nell,' he whispered.

'I love you too,' she said, fighting back her tears.

As he reached the entrance to the ward he turned and waved and was surprised when Josie put her arms round him and kissed him on the cheek. 'Fanks fer comin', Dad,' she said.

Frank patted Tommy's head and leaned down to plant a kiss on Kathy's cheek. 'I'll see yer soon,' he said cheerily before turning on his heel and marching quickly towards the stairs.

Wilco Johnson was not a man to be put off by trivialities, and knowing that his old drinking partner was now encamped some-where in Stepney he decided to take the bull by the horns. The East Indiaman was the most likely place to start, he thought, but getting no response from a landlord who mistook him for a detective he went on to the next pub on his list.

'Frank Bailey yer say? What's 'e done?'

'Nothing that I know of,' Wilco told another suspicious landlord. 'We're old drinking partners and I want to locate him. Here I'll show you a photo. There's Frank next to me. That was taken at our local pub's outing a couple of years ago.'

The sight of the photograph seemed to allay the landlord's fears. 'Frank used this pub at one time,' he admitted, 'but 'e got involved in a bit o' bovver an' 'e stopped comin' in. It was nuffink of 'is makin' but 'e prefers the Lighterman now. That's where yer'll find 'im, pound to a pinch o' shit.'

'Where's that, old son?' Wilco asked.

'Down by the riverside. Yer go down Commercial Road towards Burdett Road an' turn left inter Friary Street. It takes yer down to the river. There's a jetty wiv tugs an' boats moored there. Yer'll see the pub. Can't miss it. It lays ter yer left.'

The sky was a mass of red and gold with a light breeze rising as Frank entered the bar and sank down on to a bar stool.

'You're early ternight,' the barman remarked as he waited for Frank's order.

'Yeah, I am,' Frank answered. 'Usual, Fred.'

'Nice evenin'.'

'Yeah it was.'

'Was?'

'It doesn't matter. Forget it.'

The barman was used to cryptic conversation from some of his barflies and he merely raised his eyes and went on to serve someone else, leaving this one to wallow in his misery.

Chance, mere chance, Frank thought as he stared down at the froth in his glass. Maybe not though. Maybe it was meant to happen, like a sign reminding him, telling him that there could be no place at the cosy family table any more. It was his family he had been dwelling on when he took a wrong turn at the foot of the stairs and walked down the wrong corridor. He heard a child sobbing and caught sight of her mother as she cradled her in her arms. The tot's fair hair was matted with blood and her feet were kicking and drawing up as the doctor tried to prise her away from her mother. Hurrying through the casualty department, following the signs to the street, Frank saw an ambulanceman rush in carrying a baby. The mother followed, covered in a white dust, distressed and shakily holding a pad to her forehead. Two more victims of an evening flying-bomb attack which were commonplace now. Frank gulped hard, suddenly feeling weak in his legs, and he leaned his arm on the wall for support. It was all coming back again.

It was night, with flames roaring up into the angry sky. The whole children's wing of the Rotherhithe Infirmary was down. They had dug into the rubble for what seemed an eternity, and then came a muffled cry. The tiny bundle was passed up through the tunnel by the squad leader into his arms. He felt the movement, heard the choking breaths and he was terrified. Nurses were running, doctors working alongside rescue squads and out of the burning hell he staggered with a tiny child in his arms.

He ran towards cover, into the bomb-blasted hospital and saw the sight that he had tried to rip out of his mind ever since. The whole floor was taken up with babies and children, all victims of the direct hit. Doctors moved amongst them, looking gaunt from sheer exhaustion, and nurses dabbed at their dripping faces with cloths, stemming their charges' blood with pads and tying bandages. Words of comfort sounded sadly hollow, and he saw the looks of helplessness as more victims arrived.

'Put the baby down here,' the doctor had said. 'That's it. I can manage now: please go outside and let us get on,' but Frank's feet were like clay and he stood turning slowly around on himself as the scene of carnage burned itself into his brain for ever. Another cry, another desperate burst of digging and the process repeated itself, all through the long night, until the last of the victims had been removed.

As he sat staring at his pint of bitter, Frank Bailey knew in his heart that he had already lost. He picked up the pint with a shaking hand and let the cool balm run down his parched throat.

'Bloody 'ell, that never touched the sides,' the barman joked as Frank pushed the empty glass his way.

'Just one more an' then I'm off,' he replied.

'Well, if it ain't my old pal Frank Bailey,' a voice called out.

''Ello, Wilco,' Frank said, looking surprised. 'What brings you over 'ere?'

'Thought I'd look you up.'

'You were lucky,' Frank told him. 'I was goin' after this one.'

'Nonsense. Me and you are going to chew the fat for a while.'

'Truly, Wilco, I'm not in the mood for reminiscin'.'

'After me taking the trouble to find you.'

'I'm sorry.'

'No need to be. Barman, two large whiskies.'

The copper sky was now fading to purple as Josie strolled through the park gardens beside Johnny Francis. 'It's all right, they'll sound the bell when they want ter close,' she said reassuringly.

He nodded and smiled. 'I wasn't worried, just a bit concerned in case we 'ad ter climb over the fencin'.'

Josie was feeling pleased with herself. It was the first time she had been able to encourage the young man to take a stroll with her, and he had even allowed her to take his arm.

'Do yer mind if we sit fer a while?' Johnny asked her.

'Of course not,' she replied. 'Are yer gettin' out o' breath?'

'No, I've 'ad no trouble wiv me breavvin' lately an' the doctor seems ter fink there'll be no lastin' damage.'

'What about yer shoulder?'

'There's a lot of movement now.'

'That's very good.'

They reached the wooden seat and sat facing a wide flowerbed.

'I was glad we didn't bump into anyone I know,' Johnny remarked.

'Why? It wouldn't 'ave made any difference,' Josie said smiling casually. 'They'd only ask 'ow yer was.'

'I can 'andle that,' the young man told her. 'It's when they wanna know the ins an' outs of everyfing I get all tightened up inside.'

'I don't fink anyone wiv an ounce o' sense would ask yer too many questions. They'd know it'd upset yer. But you gotta realise that some day yer gonna 'ave ter talk about it, Johnny,' she reminded him in a quiet voice.

'Yeah, but not yet.'

Josie thought about how close he was, sitting next to her and she sighed. She remembered only a couple of years ago when the handsome Johnny Francis had sat on the windowsill of his house chatting to some young women. His fair wavy hair was brushed back and his ice-blue eyes seemed bright with mockery as he flashed his smile at the girls. Across the street Josie had watched as she stood chatting with Billy Emmerson, outwardly disinterested but secretly yearning over the young man who had never even given her a smile. Now she was alone with him and her heart was light with hope.

'Do you remember the dance nights at the youth club?' she asked after a while.

He nodded. 'Did you go too? I never saw yer there.'

'I wasn't in your circle o' friends,' Josie told him. 'I used ter go wiv Billy Emmerson's crowd.'

'So we never danced tergevver,' Johnny said smiling.

'No, but I wished we 'ad. I was a pretty good dancer.'

'Was?'

'Maybe I still am, but I've 'ad no chance lately ter find out.'

'It'll still be there.'

Josie turned to face him. 'That's an idea. Why don't we go ter the dance at the Co-op on Saturday night?'

'I couldn't face it, Josie,' he said quickly.

'It'll be anuvver landmark,' she persisted. 'If it gets too much we could always leave.'

He shook his head. 'You don't understand what it's like.'

'I'm tryin' to,' she replied, feeling suddenly deflated.

'It's noise that gets ter me,' Johnny said, looking upset. 'The noise o' traffic durin' the day, an' when me muvver 'as the wireless blarin' out. It'll be the same at the dance 'all, the noise o' the music, an' everyone chattin' an' laughin'. It all gets ter me. It's like the landin's all over again.'

'Facin' what troubles yer might be the right fing ter do, but then I'm not a doctor,' she said quietly.

He gave her a hard look. 'You don't fink I'm a nutcase, do yer?' he asked quickly.

'No, of course not, but I do know that yer need 'elp an' encouragement ter get back ter bein' the Johnny Francis we all chased after.'

He snorted dismissively. 'I don't need doctors, psychiatrists or anyone else; I just need time,' he growled, standing up. 'I need time ter get used ter bein' a civilian again, ter get used ter the fact that I'm not puttin' me life on the line any more, no more shells an' bullets. I'll beat this, an' then yer'll see the real Johnny Francis. It'll be like it used ter be.'

Josie stood up and walked beside him, not bothering to take his arm. Her evening had been suddenly spoiled by his angry words. A few minutes ago her young heart had been light and open and now it felt as heavy as lead. She wanted to cry but steeled herself not to. She guessed that Johnny would despise her for her tears, for feeling sorry for herself. She had walked into a difficult situation with her eyes wide open, and if it led her nowhere then it was her fault and her fault alone.

They spoke little on the way back to Quay Street, and as they reached her door Johnny Francis gave her a weak smile. 'I'm sorry if I've not bin much company ternight,' he said. 'I've got a bit of an 'eadache.'

'It's all right, Johnny, I understand,' she said flatly. 'I'll pop over some time termorrer an' pick up that library book.'

He nodded then turned away and walked to his own front door with not a backward glance as Josie stood watching him. With a deep sigh she let herself into the house, but there was no time to sit moping over things. Kathy met her in the passageway looking very agitated.

'Tommy's not 'ome, Josie,' she told her. 'I'm really worried. 'E said 'e'd be in by quarter past nine an' it's nearly ten o'clock.'

Chapter Twelve

Even before Josie let herself into the house she had decided that it was a day she wanted to forget. Things had not gone very well at work and she had rushed home to get the tea before visiting the hospital, forgetting to call in at the watchmaker's, and then the evening with Johnny Francis had ended miserably. Now though it all paled into insignificance as she stood looking at her distressed younger sister. This was a family crisis and their mother was not on hand to take charge. It was a role she had to fulfil and she drew a deep breath as she took Kathy by the shoulders. 'Now look, don't panic,' she said as calmly as she could. 'Tommy might be at the Taylors' 'ouse.'

''E's not, I went along an' knocked,' Kathy told her quickly.

'Was Dennis in?' she asked.

''E's bin in fer hours.'

''E wouldn't 'ave gone over the water ter see Dad, surely,' Josie thought aloud.

'I 'ope 'e's not bin playin' down by the river,' Kathy said fearfully.

'No, I shouldn't 'ave thought so,' her sister said reassuringly. 'Tommy knows I've ferbidden 'im ter go anywhere near the water.'

''E's gotta be somewhere,' Kathy sighed, her face flushed with concern and fear.

'Did 'e 'ave 'is coat wiv 'im when 'e went out?' Josie asked.

'Yeah.'

'Did 'e say 'e'd be wiv the Taylor boy?'

'No, 'e just dashed off out. You know what Tommy's like.'

Josie slipped her arm round her younger sister's shoulders. 'Now look, I want you ter stay put while I ask the neighbours if anyone's seen 'im.'

'I'm comin' wiv yer,' Kathy replied spiritedly.

'No, you stay here. If Tommy comes 'ome while we're out 'e won't be able ter get in, an' it's a dead cert 'e'll be tired an' 'ungry.'

'But we'll only be in the street.'

'Be sensible, Kathy, I'm gonna 'ave ter go lookin' for 'im.'

'I'll kill 'im when 'e does get in,' Kathy growled.

'No you won't, I will,' Josie told her with a brief smile.

That Wednesday had been a bad day for Stymie Smith. His horse had cast a shoe and the collection round had been a waste of time. One of the cart's wheels had constantly squeaked for want of grease and he had accidentally left the tin of lubricant behind. The man at the oil shop had squirted some machine oil on the offending axle but it had soon dried out with the friction and Stymie was left feeling that he should never have got out of bed that morning.

It was not destined to get any better in the evening, for as the totter stepped into the house he trod on a letter, and that immediately made him feel a little uneasy. The postman had already been twice that day, passing by his front door the first time. The second post had only brought a bill for his horse feed, so this had to be a private delivery. It could be from Bel, he thought. No, she wouldn't take the trouble to write to him when they lived in the same turning. Stymie finally made up his mind to open it. He had never fully mastered the art of reading and any unusual letter made him feel unsure of himself, but when he opened the envelope and took this letter out he felt decidedly nervous. It had an official heading and a coat of arms printed on the top of the page. Realising that it was as good an excuse as any to see Bel Fiddler he left the horse blowing into his nosebag outside the yard while he hurried along to number 18.

'I can't ask yer in, Fred,' Bel told him. 'Our Chloe's in the bathtub in the parlour.'

'That's all right,' he said with a quick smile. 'I just wanted yer ter read this an' tell me what it's all about.'

Bel took the letter from him and frowned. 'It's from Abbey Estates,' she said.

'What's it say?'

'It ses the lease runs out at the end o' September an' the owner 'as decided ter sell the property.'

'They can't do that!'

Bel gave him a sympathetic smile. 'I reckon there's not much you can do about it, apart from offerin' ter buy the place.'

'Not a chance, I ain't got a pot ter piss in,' Stymie growled.

'I'm sorry, luv, but there's nuffink I can suggest, ovver than goin' round ter see the estate agents,' Bel said sighing.

Stymie nodded. 'Well fanks anyway,' he told her.

She gave him another big smile. 'It'll turn out all right, you'll see,' she said.

'I bloody well 'ope so,' he replied quickly. 'This could put me out o' business.'

'Is it still all right fer termorrer night?' Bel asked hesitantly.

'Yeah, course it is,' Stymie replied.

'You won't be 'angin' up any more lavatory seats, will yer?'

'Certainly not. We'll go to a civilised pub fer a change.'

'Seth.'

'Yeah?'

'D'you like dancin'?'

'Ain't bin fer years.'

'Fancy the Co-op on Saturday night?'

'You askin'?'

'Are you acceptin'?'

'Yeah, why not.'

'Good. Anyway see yer termorrer night.'

Stymie walked back to his house and was about to back the cart into the yard when an idea struck him. A few of his totter friends had managed to hire arches in Druid Street recently and he thought it might be worth his while going along to the pub they used in Long Lane and making a few inquiries.

Tommy Bailey ambled along Dockhead feeling angry and upset. It was nearly ten o'clock according to the church clock and he was supposed to have been back indoors three quarters of an hour ago. What chance did he ever get to do anything? It was all right for Josie. She had rushed out to see Johnny Francis as soon as they got back from the hospital and Kathy had gone along the street to see Patty Simms, yet when he told her he was going out she made him promise to be back home by a quarter past nine. It wasn't fair. He could look after himself better than Kathy. He was a boy and boys knew more things than stupid girls.

Tommy kicked a stone and watched it skid along the gutter, still griping inside. Denny Taylor usually stayed out till nine thirty when it was school holidays but tonight his mother had made him stay in for being cheeky. It wasn't fair. They could've gone on the barges or down the steps at low tide to search for coins in the muddy foreshore. Denny found a coin once and the man sitting outside the pub gave him a sixpence for it.

The young lad felt the sole of his shoe flapping and brought his leg up to examine the damage. He knew this was yet one more thing he would get a telling-off for. He had been playing football with the Paradise Street boys and the time had flown. He reached Jacobs Wharf and stopped to look over the high wall which hid a muddy creek and remembered that his teacher had pointed it out one day when the class were coming back from swimming lessons. He had said it was where Bill Sykes used to live. The houses were gone now but the warehouses looked just as scary, and as his eyes took in the opposite bank Tommy thought about his father over there in Stepney some- where. Perhaps he would be sitting with his friends in a pub, or maybe he had spent all his money and was sitting by himself in that horrible, dirty flat in those old buildings. Why didn't he come home? Mum would take him in. She missed him, it was easy to see. He had heard her crying one night when he couldn't sleep. It would be good if Dad did come back, espe- cially now Mum was in hospital. He could help her, like lifting her into a chair or getting her cups of tea. He could chop the wood and light the fire.

Tommy raised himself on to the wall by his forearms, his feet hanging a few inches off the ground, wondering how long it would take him to get over to Stepney. He didn't have any money so he would have to walk there and back. Then he would have to look for Dad if he wasn't in the flat. No, it would take too long. He wouldn't get back before midnight and Josie would be sure to go to the police station to report him missing.

Suddenly the air-raid siren blared out from the top of the Tooley Street police station and the young lad looked up at the darkening sky. He saw it far away downriver, a dark object that looked like a cigar spitting flame. He heard a policeman's whistle and a shout to take cover and he hurried into the deep recess of a tea-warehouse entrance and pressed himself against the cold metal door. The whole street was deserted now and he felt suddenly frightened. The roar was getting louder and he waited for the ominous sputtering of the flying bomb's engine. 'Keep goin',' he said aloud. 'Don't stop yet.'

The noise was almost deafening now, and as the engine started to cough Tommy saw a policeman running. He was wearing a steel helmet and making for the large block of flats opposite the warehouse. With the danger immediately over-head Tommy knew that he should stay under cover, but he suddenly imagined the vast empty blackness of that dark warehouse swallowing him up like a giant coffin. With a nervous cry Tommy ran from the cold recess across the wide Tooley Street and straight into the arms of the policeman who had seen him coming. The constable dragged him into a block and pushed him under the stone stairs just as the roar of the bomb's engine died. There was a loud rushing noise and a deafening explosion that hurt his ears as the whole block seemed to shake violently and acrid dust filled the entrance. For what seemed like ages he lay where he was, protected by the body of the policeman.

'Are you all right, son?' the constable asked finally.

Tommy nodded as he followed him out from under the stairs. 'I was over the road in a doorway an' I got scared,' he said simply.

The policeman looked at him closely. 'Well, I don't know what made yer run over 'ere, but whatever it was saved yer life,' he replied.

They stood together, the large guardian of the law and the small boy, both staring over at the ruins of the tea warehouse which were burning fiercely.

'What are you doin' out at this time o' night anyway?' the policeman asked him.

'I was on me way 'ome,' he protested. 'It's school 'olidays yer see . . .'

'Yeah, yer don't 'ave ter tell me it's school 'olidays,' the policeman replied. ''Olidays or not, you young striplin's should be in bed by now. Where d'yer live, son?'

'Quay Street.'

'Well I suggest you get back ter Quay Street quick as possible. I should fink yer muvver's worried sick by this time.'

'Me muvver's in 'ospital,' Tommy told him. 'She was in that Rayburn's bombin'. She's gettin' better though.'

'Well, yer dad'll be worried.'

''E don't live wiv us any more.'

'Oh I see.'

'I expect I'll get a good tellin'-off from me sister though.'

'Well, yer can't blame 'er if she larrups yer, can yer?'

'No, I s'pose not. But she wouldn't larrup me. Only tell me off.'

'An' keep yer in fer a week.'

'I 'spect so.'

The fire engines were arriving opposite and a loud wail started up again. The policeman nudged Tommy gently. 'Come on, son, on yer way, there's the all-clear.'

'Goodnight then.'

'Goodnight, son.'

Tommy set off for home not realising that he was white with dust, though he couldn't really have cared. He had come so close to being blown to pieces and yet he had escaped, and that made him feel pretty special.

'Oi, you. What you doin' out this time o' night?'

Tommy had been totally preoccupied and was surprised to see the cart draw up beside him. 'I'm goin' 'ome, Mr Smith,' he said with a cheeky smile.

Stymie burped loudly and chuckled. 'You look like you just done a shift at the flour mills. Come on, jump up 'ere.'

The young lad stepped on to the wheel and Stymie caught him by the arm and yanked him up beside him. 'Giddy-up, you lazy ole flea-bag,' he growled, flicking the reins.

The horse moved off at a steady walk and Stymie turned to Tommy. ''Ow d'yer get that colour?' he asked.

Tommy told him what had happened and the totter shook his head. 'All I can say is, somebody up there's lookin' after you, lad.'

Tommy grinned at him. 'I'm really gonna say me prayers ternight, Mr Smith.'

'An' so yer should, son. So yer should. By the way, 'ave yer seen anyfing o' the ole man lately?'

''E came in ter see Mum this evenin',' Tommy replied.

'An' 'ow is 'e?'

''E's all right now. 'E's comin' 'ome soon.'

'Well, I'm glad to 'ear it.'

The horse swung into Quay Street without any prompting from Stymie who kicked down on the brake outside the Bailey house. The front door flew open and at the same time Josie came running back along the turning.

'If yer gonna read the riot act I'd wait till termorrer, darlin',' the totter said quietly.

Kathy looked at him sternly but Josie gave him a smile. 'Just as long as 'e's safe,' she sighed thankfully. 'We were worried 'e'd bin caught up in that last bomb. Someone said it caught the tea ware'ouse in Dock'ead.'

'Fanks fer the lift, Mr Smith,' Tommy said as he clambered down on to the pavement.

Stymie winked at him. 'An' don't ferget yer prayers.'

'No, I won't ferget.'

It was nearing midnight when Josie crept into Tommy's room

and looked down on the angelic face of her sleeping young brother. She had wanted to tell him off for causing her and Kathy so much anguish but she hadn't been able to. He was home safe and sound and that was all that mattered for the time being. Time enough tomorrow for the recriminations.

Chapter Thirteen

Saturday morning was warm and sunny, and while some of the street folk were still rousing themselves the widow Meadows had already whitened her front step and was busy cleaning the outside of her parlour windows. Opposite, the Fiddler girls were chatting to Dot Simms, their next-door neighbour.

'We was feelin' so guilty we 'ad ter go over an' see 'er,' Bel was saying. 'Anyway we 'ad a word wiv Josie an' she said it'd be best if we went in this afternoon. She was sayin' the Woodleys wanna go in as well an' so does Polly Seagram, so 'er an' Kathy are gonna leave it an' go this evenin'. They was a bit worried about their farvver too. 'E ain't bin in since Wednesday an' she said it's possible 'e might turn up this afternoon.'

'Yeah, it could be awkward,' Dot said as she folded her chubby arms over her fresh apron. 'They don't like too many round the bed neivver, weekends or not.'

'I mean ter say, yer feel so 'elpless at times like these,' Chloe remarked. 'We asked if there was anyfing we could do, but Josie said it was all under control.'

'I asked 'er if she wanted any shoppin' got but she said no,' Bel went on. 'Still she knows we're 'ere for 'er if the need arises.'

'By the way, did you get that job at the vinegar factory?' Dot asked.

Chloe shook her head. 'We're doin' some 'ome work. We start next week.'

'What sort of 'ome work?'

'Sewin' cards.'

'What, those fings they 'ang up in shops wiv fings fixed to 'em?'

'Yeah. We're gonna be on corn plaster cards. They pay ten bob per 'undred.'

'Gawd 'elp yer,' Dot said pulling a face. 'D'yer realise'ow many corn plasters are fixed on those cards? Two dozen. That's two dozen loops an' all that tyin' off fer one card. I know, I tried it. I was workin' from mornin' till night an' I still couldn't earn enough ter make it werf me while.'

Bel and Chloe looked disheartened. 'Well, we'll give it a try an' see 'ow it goes,' Bel replied gamely.

Gladys Metcalf came into the street with Ginny Allen. ''Ere, I was just talkin' to Annie Francis when we was down the market,' Ginny said as they drew level. 'Stymie's got notice ter quit by all accounts.'

'No!'

'It's true,' Ginny went on. 'Annie's got no reason ter lie. It turns out the lease is up an' it's not bein' renewed.'

'That's right. Stymie showed me the letter,' Bel added.

'What's 'e gonna do?' Dot asked.

'Not much 'e can do,' Bel replied, ''cept go round the estate office an' see if they've got anyfing else suitable.'

'P'raps the bloke who owns the place might change 'is mind,' Dot ventured.

'I reckon Stymie should get a petition up,' Gladys said. 'I'd sign it. I fink we all would. 'E don't trouble us none an''e does try ter keep that yard clean. Always swillin' it out, 'e is.'

Iris Meadows had finished cleaning her front windows, and spotting the gathering across the street she decided to find out what was going on. She slipped on her coat and bonnet and took up her large handbag which she cradled under her arm as she stepped out and walked casually up the turning.

'Mornin', ladies.'

'Mornin', Mrs Meadows.'

'Nice day.'

'Very nice. Just goin' ter get me bits an' pieces.'

'I'm goin' down the market later, Mrs Meadows,' Bel said courteously. 'I can get a few bits for yer, save yer makin' the trip.'

'No, I prefer the walk, fanks anyway,' Iris said stiffly.

'We was just talkin' about Stymie Smith,' Dot Simms said. 'Apparently 'e's got notice ter quit.'

'Well, at least the street'll look a bit tidier wiv 'im out of the way,' the widow growled.

'That's a bit 'ard, Iris,' Gladys Metcalf remarked. 'The poor sod's gotta earn a livin'.'

'Yeah, an' we was just sayin' 'ow 'e keeps the yard spotless. 'E's always swillin' it out,' Chloe told her.

'I was sayin' it might be a good idea if we got up a petition. I'm sure none of us'd mind signin' it,' Gladys added.

Iris Meadows realised that she had miscalculated the general feeling and she sought to make amends. 'Well, ter be honest I never 'ad reason ter dislike the man,' she replied, 'an' as yer say, 'e's entitled to earn a livin'. I was only talkin' about the 'orse shittin' the street up. Mind you, it's good fer tomatoes, if yer growin' 'em an' can stand the smell.'

The women chuckled and Iris felt better. 'Well, I must be off. If yer get up a petition I'd be only too glad ter sign it.'

'Fanks, luv, that's nice of yer,' Dot said as Iris Meadows walked off. When she was out of earshot she curled up her lip.

'Crabby ole cow. She's better than a dose of syrup o' figs when yer bound up.'

Josie Bailey walked along Jamaica Road to the watchmaker's, feeling slightly guilty for not calling in before. 'Mornin', Mr Stephens,' she said above the clatter of the door bell.

'Mornin', Miss Bailey,' George Stephens replied, smiling back at her. 'Well, it's fixed. New hands, new glass. I've oiled it too and adjusted the spring. It was losing quite a bit.'

'That's nice of yer,' she remarked.

'All part of the service,' he said, reaching under the counter. 'There we are.'

Josie noticed how nimble the man's large hands seemed as he gently turned the winder a few times. He was broad and fresh-faced, with dark curly hair, not at all how she would have imagined a watchmender. 'You said twelve an' six.'

'That's right,' he said smiling easily.

Josie fished into her purse. 'I expect yer get a lot o' these sort o' jobs,' she ventured.

'Quite a few,' he replied, 'though most of my repair work comes from the docks, would you believe? I get ships' clocks and chronometers to service, and I sell a few of those cuckoo clocks to the seamen who come in. A cheap souvenir to take home to Russia, Norway, Finland or wherever.'

Josie paid the money and slipped the watch into her handbag. 'I was wonderin',' she said a little uncertainly. 'Do you sell those chains fer watches?'

'You mean fob chains?'

'Yeah, that's right.'

The watchmender reached under the counter again and took out a small tray. 'These ones aren't expensive. They're silver-plated. But these few are solid silver. If you look closely you can see the hallmark.'

''Ow much is that one?' Josie asked, pointing to a thick silver chain.

'That's the dearest one, actually,' he replied. 'It's two guineas. It'll look nice on that watch.'

'I'm afraid it's a bit too much,' Josie answered.

George Stephens smiled indulgently. 'Look, I'll tell you what I'll do. If you really want this chain I'll take seven shillings down and you can pay me the balance at seven shillings a week over five weeks.'

Josie nodded enthusiastically. 'I can manage that,' she said smiling. 'It's very good of yer ter trust me.'

'Look, my dear, I know an honest face when I see one. Now hand me the watch and I'll put the chain on.'

Josie did as she was bid and when he had clipped the chain on he went to a small drawer and took out a tiny silver fob with a bronze setting. 'I'll throw this in for luck,' he said smiling broadly.

'That's very nice of yer,' Josie told him. 'I'm sure my dad could do wiv some luck.'

'Couldn't we all,' he said with feeling.

The young woman left the shop thinking about her father, imagining the look on his face when he saw the watch with its new chain and she hoped she would soon be able to give it to him. He should have paid another visit to the hospital before now, and she prayed that he had not slipped back into his old drinking habits.

Ralph Hennessey finished shaving in his hotel room and dabbed a few drops of aftershave on his face. He was due to leave for Lisbon early the following morning and he felt pleased with the progress he had made. The agent had been in touch with him to let him know that the plan had been accepted and he now had to finalise the financial side of things before his next trip to London.

As he ran a comb through his thick fair hair Hennessey thought about his part in all this. He had been entrusted with delivering a far-reaching, desperate plan, for which he had been well rewarded. His own bank account in Zurich was growing nicely and soon he would be in a position to sever all the ties with the Field Operations Unit in Berlin and disappear to start a new life with a new identity before Germany went under. Ralph Hennessey, alias Werner Reismann, would become a Swiss national, Philippe Korner, the name of his deceased cousin on his mother's side.

Hennessey left the hotel and ambled over to the Grapes public house opposite. It was his usual watering-hole while he was on diplomatic business and it was there that he was due to meet his ladyfriend for the evening.

'Hello, Norman. The usual if you please,' he said to the barman.

While he waited Hennessey looked around the bar and saw the two barflies in their usual spot, propping up the counter with their elbows, their flushed faces indicating a certain alcoholic over-indulgence.

'They want me to open the innings tomorrow,' the taller of the two regulars announced.

'Good Lord. Quite a responsibility there, Toby.'

'Too true, Cyril. Tilden Green haven't beaten us for yonks. I don't want to be the bounder who breaks the sequence. My opening partner invariably gets his half century. Trouble is when one opener goes the other soon follows, in my experience.'

'You'll be all right, Toby. Take my advice. Settle with the umpire for middle and off and block up. Let your partner go for the runs.'

'Actually I've always been good for a few runs myself,' Toby replied, somewhat peeved. 'Just a little out of practice, what.'

'Is the vicar playing tomorrow?' Cyril asked.

'Yes. Manvers too. We've also got Cardwell back from his shoulder sprain. He should prove invaluable with his leg spin if the weather holds. Give him a nice dry wicket that's inclined to break up and Cardwell is quite likely to skittle them out.'

Cyril nodded, suddenly distracted by the stunning redhead who swayed provocatively into the bar. 'Good Lord, there's something that has nothing at all to do with cricket, old chap,' he gulped.

The two watched as the redhead ambled up to Hennessey and they looked on enviously as he put his arm around her waist and she pressed herself close to him.

Play was suspended as the two barflies waited patiently. Then, as Hennessey and his ladyfriend left the pub, their vapid demeanour and sloppy posture were discreetly replaced by the sense of urgency and resolve natural to MI5 operatives.

'Right, old man, yours I believe,' Toby said.

Cyril patted his coat pocket and nodded briefly before leaving. Toby waited a few minutes then he crossed the wide thoroughfare and entered the hotel. 'My name's Mr Eastham. I've a meeting with Mr Congrieve. It's Room 224 if I'm not mistaken,' he said to the receptionist, who picked up the phone.

'I'm sorry, sir. Mr Congrieve doesn't appear to be in his room.'

'He should be back soon. Do you mind if I wait?' Toby asked.

'Certainly not. Can I get you some tea?'

'No, I'm fine thank you.'

A few minutes later the receptionist left the counter and Toby immediately made his way up a carpeted flight of stairs to the first floor. Room 224 did not interest him. The man staying there was a visiting official from South Africa and at that moment he was taking tea with a delegation at the Foreign Office. It was Room 226 he wanted and, knowing its occupant was otherwise engaged, Toby applied his skills on the lock with a set of skeleton keys.

Nell Bailey looked very cheerful when Josie and the two younger children walked into the ward. She was sitting up in bed and had had her hair done. 'They're gonna let me get up fer an hour termorrer,' she announced.

'That's good,' Josie enthused. ''Ow did this afternoon go?'

'Don't ask me,' Nell replied, her eyes going up to the ceiling. 'The Fiddler gels came in first, then Dot Simms an' Gladys Metcalf. Then Ellie Woodley an' Annie Francis, an' ter top it all Polly Seagram turned up. I swear there was six round the bed at one time an' the sister made some of 'em leave. Polly stayed, as you might 'ave guessed. She 'ad me in stitches, talkin' about 'er Bernie an' 'er sister.'

'Did Dad come in?'

Nell shook her head. 'Ter be honest I was glad 'e didn't. There was too many 'ere. P'raps 'e'll come in later.'

Josie saw the look on her mother's face and felt sad. She was trying to make light of it but was obviously disappointed at not seeing him. 'Yeah, I fink 'e will,' she said.

Tommy was looking subdued and Nell noticed it. 'Are you all right, boy? You look troubled,' she remarked.

'I'm all right, Mum,' he replied quickly, having been warned by Josie not to mention his experience the previous night.

'Are yer feelin' well? Yer look like yer in fer somefing.'

'A right-'ander if I don't do me bedroom,' he said in a put-upon voice.

Everyone smiled and Josie was proud of her young brother for his little feint.

'We're goin' dancin' ternight, Mum,' Kathy told her.

'You an' Josie?'

'Yeah. She's goin' wiv Johnny Francis an' I'm goin' wiv Patty Simms.'

'An' what you gonna do?' Nell asked Tommy.

'I'm stayin' wiv Dennis Taylor ternight,' the lad replied. 'We're gonna make this model up. It's a bomber an' we'll be able ter paint it. Dennis ses . . .'

'Don't go on about it,' Josie cut in.

'It's all right, let 'im talk,' Nell said indulgently. 'Boys are naturally bloodthirsty. Most o' the lads in the street collect shrapnel an' shell cones. When 'is dad took 'im ter the pictures it always 'ad ter be a war film. No musicals fer our Tommy.'

'I got a big box o' shrapnel,' the lad said quickly. 'I got bits wiv numbers an' letters on.'

Nell eased her position in the bed, looking a little uncomfortable. 'I'll be better when I can get up fer a spell,' she puffed. 'I'm really stiff.'

Just then Tommy caught sight of his father who was peering into the ward. 'There's Dad!'

'Come on, gang, let's get goin' an' give Mum some time on 'er own wiv Dad,' Josie urged them.

As they filed out Frank stepped forward and hugged each of them in turn. 'I made it,' he said smiling.

Josie smelled the drink on him and saw his creased shirt and the coat lapels that needed a stiff brush. His tie was crooked and she reached up to adjust it. 'Mustn't let Mum see yer wiv yer tie like this,' she said.

'I'll see yer later, kids,' Frank told them.

Josie motioned to Kathy and Tommy to walk along the corridor then she reached into her handbag. 'I got yer watch 'ere, Dad,' she said. 'I bought yer a chain for it. 'Ope yer like it.'

His eyes clouded as she gave it to him. 'That was a nice thought,' he murmured.

'That fob's fer good luck,' she told him.

'Well, I'm gonna need it, luv,' he replied.

'Dad, you ain't back on the booze, are yer?' Josie said sighing.

'I ain't kicked it yet, darlin', but I'm tryin', really I am. I promise yer I'll beat it. I will, as God's my judge.'

'I'll see yer, Dad,' Josie said as she stepped away from him.

'See yer, Josie, an' fanks very much fer the chain, an' the good luck piece.'

She watched him walk into the ward then turned on her heel and caught up with Kathy and Tommy. Her father had slipped back to heavy drinking, she felt sure. All the signs were there.

''E stunk o' booze,' Kathy said uncharitably.

'Yeah, I could smell it too,' Tommy added. 'I bet Mum will an' all.'

'That's what's worryin' me,' Josie sighed as they left the hospital.

Chapter Fourteen

Sidney Holman swung the steering wheel over and the car left the main London-St Albans road. As he accelerated along the narrow country road in the gathering dusk he was glad he had not used the ageing Vauxhall lately. Charles Pelham had sounded troubled when he phoned from his home in Hertfordshire, wanting to talk on an urgent matter, and he had not liked the idea of his old friend coming by train as it meant getting a local taxi to the remote farmhouse. 'People talk, old chap, and I wouldn't want any casual inquirers knowing that you came to see me,' he said. 'Believe me, I have reason to be extra careful.'

Holman smiled to himself as he slipped into top gear. Pelham had sounded very relieved when he explained that he had some petrol in the Vauxhall and enough coupons left to cover the trip. What was it that the banker had become so paranoid about? He had his suspicions, but did not want to dwell on them unnecessarily. After all, it might be something quite unconnected with the League.

A couple of miles later he saw the farmhouse up ahead. It lay back off the road, the walls glowing purple-white in the light of the full moon. He had been there on a few social occasions and liked the place. It had an old-fashioned charm and Pelham had had many improvements carried out to make it comfortable and homely. The honeysuckle around the door and over the leaded windows smelled sickly sweet as he climbed out of the car and ducked under the low weather arch above the door to ring the bell. Getting no answer he rang again and then stepped back to peer through the window. There was plenty of light in the house and everything seemed in place. A log was burning in the hearth and he could see the partly filled decanter standing alongside two goblets on the small table by the deep leather armchair. Something was wrong and he should have guessed it as soon as he rang the doorbell. Pelham's retriever Lady should have immediately started barking. But it was deadly quiet.

Holman stood looking into the room for a few moments stroking his chin thoughtfully. Apart from his housekeeper, who would have left by now, Pelham had lived alone at the farmhouse since his wife died. He had often said the solitude was welcome after the busy, stressful time he spent in the City all week. Perhaps Charles was in one of the outhouses with Lady. Treading carefully he made his way to the back of the house and called out. The barn seemed to be empty, and so did the tractor shed and the large lean-to. Where was Pelham? What could have happened to him? Holman thought as he made his way to the back door of the house. He found it unlocked. Charles must have come out this way, unless he was still inside somewhere, upstairs asleep maybe. But where was the dog? Lady would have been roused as soon as she heard the car drive up over the chippings.

Sidney Holman walked slowly into the kitchen and his heart suddenly missed a beat as he stared down at the dead animal. It had a film of froth around its mouth and beside its head was a half-eaten chunk of raw meat. It had obviously been poisoned. 'Charles,' Holman called out loudly. 'Charles, are you there?'

When he got no answer he hurried into the hall and bounded up the stairs, going from room to room. Finally he came back down and slumped into the settee facing the log fire. He lit a cigarette and took a deep drag. Something must have happened to Pelham, but there was no sign of a struggle. He had to be somewhere out there. Holman decided he would have to go back and make a detailed search of the outbuildings once more but he would need a torch. Pelham was sure to have one, and he'd most likely keep it in the kitchen.

When he had finished his cigarette Holman flicked it into the fire and soon found a large flashlight standing on the Welsh dresser. Making sure it was working he went back out into the dark and made his way to the large barn. Previously he had just poked his head through the opening and called out, but this time he went inside and shone the torch around. The beam of light picked out a pair of shoes and Holman's heart rose into his throat. The search was over. Charles Pelham, banker and White Knight, was hanging by his neck from a lofty beam, his feet just above eye level. His sightless eyes were popping and his swollen tongue stuck out grotesquely.

Holman knew that it was too late to do anything. Getting the banker down would require a ladder. Better to leave things as they were. No one would know he had been there. Wait a minute. The torch. He would have to put the torch back first. 'Don't panic,' he told himself aloud as he wiped the flashlight vigorously with his handkerchief. What else had he touched? Only the door handles.

Five minutes later Holman sat down in the settee once more to smoke another badly needed cigarette, endeavouring to make sure he had covered everything. Charles Pelham had not committed suicide, he was sure of that. Whoever killed him had set it up to look that way: no forced entry and no disturbance told him that Pelham had let the killer, or killers, in. Was he expecting them or had he been taken by surprise? It was possible that he had been expecting visitors and had wanted someone else he could trust to be there with him when they called. It must have been more than one person, Holman figured. After all it would have taken more than one to get Pelham up into the gallery of the barn and knot the rope round his neck before kicking him off.

Still feeling sick and shocked by his discovery Holman drew hard on the stub of his cigarette and tossed it into the flames. Then as he got up to leave his eyes alighted on the opened novel lying face down on the low coffee table. *My Endless Love* by Lucy Albright. That would hardly be Charles's cup of tea, Holman thought. Probably one of his dead wife's novels. But what was it doing lying there open on the coffee table? Using his handkerchief he picked it up and scanned the open page, immediately spotting the sentence which had been underlined. 'I'll love you forever and a day, my darling, with all my heart and with every fibre of my being. My dedication to serving your every need and my undying devotion will know no bounds and together we will soar to the stars.'

Flowery stuff and certainly not for Charles, Holman thought. Why had the sentence been underlined? And why the more prominent pencil line under the word 'dedication'. Of course! He quickly turned to the front of the book, taking care not to leave any fingerprints on the pages, and found the dedication. 'To my Mother and Father, with love.' It told him nothing, but the signed message below certainly did. It had been written with a fountain pen. 'To my dear friend, Aubrey. With fond memories of those halcyon days chasing the impossible dream in Shangri-La.'

As he read the inscription Holman knew that Charles

intended it as a cryptic message. The banker was one of the few people who knew that his middle name was Aubrey. But what of Shangri-La? A book maybe. He quickly went over to the tall bookcase and scanned the shelves, but there was no book with that word in the title. Then as he turned away he saw it, a piece of sheet music sitting on the frame above the keyboard of the Steinbeck piano that Charles' wife Melinda used to play so well. *Shangri-La* by Robert Maxwell and Matty Malneck. As he picked up the score a long envelope fell from it and landed at his feet.

The sound of a passing car reminded Holman that he should be leaving and, tucking the sealed envelope in his coat pocket, he hurried out of the house by the back door and got into his car. It was not until he was moving at a steady speed down the almost deserted London road that he began to feel a little more relaxed. Soon he would be able to study the contents of the envelope, which might throw some light on the tragedy he had stumbled into that evening.

The Co-op dance hall was situated above the large Co-operative grocery store in Rotherhithe and it was a favourite haunt of the younger local folk. The visiting bands were usually good and there was a small bar that sold beer and lemonade. Even those young men who had no dancing skills went along anyway. They usually sat around drinking or stood in groups ogling the young women, and looking enviously at the accomplished dancers performing on the circular dance floor.

Stymie Smith looked smart in his brown pinstriped suit and large brogues, while Bel Fiddler turned a few eyes with her tightly fitting royal-blue dress and very high-heeled black shoes. Her fair hair was piled up on top of her head and held in place with a bone comb, and she wore a deep red lipstick which contrasted with her pale skin as she stepped across the floor with Stymie to the strains of *I'm in the Mood for Love*.

Josie Bailey stood by the bar with Johnny Francis who was wearing his grey suit and black shirt, set off with a narrow cream tie. 'Are yer sure you're all right?' she asked with concern, mindful of the effort it had taken on his mother's part as well as hers to get him along to the dance.

He smiled and nodded, his attention drawn to Bel Fiddler's complicated steps which were obviously confusing Stymie. 'The band's good,' he remarked after a while.

Josie remembered how Johnny Francis had never been off the floor before he went to war. He had seemed perfectly at home with a quickstep, foxtrot or even the more energetic South American dances. Now though it looked like she would have to use all her powers of persuasion to get him to stand up even for a waltz. 'Care ter try this one?' she asked, already knowing the answer.

'Nah, it's too fast.'

Josie sipped her light ale, noticing that Billy Emmerson was there with a few of his friends. Billy never went on the floor to her knowledge but he seemed relaxed as he stood watching with a glass of beer in his hand. Kathy was dancing, held tightly by a tall thin youth who looked embarrassed, and there were various other faces she recognised.

After a while the band struck up with a waltz and Josie caught Johnny's eye. 'Come on, let's see 'ow good you really are,' she said encouragingly.

He hesitated for a second or two then quickly put his half-empty glass down on the counter and took her by the hand. He moved stiffly at first, holding her slightly away from him but as the music continued he seemed to relax. She drew closer, moulding herself against him and she could feel his tension draining away. He was certainly a very good dancer and she found it easy to follow his steps. The other women dancing were resting their heads on their partners' shoulders and she did the same. She could smell his aftershave and the starch of his shirt and feel the pressure of his hand on her back. It was delicious and she closed her eyes, letting the music weave its special dream for her.

Billy Emmerson gulped his drink and ordered another. Before the night was out he was determined to ask Josie to dance with him, and if Johnny Francis didn't like it he could take a running jump.'

'What's up, Billy?' Frankie Morgan asked. 'You look gutted.'

'Yeah, I am,' he replied. 'That's the gel I'm gonna marry over there an' just look at that flash git 'angin' all over 'er.'

'You, get married? Do me a favour. Yer'll be in the Kate Carney before long. It'll 'ave ter wait, pal.'

'Just dreamin', Frankie,' the young man told him. 'She don't know I'm around.'

Frankie Morgan took a gulp from his glass. 'What you should do is wait till the excuse-me waltz then go up an' cut in.'

'Yeah, I would do, if I could dance,' Billy scowled.

'Don't give me that, anyone can do the waltz.'

'Yeah, 'cept me.'

The dancers were walking off the floor while the band took a break and Billy caught Josie's eye as she and Johnny came towards the bar. ''Ow's yer dad, Josie?' he asked.

''E's much better fanks, Billy,' she replied. ''E's bin in ter see me mum.'

'Well, if yer want any more lifts yer know where I am.'

Johnny Francis gave the young man a disdainful look. 'You still got that ole bike?' he asked.

'It's not that old,' Billy retorted. 'At least it gets me around.'

'What's it run on, paraffin?' Johnny remarked with a superior glance Josie's way.

Billy flushed up with anger, but Frankie Morgan beat him to a sharp reply. 'I wouldn't go makin' fun o' people's means o' transport if I were you,' he said calmly.

'Why's that then?' Johnny asked him.

'Well, yer might come unstuck if yer say fings like that ter the wrong bloke,' Frankie told him, moving a little closer to him. 'Stymie Smith goes everywhere on that 'orse-an'-cart of 'is, an' if yer tried ter take the piss out of 'im 'e'd probably 'ave no 'esitation in kickin' six buckets o' shit out o' yer.'

Josie could see the situation turning ugly and she took Johnny's arm. 'Come on, it's my turn, I'll buy us a drink.'

As they moved to the counter Frankie turned to Billy, and in a voice loud enough for Johnny Francis to hear he said, 'The first rule, Billy, is not to let yer gel buy yer a drink. It ain't right.'

Johnny heard the comment and pulled his arm from Josie. 'Are you after takin' the piss out o' me?' he asked menacingly.

'I wasn't talkin' ter you, so get lost,' Frankie growled.

'Don't you tell me ter get lost.'

'Why? What you gonna do about it?'

'I'll soon show yer,' Johnny said, grabbing at Frankie's lapels.

Josie and Billy jumped in quickly. Between them they managed to separate the two and Billy pushed his friend away to a corner of the drinking area. 'You done me up like a kipper, Frankie,' he growled. ''Ow can I ask Josie ter dance wiv me now?'

'Well, I would,' Frankie told him sharply. 'The trouble wiv you is yer too soft. You should 'ave given that flash git a smack when 'e started on about yer bike. Gels like a feller who can stick up fer 'imself.'

Billy sighed in resignation and leaned on the bar counter. 'Give us two light ales, will yer, Tom,' he asked.

Josie sensed that Johnny had actually enjoyed the confrontation. He was sitting back in his chair looking quite at ease, and she wondered if she should feel happy or sad. For some time now she had worked hard at encouraging him to get out and about but, having managed to get him to the dance, she had hardly expected him to pick a fight. 'Are you all right?' she asked in an effort to break the awkward silence.

'Yeah, I'm fine. Never felt better.'

Josie smiled half-heartedly and looked around the bar area. She could see Billy Emmerson and Frankie Morgan in close conversation, and her sister Kathy chatting to a girlfriend, and when she looked back at Johnny she saw that he was staring over towards two young women who stood whispering together. Each in turn was nodding and then they looked over and smiled. Josie half turned her head away but she saw Johnny return the smile and she tightened up inside. This was the old Johnny Francis she had once coveted; but things were different now, he was with her and it hurt to discover him openly flirting in front of her. 'Shall we dance?' she said quickly.

'Nah, I fink I'll sit this one out,' he told her. 'You dance if yer like.'

'I fink I will,' she replied coldly.

Billy Emmerson was taken by surprise when Josie walked over to him. 'Come on, Billy, you've never danced wiv me,' she said smiling. 'Let's see 'ow good you are.'

The young man got up quickly, determined not to let the opportunity pass. 'I'm not very good at all,' he said.

'Nor am I, so that makes two of us.'

When the dance ended Billy led her back to the table. 'Where's Johnny gone?' he asked.

'Over there,' Josie replied, nodding towards the two young women who had made eyes at him earlier. Johnny was with them and they all seemed to be enjoying themselves.

'Well 'ow did I do?' Billy asked, feeling embarrassed for her.

'You did very well,' she replied with a smile. 'It just takes practice.'

'I don't get enough of it,' he said sheepishly. 'I come 'ere pretty often wiv Frankie an' a few ovvers but we never seem ter dance. We just sit watchin'.'

'You should ask the gels ter dance,' she told him.

He shrugged his shoulders. 'It was different wiv you. It seemed easy, but then you're a very good dancer.'

'Well, then you should ask me ter the dance sometime,' she responded.

'You really mean it?' he said unbelievingly.

'Of course,' Josie answered, glancing over briefly towards her erstwhile escort and the two girls he was amusing.

Her look was not lost on Billy. He knew she was encouraging him out of anger, and he could understand it. Everyone in the street had been shocked by the change in Johnny Francis when he came back from the war. Morose and idle, with no pride in his appearance, he had been ignored by the very girls who had swarmed around him before. Only Josie had taken the trouble to spend time with him, encouraging him, running errands and generally making him feel more confident, and by the look of it she had done a remarkable job. The word would go out now. Johnny Francis was back on the scene.

'Billy?'

'Yeah?'

'Are you takin' anyone 'ome from the dance?'

'Only Frankie,' he said grinning.

His grin and the flash of his green eyes made her smile. 'I may need you to escort me 'ome, if yer want to that is.'

'Well, we do live in the same street,' Billy said casually, and seeing Josie's expression he smiled broadly again. 'Even if I lived miles away from Quay Street, I'd be only too glad ter take you 'ome,' he told her sincerely.

'Won't Frankie mind?' she laughed.

'Just look at 'im downin' that drink,' Billy answered. 'By the time they play the last waltz 'e'll be too pissed ter care.'

Josie saw Johnny Francis take one of the girls by the hand and lead her on to the floor and she grabbed Billy by his arm. 'Come on then, lesson number two.'

Chapter Fifteen

Sidney Holman sat in the comfortable study of the flat he rented at the Albany in Piccadilly. It was the haunt of writers, lawyers and people in the professions and it more than suited his personal needs. Tonight he appreciated the peace and quiet of the place as he tried to take in all that he had seen that evening, and digest the letter lying open in front of him on the low table.

'My dear Sidney,
Should your astute powers of deduction lead you to find this letter you will already have learned the worst. In the words of the bard, I will already have shuffled off this mortal coil. You will also be satisfied that I did not ask you to make the visit out of panic or hysteria. As I write this letter I fear that moves are afoot to have me taken out of circulation just as poor Herbert Millington was, but unlike my old and dear friend, whose death was shrouded in mystery, I would wish my demise to be an open book, if you'll pardon the pun.

First and foremost, Sidney, I have neither desire nor reason to take my own life. My death will undoubtedly have been one of murder. Like Herbert I know too much and consequently pose a danger to those who profess to swear their undying allegiance to the League and all it stands for. Sidney, old chap, the League is at this moment in the hands of those whom our American cousins would vulgarly describe as conmen. Herbert Millington uncovered fraudulent dealings quite by chance through his contacts in the City, who had asked him to check out the validity and credibility of one or two new companies being floated on the Stock Exchange. Herbert had chosen the Lord Mayor's banquet to seek out some business associates with whom he could converse in what he believed to be total confidence. Unfortunately for him someone must have informed our First Knight who, as you know, has many friends in the City.

Bear with me, Sidney, and I will try to put you in the picture as concisely as I can. Suffice it to say that Sir Barry Freeman and the League's current treasurer, Sir William Robinson, are systematically filching considerable sums of money from our extensive funds and routing them through these new companies of which both Freeman and Robinson are executive directors. Millington confided in me as soon as he became suspicious and asked me to assist him by making my own inquiries, which I did. There is no doubt about it in my mind, Sidney. Despite the verdict pronounced on Herbert Millington, he was murdered.

You will by now understand why I asked you to call in secrecy. I did not want to put you at risk, but at the same time I wanted to make you fully aware of the danger so that you don't fall into the same trap that Herbert and I did. I know my days are numbered, unless the League members can act together to bring this unholy mess out into the open, which I'm afraid is a virtual impossibility. Understand too, Sidney, that I do not fear leaving this world behind, only the method of my going. Since Melinda's death my life has become empty and meaningless. I no longer have the desire or motivation to support and further our early aims and objectives. We are living in a fast-changing world, and I'm convinced that the Fascist movement will go the way of all history's other grandiose, Ozymandian schemes.

In closing I would say, do not grieve for me, Sidney. Before long you may come to feel that I was one of the lucky ones. Be alert and always on your guard. Beware too of Victor Anderson. This may surprise you, but Millington suspected him of being in on the intrigue. I do too. It makes him very dangerous.

Goodnight, old friend, and remember what I have written. I'm sure that you will seek salvation in your own way, but do it before the deed is done. After will be too late.

Yours affectionately,
Charles Pelham.'

Holman drained his brandy and sat for some time staring into the empty grate. The mention of Victor Anderson in Pelham's letter was surprising, but on reflection he felt that it might well be justified. Anderson had half joked about the loaves and fishes that were there for the taking and it added up now. It was as though he was searching for some commitment either way and Holman felt relieved that he had been fairly ambivalent in his response. Things would be moving soon, and as Pelham had been at pains to point out, if he was going to get out it would have to be now. Once Churchill had been assassinated it would be too late. If one fell they would all fall.

Another brandy did nothing to relieve the anxiety that was eating away at his insides and Holman turned his friend's words over in his mind again. Charles had said that unless the members acted together there was no solution, but maybe there was. Any move would be very difficult and fraught with peril, but it had to be considered, however dangerous. He would have one last brandy and sleep on his troubled thoughts. Tomorrow he would decide on what action to take.

On Saturday night Frank Bailey went into the Lighterman seeking the company of his old friend Nobby Swan. He had managed to get to the hospital in a reasonable enough state, but he was finding it exceedingly difficult to stay away from the drink and the elderly doctor who had treated his cuts and bruises had spelled it out in no uncertain terms.

'If you can't get through a day without taking a drink of beer, wine or spirits then you can consider yourself an alcoholic.'

Frank knew that until he took that first drink his hands would shake and his stomach would churn painfully. There was no hiding the fact – he was an alcoholic. He knew that if he wanted to be reunited with his family he would have to fight through the pain and discomfort of drying out, however much the thought distressed him. That would have to wait for another day though. Tonight he needed the company of someone who understood him and the personal problems he was facing.

''Ow's Nell?' Nobby asked as soon as Frank joined him at the counter.

'She's doin' well,' Frank told him. 'She reckons she'll be allowed up fer an hour or so a day now.'

'So all bein' well she should be out soon.'

'Anuvver couple o' weeks, Nell reckons.'

'Well, that's good news,' Nobby said, packing his clay pipe with dark tobacco.

Frank took a large gulp from his glass. 'Been out terday?'

Nobby shook his head. 'Saturdays are pretty quiet these days but I got some ferryin' ter do on the tide termorrer. Couple of ship's officers off the *Claymore* that's moored downriver.'

'Is that the Scottish tramper that goes inter the pool?'

'Yeah. Hibernia Wharf.'

'Thought it was.'

Frank studied his half-empty glass for a few moments, then he looked up at Nobby. 'Tell me somefing,' he said. 'Can you go frew a day wivout 'avin' a drink?'

'Yeah if need be, but I try not to.'

''Ave yer tried?'

'Not lately.'

'I can't, Nobby.'

'I shouldn't worry about it.'

'But I am. Me doctor finks I'm an alcoholic.'

'Who's yer doctor?'

'Doctor Samuels.'

Nobby chuckled as he drew on his pipe and was suddenly reduced to a fit of coughing. 'Well 'e should know,' he managed after he had composed himself.

'What d'yer mean?'

'Doctor Samuels is a piss-artist if ever there was one,' Nobby told him.

'I gotta get meself straightened out,' Frank said earnestly.

'Only you can do it,' Nobby reminded him. 'Now you take me. I'm on me own an' I can 'andle that ole tub o' mine drunk or sober. I ain't got no one to answer to so I don't worry. But fings are different wiv you. You've got a good reason ter lay off the booze – Nell an' the kids. All I would say ter yer is, if yer gonna try an' knock it on the'ead don't wait too long. The longer yer wait the 'arder it's gonna be, an' yer gotta remember too that Nell's still an attractive woman. Sooner yer get straight the sooner yer'll get yer feet under 'er table again, before some ovver glib bastard does.'

'My Nell wouldn't take anuvver man in while I'm still around,' Frank said quickly.

'Don't you be so sure,' Nobby countered. 'Don't get me wrong. I don't fink your Nell's flighty or man-mad, but she's only human after all an' a woman needs a man about the place. If she can't 'ave you then she could well look at what's on offer.'

'But she can 'ave me,' Frank replied. 'I didn't leave, she kicked me out. She's only gotta say the word an' I'll go back straight away.'

'Yeah, course yer would, but it wouldn't do neivver of yer any good. It'd be back ter the way it was, the way yer told me it was.'

Frank lapsed into a sullen silence for a while and Nobby sat back puffing away contentedly on his stained clay pipe. Presently a well-dressed man entered the bar and stood chatting to the landlord. Nobby Swan sat watching for a few minutes then he turned to Frank. 'See that tall geezer wiv the smart suit on? That's Ben Thorburn. 'E's one o' those big nobs in the City. 'E was a right 'andful in 'is younger days, accordin' ter the landlord. 'E used ter be in the Blackshirts. They say 'e's cracked a few Jew-boys' skulls in 'is time. Wouldn't fink so, just lookin' at 'im, would yer?'

Frank pushed his empty glass across the counter and pointed to Nobby's near-empty one. 'Drink up, mate. There's time enough ter worry about kickin' the booze termorrer. Ternight me an' you are gonna get nice an' merry.'

Nobby smiled. 'Well, you know best. Anyway yer don't need ter go back ter that flea-pit ternight. You can kip in the spare bunk on the *Marigold*, as long as yer promise me yer won't fall overboard.'

'Don't worry, pal, I ain't plannin' ter drown meself, only me sorrows.'

'What d'yer mean drown yerself?' Nobby queried with a crooked smile. 'If yer fell in at Stepney Reach yer wouldn't drown, yer'd suffocate. My ole *Marigold's* sittin' in one foot o' water an' six feet o' mud.'

The drinks followed one another and the pub began to fill up. Seamen, Thames rivermen and well-dressed visitors to the seamy side of London rubbed shoulders with a few locals, who often earned a drink by relating stories of the river, its hidden dangers and treacherous moods. One young couple who appeared to be very close stopped looking adoringly into each other's eyes long enough for an old salt to tell them that whenever a body was taken from the river it invariably went to Wapping morgue, and that every life lost at sea was registered in the nearby Limehouse Church. They also learned that the river tide flowed at six knots most of the time and even the strongest swimmer could quite easily be sucked under the fast-swirling eddies. The young couple were intrigued and eager for more information, which was soon forthcoming, at the price of a pint of bitter. 'There's a bend in the river not far from 'ere called Galleon's Reach,' the old man explained. 'In the old days the sailin' ships moored there in midstream while they waited ter dock. Now there's a pub along the reach on this side o' the water called the Town of Ramsgate, an' just past there is what's known as Execution Dock. They used to 'ang the pirates there from gibbets an' leave 'em ter rot so the returning sailors could see 'em. It was done ter frighten'em off o' becomin' pirates. As a matter o' fact Captain Kidd was 'ung there.'

The night wore on, and by closing time Frank Bailey and Nobby Swan were too drunk to worry about anything except a place to lay their heads for the night. 'Nah, it's nice o' yer but I gotta get 'ome,' Frank slurred. 'Our Josie might call termorrer.'

'You ain't in no fit state ter walk that far,' Nobby told him.

'Who ain't?'

'You ain't.'

Frank stood up to prove a point but immediately fell back into his chair. 'I fink yer right,' he said, his eyes rolling.

Nobby helped him up and took him by the arm for the short walk down to the jetty. 'Come on, ole son, mind yer step.'

They managed the precarious walk up the short gangplank and soon both men were comfortably settled in their makeshift bunks, snoring loudly and lulled by the gentle rocking of the ferry.

Overhead the moon shone down on the quiet river and the cobbled waterside streets as Ben Thorburn made his way back to his London house in Stepney Green. Things were looking up, he thought. Sir Barry had indicated to him that he was in line for a place on the cadre as the League's new treasurer, after Sir William Robinson retired in September. Poor old Charles Pelham would no doubt be most put out.

Chapter Sixteen

On Sunday morning Billy Emmerson whistled happily as he stripped down the magneto of his motorcycle. It had turned out to be a very pleasant Saturday evening, and he smiled to himself as he remembered how Josie had taken his arm when they walked home from the dance. Johnny Francis had upset her by dancing most of the evening away in the company of Sadie Maguire and her giggly friend, and Josie had been quick to suggest that maybe he should see them home and Billy could walk her home. Johnny Francis had seemed quite happy with that and Josie had been at pains to make Billy see that she wasn't using him to make Francis jealous. 'I should 'ave realised right from the start that this was gonna 'appen sooner or later,' she had told him, 'but I fink I knew deep down I was never gonna be Johnny's steady gelfriend. I was just around when ovvers weren't.'

'Yeah, well I fink yer done the best fing,' Billy replied. 'That feller's back on the scene by the looks of it an' I'm sure 'e's gonna play the field like 'e always did, till someone gets their 'ooks into 'im. 'E'll most likely end up wiv some ole plum.'

'Billy, that's not nice,' Josie said smiling.

'Maybe not, but it's on the cards,' he went on. 'The way 'e performs, no decent gel's gonna take 'im seriously.'

'What about you? Do you like playin' the field?' she asked mischievously.

'You know me well enough not ter fink that,' he said with a defensive smile.

'I know, I was only jokin', Billy.'

'That's my downfall,' he replied with feeling. 'No one ever takes me seriously eivver.'

'I do, Billy.'

'You might, if you knew just 'ow I felt about yer.'

''Ow do yer feel about me?'

'I'd like ter fink you knew that already,' he said quietly.

'I know yer like me, it shows,' Josie answered, 'but even though feelin's are difficult ter put inter words at times, a gel can't afford ter take fings fer granted.'

'The way I feel about you goes deeper than that,' he told her. 'I've always felt you were special, but I never really thought you 'ad any special feelin's fer me.'

'So yer never let me know in case you got 'urt in the process.'

'Yeah, that's partly it, but there's ovver fings ter take inter consideration too.'

'Such as?'

'Well, I'm waitin' fer me call-up papers. I can't afford ter get serious yet.'

'Why not? What's gettin' called up got ter do wiv it?'

'Supposin' I get crippled, or killed in action.'

'Listen, Billy, life's a gamble, fer civilians as well as servicemen an' women,' Josie said earnestly. 'None of us know if we'll be around termorrer or the next day. All any of us can do is get on wiv our lives an' 'ope an' pray we'll come frew the war. 'Avin' someone to 'old on to is very important.'

Billy nodded slowly. 'When I do go in the army it'd be nice ter know that there was someone back 'ome who cares about me.'

'People do. There's yer family an' yer pals, an' there's me. I care about yer.'

Billy recalled the effort it had taken for him to come out with what was on his mind. 'Look, I know yer said I should ask you out to a Saturday night dance sometime, but would yer walk out wiv me, on a regular basis I mean, knowin' I'm gonna be called up soon? There'd be no strings attached.'

'I'd be very 'appy to,' Josie replied.

As the sun rose above the rooftops Billy gathered up his tools, still dreaming about the previous evening. He had walked Josie to her front door and she had let him kiss her goodnight. Her lips had tasted sweet as honey and he had woken up that morning fearing at first that it had all been a dream.

Wilco Johnson was up early that Sunday morning and as he walked along the turning on his way to get the *Sunday Pictorial* he encountered the widow Meadows brushing the dust from her front door. 'Morning, Iris,' he said cheerfully.

The old lady gave him a hard look. She had always been particular about who called her by her Christian name and the street's drunk was not in that category. 'Mornin', *Mr* Johnson,' she replied with emphasis.

Wilco was still recovering from his Saturday night drinking session and her irritation went over the top of his head. 'It's always nice to see people take pride in their place,' he said, putting his hands in his trouser pockets. 'You always seem to be working. If you're not sweeping the front you're whitening the doorstep, or cleaning the windows. You're a credit to the street, my dear.'

Iris Meadows suddenly felt quite young again. She couldn't remember the last time anyone called her 'my dear', and she forgot her quick anger at Wilco's familiarity. 'Well, I do try ter keep my 'ouse nice an' tidy. Yer know the ole sayin', cleanliness is next ter godliness.'

'I'm sure it's true,' Wilco said smiling. 'It's nice to know you can smile at us poor sinners.'

Iris didn't know when she had last given him a smile but the remark was appreciated anyway. Perhaps she had been a little hasty in ignoring the man. He was being very neighbourly that morning and he had noticed her efforts. It couldn't be very nice for him living alone the way he did. It was probably the reason he drank so much. 'I 'ear Nell Bailey's doin' well,' she offered by way of returning his friendliness.

'So I gather. Frank Bailey's not looking so good though.'

'You've seen 'im?'

'Yeah, the other night. We had a few drinks together.'

'Where's 'e livin' now?'

'Over Stepney.'

Iris decided to probe a little further, thinking how nice it would be to know a bit more than the rest of the street. 'Did 'e mention if 'e's intendin' on comin' back 'ome?' she asked as casually as she could.

'He wants to, but unfortunately there's a few problems.'

'Oh?'

Wilco leaned on the wall and looked up and down the turning before answering, which made the widow even more avid to hear. 'Frank's been a good friend of mine for a few years now, and as you know me and him used to have a few drinks together,' he went on. 'Trouble was he got too fond of it and it caused barneys between him and Nell.'

Iris narrowed her eyes in irritation. That was common knowledge. Everyone in the street knew why Nell had told him to go. 'We all know that,' she said quickly. 'You said problems. What ovver problems are yer talkin' about?'

'Well, he's lost his job for a start, and I'm afraid he's got into bad company.'

'Bad company?'

Wilco nodded. 'Far be it from me to criticise people unnecessarily, but this chap Frank's got in with is a bad influence on him. As a matter of fact I met him when I was with Frank in the pub and I didn't like the look of him. One of those old rivermen, drinks like a fish, never sober. You know the sort.'

Iris Meadows looked at him haughtily. She didn't know the sort and had no desire to. 'And yer fink 'e's encouragin' Frank Bailey ter get sozzled.'

'Exactly.'

'Well, I blame Frank 'imself,' Iris told him. 'After all 'e ain't a kid. 'E's got Nell an' those lovely children, an' 'e's chuckin' it all away – fer what, I ask yer? I can't make it out, really I can't.'

Wilco could have told her what had turned Frank towards the bottle but he thought better of it. The silly old cow wouldn't have understood anyway. 'By the way, what's all this business about Stymie Smith?' he asked.

'The estate's chuckin' 'im out by all accounts,' Iris told him.

'Yeah, I heard something about it in the pub last night,' he remarked.

Iris did not know which way his sympathies lay but she guessed correctly that they would favour the totter. 'I suggested it might be a good idea fer 'im ter get up a petition,' she said. 'After all a man needs ter work, even if 'e's only got 'imself an' that ole flea-bag ter feed.'

'Quite right too,' Wilco replied.

'Mind you, I dunno if they'll take up me idea but I fink it's werf a try.'

'Well you can count me in, luv,' Wilco told her.

Iris raised her eyebrows slightly. The man was getting more familiar by the minute, she thought. 'If they come round wiv the paper I'll tell 'em ter give yer a knock.'

'I'll be happy to oblige,' he said. 'Well, I'd better be on my way before all the papers go. Cheerio, Iris.'

'Cheerio, Mr Johnson.'

Josie Bailey and Ellie Woodley were having a chat over their adjoining backyard wall. 'Me mum was very pleased wiv the nightdress yer bought 'er,' Josie remarked. 'She said it was a perfect fit, not too skimpy an' not too loose.'

'I wish there was more I could do, luv,' Ellie replied. 'Yer mum's always the first to 'elp anyone else out. Yer don't ferget those fings.'

Kathy called out a question and Josie looked at Ellie and raised her eyes in resignation. 'Yer clean knicks an' bra are in the same place they always are.'

'No, they're not,' Kathy replied irritably.

'Well look again.'

A few minutes later Kathy came out into the yard. 'I found 'em,' she announced.

'Good.'

'They was in the ovver drawer by the way.'

'Well, at least yer won't go out wiv dirty knickers on now.'

'Do you mind!' Kathy said indignantly as she went back into the house.

Ellie was smiling. ''Ow they bin while Nell's not 'ere?'

'Pretty good really,' Josie admitted. 'Kathy goes on a bit but she does a lot round the place. Tommy's bin a bit difficult, though I can understand it. I'm not as easy as me mum is wiv 'im an' 'e resents it. I 'ad ter keep 'im in fer a few nights over 'im comin' in late. Worried out o' me mind I was at the time.'

'Well I fink yer doin' a good job, Josie,' Ellie told her. 'Please Gawd it won't be fer much longer.'

'Me dad's bin in the 'ospital a few times. I fink it really bucked Mum up.'

'That's nice,' Ellie replied. 'I do 'ope fings work out fer the two of 'em. It's such a shame.'

'I fink they will,' Josie said. 'Me dad's tryin' really 'ard ter get 'imself sorted out. I've bin over ter see 'im a few times lately. I got 'im a nice chain fer 'is watch. 'E'd busted it yer see an' I took it in ter that feller in Jamaica Road. That's where I saw the chain.'

''E's a strange bloke,' Ellie remarked. 'I bought an alarm clock in there a few weeks ago. Likes a chat, don't 'e?'

'I thought 'e was nice,' Josie replied.

'Oh yeah 'e's nice enough, but there's somefing about 'im,' Ellie went on. ''E lives in the rooms above the shop, so 'e told me. I s'pose I was a bit nosy. I asked 'im if 'e was married an' 'e made a joke of it. 'E told me 'e 'adn't found the right gel. Asked me if I was fancy-free, would yer believe? Course 'e was only jokin' but I got ter finkin'. 'E's not a bad-lookin' bloke an' I'm sure 'e'd 'ave no trouble findin' a nice gel.'

'P'raps 'e prefers 'is own company,' Josie suggested.

'Yer could be right,' Ellie conceded. ''E's bin in that shop since the ovver ole feller retired, just before the war started. I remember it 'cos that was when all the shopkeepers were puttin' that brown sticky paper on their winders. I went in there around that time ter get a wristwatch fer Larry's birfday an' the ole feller served me. I asked 'im if 'e was gonna put any paper up an' 'e said 'e wouldn't be there long enough. Told me then 'e was closin' down. A few weeks later when I was passin' I looked in the winder ter see if the ole boy was still there an' I saw the new bloke be'ind the counter.'

Josie saw that Tommy was hanging about by the yard door and she picked up the clothes-peg box from a rickety chair. 'Well, duty calls,' she said smiling. 'Now what d'you want, young man?'

'Not money, is it?' Ellie said grinning. 'See yer later, Josie. I gotta get me work done while it's quiet.'

Josie understood what she was alluding to as her next-door neighbour scanned the empty sky above. 'Yeah, it 'as bin quiet this last few days,' she remarked.

'Josie, can I 'ave a tanner?'

'What for?'

'I'm gonna go down the Lane wiv Denny an' 'e's got a tanner ter buy somefing wiv.'

'So you wanna get the same?'

'Yeah, I wanna get a metal strap fer that watch Mum bought me.'

'But the watch don't work an' the man on the stall where Mum bought it said it was past repair.'

'Yeah, but I still like ter wear it. It looks smart an' it'll look smarter still wiv a metal strap.'

'Well, yer won't get a metal strap fer a tanner.'

'Yeah, I know. They're two bob, but I've already got one an' six.'

'I don't like the idea o' you goin' all that way,' Josie told him. 'There might be an air raid while yer gone.'

'Ah go on, sis, be a sport,' Tommy pleaded. 'Yer can't expect me ter stay indoors all the time just in case of air raids. Anyway I know what ter do. If one comes over I'll get off the street or chuck meself down till it goes by.'

''Ere, there's a sixpence. Now don't be too long.'

'Fanks, Josie,' he said. 'I'll clean me room up terday, I promise.'

'You make sure yer do,' she growled, unable to stop herself smiling.

After the Blitz had ended some of the museums and art galleries around London opened to visitors once more, although many of the priceless treasures they had once contained were still in bank vaults and places of safety. The start of the flying bomb attacks had posed a problem for their curators but on Government instructions they stayed open, offering shelter to the visitors during a raid.

People could still wander through the Palladian rooms and classical colonnades of the Maritime Museum at Greenwich, and the Nelson Room was one of the main attractions for visitors. Servicemen and women mingled with families on a day out, and amongst the exhibits on show was the bloodstained jacket which Horatio Nelson had been wearing when he received his mortal wound at the Battle of Trafalgar.

'A bit of heritage there,' Sir Barry remarked to the tall lean man who had sidled up to look into the high class case.

'To be sure,' he answered in an Irish brogue.

'The trouble with these exhibitions, good as they are, is the strain on the feet getting to see everything,' Sir Barry went on. 'As a matter of fact I'm fair bushed. Think I'll take a pew for a while.'

'A good idea, I think I'll join you, if you have no objections,' the tall man replied.

The First Knight looked at the man and noted that he was wearing a light-brown summer suit and an open-necked cream shirt, but as he met the stranger's eyes he had to suppress a shudder. It was as though he was looking into evil itself. The eyes were small and wide-spaced, and cold as ice.

'Thank you for coming,' Sir Barry said as they sat down together on a long leather-upholstered bench in the high panelled hall.

'Thank you for inviting me,' the man replied.

'I wasn't sure that you'd turn up.'

'Why's that?'

'For all you knew it might have been a trap, an ambush, to use a military term.'

The tall cold-eyed one smiled cynically. 'I've survived this long by not taking chances,' he answered. 'You were observed long before I came into the museum, and at the first sign of treachery my men would have . . .' He paused and smiled again. 'Made sure that I got away safely, shall we say.'

Sir Barry smiled back. 'I guessed you had a back-up. The man by the door?'

The stranger nodded. 'He's one of them.'

'I understand your reasons. Our mutual contact told me you were hiding out in London and go in fear of your life.'

'Life can be balanced on the edge of a pin in a profession such as mine. I can't afford to make one slip-up. When I was contacted my immediate worry was how the caller had learned of my hideaway? I had to move immediately.'

'It's my understanding that you still have loyal people out there,' Sir Barry told him. 'Our contact is only a voice on the phone and it suits me. I have to be careful about whose company I choose to be seen in.'

'It doesn't trouble you that you might be seen talking to me?'

'Not in the slightest,' Sir Barry replied calmly. 'For all intents and purposes I've just met a very sociable young man who shares the same taste in art and history as I. We're having a comfortable chat and then when I get up to leave it will be the last time I ever see you.'

The Pedlar nodded slowly. 'Why did you select me for the task?'

'According to our mutual contact your reputation is legendary among the warring factions in Ireland. I know too that you've managed to slip out of America, where you're wanted for armed robbery, and word has it that you always get the job done. I need the best. Failure would most certainly mean the end for me, and for the people I represent.'

'I would hope that your favourable assessment of my capabilities will be reflected in my fee?'

'Yes of course. The figure I'm authorised to offer you is

five thousand pounds. Two down on acceptance and three when the task has been completed.'

The Pedlar smiled mirthlessly. 'We're talking about removing the most charismatic and successful leader this country has ever known. A man who has his own secret service agency and who rides around in an armoured car. We're talking about a task that could well change the course of history, even more so than the assassination of the Archduke Franz Ferdinand in Sarajevo that led to the First World War.'

'We are.'

'Then I suggest that you seek authority to double the offer. Five down and five on completion.'

'That will not be necessary,' Sir Barry replied. 'My organisation will bear that cost. The money will be paid into a Dublin bank account, details of which will be made available to you in a few days' time, following your instructions of course.'

People were passing through the Nelson Room and the two conspirators sat silent until they were alone once more.

'I'll phone the number you gave me with my instructions,' the Pedlar said. 'Tomorrow morning, if you've no objections.'

'That will be fine,' Sir Barry told him. 'What's more, I do appreciate how difficult the task is going to be.'

'Everyone has an Achilles heel,' the Pedlar said quietly.

Sir Barry stood up and held out his hand. 'Well, it's been a pleasure,' he remarked.

'Mutual.'

The First Knight left the Maritime Museum feeling cold inside despite the heat of the day, and he hoped that he would never have to meet the assassin again, never again have to look into those cold dead eyes.

Chapter Seventeen

The Bermondsey Tradesmen's Guild had been formed back in the twenties and its members met together on the third Monday of every month. Even during the dark days at the beginning of the war and throughout the Blitz the guild never failed to hold their meetings, and for some it was the most important element of their lives outside of their families. Holidays were planned around the meetings, and if any member was unable to attend for any reason then a formal apology for absence was forwarded to the Rose and Crown in Abbey Street where the guild assembled in a room above the public bar.

On Monday the twenty-first of August the regular meeting was convened as usual. Jack Hamil the butcher was there, along with Fred Alladyce the greengrocer and Charlie Hornby who ran a hardware shop in Jamaica Road. Other members from Jamaica Road included Joe Bryce the groceryman, the Sanders brothers who ran the fish shop and George Stephens the watch-mender. Daniel Foden the carpet man and Stan Wickstead the haberdasher represented the Tower Bridge Road market, as did Joe Jackson the pie man.

Along with the tradesmen there were others, men who had

become Bermondsey councillors from trading backgrounds. Honorary members included the mayor and the town clerk, as well as Matthew Crittenden who headed a firm of solicitors at Dockhead.

On that Monday evening the large room above the Rose and Crown was full as the current chairman, Charlie Hornby, opened the meeting. Minutes were read and business arising fully aired before items on the agenda were discussed. Future plans to move the Tower Bridge Road market to a new location behind the Trocette Cinema elicted the usual heated protestations and the vote to oppose it was unanimous. Things became a little more serene when the meeting moved to other matters, and a vote in favour was taken regarding the question of whether the tradesmen would display War Orphans' collection boxes on their premises. Another item discussed was the annual social evening, which always took place in November. As usual the evening would include fundraising schemes, and those assembled spent some time deliberating over whom the proceeds should benefit. Still undecided, the members agreed to defer a decision until the September gathering and the chairman then asked the assembly if there was any other business. Councillor Reginald Springer raised his hand and was given the floor.

'I am now able to pass on an important bit of news,' he began. 'I know that everyone here was devastated and heart-broken when the children's wing of the Rotherhithe Infirmary was hit during the Blitz. But like a phoenix rising from the ashes a new children's department has grown up from the rubble. We have all seen the rebuilding taking place during the past year, and I'm happy to tell you this evening that the new wing will be completed within a few days. I've been privileged to be shown around, and I was very pleased to see that a plaque has been installed to the memory of the children who died on that fateful night.

'The opening was discussed at the last full Council meeting and it was decided to ask the Prime Minister to cut the tape when he makes his next visit to our borough. As we all know, Winston Churchill visited the riverside boroughs frequently during the Blitz to boost morale and he has continued the practice ever since the first flying bomb attack. I can tell you now that our request was successful. The Prime Minister has said that he would be delighted to officiate at such an important occasion.'

The murmur of voices and a few handclaps prompted the councillor to raise his hand for attention. 'National security prevents me from giving you a specific date and time,' he went on. 'Suffice it to say that it was five days after the start of the Blitz that the hospital was hit. The eleventh of September nineteen forty to be exact. It would be nice to think that the opening ceremony would take place on the same date this year, Monday the eleventh of September. In so saying I would urge you to remember that this information is top secret and must not go beyond these four walls. Such discretion will not prevent the people of Bermondsey from seeing the Prime Minister on the day, as we know from experience. A large police presence and the diversion of traffic will not go unnoticed, and once the Prime Minister makes his first stop en route word will spread faster than the cavalcade, as in the past. Unless I'm very much mistaken, by the time Winston Churchill cuts the tape the streets will be thronging with people waiting to catch a glimpse of him when he leaves the hospital.'

'The way I see it, the people of Bermondsey should be made aware of the day of the Prime Minister's visit in advance,' Stan Wickstead cut in. 'Surely he would be in no danger walking through our streets. After all, he's done it many times before.'

'Yes, but always unannounced, you must remember,' the councillor replied. 'I've been sworn to secrecy and I've put myself in jeopardy by saying as much as I have. I have to rely on your sense of public duty.'

George Stephens raised his hand for attention. 'I'm sure I speak for everyone present when I say that your confidence in us will be respected and the secret closely guarded,' he said, looking round the room.

'Well then, if there are no other matters I call this meeting closed,' Hornby announced.

The members made their way down into the bar and began to form themselves into small groups. The watchmender got a round of drinks in for Joe Bryce, Fred Alladyce, Charlie Hornby and himself and they moved to a corner table.

'It'll be nice ter see that children's wing opened once more,' Fred Alladyce remarked. 'I was there that night. If I live ter be 'undred years old I'll never ferget it.'

'It's good that the Prime Minister 'imself is openin' the new place,' Joe Bryce said.

'Yeah, it'll bring the people out,' George Stephens added. 'I think I'll hire out my rooms over the shop. Pack a few families in and come round selling tea and biscuits.'

The men chuckled and Fred Alladyce glanced over at the close conversation taking place between Councillor Springer and the Sanders brothers. 'I thought ole Springer was takin' a chance ternight,' he told them. 'If the news leaked out it could well cost 'im 'is place on the Council.'

The watchmender shrugged his shoulders. 'I don't think he's got anything to worry about,' he remarked. 'In any case it'd be difficult to prove that he was the one who opened his mouth.'

'No, I fink 'e's on safe ground,' Joe Bryce said.

The evening wore on and before last orders were taken one or two members left. One member went to the nearest phone box and made a call. He then walked home through the empty streets to make another call, a transmission to Berlin. The meeting that evening had produced a surprising piece of information which would more than please the Field Operations team. The other two items of news sure to be welcomed were that a first-class operator had now been recruited to execute the first phase of the plan at just the right time, a few days before the second phase was set in motion, and the indication was that more flying bombs were now falling in the centre of London since the last communication.

Von Mannheim studied the decoded information and smiled with a sense of gratification. 'Read it, gentlemen.'

'This is more than we could have hoped for in such a short time,' Hoess said with enthusiasm.

'Well, this will certainly help to raise the Fuehrer's spirits,' Mannheim remarked. 'Today he was like a bear with a sore head. News from the Eastern Front gets worse by the day and he rants and raves at the generals. I fear for his sanity.'

Mannheim's aides Hoess and Lindsdorf both nodded gravely, each worrying about the rumour that was doing the rounds at the officers' club that the Fuehrer had indeed become insane and was intent on sending new, untried officers to the Eastern Front to aid and assist the beleaguered front-line generals. Both Hoess and Lindsdorf were administrators with no battle experience and, fearing they would be among those selected, they sought to strengthen their position on Mannheim's team.

'It's good that our flying bombs are now falling where they should,' Lindsdorf stated, reminding the general that he had been responsible for overseeing the operation.

'You did well,' Mannheim told him. 'I'll be informing our Fuehrer of your part in this. I'm sure he'll be impressed. It could mean a promotion and transfer to the Eastern Front. Are you up to it?'

'Of course, general,' Lindsdorf said quickly as the blood

drained from his face. 'Though much as I would welcome a field appointment I would still prefer to remain on your staff.'

Hoess felt sorry for his colleague and decided that the less said the better in the current fluid situation. 'That goes for me too, general,' he ventured.

Fifteen minutes later, at the appointed time, General Mannheim walked the short distance to the Chancery. His credentials were checked and then he was escorted to the inner chamber which led down to the bunker. Once again his papers were scrutinised and Mannheim was offered a seat while a messenger went to inform the Fuehrer's secretary that he had arrived. There was one other senior officer waiting in the room, wearing an eye patch and with his arm in a black cotton sling. Mannheim smiled at him. 'General Mueller, I believe.'

'General Mannheim. It's a pleasure.'

After the two exchanged handshakes they sat down next to each other. 'I was transferred to Poland,' Mannheim told him.

'I went to the Eastern Front,' Mueller replied.

'Is that where you met with your injuries?'

Mueller smiled. 'No, as a matter of fact I got caught up in the air raid a few nights ago.'

'Are you here to see the Fuehrer?' Mannheim asked.

A look of distaste appeared on General Mueller's face. 'I carry a communique compiled by the field commanders on the Eastern Front,' he said heavily, 'and every evening for the past week I've been here waiting to present it to our leader. It appears he is purposely disregarding their reports and suggestions. His recent directive seems designed to make their observations irrelevant. "Not an inch to be given." Mannheim, we are losing the war and our gallant troops are near to exhaustion. Field generals say that the only way is to retreat and regroup, but our leader will have none of it. "Be proud to die for the Fatherland." "Fight till the last bullet." How do you tell our starving, half-frozen soldiers that maniacal rubbish with the Red Army breathing down their necks? It's a lost cause, Mannheim.'

The Chief of Field Operations smiled sympathetically, not needing to be told. He himself was overseeing one of the Fuehrer's grand schemes, a plan so outrageous in ambition it defied logic. The British leader Winston Churchill might well be assassinated and the new weapon due to be unleashed on London might well cause some panic, but like the Berliners during the past weeks the Londoners would suffer and carry on regardless. The Fascist movement might make some ground politically, but to think that the Americans would pull out of Europe and leave the British and their colonials to line up with the German forces against the Red Army was like fishing for the moon in a puddle. But such thoughts would have to remain private, so as not to incur a firing squad in the bunker yard.

'The Fuehrer will see you now,' the messenger announced to Mannheim.

'Good luck, General Mueller,' he said as he walked from the room.

Chapter Eighteen

It was Sunday the twenty-seventh of August when Nell Bailey arrived back home in Quay Street. Still feeling very stiff and holding on to Josie and Kathy she smiled at the solicitous neighbours and waved her hand, hoping she wouldn't look too much like the Queen acknowledging her husband's subjects. 'Yes, I feel fine. Gotta take it easy fer a few weeks though,' she told Ellie and Larry Woodley from next door.

Polly Seagram was standing at her front door. 'Lovely ter see yer 'ome again, luv,' she beamed. 'You take it easy now. No flyin' up an' down that market. Anyfing yer want I'll get while yer gels are at work.'

The Fiddler girls were at their door at the other end of the street and they waved cheerfully.

'She looks pale, don't she?' Bel remarked.

''Ow the bloody 'ell can yer see from 'ere?' Chloe said quickly.

'I got sharp eyes, I don't need goggles,' Bel told her cuttingly.

'Nor do I, most o' the time. I only wear 'em fer close work,' Chloe replied.

'Pity yer didn't wear 'em when we was doin' those cards,' Bel growled.

'It wasn't me what ballsed the job up,' Chloe said defensively. 'It was Sandra what done it. She's useless at anyfing like that.'

'Come on, Chloe, yer can't blame 'er fer us not gettin' any more work,' Bel protested. 'She was only tryin' to 'elp us out when we got be'ind.'

'Yeah, I s'pose so, but the card people are very fussy,' Chloe went on. 'Sandra didn't leave the loops big enough, an' then there was the ones wiv the tea stains.'

'Well, don't blame me fer that,' Bel replied quickly. 'That was your fault. I managed ter clean the ones I spilt cocoa on before it dried.'

'Anyway it didn't pay an' I for one am bloody glad we got shot o' the job,' Chloe declared. 'Just fink of it. We sat there from mornin' till night all week, an' fer what? Bloody coppers. Slave labour, that's what it is. We'd 'ave bin better spendin' the time lookin' fer a decent job.'

'Ne'er mind, maybe we'll 'ave a bit o' luck next week,' Bel said cheerfully.

'I 'ope we do, if it's only ter stop Farvver moanin',' Chloe grumbled. ''E reckons we're eatin' 'im out of 'ouse an' 'ome an' not puttin' a penny in the kitty.'

'Yer gotta make 'im right.'

'I know, but 'e does go on a bit.'

''Ow much we got comin' on the cards, if they pay us?'

'Fifteen an' a tanner,' Chloe told her.

'Between us?'

'Yeah.'

'P'raps we could buy 'im an ounce o' tobacco an' some fag papers out of it,' Bel suggested. 'It might 'elp shut 'im up fer five minutes.'

'Good idea.'

'We could borrer the money out o' the jug an' get it terday.'

'Yeah, let's.'

'We'll 'ave ter make sure we put it back by Tuesday fer the rent man though.'

'Course.'

'Chloe! Bel! Are you gonna leave these breakfast fings in the poxy sink all day?' Charlie called out irritably.

'Just comin', Dad,' Bel yelled back. 'We're wavin' ter Nell Bailey. She's just got 'ome.'

Nell had already been settled in her favourite chair with a pillow to support her back and she was sipping a cup of tea. 'They was a bit reluctant ter let me come 'ome so soon,' she was saying to her daughters, 'but the wards are chock-a-block an' there's a shortage o' beds after those buildin's in Long Lane copped it. Anyway it's only rest that I need. Give us a week an' I'll be good as new.'

Tommy was sitting facing her, watching her as she sipped her tea. 'D'yer fink it'll be long before Dad comes 'ome, Mum?' he asked. Josie gave him a blinding look but he ignored it. 'Why can't it be like it used ter be?'

Nell smiled sadly at him. 'I know yer miss 'im, boy. We all do, but the move's gotta come from yer dad. You're old enough to understand. Fings couldn't go on the way they were. Yer dad knows that soon as 'e's sobered up fer good there's a place for 'im 'ere. It won't be long, 'e is tryin' very 'ard.'

Josie glanced briefly at Kathy and knew by the look on her face that her younger sister felt as she did. Their father had only visited the hospital twice during the past week and then only for a brief spell. He looked as though he had tried to tidy himself up a bit but it had not fooled either of them, and certainly not their mother. It was going to need a miracle for him to beat his addiction and miracles were in short supply.

'Can I go out an' play?' Tommy asked.

'Yeah, but be back 'ere by two sharp, or yer'll not get any dinner,' Josie told him sternly.

Nell smiled at her daughter as Tommy skipped out of the parlour. 'Yer sounded just like me then,' she joked.

'We managed quite well really,' Kathy remarked quickly. 'Me an' Josie done it all between us, an' we kept a tight rein on Tommy.'

'No arguments?'

'No, not one.'

'Well, I'm glad to 'ear it,' Nell said smiling. 'It seems my two gels 'ave grown up all of a sudden.'

Kathy looked particularly pleased. 'I'd better put the spuds on,' she said, taking the initiative.

When she had left the room Nell turned to Josie. 'Are yer still seein' that Francis lad?' she asked.

'Not so much,' Josie replied. 'In fact not at all. There was nuffink in it anyway. I just felt sorry fer 'im I was shocked when I first saw 'im after 'e came 'ome. All those gels who used ter chase after 'im seemed to 'ave vanished an' I took 'im a couple o' books ter read after 'is muvver told me 'e was just sittin' round the 'ouse all day an' wouldn't go out.'

'Yeah, I remember it,' Nell said. 'An' I s'pose 'e's back to 'is old self now.'

'Almost,' Josie admitted. 'The night o' the dance spelt it out fer me. Johnny took me an' I only got to 'ave one dance wiv 'im. All the gels were flockin' back.'

'Yeah, I can imagine,' Nell replied. 'So you came 'ome by yerself?'

'No, Billy Emmerson was there. 'E saw me 'ome.'

'Now there's a nice young man, an' livin' only two doors away,' Nell said smiling. 'You could do a lot worse.'

'As a matter o' fact Billy asked me ter walk out wiv 'im last week,' Josie remarked, looking down at her clasped hands.

'And?'

'I said yes.'

'Good fer you,' Nell said smiling. 'Shame 'e's waitin' fer 'is call-up, but at least it'll be somefing fer both of yer to 'old on to. Please Gawd the war'll be over before Billy finishes 'is trainin'.'

'They say it'll go on inter the new year,' Josie replied.

Nell suddenly shuddered. 'I 'ope we 'aven't gotta put up wiv those doodle-bugs till next year. One minute I was talkin' ter Janice Groves an' the next minute they was diggin' me out from under all that rubble. It 'appened so quick.'

'Look, Mum, yer gotta try an' put it ter the back o' yer mind,' Josie urged her gently. 'You're safe an' back 'ome, an' that's all that matters as far as this family is concerned.'

'Is it?' Nell said quietly.

Josie wished she had been more subtle. 'Well at least we can be a whole family again, once Dad sorts 'imself out, an' 'e will do, Mum, I'm sure of it.'

'I wish I was so sure,' Nell replied. 'Those visits of 'is showed me 'ow far 'e's gone. All right, 'e made an effort, but I could see the effect the booze was 'avin' by 'is eyes, I could smell it on 'is breath an' see by the way 'e walked. It's killin' 'im slowly, Josie, an' I don't know what ter do about it.'

Josie stood up and went to her mother, patting her back gently as Nell broke down in a flood of tears. Kathy hurried into the parlour and stood to one side looking distressed. 'Don't cry, Mum,' she managed.

Josie caught her eye. 'Kathy, go an' make a pot o' tea. D'yer 'ear me?'

The younger girl jumped at her sister's raised voice and did as she was bid, feeling at that minute she could cheerfully use the carving knife on her father if he showed his face in the house.

★

191

Stymie Smith had had a bad week. His total earnings were less than the week before and the horse had gone lame on Friday morning. 'A strained back tendon below the hock,' the vet had told him. 'Hot linseed poultices and a week away from the cart should do it.'

Stymie had decided to go to the estate office on Friday afternoon and had come out feeling even more depressed. The clerk was civil enough but in his opinion there was little Stymie could do except write to the owner of the house and attached yard to apply for an extension of occupancy until there was a firm buyer. The totter explained that he wasn't very good at writing letters and the clerk, feeling sorry for him, agreed to write the letter himself, stressing that it would be foolish to harbour any real hopes.

Bel Fiddler was more optimistic when Stymie explained his predicament. 'Get that petition started,' she told him. 'If the owner knows 'ow people round 'ere feel about yer, 'e might let yer stay there fer the time bein'.'

'Could yer do it for me?' he asked her.

'Yeah okay, but you gotta take it round yerself, Seth. I'll come round the doors wiv yer, but yer gotta let people see you're determined ter stay.'

True to her word Bel Fiddler had the petition ready in no time at all but when she handed it to Stymie on Sunday morning he baulked at going round the street immediately. 'Sunday's a day o' rest,' he said weakly. 'I'll start termorrer.'

'I'll 'elp yer, as soon as I find out what's 'appenin' down at the labour exchange,' Bel promised.

Satisfied with the progress, Stymie went to the Star and Garter at lunchtime and got drunk, staggering home at closing time with two quarts of brown ale in a paper bag. 'There you are, me ole mate,' he mumbled to the horse as he poured the beer into a rusty bucket. 'Yer need this as much as I do.'

★

The tall man with the cold grey eyes limped into the Rotherhithe Infirmary on Sunday morning leaning on a walking-stick and made his way to the casualty department. 'It's my knee,' he said in answer to the duty nurse's inquiry. 'I'm afraid I've twisted it.'

'If you'll take a seat the doctor will see you as soon as he can,' the nurse told him.

The Pedlar sat down some way apart from the other two people waiting and glanced casually around the large reception area. This part of the building looked old and in need of renovation, but adjacent to it was the new children's wing, a fine reconstruction waiting to be brought into use as soon as the Prime Minister cut the tape in ten days' time. Sir Barry Freeman had passed on the information about the probable date over the phone, after he had been instructed to transfer the blood money into an account held in the name of William McGarry in a Dublin bank.

At last a tired-looking doctor examined the Pedlar's knee and shook his head. 'There doesn't seem to be anything severely wrong with it,' he announced. 'I don't think there's any cartilage damage, but just to be on the safe side I'd like you to have an X-ray. Nurse, can you get Mr McGarry fixed up with the orthopaedic clinic on Monday week? Yes, that's right, Mr Charles. He's there every Monday.'

Feigning absent-mindedness the Pedlar got the nurse to write out the date of his next visit on an appointment card, and after being prescribed some painkillers and having his knee supported with a crepe bandage he left the hospital feeling satisfied with his progress.

The occupants of Room 13 at the Foreign Office had long ceased to consider Sunday a day of rest, and Commander Jock Barratt looked particularly businesslike as he eyed the other two people in the room from across his wide desk. A large, craggy-faced man in his fifties with a mop of white hair, Commander Barratt headed the MI5 anti-espionage team and his successes over the years had served to place him in high esteem amongst his colleagues. 'The two tapes we had installed in Hennessey's hotel room failed to give us any clues as to his accomplices,' he said in his gruff voice. 'There was one incoming call that stank louder than Billingsgate however. A message to say that Hennessey's mother would be arriving home that midday. Most likely a coded request for him to make contact with someone.'

Sir Benjamin Holloway nodded. 'I think we should give our Mr Hennessey all the rope he needs for the time being. I also think we should allow Miss Winkless full licence to further the relationship. She's very good.'

'When's he due back in this country?' Dan Forester the section leader asked.

'On Saturday,' Jock Barratt told him. 'He'll be bringing lists of displaced persons residing at present in Portugal for department scrutiny.'

'Does Miss Winkless know?'

'Oh yes,' the commander replied with a sly smile. 'There'll be a social evening here next Saturday and she'll be present in her role as my secretary. God, it's a good thing my wife never shows any interest in coming along to these functions. How could I explain Miss Winkless to her?'

The men chuckled and Commander Barratt got up to pour them a drink. Good men both of them, he thought, but in the dangerous and shape-shifting business they were in it was sometimes necessary to withhold some of the cards, even from the most trusted of colleagues. After all, this was not just any operation. It was the most important and perilous enterprise he had been involved with in all of his twenty years at MI5, and nothing must go wrong. Apart from himself, only two other men knew the whole plan, and one was the Prime Minister himself.

On Sunday afternoon Tommy Bailey sat on the kerbside next to Dennis Taylor with a long face. 'I never like Sundays,' he said, scratching in the dirt.

'No, neivver do I,' his friend agreed. 'Yer made to wear yer best clothes an' yer can't do any climbin' an' fings.'

'When I got kids I'm gonna let 'em wear all their ole clothes on Sundays,' Tommy vowed.

'Yeah, me too.'

'Mums are all the same, ain't they?'

'Yeah. Bloody spoilsports.'

'I reckon it's the worst day o' the week, Sunday.'

Dennis looked along the deserted summer street and scowled. 'My dad's just as bad. 'E should see fings my way, but 'e don't. Everyfing me muvver ses 'e agrees wiv. I fink 'e's scared she'll 'ave a go at 'im.'

'Well, at least yer got a dad.'

'So 'ave you.'

'Yeah I know, but 'e ain't livin' at 'ome,' Tommy said glumly. 'If my dad was livin' wiv us I bet 'e'd let me go out in me ole clothes on Sundays.'

'Will 'e be comin' back?' Dennis asked.

'Yeah, soon.'

'Next week?'

'Maybe.'

'Do yer ever see 'im?'

'Yeah sometimes, but 'e moves about a lot.'

'Moves about? What, different 'ouses?'

'Nah, different pubs.'

Dennis looked at his friend's sad face and it made him feel

sad too. 'I never ever called your dad a drunken ole bastard,' he said.

'Nah, I know yer never,' Tommy replied. 'There was plenty who did though. I bashed Lennie Smivvers up over what 'e called 'im an' yer remember that fight I 'ad at school wiv Georgie Pimples? That was over what 'e said about me dad.'

'Yeah, I know,' Dennis laughed. ''E went 'ome cryin' an' all the kids took the piss out of 'im the next day.'

'I might go an' see me dad soon,' Tommy told him.

'What, on yer own?'

'Yeah. I'll tell 'im ter come 'ome now, not next week or the week after. It used ter be really nice when 'e was around. It's bloody miserable now most o' the time.'

'When yer go I'll come wiv yer,' Dennis volunteered. 'It's better if there's two of yer. That place you said yer dad was livin' is where the Chinks live. My dad told me.'

'When I go over there I'll let yer know,' Tommy agreed.

Dennis Taylor breathed in deeply and let the air out of his lungs slowly through pursed lips. It felt good to be best friends with someone, someone you could share adventures with. ''Ere, Tommy, I got somefing for yer,' he said impulsively, despite himself.

'What is it?' Tommy asked.

Dennis held out his hand and Tommy's eyes lit up. He had always admired the small, pearl-handled clasp knife that now lay in his friend's outstretched palm.

'You can 'ave it.'

'Cor! Can I?'

'Yeah, take it. I don't want it any more.'

Tommy took the knife and opened the blade. 'It's dead sharp,' he said. 'Cor fanks, Den.'

'It's all right,' the lad said, knowing he was going to miss that knife. 'We're best friends, ain't we?'

'Yeah, best friends.'

'Yer better take that knife wiv yer when yer go over the water,' Dennis advised him. 'Some o' those Chinks carry knives round wiv 'em, so my dad said.'

'I'll keep it on me all the time,' Tommy replied.

'I don't want it, but if yer ever get fed up wiv it I'll 'ave it back.'

'Yeah okay, Den.'

The sound of his mother calling out for him made Dennis jump up quickly and he brushed the seat of his trousers. 'I gotta go,' he puffed.

'See yer, Den.'

'See yer, Tommy.'

Chapter Nineteen

Sir Barry Freeman met with his three League associates on Monday lunchtime at his favourite haunt, the Savoy Grill. Victor Anderson and Sidney Holman were already waiting in the ornate lounge when the leader arrived, and a few minutes later Ben Thorburn stepped out of a taxi after cutting short a meeting of bankers in the City. This was priority business and things were moving fast.

Sir Barry looked around at his colleagues after they had made themselves comfortable at the table. 'Well, gentlemen, everything is in place now,' he began. 'The Pedlar's gone to ground and there'll be no more contact with us, I'm pleased to say. We'll hear the tragic news in the normal way and act accordingly. The meeting I had with him was a civilised affair but the man sent shivers down my spine, I don't mind admitting. I looked into his cold eyes and found myself thinking that he had even less heart than most of the company chairmen I've known over the years! I'm certain we've picked the right man, but not one I would want to meet again, ever.'

Anderson smiled appreciatively and Holman and Thorburn exchanged brief glances, each aware that it would take a singular kind of person to measure up to the enormously difficult task of the assassin. He would have very little time and opportunity to target Churchill, to pull the trigger and then make his getaway. People would be milling around and all vantage points would have been checked out by the Prime Minister's own security team. The police too would be there in numbers and the local bobbies would be alerted to watch for any strangers acting suspiciously.

'I don't envy him his job,' Thorburn remarked.

'Well, he'll certainly earn his fee,' Sir Barry replied. 'Now gentlemen, to the task in hand.' The waiter interrupted the conversation and the leader ordered a bottle of '37 St Emilion and delayed ordering the meal. 'Our contact has confirmed that Hennessey will be arriving in the country on Saturday morning,' he continued. 'I'd like you three to meet with him during the evening. He should have the necessary information on the money transfer with him, and I would urge you to make sure that the Pedlar's account is topped up by Wednesday or Thursday at the very latest. He'll be checking it next Friday, and if there's any hitch then the whole plan falls down. I have the details of the account here.' He took out a black leather wallet from his coat and pulled out a small card which he placed in front of Ben Thorburn.

'I'm sure everything will go like clockwork,' the prospective treasurer said with a smug smile.

'Let's hope so,' Sir Barry answered. 'We have no way of contacting the Pedlar to warn him of any delay.'

Anderson caught the leader's eye. 'I don't want to sound alarmist, but if there's any problem with the money from Hennessey, do we have funds available to cover the Pedlar's payment?'

'I suppose we could use League funds for the time being,' Sir Barry told him. 'I just hope Hennessey will come up with the money on Saturday evening. Let's be positive, gentlemen,' he enjoined them, holding up his glass in a toast.

★

Don Brady took a sip of tea from his large cracked mug and put it down on the desk in front of him. 'Yer let me down, Frank,' he said, eyeing the dishevelled figure standing in front of him. 'I wanted you ter get those fires roarin' by the time the lads came in ter work last Friday mornin'. There was some cuttin' ter do as well. You could 'ave coped wiv that if yer'd 'ave bin 'alf sensible. But what 'appens? Yer don't show up, an' now yer come in 'ere lookin' like a poxy tramp an' expect me ter say it doesn't matter. It bloody well does. If you wanna get back ter cooperin' yer'll 'ave ter pull yerself tergevver an' quick. Dick Foss goes in two weeks' time an' I told yer you could 'ave 'is job, if yer prove ter me yer capable. Yer couldn't blame me if I told yer ter piss off an' don't come back.'

Frank screwed his cap up in his shaking hands and shuffled uncomfortably. 'No, I couldn't blame yer, Don,' he said quietly. 'Nobody's bin more patient than you. Anuvver bloke would 'ave chucked me out before now.'

The wiry cooper ran his hand over his bald head and puffed loudly. 'Sit down fer Gawd sake an' stop twistin' that bloody cap,' he growled. 'Yer make me feel nervous.'

Frank Bailey did as he was told and put the cap under his leg, clasping his hands to keep them still. 'Don't fink I'm not tryin' ter kick the booze, Don, 'cos I am,' he said. 'I got a family ter fink about. Nell's a diamond, an' those kids o' mine are the best. I could 'ave it all back if I try really 'ard, an' that's what I'm gonna do.' He looked up at the wall clock behind the desk. 'It's nearly two o'clock an' I ain't 'ad one drink terday. Normally I'd be 'alf sloshed by now.'

'Yeah, but 'ave yer 'ad anyfing to eat?'

'A slice o' toast.'

'Yer need more inside yer than one slice o' poxy toast,' Don Brady laughed. 'If yer serious about givin' up the boozin' yer gotta eat, an' regular. Come on, let's go.'

'Where we goin'?' Frank asked.

'Ter Buckley's cafe. 'E'll still be servin' dinners if I know Tom Buckley.'

'I couldn't,' Frank said, pulling a face.

'Yes yer can, so don't argue, let's go,' the cooper said firmly.

While Frank tucked into a meat pie and two veg Don Brady sat watching him, puffing on a hand-rolled cigarette. ''Ow's Nell?' he asked after a while.

'She's back 'ome,' Frank told him. 'She's still very stiff but the doctors said it'll pass off after a week or two.'

''Ave yer bin over the water ter see 'er?' Don asked.

'Nah, but I spoke ter the doctor at the 'ospital.'

'Go on, finish it up,' the cooper urged him as Frank put down the knife and fork.

'It's a bit too much fer me,' he said puffing.

'It's only a kid's dinner, eat it up.'

Frank picked up the utensils once more, and when he had cleared his plate he leaned back on the wooden bench. 'That was a very nice meat pie,' he remarked. 'Just like Nell makes.'

'Yeah, I always come 'ere fer me grub,' Don said. 'What yer doin' now?'

'I fink I'll go an' sit in the church gardens fer a while,' Frank replied. 'Then I'm gonna go 'ome an' get a shave.'

'An' down the pub ternight?'

'No, Don, I'm gonna give it a miss. I can do it.'

'Well, if yer can, an' yer get a good night's sleep, yer can come in early an' get those fires started termorrer,' Don told him. 'Like I said, there's some cuttin' ter do an' some bands ter shape.'

Frank watched the stream of cigarette smoke curling up to the ceiling and subconsciously felt for his makings. Don noticed and pushed over his tobacco tin. 'Can yer manage ter roll it?' he asked.

Frank nodded quickly, but after trying unsuccessfully to spread the tobacco out along the paper he looked up helplessly.

'Come 'ere, I'll do it,' Don said.

'Why d'yer bovver wiv me?' the drunkard asked as his friend expertly twirled the paper around the tobacco and made a smooth even cigarette.

'Normally I wouldn't give a piss-artist five minutes o' me time,' the cooper replied.

'So why me?'

''Cos you're a different case, an' I know the 'istory.'

Frank lit up and took a deep drag. ''Ow d'you know?'

'Swanny told me.'

'Lots o' people who get pissed all the time 'ave a reason,' Frank remarked.

'Or an excuse,' Don said quickly. 'Trouble is a lot of 'em are past redemption. You ain't.'

'I'm glad o' yer confidence in me.'

'I wouldn't be sittin' 'ere now if I didn't fink you could kick it,' the cooper said. 'Come ter terms wiv the reason yer started an' yer 'alfway there. Try ter drown it in drink all the time an' yer just make it worse.'

'What can I do?' Frank asked desperately. 'Tell me, Don, what can I do ter come ter terms wiv it? The memory 'aunts me day an' night.'

'I dunno, I ain't no psychiatrist,' Don replied shrugging his narrow shoulders, 'but in my 'umble opinion yer punishin' yerself 'cos you're too decent a bloke ter take it out on anyone else. As a rescue worker you was no stranger ter the terrible sights yer saw, the children's 'ospital was different. They were all sick kids, an' seein' somefing as evil an' sickenin' as that probably brought up all the bad experiences yer'd buried away in yer mind, an' yer still tryin' ter put the lid on. There's the feelin's o' guilt ter consider as well. Did yer do all yer could ter get those kids out from under the debris while there was still life in their little bodies? Did yer do all yer could to 'elp 'em once they were out? Fings like that.'

Frank stubbed his cigarette out in the tin lid which served as an ashtray and coughed nervously. 'Ter be honest, Don, I don't fink I was the right man fer the 'Eavy Rescue Squad,' he said. 'Every time we come across someone under the wreckage I used ter shake terrible. I 'id it from the rest, but I 'ad this terrible panic inside.'

'Don't yer fink we all felt like that?' Don asked him. 'I was in the rescue squad fer a short while an' I used ter break out in a cold sweat every time we went out on a job. Fortunately fer me I was stood down frew medical reasons. They reckon I've got a dicky 'eart.'

'I never knew you was in the rescue squad,' Frank said looking very surprised. 'Yer never talked about it.'

'I didn't want to. I'm just tryin' ter ferget it, like you, but I still get nightmares, an' wake up in a cold sweat in the dark wonderin' where I am. I'm in the same boat as you, Frank, but gettin' pissed ain't the answer.'

Frank put his hand in his coat pocket and took out a handful of coppers. 'I wouldn't fink of offerin' yer a beer, but I'm gonna buy yer a mug o' tea. D'yer take sugar?'

Don nodded. 'We'll 'ave ter make it a quick one though, Frank, I've got a cooperage ter run, in case yer've fergot.'

Stymie Smith replaced the poultice on his horse's sore tendon and mucked out the stall, then he washed down the cart and oiled the axles. Still feeling energetic he sorted out the copper and brass from the scrap metal and worked at stripping down a couple of old iron gas-stoves for spare parts. Resisting the urge to go to the Star and Garter for a lunchtime drink he made himself a cheese sandwich instead, which he washed down with a mug of sweet tea. Later there was some sheathed copper wire to be stripped but he felt it could wait. There was another task that awaited him, one he was loath to tackle.

The totter had a shave, combed his thin sandy hair back from his forehead and used a tiny smear of tallow to hold it down. He was a totter of the old school and when he went out socially he invariably wore an open-necked shirt with a red-spotted scarf tied round his neck. Polished brown boots, grey slacks and a fawn tweed coat adorned with a wilting sprig of heather completed the outfit, and when he took a brief look at himself in his wardrobe mirror he felt as ready as he ever would.

Hoping that Bel Fiddler was available Stymie knocked at her front door and stood looking down at his boots while he waited.

'Well, well, you look smart,' Bel said as she opened the door to him.

'I thought we might get started,' he said in a voice lacking all enthusiasm, which did not go unnoticed.

'Don't look so glum, Seth,' Bel replied with a smile. 'You ain't gotta do it yer know.'

'Yeah, I wanna do it but I'm just a bit nervous, I s'pose,' he confessed. 'I ain't never spoke to 'alf of 'em in the turnin'.'

'Don't worry, I'll explain if yer want me to,' she told him, 'but it's a bit early if you ask me. Some are still at work an' some'll be 'avin' a lie-down.'

'D'yer fink we should wait till ternight then?' he asked.

'No, come on,' Bel said. 'It'll be a start anyway. Come in fer a minute while I get ready.'

Stymie followed the young woman into the parlour and stood by the table.

'Well, don't just stand there, sit down,' she said grinning. 'Yer makin' the place untidy.'

'Where's Chloe?' he asked as he made himself comfortable in an easy chair.

'She's gone ter take the cards back,' Bel told him. 'Why d'yer ask?'

'I just wondered. You an' 'er are always tergevver,' he replied. 'Yer say she's gone ter take the cards back. What cards are they then?'

'You wouldn't be interested.'

'I might be.'

Bel sat down facing him. 'Me an' Chloe got this 'ome work to earn some money while we were lookin' fer a job. What you 'ave ter do is sew loops in the cards. The ones we got were corn plaster cards, you've seen the sort 'angin' up in the shops. Anyway we was doin' 'em all last week an' Sandra 'elped us. We even got our dad ter give us an 'and. Trouble was when we took the first batch back the firm wouldn't pay us.'

'Why not?' Stymie asked.

'Well, fer a start me dad spilt some tea on a pile of 'em, an' Sandra made the loops too small. Anyway Chloe's took the rest back an' she's gonna demand they pay us the full amount. I was gonna go wiv 'er but she said it'd be better if she went on 'er own. She knows 'ow I blow me top.'

'Yer'd 'ave bin better wiv the soldiers,' Stymie remarked.

'Soldiers? What soldiers?'

'There's a place in Tower Bridge Road that makes little soldiers an' they get outworkers ter do the faces on 'em. All yer 'ave ter do is make a round blob wiv pink paint an' when they're dry yer put two eyes on 'em wiv a pen.'

'An 'ow's it work out in money?'

''Alf a dollar a box, so this woman told me.'

'An' 'ow many in a box?'

'I dunno. The box is this size.' Stymie showed her with his hands.

'An' 'ow big are the soldiers?'

'About an inch long.'

'Bloody 'ell, Seth, that sounds even worse than the soddin' cards,' Bel said quickly. 'No, me an' Chloe are gonna go out termorrer an' get some work, whatever it is. Anyfing is gonna be better than spendin' all our spare time doin' those poxy loops.'

Stymie looked down at his boots for a few moments. 'I really appreciate what yer done, Bel,' he said hesitantly.

'I ain't done nuffink yet,' she replied.

'Yes, you 'ave. Yer done the petition an' yer willin' ter come round door-knockin' wiv me.'

'I'm yer friend. That's what friends are for,' she told him with a smile.

'I've never 'ad a ladyfriend,' he said nervously. 'Not like you anyway.'

Bel leaned forward and laid a hand on his knee. 'What d'yer mean, not like me?' she asked.

Stymie coloured up. 'I can't imagine anyone else goin' fer a ride on me cart.'

'D'you really like me?' Bel prompted him.

'Course I do. I just said so, didn't I?'

'No, I mean in that way,' she pressed.

'What way?'

'You know, the man an' woman way.'

'Course I do. I fink yer a good sport.'

'D'yer like the look o' me?'

'Yeah, course I do.'

'Then why ain't yer tried anyfing?'

'Like givin' yer a kiss?'

Bel puffed loudly for his benefit. 'Tell me, Seth. 'Ow many gels 'ave you bin out wiv?'

'One or two.'

'An' when was that?'

'A few years back.'

'An' did yer fancy them?'

'I kissed one an' she slapped me face.'

'God Almighty,' she sighed. 'Do you really know what yer got it for?'

Stymie flushed up again. 'Just because I ain't kissed yer yet doesn't mean I don't want to,' he said quietly. 'I didn't fink yer wanted me to.'

Bel shook her head slowly. 'I've bin on that cart wiv yer an' we've bin out a couple o' times ter the pub an' yer've still not tried ter kiss me. I'm beginnin' ter fink there's somefing wrong wiv me.'

'There's nuffink wrong wiv you, Bel,' he told her firmly. 'I just ain't good at that sort o' fing.'

She stood up and reached out her hands. 'Stand up, you dopey git,' she growled good-naturedly. 'Put yer arms round me an' kiss me on the lips like yer mean it. Like they do in the films.'

'In the films?'

'Kiss me, fer Christ sake,' she almost screamed.

Stymie wasn't sure which way to bend his head to avoid their noses touching but he managed to oblige the young woman and she held on to him until he grew short of breath.

'There you are. It wasn't so bad, was it?' she said, smiling as she felt how excited it had made him.

Stymie sat down quickly to cover his embarrassment. 'Was it okay?' he asked.

'It'll do, fer the time bein',' she replied. 'I tell yer somefing though. There ain't nuffink wrong wiv you that a bit o' practice won't put right. Now come on an' let's make a start wiv the petition before I drag you upstairs.'

Stymie walked out of the house in a state of shock and

crossed the street behind Bel, his eyes fixed on her wide hips and shapely calves.

'We'll start at Wilco's an' work along the street,' she told him. 'Seth, are you listenin'? Right then, bang on the door.'

Their first respondent was enthusiastic. Fortified with a few drinks that lunchtime, Wilco Johnson was in a carefree mood. 'Sign it? Course I'll sign it. Bloody disgrace what they try to get away with,' he sounded off. 'If anybody refuses to sign this petition just you let me know and I'll give 'em a piece of my mind. Bloody disgraceful the carryings-on. A land fit for heroes indeed. More than happy to oblige. I'd go round with you myself but for my leg. Piece of shell actually. Plays me up at times. You've got my support though. Good luck to you, old chap. Happy hunting.'

Bel looked at Stymie and shook her head slowly as the door shut in their faces. 'All that bloody codswallop an' 'e didn't even sign the poxy paper,' she said incredulously. 'Well, don't just stand there, knock on the door again, yer silly git.'

Chapter Twenty

The two young lads from Quay Street walked home at teatime with worried looks on their faces. They had been in forbidden territory in Dockhead and realised that it was going to be difficult to hide it from their parents. Dennis Taylor frowned as he saw the white patches forming on his boots from the salty Thames water. 'Me mum'll go mad,' he groaned. 'She told me I mustn't go near the water after what 'appened ter that kid from Maltby Buildin's.'

'P'raps I might be able ter sneak the blackin' an' a brush out ter yer before yer go in,' Tommy Bailey suggested.

'Yeah, but it's me socks as well,' Dennis said in a worried voice. 'They're soakin' bloody wet.'

'I ain't got no spare socks the same as them, Den, or I'd let yer 'ave 'em,' Tommy told him.

'It's all right, Tommy, I'll just tell 'er I slipped off the steps.'

'Won't she go off at yer fer goin' where yer shouldn't?'

'Yeah, but I'll make up some excuse. I know, I'll tell 'er we was just goin' over the bridge ter watch the ship bein' unloaded an' we saw these boys chuck a little puppy in the river.'

'Cor yeah! Yer could say we run down ter Shad Thames steps an' got the puppy out the water wiv a big long pole.'

'An' I slipped on the muddy steps an' got me boots an' socks wet.'

'It wouldn't be all lies, would it?' Tommy remarked. 'Yer did slip on the steps.'

Dennis nodded. 'If me mum goes off too much I'll tell 'er that kids 'ave ter play somewhere. If we play football or tin-can-copper in the street we get told ter piss off, an' then we're told we mustn't go near the river or places like the Borough Market. What we s'posed ter do, sit readin' comics all day?'

'Parents ain't got no sense most o' the time,' Tommy scowled. 'They stop yer doin' everyfing, an' we'll be goin' back ter school in a few days' time.'

'Look at my boots, they're gettin' worse,' Dennis said anxiously.

'Don't worry, I'll get yer the blackin' some'ow,' Tommy reassured him as he looked down at the growing white patches on the black leather.

They turned into Quay Street and Dennis sat down at the kerbside to wait while Tommy crossed the road and let himself into the house opposite.

'Is that you, Tommy?' Nell called out.

'Yeah, Mum,' the lad replied as he put his head round the parlour door.

'Don't get goin' out again,' Nell told him. 'Josie'll be in soon an' she'll be gettin' yer tea.'

'I'm only gonna give Dennis a comic I promised 'im,' Tommy said quickly. ''E's waitin' outside fer it.'

'Well, don't stay out there chattin',' Nell replied. 'Yer gotta get cleaned up. Yer look like yer bin climbin' up chimneys.'

Tommy rummaged through the cupboard in the scullery and looked under the sink for the biscuit tin which contained the shoe brushes and polish but it was nowhere to be seen. 'Where's the shoe brushes, Mum?' he called out.

'I dunno, Josie's 'ad a clear-out, she'll know.'

'Why can't they leave fings where they are,' Tommy said aloud as he searched through the various odds and ends in the cupboard beneath the Welsh dresser.

''Ave yer found 'em?'

'Nah.'

'Well, it doesn't matter, you can clean yer boots after tea,' Nell told him. 'Now come on, wash yer grubby 'ands an' face.'

Tommy gave up looking and was creeping towards the front door to let Dennis know, when he heard footsteps outside and Josie's voice as she said something to one of the neighbours. He hurried back into the scullery and as soon as his sister had come in and walked through to the parlour the lad slipped out of the house. There was no sign of Dennis and Tommy guessed that his friend had been spotted and ordered in.

Nell eased her position in the easy chair and grimaced. 'I peeled the spuds an' done the greens but I 'ad ter sit down, me back was startin' ter play me up,' she said morosely.

'Look, I said not ter worry,' Josie reminded her. 'It's early days yet. They said yer'd be very stiff fer a while.'

'Yeah, but I can't just sit 'ere all day doin' nuffink, I'll go right round the twist,' Nell moaned.

'You could read, or listen ter the wireless,' Josie suggested. 'It's no trouble fer me an' Kathy ter get the tea an' do the 'ousework till yer feelin' stronger. We don't want you strainin' yer back an' 'avin' ter go back in the 'ospital.'

Nell stared into the empty grate. 'There's fings I can't expect you an' Kathy ter do,' she said.

'Like what?' Josie asked.

'Like black-leadin' the grate an' the gas-stove, an' changin' the curtains.'

Josie slumped down in the chair facing her mother. 'Look, Mum, you only 'ave to ask. We can't fink of everyfing.'

Nell pulled out a handkerchief and blew her nose. 'Four days I've bin 'ome. I expect yer farvver knows by now.'

'Yeah, I reckon so, but I don't fink 'e'd call 'ere, not till 'e's ready ter come back,' Josie remarked.

Nell dabbed at her eyes. 'I worry over 'im,' she said. 'Is 'e gettin' enough food? Is 'e sleepin' rough? I dunno, I s'pose I shouldn't. After all, I chucked 'im out, but we couldn't go on any longer the way it was. We were the laughin'-stock o' the street.

Josie stared down at her fingernails for a few moments. 'I fink I'll go over the water an' see 'im on Saturday,' she said.

Nell sniffed loudly and blew her nose again. 'I bin worried sick,' she confessed, suddenly breaking down. 'I miss 'im so much.'

'We all do, Mum, but it won't be fer long, you'll see.'

'If 'e showed up 'ere pissed I couldn't send 'im away again.'

Tommy had been standing in the passage and heard most of the conversation. Hearing his mother crying upset him and made his stomach knot up. He chewed his lip, suddenly wanting to get out of the house and run hard and fast. Somewhere, anywhere. He slipped out into the street quietly, but instead of running he simply squatted down in the kerb with his chin propped on his hands.

'What's the matter, Tommy, you look very pensive?'

The lad looked up to see Wilco Johnson standing over him. 'I was just finkin',' he replied.

'About going back to school?'

'Yeah, sort of.'

'Never mind, at least it'll keep you young lads out of trouble,' Wilco remarked with a grin.

'Me an' Dennis don't get inter trouble,' Tommy said defensively.

'Well, good for you. By the way, how's your dad?'

Tommy looked up at the tall figure with the handlebar moustache. ''E's okay, Mr Johnson.'

'Have you seen him lately?'

'Not lately.'

'I have.'

'Where?' Tommy asked quickly.

Wilco squatted down in the kerb next to the young lad, puffing with the effort. 'You know me and your father are pals,' he said, and Tommy nodded. 'Well, I got a bit concerned at not seeing him for a few weeks so I went over the water to look him up. I found him after a bit of a search and we had a few drinks together and a long chat. It was very nice to see him again.'

'I'm finkin' o' goin' over there ter see 'im,' Tommy replied. 'I'm gonna ask 'im ter come back 'ome.'

'Very good too,' Wilco said smiling.

'Trouble is I don't know 'ow ter get ter the buildin's where 'e lives,' Tommy confessed. 'I've only bin there once. I know it's somewhere the ovver side o' the tunnel.'

'I don't think you'll find him there,' Wilco told him. 'Your dad's got a mate who he drinks with. They use the Lighterman at Stepney Reach and this man has a small boat moored there. That's where your dad sleeps most nights.'

'Could I find it?' Tommy asked.

Wilco nodded. 'Are you good at directions?'

It was the young lad's turn to nod. 'Me an' Dennis go all over the place, an' we go on the underground an' foller the maps.'

'Right then,' Wilco said twirling his moustache. 'First you catch the number eighty-two bus through the tunnel . . .'

The tall lean man with the ice-cold eyes walked stiff-legged into the grounds of the Rotherhithe Infirmary with the aid of his stick and stood for a while watching the builders putting the last touches to the children's wing. He wore two pairs of trousers, a thin pair of cashmere next to his skin and over them a pair of rough twill, the sort favoured by manual workers. He had strapped a shortened broom handle to his left leg at the ankle and thigh and it was not noticeable beneath the heavy twill cloth. The man leaned on his stick as he looked up at some scaffolding where a workman was grouting an air vent in the brick wall. 'A very nice job,' he said amicably.

The workman nodded. 'It'll be much better than the last buildin',' he remarked. 'All modern this one is.'

'I noticed it's got a flat roof,' the Pedlar said.

'Yeah, it's 'andy as an extra escape route in case o' fire.'

'Good Lord.'

'Oh yeah, up one flight o' stairs, across the roof an' down the ovver flight,' the workman explained as he cleaned the cement from his trowel.

'Are any of your lads invited to the opening ceremony?' the Pedlar asked.

'Only the boss,' the workman told him. 'The rest of us'll be workin' on anuvver site by then.'

'I wonder who's going to open it? Nice if it was the King or the Queen. It'd give the people round here something to look forward to.'

The workman crouched on the planking just above the Pedlar's head. 'I 'eard it was gonna be old Churchill, but it's only rumours,' he said.

The Pedlar smiled. 'It could well be. The Prime Minister often visits Bermondsey and Stepney on those walkabouts of his.'

The workman threw his clean trowel into a grubby canvas bag. 'If yer interested yer can see a bit o' what it looks like inside. It's all marble floorin', yer know.'

'Yeah, I'd like to take a look.'

'Go in the main entrance, turn left an' walk right ter the end o' the corridor, then turn left again an' yer'll see the barrier. Yer can see the long corridor of this wing over the barrier. It'll give yer some idea o' what it's like. I tell yer, it's lovely inside.'

'Well, thanks for the info,' the Pedlar told him. 'If I'm up to it I'll take a gander, after I've got my leg looked at.'

Following the directions he made his way to the barrier and noticed that there was a small black curtain fixed nearby at eye level on one of the walls. It was quiet and the long marbled corridor ahead seemed deserted. The Pedlar looked quickly around him and then ducked under the barrier and walked along the corridor of the children's wing. There were fire doors on each side at intervals and when he reached the far end he turned to look back. Seventy yards from here to the barrier, he estimated. Carrying on he turned left and saw that the main front doors were propped open, and without being challenged he walked out into the sunlight, down a few steps and along a short path to some iron gates that led out into Jamaica Road.

It had been a good exercise, he thought. He had started to familiarise himself with the location and was getting quite used to walking stiff-legged. Today it was a piece of wood that was strapped to his leg, but on the day of reckoning it would be something a little more powerful, the Schreider hunting rifle with its clip-on telescopic sight. Deadly accurate in the right hands and with little recoil, the rifle had become his favourite tool of trade and the Pedlar smiled contentedly as he hobbled along Jamaica Road in the early evening sunlight.

Billy Emmerson saw the worried look on his mother's face as he walked into the house on that Thursday evening and his eyes instinctively went to the mantelshelf. It had come. The official buff envelope was unmistakable and Billy tore it open to find that he had been called up into the Royal Corps of Signals.

'When d'yer 'ave ter go?' his mother asked, trying to hide her concern.

'Thursday the twenty-first o' September,' he replied with a smile.

'It's nuffink ter laugh about,' Rose told him.

'Well, there's no use cryin' over it,' Billy remarked, his smile broadening.

'You really wanna go, don't yer?' Rose said in exasperation. 'Don't leave me out. Give me a bit o' the action. It's a bloody game wiv you blokes. There's yer farvver last night, glued ter the wireless, maps on the table. Like a bleedin' big kid.'

Billy put his arm round his mother's shoulders. 'Now listen, Ma,' he replied calmly in an effort to reassure her. 'It's not like that at all. Now I've finished me apprenticeship I'm duty-bound ter go in the services. I've just gotta be fankful that I was allowed the deferment. Anyway I've got trainin' ter do, an' by the time I'm ready fer the off the war could be all over.'

'I bloody well 'ope so,' Rose Emmerson said sighing.

As Billy went into the scullery rolling his sleeves up to his elbows Rose followed him and picked up the simmering kettle. 'Where is it yer gotta report to?' she asked as she poured the hot water into a tin bowl lying in the large stone sink.

'Catterick in Yorkshire,' he told her as he grabbed the large block of Sunlight soap and dipped it into the water.

Rose stood behind him as he scrubbed his hands and fore-arms. He was just a boy, she thought sadly. They all looked like boys. A few years on from learning their sums and grammar and they're learning again – how to kill. It seemed as though the whole world had gone mad.

'Where's the towel, Ma?'

'On the drainin'-board beside yer.'

'I'm takin' Josie ter the pictures ternight. She'll be surprised.'

'Wait till yer come out before yer tell 'er.'

'Why?'

'Yer don't wanna spoil the picture for 'er.'

'Josie's not like that,' Billy said grinning. 'She knows I gotta go in some time.'

'An' she won't be upset?'

'If she is she won't let me see it.'

Rose shook her head slowly. 'I don't understand you young people. There's you goin' off ter fight an' yer gelfriend won't even be upset.'

'I didn't say she won't, Ma, but she won't make a fuss about it,' Billy replied with a deep sigh.

Rose could see that it was pointless going on about it and she made an attempt to brighten up. 'Yer farvver'll be in soon. Go an' sit down an' I'll serve up. It's pork chops. I made an apple pie too. I know yer like apple pie.'

Billy put the towel back on the draining-board and turned down his shirt sleeves. The atmosphere in the house was going to be difficult for the next two weeks, he thought. There was no use in being awkward and upsetting everyone before he left. Better to go along with the flow and let his mother fuss over him. 'Ma, is my blue shirt ironed?' he asked.

'It's up in yer wardrobe,' she told him. 'I've done 'em all this afternoon. I just couldn't sit still after that letter came this mornin'.'

Billy saw that his mother was near to tears and he searched desperately for something to say. 'I'm finkin' o' sellin' me bike,' he announced.

'Why?'

'It'll get in the way stuck in the yard all the time.'

'No, it won't. Anyway who'd buy that ole contraption?'

Billy smiled as he watched his mother take the chops out of the oven. 'Colin Knight made me an offer not so long ago,' he replied. 'If 'e comes 'ome on leave before I go in I'll tell 'im I'm sellin' it.'

Rose bit on her lip as she straightened up. 'Course you wouldn't know; I was gonna tell yer but that letter took it right out o' me mind.'

'Tell me what, Ma?'

'Colin's bin wounded. 'E's back in a military 'ospital in Sussex.'

'Is 'e badly 'urt?' Billy asked quickly.

''E's lost a leg,' Rose said, her eyes brimming.

Chapter Twenty-One

On Thursday evening Josie showed Mrs Taylor into the parlour and went out into the scullery to put the kettle on. She could tell by the stern look on their neighbour's face that all was not well and she listened in the doorway.

''Ello, Nell, 'ow are yer?'

'Not so bad considerin', Eileen, but I'm fed up wiv sittin' about,' Nell told her. 'Sit down fer a minute, join the club.'

Eileen made herself comfortable in the chair facing Nell. 'I don't wanna worry yer, Nell, considerin' all yer've bin frew lately,' she began, 'but I 'ad ter come over. My Dennis an' your Tommy 'ave bin down the river terday, despite me warnin' Dennis ter keep away. Far be it from me ter stop their fun, but after that little boy got drowned last week I 'ad ter put me foot down. Trouble is, it seems I've bin talkin' ter meself. They went anyway. I wouldn't 'ave known but Dennis came 'ome wiv 'is boots all soppin' wet, an' 'is socks too. 'E said they were goin' over London Bridge ter watch the ship bein' unloaded an' they saw this bloke chuckin' a dog in the water, so they run down ter save it an' my Dennis slipped on the mud an' fell down the steps. Mind you, I don't believe a word of it, an' I told 'im so. They was just playin' there, yer can bet yer life. Anyway I've punished 'im. 'E's gotta stop in all weekend. Fank Gawd they're back at school next week.'

Nell shook her head slowly. 'I've warned Tommy ter keep away from the river too,' she replied. 'I've just sent 'im fer an errand but I'll 'ave a word wiv 'im as soon as 'e gets back.'

Eileen Taylor was a slim woman with doleful eyes and a nervous disposition and it irked Nell the way she fidgeted in the chair, with her hands moving all the time and blinking frequently behind her glasses. She was a decent neighbour however and Nell appreciated her visit. 'Well, at least they come 'ome in one piece,' she said smiling. ''Ave a cup o' tea. Josie's just makin' it.'

Eileen pushed her glasses up on to the bridge of her nose, dabbed at her curlered hair and tried to capture her hands. 'My Dennis worries the life out o' me at times,' she went on. ''E's so darin'. I told 'im 'e was leadin' Tommy on an' if anyfing 'appened to 'im it'd be 'is fault.'

'I don't fink Dennis leads my Tommy on,' Nell replied. 'I tend ter fink it's the ovver way about. Still I'm glad yer came over ter tell me. I'll certainly 'ave words wiv the little bleeder.'

Josie came in with the tea on a tray and sat down at the table. 'Sugar, Mrs Taylor?'

'Two please, luv.'

'Did you 'ear what Eileen was sayin'?' Nell asked her.

'Yeah, I did,' Josie replied. 'The little sod.'

'I wouldn't mind but it's so dangerous down by those steps,' Eileen Taylor carried on. 'I fink they must 'ave lost count 'ow many kids 'ave fell in there an' got drowned. If I've told our Dennis once I've told 'im a fousand times ter keep away from there, but 'e takes no notice. Those steps by London Bridge was where ole Daisy Maggot got drowned. She just walked down the steps an' in she went.'

'Daisy Maggot?' Nell queried. 'I never 'eard about 'er.'

'It's a funny name,' Josie remarked.

'It wasn't 'er real name,' Eileen told her. 'They called 'er Maggot 'cos o' the state of 'er place. Runnin' alive wiv maggots it was. They reckoned she used ter keep meat an' fish in 'er cupboard fer weeks. She 'ad four or five cats an' she used ter feed 'em the rotten food. Very strange woman. She used ter live over the bootmender's in Jamaica Road, till the landlord chucked 'er out. Then she went ter live Downtown. I did 'ear that she was on the game when she was younger. Caught a dose an' it turned 'er brain. It was only rumours, mind, but there's often some trufe in rumours, as yer know.'

Josie and her mother exchanged quick glances. Eileen was sipping her tea like a bird dipping its beak in a puddle.

'Is yer tea all right?' Nell asked with an amused expression on her face.

'Very nice,' Eileen replied. 'Nuffink like a nice cup o' tea when yer worried, is there?'

'It's no good you gettin' worried,' Nell said with a hint of irritation in her voice. 'Yer've punished the lad an' that should stop 'im doin' it again. As fer my Tommy I'll punish' im too. What's good fer one's good fer the ovver.'

Eileen drained the cup and set it down in the saucer. 'That was very nice,' she remarked.

'Can I get yer anuvver one?' Josie offered.

Their neighbour nodded. 'If it's not too much trouble.'

Nell eased her position in the chair. ''Ave they bin round ter yer wiv the petition yet?' she inquired.

'I wouldn't sign it,' Eileen said quickly.

'Oh. Why?'

'I've never spoke ter the man but I don't like a totter's yard in our street,' Eileen replied. 'I fink it encourages rats an' mice, the sort o' stuff 'e stores there.'

'Was Stymie upset yer didn't sign?' Nell asked.

'I dunno. I saw 'im comin' round from the winder so I never opened the door.'

''E'll call again.'

'Yeah, that's what my Sid said. I'll just 'ave ter tell 'im no.'

'We signed,' Josie said as she handed her the refilled cup.

'I bet Iris Meadows didn't sign,' Eileen remarked. 'She was tellin' me she didn't agree wiv it.'

'She signed in the finish,' Nell informed her. 'She told me so.'

'The bloody turncoat,' Eileen grumbled. 'After all she said ter me.'

'Wilco signed as well,' Josie added impishly. 'An' Mrs Metcalf, an' the Baineses, an' Ginny Allen.'

'You must be the only one who ain't signed,' Nell said grinning. 'You mind Stymie don't let that nag of 'is do its business outside your front door.'

The blinking of Eileen's eyes was even more pronounced and she sipped her tea noisily before replying. 'I don't care. Yer gotta stick ter yer principles no matter what everybody else does. I'd sooner 'im go than our buses get ovverun wiv vermin.'

'Trouble is, we don't know who'll be the next tenant,' Nell reminded her. 'I do know there was a rag sorter after the place when Stymie Smith got the tenancy. He could get it next.'

''Eaven ferbid,' Eileen gasped. 'It'll be even worse.'

'Exactly,' Nell said, feeling that she had made her point.

Tommy strolled in and put the wrapped-up brawn on the table, a worried look suddenly crossing his face as he saw Eileen Taylor sitting there. 'Is Dennis comin' out ternight, Mrs Taylor?' he asked.

'No, 'e's not,' Nell answered for her. 'An' nor are you. I'll be wantin' a few words wiv you in a minute, young man.'

Tommy left the parlour and climbed the stairs to his room, realising that the little adventure that afternoon had been found out and it now looked like he was for it. 'Silly ole cow,' he growled. 'Fancy 'er comin' over snitchin'.'

Fifteen minutes later the front door went and then Nell's voice boomed out. 'Tommy. Get down 'ere this minute.'

Putting on his best face and using all his guile the lad explained just what had happened. 'I told Dennis not ter make up stories,' he lied. 'I told 'im ter tell the trufe an' 'is muvver would most likely let 'im off.'

'It's a wonder you didn't fall in too,' Nell told him. 'Do you realise just 'ow dangerous those currents are by that bridge? You could easily get sucked under, no matter 'ow good a swimmer you are.'

'Are they as bad at Stepney Reach?' the lad asked.

'Course they are. But why Stepney Reach?'

'I just wanted ter know,' Tommy said, lowering his head.

Nell read the signs. 'Come on, out wiv it.'

Tommy looked into his mother's pale blue eyes inquiringly. 'I was just finkin' about Dad,' he said. 'Dad's a very good swimmer. I bet 'e could swim across the river easy.'

'Dad wouldn't be silly enough ter try it,' Josie cut in.

'Yeah, but s'posin' 'e fell off that boat when 'e was drunk.'

'What boat?' Nell asked quickly.

'Mr Johnson told me Dad stays on a boat at Stepney Reach some nights, wiv this man who 'e drinks wiv.'

''Ow does Mr Johnson know?'

''Cos 'e went ter see Dad an' they 'ad a drink tergevver.'

Nell looked briefly at Josie. 'When did 'e tell yer this?' she asked Tommy.

'This evenin',' he replied.

Nell's expression suddenly grew very stern. 'I'm fed up wiv you defyin' me, 'specially after spellin' out all the dangers, so you can stop in now, all weekend. Don't look so shocked. Mrs Taylor's keepin' Dennis in too. You boys 'ave gotta learn ter do as yer told. I'm not gonna 'ave you disobeyin' me all the time.'

'Aw, Mum.'

'Never mind "aw Mum". You get yer room cleared up as well before yer go ter bed. I can't do it yet awhile an' yer can't expect yer sister ter do it. She's got enough on 'er plate.'

Tommy went out of the room with a sour look on his face and Josie got up and stretched. 'I'd better get ready,' she remarked. 'Billy'll be callin' any minute.'

When Eileen Taylor left the Baileys' she made her way to the totter's yard. It was locked, but undeterred she knocked on the front door. Stymie looked surprised to see her standing there. 'What can I do fer yer, luv?' he asked.

'I'm sorry ter trouble yer, Mr Smith, but I understand yer've bin round wiv the petition,' she said.

'Yeah, that's right,' he replied.

'I must 'ave bin out at the time so I've come ter put me an' Sid's names down.'

'That's very nice of yer,' Stymie told her. 'Just a minute an' I'll go an' get the paper.'

He was soon back. 'Would yer care ter step in the parlour? It's easier ter write on the table.'

Eileen followed him into the house and was surprised by the tidiness and the fresh smell of disinfectant.

'There we are. If yer'll just put yer name under the last one,' Stymie invited her.

Eileen took the pencil from him and quickly added her and Sid's names to the list. 'I do 'ope this petition'll 'elp,' she said.

'I'm sure it will,' Stymie replied. 'I'm just took back by all the support people round 'ere 'ave bin givin' me. Like you an' Sid, makin' the effort ter sign after missin' me earlier.'

Eileen smiled smugly. 'We both wish yer all the best. It wouldn't be the same round 'ere wivout yer.'

Stymie looked embarrassed and he shuffled his feet. 'Well, fanks again,' he said.

Eileen Taylor left the house and walked quickly back along the street, observed by Iris Meadows, who happened to be fiddling with her parlour curtains. The mere sight of the Taylor woman coming out of the totter's house posed all sorts of questions. Iris knew from experience that Eileen Taylor did not hold with a totter's yard in Quay Street and she had been vociferous in the past about the effect the place was having on the turning. What was she up to? Was there something going on? After all, Stymie Smith was a single man and obviously not short of a bob or two. Had he doffed his cap in the Taylor woman's direction? Granted she was married, but that wouldn't necessarily deter her. Sid Taylor was a dopey git who always seemed to have his head in the clouds. Maybe his wife was looking for a bit of spice in her life. Plenty had before her and plenty would after.

Iris made herself a cup of tea and sat mulling over the conundrum, finally deciding to sound out others in the turning as soon as possible. One or two might have seen Eileen Taylor come out of the totter's place and they too would be just as eager to find out what was going on.

Charlie Fiddler worked at the local brewery as a loading foreman and often he spent the evening in the firm's drinking club. The beer there was cheap and it gave him a pause from his three demanding, tiring daughters. Not that he wanted to be away from them for long, rather the opposite. Leaving them alone for too long in the house was like letting children play with matches in a petrol station, he thought. Nevertheless he relished the time spent in the club with his mates and after a few pints Charlie usually walked home feeling quite contented.

Tonight though he was a little angry with his brood. For two weeks Chloe and Bel had wasted their time on those stupid cards and ended up earning next to nothing. They had contributed nothing whatsoever to the housekeeping money which he kept in the glass mug on the scullery dresser, and to top it all he had found a deficit there when he sorted the rent money out. It wasn't that any of his girls was dishonest. Anything they took out of the jug they would replace, of that he had no fears. It was just the inconsiderate ways they seemed to have adopted; they just took liberties. Chloe and Bel were the worst offenders. Sandra was in regular employment and at present courting one of the clerks at her office, but even she was not above taking the mickey at times.

It was getting dark when Charlie Fiddler walked home from the club and decided to stop off at the fish shop in Dockhead for cod, chips and a nice juicy wallie. It would go down well with a couple of slices of the crusty loaf he had got that morning before setting off for work. At least he would have the house to himself. Bel was going out for a drink with Stymie and Sandra was having a night off from her boyfriend and treating Chloe to the pictures.

Charlie took a short cut home from the fish shop, making his way through the deserted River Lane into Quay Street, and just as he was passing Iris Meadows opened her front door. ''Ello, luv, everyfing all right?' he asked pleasantly.

'Yes, fanks,' Iris replied, ready with her excuse. 'There's bin a strange cat sittin' on me windersill this evenin' an' I took it out some milk earlier. I just come out ter see if it's still there but it's gone. I was wonderin' if it was lost or abandoned. I can't stand ter see animals suffer.'

'No neivver can I, luv,' Charlie told her. 'It won't be lost though. Cats can always find their way back 'ome, no matter 'ow far away it is. They got this sixth sense.'

'Yeah, I expect yer right,' Iris said grudgingly. 'Anyway it enjoyed the milk. Lapped it up like it was parched. Funny fing, when I came out before I saw Eileen Taylor comin' out o' Stymie Smith's place. She didn't see me but she looked sort of shifty, as if she didn't want anyone ter know where she'd bin. Course I might be wrong, but I don't fink so. I wouldn't 'ave took no notice if it'd bin someone else, but it's common knowledge in the street that she don't like 'im bein' 'ere. It makes yer fink.'

Charlie felt pleased with the news. He had been on to Bel not to get too attached to the man. He was a lot older than her and in a chancy business. She deserved better in his estimation and if he could influence her to reconsider then he would. 'Yeah, it seems a bit fishy,' he replied. 'I wonder what Sid Taylor would make of it?'

'Not a lot, I imagine,' Iris said, taking the subtle hint.

'Well, I'm sure 'e'll get to 'ear of it one way or anuvver,' Charlie went on. 'Whoever lets 'im know would be doin' 'im a favour, wouldn't yer fink?'

'Yes, I would,' Iris agreed. 'Anyway I'd better get indoors or it'll be me they're talkin' about.'

'That would never do, Mrs Meadows,' he replied with a grin, suddenly realising that the fish and chips were getting cold. 'Bye fer now,' he said, tucking the bundle under his arm and hurrying off.

Chapter Twenty-Two

Councillor Reginald Springer was a long-standing member of the Bermondsey Trader's Guild and he felt pleased that his knowledge of Council matters was beneficial to the members. He also believed that he was held in esteem by them for his discreet manner. The last meeting had been rewarding for him in that respect, he imagined. Revealing the information about the Prime Minister's proposed visit to Bermondsey had given him a feeling of importance and Councillor Springer liked to feel important.

On Saturday morning he felt rather consequential as he made his way to the Tower Bridge Road market, where he called in at Daniel Foden's carpet shop and told him in strictest confidence that the special executive committee had met and been informed by the leader of the Council that the date of the Prime Minister's visit to Bermondsey had been confirmed as the eleventh of September. Springer then made his way to Stan Wickstead's haberdashery and Joe Jackson's pie shop and told them the same. On to Jamaica Road, where the councillor spoke to Jack Hamil the butcher, Fred Alladyce the greengrocer, Joe Bryce the grocery-man and then Pete and Vic Sanders at the fish shop. Lastly Springer called in on George Stephens the watchmender.

'Does everyone else know?' Stephens asked.

'I've just come from Tower Bridge Road,' Springer replied. 'All the traders have been told and I'm due to have a lunchtime drink with Matt Crittenden in the Crown. He's been out on business this morning and I left a message with his secretary. I expect Charlie Hornby'll be there too, so I can kill two birds with one stone. According to the report the police are going to liaise with us on security and safety, so be prepared for a visit, George, being as your shop is the nearest to the hospital.'

'Well, I sincerely hope that everyone heeds the need for discretion,' the watchmender replied.

Springer shrugged his shoulders. 'Regardless of how I impress it on everyone, the news will leak out,' he said sighing. 'The police know and they'll be talking to people. The council maintenance men have been told to prepare the barriers and there'll be the usual try-out road diversions a day or two beforehand. It happens every time someone of importance visits the borough.'

'I expect the police will be drafting in extra men too,' George remarked. 'They'll be in evidence on the streets as well.'

'Precisely.'

A customer came in with a defective alarm clock and Springer took his leave. It had been a tiring morning in all and the lunchtime drink would be very welcome.

That afternoon a member of the Bermondsey Tradesmen's Guild made an important phone call to a pub in north-west London, and by early evening the information he had imparted was relayed to the Pedlar himself when he phoned the pub as usual. Later that evening a small aerial was wound up through an open skylight in Bermondsey and a transmission in encrypted Morse code was flashed to Berlin.

General Mannheim read the decoding with mixed feelings.

The day of the assassination had been confirmed as the eleventh of September, which by the normal planning of things would have tied in excellently with the commencement of the rocket bombardment of London two days later, but down in the concrete bunker of the Chancery the Fuehrer was becoming more and more disorientated as the disastrous news from the Eastern Front trickled through. Impatient for his master plan to come to fruition he had sent out instructions to bring forward the first launching of the rockets to the eighth of September. Furthermore, he had sent a communique to the High Command on the Western Front, ordering them to counter-attack forthwith. The reply, stating that this was impossible until sufficient reserves had been brought up into the battlezone, infuriated the Fuehrer still further and General Mannheim, having been privy to the exchange of messages, was loath to visit the leader again, even though the latest news from London was more encouraging.

Totally oblivious to all the intrigue and military planning, and ignorant of the fact that there was a German agent in their midst, the people of Bermondsey got on with their lives. On Saturday night the Co-op dance at Rotherhithe was packed with hot, excited faces, and the new band made many fans when they played jive music.

Josie and Kathy had been practising the jive and jitterbug with not a little difficulty in their backyard for the past week and were eager to show off their newly acquired skills. Billy Emmerson had decided that it was beyond him and was prepared to sit out the energetic dances while Josie and Kathy 'cut the rug' as they put it.

The evening was well under way when Johnny Francis entered the hall along with two young women who Josie knew fairly well. They were both very good dancers and before long they were demonstrating their jitterbugging for all to see. Francis looked at ease as he partnered Claire, the better dancer of the two and soon the other dancers moved back and formed a circle to watch the pair gyrate.

'Look at that big flash git,' Frankie Morgan growled. 'Don't 'e fancy 'imself.'

'I'd fancy myself if I could dance like that,' Billy said sighing enviously.

Josie was standing in the circle with her partner and when the dance ended she came back to the bar and sat down beside Billy. 'Did you see Johnny Francis dancin'?' she asked.

Billy nodded, not wanting to seem jealous by making some trite remark.

''E wanted a lot o' room, didn't 'e,' Frankie said sarcastically.

'I couldn't 'ave imagined 'im doin' that a few weeks ago,' Billy said, looking closely at Josie.

'I fink it was only a matter o' time,' she replied. 'Once 'e got 'is confidence back.'

Another jive number started up and Frankie Morgan turned his head sideways towards Billy. ''Old tight, 'ere comes Flash 'Arry.'

Johnny Francis walked up and smiled at Josie. 'Fancy this dance?' he asked amiably, and turned to her escort. 'All right, Billy?'

'Yeah, sure.'

Josie was about to refuse but thought that it might create some tension. 'I'm not too good at this,' she told him.

'Come on, it's easy,' he said smiling.

'Why didn't yer tell 'im ter piss off?' Frankie said gruffly as the couple made their way on to the dance floor.

'There's no worry,' Billy said casually. 'Josie knows who she came with.'

The tune was a hot number and Josie felt confident as Johnny

Francis executed the fast movements, to the appreciation of the other dancers. As before they moved back and formed a circle around the two, clapping their hands in time with the music. Johnny smiled and looked totally at ease as he moved expertly, guiding Josie and letting her respond to his rhythm. At the finish the applause was genuine and the exhausted young woman smiled at her partner and let him squeeze her to him before they walked off the floor.

'You were very good,' he said.

'So were you,' she told him breathlessly.

'We must do this again.'

Josie did not reply, noticing the hard stare from Johnny's girlfriend Claire who was standing at the bar area.

The band struck up with a waltz, allowing the dancers to catch their breath, and Billy gave Josie a quick glance. She still looked a little flushed and he decided not to ask her, but she reached out her hot hand and smiled. 'Come on, you can't sit 'ere all night.'

He held her close as they glided slowly across the floor. Her hair smelled sweet and her movements were sensuous and exciting. She was a delight to dance with. The steps seemed easy with her and he promised himself that somehow he would brush up on his dancing skills.

Josie let her head rest on his shoulder. Dancing with Billy was very nice. His strong arms held her firmly but comfortably, and he was very careful to avoid standing on her toes. With Johnny Francis it was another thing entirely. He dominated her on the floor, coaxing and teasing and pressing himself to her passionately as he paraded himself like some exotic animal. He was back to normal, an exhibitionist who had the girls pestering him to partner them. Johnny was exciting to dance with and it brought out something inside her that tended to frighten her. For a few moments while she was dancing with him she had felt complete abandonment. It mattered not that the other dancers were watching. All she could see was the man with her, his carefree smile and his lithe body. It would be easy to vamp him now, she had thought. They had been close, after a fashion, during his first days back home and it would count for something, even now he was back to being the old Johnny Francis, totally unreliable and unable to resist the attention that the local young women paid him. He was like a fantasy though, an apparition from a world of pleasure and licentiousness that did not belong to the real world she was living in. The real world was made up of people like Billy Emmerson. Here, holding her tightly and protectively, was the real man: cool, calm, and with his two feet planted firmly on the ground. Dependable, that was the word.

'I beg yer pardon?' Billy said.

Josie realised that she had said it aloud and she looked up into his wide grey eyes. 'Dependable,' she repeated, and seeing his confusion she said, 'I'll explain later. Just 'old me, Billy.'

Tommy Bailey sat propped up on his bed reading a tattered comic. It was early evening and the house had grown quiet after his sisters left for the dance. His room was neat and tidy and his clothes were put away. Beside him on the chair was a half empty glass of Tizer and a screwed up potato crisp packet. Josie had felt a little sorry for him and had given him the crisps and the drink before she went out, but the lad was still feeling hard done by. He and Dennis had been punished for something which wasn't really bad. Lots of kids went down by the river to see the ships and watch them being unloaded. It was all right if the kids were careful not to do stupid things. He and Dennis had enough sense not to get themselves drowned and they would certainly not take stupid chances. It was always the same. He could be punished but never Kathy, and she deserved to be punished sometimes, the way she carried on. It wasn't fair having to sit in on Saturday nights with nothing to do. It was much too early to go to bed and there was nothing he wanted to listen to on the wireless. He could hear it playing that miserable squeaky music and he guessed that his mother would be nodding off in her chair by this time.

Tommy threw down the comic and slipped his legs over the edge of the bed. It must be getting on for eight o'clock, he thought, though it was still light out. He had heard Josie saying that Billy would be knocking for her at seven and she must have been gone nearly an hour. He stood up and went over to the window and looked down into the backyard. It was very quiet and he could see dark clouds passing above the rooftops. Nobody would know if he slipped out of the house very quietly, he thought suddenly. His mother would be fast asleep in the chair until the girls came home and roused her with a cup of tea. Pity he couldn't get Dennis to slip out as well. If he could get into his backyard he could throw a stone up at the window, but Dennis might not be there, and in any case he couldn't get into his backyard without going over other people's walls. They might think he was a burglar.

Tommy thought for a while and then made a fateful decision to visit his father. If he could slip out of the house undetected and was lucky with the bus he could be over Stepney in no time at all. He could find his dad easily now from the instructions Mr Johnson had given him, and if his mother woke up while he was out and called up the stairs without getting an answer she would think that he had gone to sleep. She might come up though and look in the room, but he could get round that. With the aid of a couple of pillows placed under the bed-clothes and a small cushion to serve as his head under the sheet the job was done, and taking all his saved pocket money from the wooden money-box on the window-ledge Tommy crept down the stairs, taking care to miss the step that creaked. His mother's gentle snoring carried out into the passage, and holding his breath he quietly let himself out of the house.

The Lighterman was filled with its usual mixed clientele that Saturday evening and the three representatives of the League of White Knights did not look out of place as they sat chatting together while they waited for Hennessey to arrive.

'The public bar's not the ideal place to discuss our business but I'm afraid we have no other choice,' Ben Thorburn was saying. 'Unfortunately the room upstairs is in the process of being renovated and the landlord suggested we use the other bar.'

'Four of us sitting huddled together is going to look rather conspicuous in the public bar,' Anderson remarked. 'Most of the locals probably use it.'

Thorburn nodded. 'Unless we can . . .' he began. 'Just a second, I'm going to have another word with our illustrious host.'

Sidney Holman lit a cigarette and exhaled a cloud of smoke towards the ceiling. 'What's he up to?' he asked, staring over at the counter.

Anderson was irritated and he let his feelings be known. 'I wouldn't mind but it was Thorburn's idea in the first place that we use this pub to meet with Hennessey. He said it was off the beaten track and we'd be unlikely to draw any attention here.'

'Well, at least he knows the area,' Holman said in Thorburn's defence. 'We have to remember that any one of us could easily be recognised by a colleague or acquaintance if we met with Hennessey up town, and we did all agree that we should avoid using our homes.'

'Well, let's see what bright idea he's come up with,' Anderson replied as Thorburn came towards them.

'It's all fixed,' he said smiling. 'We can use the *Winslade*.' He waited for the puzzled looks. 'It's one of the tugs moored down the jetty. The old watchman who looks after them is in the public bar and the landlord had a word with him. I slipped him two pounds and he's well pleased. We've just to remember to dowse the light when we leave.'

Anderson glanced over towards the door and spotted Hennessey. 'Here's our man now,' he said. 'I'll get us all another round and then we can get going.'

Tommy stepped down from the number 82 bus at the stop just through the Rotherhithe Tunnel and set off towards Stepney Reach. Mr Johnson had said it was only ten minutes' walk, he remembered. With a bit of luck he would spot his dad in the Lighterman pub and he would tell him that everyone was missing him very much and he should come home straight away. He would also tell him it wasn't right for him to be living a lonely life in Stepney and spending all his time sitting in pubs and getting drunk because he was miserable. Dennis's dad didn't get drunk all the time and nor did the other kids' dads. That would help make his mind up, Tommy thought with a smile.

The lane leading down to the jetty was flanked by grimy warehouses on either side and with the dusk now settling in the place looked ghostly. Tommy listened to his footsteps echoing back at him and he was relieved to see the patch of light from the pub spreading out over the damp cobblestones. He could see the boats now, gently rocking in their moorings. One had a kerosene lamp burning in the small forward cabin and Tommy guessed that it would probably be the one which his dad slept on some nights.

As he reached the Lighterman the lad chewed on his lip in agitation. The windows were all of figured, sanded glass and it was impossible to see inside. He walked to the door marked 'public bar' and stood thinking hard. He dared not just walk in. Better to wait until someone came out, he decided.

A few minutes later he spotted a large woman coming towards the pub wearing a fur coat and with a huge mop of ginger hair which had been set in large waves. She carried a large handbag and seemed to be having trouble walking in her very high-heeled shoes. ''Ello, luv, waitin' fer yer dad, are yer?' she asked.

Tommy looked at her and saw the heavily made-up face and the long eyelashes fluttering at him. 'I've come ter find'im,' he told her.

'An' yer fink 'e might be in 'ere, do yer?' she went on.

'Yeah, 'e could be,' Tommy answered.

'Poor little sod,' the woman said, showing a row of very large pearly white teeth as she smiled at him. 'What's yer farv-ver's name, son?'

'Frank Bailey.'

'I don't believe it,' she whistled, chuckling as she shook her head. 'So you're Frank Bailey's boy? Come ter fink of it, yer do resemble 'im round the eyes. Frank's dark though, so I s'pose you favour yer muvver.'

'Are you me dad's friend?' Tommy asked.

'I wish I was, luvvey,' the woman replied.

'Are yer goin' in the pub?'

'I most certainly am.'

'Can yer see if me dad's in there, an' if 'e is could yer tell 'im Tommy's outside?'

The woman chuckled again. 'I can tell yer now, luv, yer dad ain't in there. 'E was in earlier, mind, but 'e was a bit tiddled an' 'e left wiv anuvver slosher. Gone ter do the rounds I expect.'

'Are yer sure?' Tommy queried.

'Sure? Course I'm sure. I was sittin' at the bar next to 'em,' the large woman replied. 'About 'alf seven it was. I thought ter meself, it's a bit early ter be tanked up. They must 'ave bin on the turps all day, if you ask me. Why don't yer go 'ome before it gets late. This ain't the sort o' place fer young sprats ter be 'angin' around. There's some very strange people knockin' about down 'ere.'

Tommy smiled at her. 'Yeah, I fink I will,' he said, watching as she pushed open the public bar door and almost fell into the pub.

There was one last chance, he thought. The tug. If his dad was drunk he would probably sleep there tonight. Best to go aboard and wait, no matter how long it took, and if they found out at home that he was missing then it was too bad. This was more important, and they would all thank him for it one day.

Chapter Twenty-Three

Nell Bailey jerked awake suddenly. She had been walking with Frank along the towpath at Richmond and the sun was hot. They were young and carefree, laughing together and holding hands, and they stopped at a little riverside pub. She waited in the shaded garden while he went for the drinks, and then the man with the bloated face sat down facing her. He smiled at her and she tried to ignore him, but his smile turned to a wide leering grin and then he leaned towards her. His eyes were red and his breath malodorous, and try as she would her legs would not support her body as she endeavoured to get away from him. She tried to call out for Frank but nothing would come out and she sat terrified as the man's face grew fatter and rounder. She turned to face the door of the pub, willing Frank to come out and saw the man staring at her from the doorway. Somehow she found her feet and ran off along the towpath. She could hear him coming after her and he was gaining on her but she knew she had to get away from him. She felt his hand on the back of her coat and abruptly woke up.

What did it all mean, Nell wondered as she wiped the sweat from her forehead? Polly Seagram had told her once that bad dreams came from harbouring bad thoughts and suppressing worries. Perhaps she was right. There were many times when Nell did not feel happy with herself. Had she been too unfeeling in the way she dealt with Frank's drinking problem? She knew that Josie felt so. The sacred oath they had taken at the altar, 'For better for worse, in sickness and in health,' had been empty words as far as she was concerned. Now Frank was gone from the house she worried over him, blamed herself, and desperately tried to justify what she had done, but she was never able to talk to anyone about it, not even Polly.

Nell got up and turned the wireless off. It was very quiet in the house and she thought about Tommy. Was she being hard on him because he was so like his father in many ways? No, the punishment was justified, she told herself. The river was a dangerous place for youngsters to play and the boy had to learn to do as he was told. She felt the stiffness in her back as she went to the bottom of the stairs and called out his name. There was no answer and she smiled to herself as she slowly made her way up to his bedroom. He would be sulking and feigning sleep, no doubt. Nell smiled as she pulled the sheet back very gently and her face suddenly dropped as she found herself staring down at the screwed up cushion. 'Just wait till I get my 'ands on that boy,' she said aloud, clenching her fists.

The young absconder walked down to the jetty and stood in the closing darkness looking at the boats moored there. He could see two tugs locked together with hawsers and another one alongside with a light burning in the cabin, all gently moving on the incoming tide. Further along there was another small craft with a cabin at the front but like the first two boats it was in darkness. The one with the light on must be the one his father used to sleep on, he figured. Maybe he was inside now.

Tommy looked around and saw that he was quite alone, and only the muffled sounds coming from the nearby pub disturbed the soft insistent swish of the current against the tugs. He hurried along the slippery jetty and stepped on to the lighted boat. 'Dad, are you there?' he called out.

Only the slap of the tide answered him and he looked into the cabin. The kerosene lamp was hanging from a hook above a small table and he could see the remains of fish and chips on some newspaper and an empty beer bottle. There was no sign of bunks, however, and Tommy knew that he had come aboard the wrong tug. He stepped out of the cabin doorway and suddenly saw the men coming down the cobbled lane towards him. There were four of them and they were talking together. He realised that he could not get off the boat without being noticed and he ducked down quickly behind the cabin. His heart started to bang in his chest as he watched them make directly for the tug he was on and he made himself even smaller by crouching down inside a coil of heavy rope. The men clambered aboard and went into the cabin and the young lad held himself absolutely still, hardly daring to breathe.

Victor Anderson sat down on the bench beneath the cabin window and screwed up the newspaper with distaste before sliding along to make room for Sidney Holman. Hennessey and Thorburn made themselves comfortable on the other bench and Holman took out a cigarette case. 'I suppose it's all right to smoke here,' he said, looking round.

Anderson shrugged his shoulders. 'It seems like the watchman does,' he replied, holding up a round tin lid which was full of ash and used matches.

Hennessey looked around at the others, a satisfied smile appearing on his face. 'I can tell you gentlemen that everything is in place. The money has been lodged in the account which our operator specified, and here is the information you'll require.' He took a small black leather wallet from the inside of his coat pocket and laid it down on the table. 'A half million in gold, ready and awaiting your instructions on the day after the deed is done.'

Anderson picked up the wallet and opened it, glancing quickly at the contents, then he put it in his coat pocket. 'I think a word of thanks is due to you for your efficiency,' he said, smiling at Hennessey.

'Yes, a very good job of work,' Thorburn added.

The agent smiled back and then his face took on a serious look. 'There is one slight change of plan,' he said. 'It seems that Adolf Hitler is getting very concerned about the way the war is moving and he's decided to bring forward the new weapon launch to the eighth of September.'

Anderson glanced quickly at his two colleagues. 'I don't see that as posing too much of a problem,' he replied. 'People will still be in shock and trying to come to terms with the new weapon sent against them when the assassination takes place.'

Holman clasped his hands on the table. 'What about the proposed military counter-attack? Has that been brought forward too?' he asked.

Hennessey shook his head. 'I've been informed that the generals are saying it's impossible before the end of the year, which has infuriated Hitler. He's running the whole business now, apparently.'

'I take it you know from our mutual contact who we've selected to carry out the job?' Anderson queried.

Hennessey nodded. 'I understand he's the best.'

'Undoubtedly,' Thorburn remarked.

Hennessey glanced slowly from one to another. 'It would seem that my job has been completed,' he said quietly. 'Everything's taken care of. The money is ready and the integrity of the League remains intact. Whether or not Adolf has correctly gauged the British response to his plan remains to be seen, but I believe that either way your aims and objectives are attainable, and let's hope sooner rather than later. For me, the future is an unknown quantity, but I hope to live a long, prosperous life, and to that end I have taken the necessary precautions. In saying this I am not implying any offence to you gentlemen. In our sphere of operations we all have to cover our backs and I'm sure that you have done so also. I'm pretty sure that if I exposed the League of White Knights I would be hunted down and dealt with accordingly. Equally, if you gentlemen decided that I should be silenced because of my knowledge of you and your organisation then you are entitled to know that there would be information forwarded to the appropriate authorities. All any of us can do is hope and pray that we all stay healthy.'

Anderson smiled. 'I think we should all look forward to a very comfortable dotage. Now if we're finished here I think we have time to drink a toast to that back at the Lighterman.'

Tommy Bailey was lying flat against the decking and had heard much of the conversation. He had wanted to slip off the tug as soon as the men went into the cabin but he knew that he would have to pass the open door and most likely be spotted. Better to wait until they left, he decided. He turned onto his side, easing his body against the coil of rope, when the penknife Dennis had given him fell out of his trouser pocket and clattered on to the planking. The lad grabbed it up quickly, painfully holding his breath as the men spilled from the cabin.

'Who's there?' a voice called out.

Suddenly Tommy felt a large hand on the back of his coat and he was dragged to his feet.

'Who are you? What are you doing here?'

'I . . . I was tired an' I . . . I, er, came on the boat ter go ter sleep,' Tommy said unconvincingly.

Anderson was holding him by the collar and he shook him roughly. 'What's your name?' he snarled.

Tommy was ready with the answer this time. 'Bob Franklin,'

he replied quickly, using the name of one of the heroes in the comic he had been reading earlier that evening.

'Where d'you live?'

'Stepney Green.'

'And why aren't you home and in bed?' Anderson pressed.

'I 'ad a row wiv me dad an' ran off,' Tommy replied.

'Have you been listening to what we were talking about?' Thorburn growled at him.

'No honest,' Tommy told him fearfully.

'How old are you, boy?' Holman asked him.

'Nearly fourteen.'

The three League men looked at each other, not knowing quite what to do, but the fourth man had no doubts. 'We can't take any chances at this stage,' Hennessey said urgently to Anderson. 'Knock him out and put him over the side.'

Tommy was fighting to control his breathing amid the rapid thudding of his heart. The men were going to kill him, that was certain. He gingerly slipped his hand into his trouser pocket and felt the folded knife. Gripping it tightly he carefully took it out while his captor was talking to Hennessey and quickly flicked open the sharp blade with his thumbnail. The men were between him and the gangplank and the lad realised that there was only one thing to do. The river was dangerous but at least he would have some chance, however slight. Staying on the tug gave him no chance at all. With a quick backward thrust he stabbed at Anderson's hand and jerked himself free as the man cursed loudly. Thorburn made a grab for him but Tommy was too quick as he jumped up and outwards over the prow of the tug, knowing the danger of being sucked under the keel. He held his breath as he went under and felt the tide dragging him along, like an ant being sucked down the drainhole. The weight of his coat and shoes was pulling him under and he kicked out, trying to swim with the current. He had been very careful not to swallow any of the water but he knew with terror stabbing into him that he was losing his battle to stay afloat. The tide was flowing too fast but suddenly his head cracked against a stanchion and he grabbed out at a cross-support timber. The cold ate into him now that he had stopped struggling and he shivered violently. Climbing the stanchion was going to be the hardest thing he had ever done in his life, but there was no other choice.

Anderson held out his hand while Holman tied a handkerchief tightly over the deep wound on his forearm. 'The little gutter-snipe,' he raged.

Sidney Holman felt sick inside as he looked over the prow of the tug. 'He must have drowned,' he said. 'He couldn't survive in this current, he'd have been dragged under.'

'We'd all better hope he has,' Hennessey remarked coldly. 'He must have heard the whole conversation.'

Holman looked across at him. 'He was just a young lad,' he said angrily.

'Lad or not, everything could have blown up in our faces had he talked to someone,' Hennessey growled.

Anderson made a fist against the shooting pain in his cut arm. 'Come on, it's no good speculating,' he told them. 'Let's get back to the pub. If the boy has drowned, which seems more than likely, we'll be reading about it in the papers.'

They made their way up the sloping cobbled lane to the Lighterman, while less than a few hundred yards downriver Tommy Bailey was pulling himself painfully up the high shoring that led to safety.

Chapter Twenty-Four

Kathy Bailey was dallying with a young man after the dance had finished and Josie smiled knowingly at Billy. 'She'll be raving over 'im when she gets in ternight,' she remarked, slipping her arm through his as they set off home.

It was nearing midnight when they turned into Quay Street, and Josie's hand tightened on Billy's arm as she spotted her mother standing at the front door. 'Somefing's wrong,' she said quickly.

'It's Tommy,' Nell told them. ''E's run off.'

'When?' Josie asked.

'I dunno, it must 'ave bin when I was noddin' off in the chair,' Nell replied. 'I didn't 'ear the little bleeder go. Just wait till 'e gets 'ome. I'll keep 'im in fer a month. I swear I will.'

'Where could 'e 'ave gone at this time o' night?' Josie said pinching her lips.

'I just 'ope 'e ain't gone over the water ter try an' find 'is farvver,' Nell said sighing.

'I don't fink so,' Josie told her. 'Tommy doesn't know 'is way around over there.'

Billy had been listening and he touched Josie's arm. 'Maybe we should search the streets,' he suggested. ''E could be just walkin' around.'

Josie nodded. 'It's where ter start,' she fretted.

Billy looked at Nell's troubled face and smiled encouragingly. 'Don't worry, Mrs Bailey, we'll find 'im. We'll use the bike, it's quicker that way.'

'There's no need,' Josie said quickly.

Billy and Nell followed her eyes and saw the hunched figure of Tommy limping into the turning.

'What the bloody . . .' Nell gasped. 'Where've yer bin? Where's yer bloody shoes? Just look at yer, yer soakin' wet. Yer've bin in the river ain't yer?' Tommy was too exhausted to say anything and he just nodded compliantly. 'Get in there, before yer catch yer death o' cold.'

''E's out on 'is feet,' Josie remarked to her mother as they ushered the sorry-looking young lad into the house.

At that moment Nell had forgotten about her aching back and generally feeling sorry for herself. There was a family crisis and she was in charge. 'Josie, run upstairs an' get 'is pyjamas, an' bring a big towel down out o' the landin' cupboard. Billy, the kettle is 'ot, can you pour it inter the large enamel bowl in the sink an' put the kettle on again? Tommy, you get in the parlour and get yer wet clothes off. Go on, no one's gonna be lookin' at yer. 'Ere, take this towel an' wrap it round yerself.'

Ten minutes later Tommy was soaking his blistered feet in front of the roaring fire and sipping a mug of steaming cocoa. Nell had looked at the bump and small cut on his head and now sat facing him while Josie sat alongside Billy on the small settee under the window.

'I wanted ter see Dad,' the lad told his mother excitedly, 'an' I knew 'e sometimes slept on a boat wiv 'is mate at Stepney Reach, so I went over there. I looked in the pub by the river but 'e wasn't there so I tried the boat.'

''Ang on a minute,' Nell interrupted. 'What sort o' boat?'

'What difference does it make,' Josie said impatiently. 'Go on, Tommy.'

'It was one o' those tugs,' the lad replied. 'There was a light in the cabin an' I called out fer Dad but there was no answer. Then I was just about ter leave when I saw these four men comin' terwards me. I got scared in case they thought I was nickin' somefing, so I 'id down by this bundle 'o rope. The men came on the tug an' went inter the cabin. They're crooks, Mum.'

'What d'yer mean, they're crooks?'

'I should fink they're worse than crooks,' Tommy went on excitedly. 'They were talkin' about money at first. A lot o' gold, then they mentioned 'itler. They was talkin' about 'im. I couldn't understand some o' the fings but I did 'ear one of 'em say somefing about assassinatin' somebody. Then they said somefing else that I remembered. One o' the men said that 'itler was gonna bring the date o' the new weapon forward ter the eighth o' September. I fink it was the eighth. Anuvver fing I remember was this name they mentioned. White Knights it was.'

Josie looked at Billy and glanced at her mother, then her eyes centred on the young lad. He looked flushed and wide-eyed. 'Yer makin' all this up, ain't yer, Tommy?' she said quietly.

'Course 'e is,' Nell told her. ''E's bin readin' too many comics.'

'It's the trufe, Mum. I swear on me life it's the trufe. Every word,' Tommy said earnestly.

'Go on then, 'ow did yer fall in the water?'

'I never fell in the water, I jumped in.'

'Go on, I'm listenin'.'

When he had finished speaking Nell had a horrible feeling in the pit of her stomach. She knew that Tommy had a good imagination, like most lads of his age, but there was something in what he said, something too extreme and yet consistent for even him to have made up and she felt uneasy and worried. 'Right then, this'll keep till termorrer. Now you get ter bed, Tommy. Josie, would yer make us all a nice pot o' tea, I fink we need it.'

While Josie was still in the scullery Kathy came in looking all wild-eyed and flushed. 'I met this smashin' feller ternight,' she started off.

'Tommy ran off ternight,' Nell interrupted. 'It's all right – 'e's 'ome now an' tucked up in bed.'

By the time Nell had told her the full story Josie had made the tea, and along with Billy Emmerson they sat discussing what should be done.

'I reckon the lad was tellin' the trufe,' Billy remarked. 'In fact I'm certain.'

'So am I,' Josie added.

Nell nodded. 'It's too far-fetched even for our Tommy to'ave made it all up.'

'Assumin' it's true I fink we should go an' see the police,' Josie declared.

'The police?' Nell said frowning.

'We've got to,' Josie went on. 'From what Tommy's told us those men could be spies.'

Billy nodded his head emphatically. 'It certainly sounds that way.'

Kathy giggled. 'Wait till I tell Douglas,' she said excitedly.

Nell rounded on her. 'You'll tell no one, an' I mean no one, about what's 'appened,' she said sharply, and seeing Kathy's disappointed look, 'If they were spies, or even villains, they know that our Tommy's on to 'em. I've told yer what the boy said. They was gonna knock 'im cold an' dump 'im in the river. We ain't too far from where it'appened, an' if word gets around they could get to 'ear of it too an' they'll come lookin' for 'im.'

Her reply was enough to convince Kathy and her face flushed up nervously. 'Mum, I'm scared,' she wailed.

'So are we all, an' that's why I'm gonna go ter the police first fing termorrer,' Nell resolved firmly. 'Now remember, all of yer. Not a word to a soul. Understood?'

They all nodded, and Josie stood up. 'I'd better get us some more tea,' she said.

Blissfully unaware of the drama moving ever closer to their little streets, the locals spent their Saturday evening uneventfully. Stymie Smith took Bel Fiddler to a pub in Deptford to meet with a few of his cronies and their wives and girlfriends, while Wilco Johnson went to the Star and Garter and got systematically drunk. Iris Meadows had declined the offer of a social evening with her daughter and son-in-law Desmond and listened instead to Saturday Night Theatre on the home service of the BBC. The creepy tale did not disturb the widow unduly. Being on her own and a little frightened was preferable in her estimation to spending the evening listening to Desmond's inane chatter.

Charlie Fiddler brought his ladyfriend Thelma back in the hope of coaxing her into his bed with tales of hardships and loneliness, but just when he thought he was making progress Sandra and Chloe came home with two young men they wanted to show off. They had brought some beer back with them and after supper, while Chloe and Sandra got into conversation with Thelma, the two beaux divulged to Charlie that they were partial to a game of cards for small stakes.

When Thelma saw Charlie spreading a blanket on the table and saw the cards appear her eyes lit up. 'Are yer gonna play poker?' she asked.

'I dunno. Are we?'

'Suits me,' one of the young men said smiling.

'Yeah, me too,' the other man said.

'In that case I'll make it a foursome, unless yer've got any objections.'

The men looked at one another in surprise and Charlie shrugged his shoulders. 'What was good enough fer Calamity Jane's good enough fer you, I s'pose,' he remarked grinning.

The game ended after one o'clock in the morning, and as Thelma pulled the pile of money towards her she had a sympathetic smile for the three she had just cleaned out. 'It 'appens that way sometimes,' she told them. 'It was just my lucky night ternight.'

'Well, it certainly wasn't mine,' Charlie muttered drily, glaring at his daughters.

Dot Simms, Gladys Metcalf and Rose Emmerson sat with Ellie Woodley, the Baileys' next-door neighbour, in the Star and Garter while their respective husbands stood at the bar chatting. Polly Seagram was drinking with Bernie in the saloon bar that evening, and their conversation had finally climbed above the realms of rationing, children, lazy husbands and flying bombs.

'I don't neglect yer,' Bernie was saying.

'Oh yes, yer do,' Polly pouted.

''Ow do I? Tell me.'

'There's times when I fancy yer an' I try ter let yer know, but yer blank me.'

'Oh no I don't.'

'Oh yes yer do.'

'Look, it might seem a bit that way but yer gotta try an' pick better times. I can't drop everyfing just at a flick o' yer fingers.'

'I don't want yer ter drop everyfing, only yer trousers,' Polly told him with a brief smile.

'Take the ovver night,' Bernie went on. 'There was I, up ter me eyes in paint an' turps, an' you said yer fancied goin' ter bed wiv me. Bloody 'ell, woman, what was I s'posed ter do, leave what I was doin' just like that? By the time I'd 'ave got cleaned up you'd 'a' bin fast asleep.'

'Oh no I wouldn't.'

'Oh yes yer would.'

Polly sighed. 'All I'm sayin' is, we should do it a bit more. After all, we ain't that old.'

'Age don't come into it,' Bernie said quickly.

'It does wiv you,' she retorted. 'Fifty-two an' it takes yer all night ter get roused.'

''Ere 'old up, gel. I ain't that bad.'

'Wanna bet?'

Bernie puffed loudly. 'Look, if you was a bit more selective when yer asked me I'd most likely be able to oblige.'

'Selective? What does that mean?' Polly frowned. 'When yer sittin' on yer arse wiv the paper, or when yer twiddlin' yer thumbs? That's the time when I'm workin'. Doin' the winders or changin' the curtains, makin' pots o' tea an' generally runnin' round after a lazy git.'

'That's what I mean about you,' Bernie growled. 'One minute yer tellin' me I'm too busy ter notice yer, then yer say I'm one lazy bastard.'

'All right I take back you bein' lazy,' Polly replied with a smile. 'Sometimes though I get a bit 'ot watchin' you work. I can't explain it, it's just one o' those fings.'

Bernie slipped his arm around Polly's ample waist. 'We need a refill,' he said. ''Ow about a green goddess?'

'Bernie, what you tryin' ter do ter me,' Polly said quickly. 'Yer remember last time.'

'Do I.'

'All right then, just as long as yer up to it,' she told him with a sly smile.

★

At the end house in Quay Street Annie and Jack Francis were talking together as the late-night music from the wireless drifted through the parlour.

'Yes, I really am pleased that our John's found 'is feet again,' Annie was saying, 'but I would 'ave thought 'e'd 'ave stuck wiv Josie Bailey. After all it was mostly 'er doin' that 'e's back the way 'e was. None o' the ovver gels gave a toss.'

'Don't get me wrong, I like the gel just as much as you do, but we can't run the boy's life for 'im,' Jack replied. 'Johnny'll settle down soon, mark my words.'

'Yeah, but wiv who?' Annie asked him. 'I don't like the sort o' gels 'e brings 'ome 'ere. Too brassy.'

'Well, I shouldn't go 'arpin' on Josie Bailey fer a future wife,' Jack told her. 'I've noticed she's walkin' out wiv the Emmerson boy.'

'Yeah, so 'ave I,' Annie sighed. 'Mind you, I fink she'd soon drop 'im if our Johnny showed 'er some real interest.'

'I dunno so much,' Jack replied. 'The gel's got 'er pride an' she ain't gonna come runnin' just 'cos John whistles at 'er.'

They heard sounds outside and Annie got up to put the kettle on. 'I expect Johnny'll fancy a cuppa,' she said.

Jack Francis puffed loudly. He could hear his son's voice above the rest and guessed how the general flow of conversation was going. It was a shame. He was convinced that he loved his boy as much as any father could, but it hurt him that his own flesh and blood could be so self-centred. It wouldn't have mattered so much if no one got hurt along the way, but they had, and Johnny's attitude nagged away at him.

Outside the wind was rising and dark clouds were rolling in to cover the stars. A distant rumble of thunder sounded and Iris Meadows looked up as she put out the solitary milk bottle. It had been a stormy night with lightning flashing in *The Caller* and as she bolted up she shivered at the thought of someone coming knocking on her front door in the middle of the night.

And so another Saturday night ended unremarkably for most folk, the lull before the storm of much bigger events soon to descend on the little riverside street in Bermondsey.

Chapter Twenty-Five

Tommy Bailey was subdued when he came down to breakfast on Sunday morning but Nell was pleased to see that he seemed none the worse physically for his terrifying experience, apart from the bump on his head. 'We're goin' ter the police this mornin' ter tell 'em everyfing,' she said as she served up a large portion of porridge.

Tommy nodded dutifully, which satisfied her. If he had made the whole story up he would not be inclined to repeat it at a police station. His face suddenly became serious however and he looked up at his mother. 'Won't I get inter trouble fer stabbin' that man?' he asked.

'Of course not,' Nell reassured him. 'You was actin' in self-defence. If you 'adn't 'a' done, they would 'ave killed yer, from what yer told me.'

'I'm not tellin' lies, Mum. It's all true, every word of it.'

'That's all the more reason ter let the police know exactly what you over'eard,' she told him.

'I'll come wiv yer, Mum,' Josie offered.

'No, it won't do fer too many ter go. Just let me do it my way.'

'What about yer back?'

'Sod me back, this is more important than a niggly backache,' Nell insisted.

It was just after nine when Nell led the way into Dockhead police station and immediately bumped into PC Woodhouse, the street bobby.

''Ello, Mrs Bailey,' he said pleasantly. 'Don't tell me Tommy's in trouble.'

'Not really, Joe,' she answered. 'I know it's Sunday but I need ter talk ter someone in charge.'

The constable frowned. 'You look worried. Anyfing I can do?'

'I'll tell yer all about it later, if yer've got time ter pop in fer a cuppa,' Nell said quickly. 'In the meantime I gotta see the boss.'

'You're lucky, 'e's in this mornin' fer a few hours,' the policeman told her. 'Ask fer Chief Inspector Malkin, yer'll find 'e's yer man.'

'Fanks a lot,' Nell replied as he gave her a reassuring smile.

James Malkin had been at Dockhead for a number of years and felt that he knew the area as well as any other copper. He had put a few villains away and been able to save a few of the young tearaways from a life behind bars. He took his job very seriously and prided himself on the fact that no one could pull the wool over his eyes.

As soon as he showed the Baileys into his office on that bright Sunday morning Malkin sent for his assistant, Detective Sergeant Ray Black. 'We're not trying to gang up on you, Mrs Bailey,' he said quietly. 'It's just that it saves me having to relay what you say to my assistant. In other words it cuts time and allows us to get on with the job we're paid for. Now, you tell me what's troubling you and the sergeant will make notes.'

Nell told him how Tommy had been confined to the house over playing near the river and how he had run off, only to come home later that night soaked to the skin, then she turned to her son. 'You'd better go on,' she said.

The young lad started nervously at first, but he soon gained confidence and tried to speak calmly and clearly, and when he was finished the inspector leaned back in his chair. 'Have you got all that, Ray?' he asked. The sergeant nodded and Malkin looked at Tommy. 'Tell me, young man, what do you think was going on last night?'

Tommy looked briefly at his mother. 'I fink they were spies an' they was plannin' a murder.'

'Um, it seems that way,' the policeman said. 'Look I've got to make a phone call. I'll only be a few minutes. Would you like a cuppa? I can get one sent in.'

Nell nodded. 'That'll be very nice.'

As he left the office Malkin nodded his head for the sergeant to follow him. 'It certainly sounds like a story from the *Wizard*,' he said smiling. 'The trouble is, I believe the lad. How do you feel about it?'

Sergeant Black looked uncertain. 'A young lad jumping in a tidal river, in the dark, alongside tugs, and surviving to tell the tale is hard to swallow,' he agreed. 'As for the story, though, I have to say that it sounds too fantastical to be made up, if you know what I mean?'

'I know,' Malkin told him. 'You and I have listened to some weird stories in our time but this one is different. It could have been concocted by an adult, but not a young boy.'

Ray Black nodded. 'How d'you intend to play it, sir?'

The inspector tapped his pursed lips. 'I'm not sure, I need a little time to think. Assuming it's true I'll be duty-bound to send the whole shebang off to Scotland Yard. They'll be in touch with the secret service and then we'll get called in to liaise with them. But if this is a figment of that lad's imagination we're going to look pretty silly.'

Nell had just put her cup down on the desk and taken Tommy's empty one from him when the two policemen came back into the room.

'There's just one question I want to ask you, Tommy,' the inspector said as he took his place behind his desk. 'When you jumped in the river what were your immediate thoughts? Can you describe them?'

Tommy looked directly at the policeman, remembering what his father had told him more than once. 'If you want to be believed look the person straight in the eye.' 'I knew that it was the only way ter get away from the men,' he said quietly. 'I knew that the river was very dangerous but I 'ad ter do it. I just gritted me teef an' jumped as far away from the tug as I could. I knew that I could be sucked under.'

'And what were your thoughts as you walked all the way home in stockinged feet and dripping wet?'

'I felt 'appy.'

'Happy?'

'Yeah, I was glad I'd managed ter get out of the water alive.'

'And you weren't worried what your mother might say, or do?' Malkin pressed.

'No, I knew that when I told 'er exactly what 'ad 'appened she'd understand.'

'Do you still have the knife you used on that man?'

'No, I must 'a' lost it when I was in the water, or when I was climbin' out up the wooden jetty.'

'It must have been hard for a young lad soaked to the skin and freezing cold to manage it.'

'I just thought o' that little boy who got drowned last week an' it 'elped me ter do it.'

The inspector turned to Nell. 'Tell me, Mrs Bailey, was Tommy worried when you told him you were coming to see us?'

'No. 'E was only worried about what you might say when you knew about 'im stabbin' someone,' she replied.

Inspector Malkin smiled at her. 'Right, I think that'll do for the time being, Mrs Bailey,' he said. 'The sergeant's got your address. I'll be coming to see you in the very near future. It'll be better than you having to drag down to the station. Before you go though I want you to promise me that you won't breathe a word of this to a soul, not even your best friend. You know yourself how news spreads. Any leakage of this affair will certainly put all of your lives in danger. It's obvious from what happened to Tommy that we're dealing with very desperate people who'll stop at nothing to achieve their aims.'

As soon as Nell and Tommy had left, Malkin turned to the sergeant. 'I'm convinced that the lad's telling the truth,' he remarked. 'Before I process it though I want to speak with the Quay Street beat bobby.'

'That's PC Woodhouse, sir.'

'Yes, I know. Is he due back before this evening?'

'At lunchtime.'

'Soon as he comes in send him straight in to me, will you, Ray?'

'Consider it done.'

Monday morning was another balmy summer day but the Quay Street totter was in no mood to appreciate the weather as he waited to be shown into the estate office. The few magazines spread about the waiting room were of little interest to him and the wall clock ticked away the seconds heavily. Stymie felt that he was just wasting his time. It could have been one of his profitable days. The sun was shining and the light breeze would have made it pleasant to be out and about on the cart. It was the sort of day when the women of the house tended to have a sort-out, and many an old wringer, piece of discarded furniture or box of chipped china had come his way on such days in the past.

'Mr Smith?'

Stymie stood. 'That's me,' he told the youthful-looking clerk.

'If you'll just follow me.'

The totter trailed down a long corridor and was shown into a small office at the end. 'Ah, Mr Smith. Do sit down,' the elderly official bade him. 'I think I've got some good news for you.'

Stymie had been expecting to present his petition to the man and he withdrew his empty hand from his coat pocket. 'You 'ave?'

'Yes. Our Mr Phelps has been dealing with your case and you may remember that he wrote a letter on your behalf to the owner of the premises that you currently occupy. Well, I can tell you that the reply has been very favourable. Providing you agree to vacate the house and yard in one year's time you can stay on as tenant at the current rent. In other words you have a year's reprieve. What do you say to that?'

'I'm over the bloody moon,' Stymie replied with passion.

'Um, yes, well,' the official faltered, striving to maintain his composure. 'I would just like to say that your attitude has helped. Our Mr Phelps was impressed and he gave you a glowing report in the letter he sent off. You see, some of our tenants, faced with the same predicament, would have gone around getting petitions up and contacting the press which would obviously put us in a bad light. Your mature forbearance was definitely a determining factor in your case. So if you'll just sign this form. It's the agreement. It allows you to stay in Quay Street until the end of September 1945.'

Stymie thanked the official and walked out of the estate office in a state of panic. Earlier that morning Bel Fiddler had been to see him and said that she was going to the *South London Press* and the *Kentish Mercury* with a story about a poor humble totter who was being evicted from his house and yard by some obscure owner who did not have the decency to make himself known, relying instead on the estate office to do his dirty work. 'It'll be a cracker,' she had told him. 'Just fink of it. They'll be queuin' up to offer you a place.'

Stymie had thought that there was more chance of pigs flying or his nag breaking into a trot but he had acquiesced. Arguing with Bel was like encouraging the Pope to play dice. Now he would have to find her quickly and hope she hadn't been successful in presenting the story.

Commander Jock Barratt of MI5 was feeling a little under the weather after his weekend at the Farringtons'. They were good shire folk and Bessie made the most succulent dinners, but Aubrey was something again. His capacity for the hard stuff was amazing, and trying to keep up with him was torture.

'Yes, that's me,' Jock said as he answered the call. Ah, Shelby. Nice to hear from you, old man. You have? Then let's meet this evening for a bevvy or two in the Carlton Grill? A hair of the dog and all that. It won't keep? Good Lord! I've not heard you so excited since Rudolf Hess landed in Scotland. Yes, I'll be there in no time at all.'

Commander Barratt picked up his astrakhan coat, despite the warm weather, and grabbed his Homburg and leather gloves. 'Take my calls, Delia. I don't know when I'll be back,' he told her as he hurried out of the room.

His official car was waiting and the tall distinguished-looking commander puffed as he almost fell into his seat. 'Scotland Yard. Fast as you can, William,' he ordered.

The large office high above the River Thames was out of bounds to all visitors except the chief of MI5 that Monday morning and the phone calls had been re-routed by the time he arrived.

'This came yesterday afternoon,' Shelby told him. 'My deputy, Commander Lansdowne, deemed this top priority and the result was a minor panic here, with everyone trying to locate me. Actually I was on the Broads with my eldest boy and the local police couldn't find me. Here, read it.'

'Good Lord!' Barratt exclaimed as he scanned the report.

'What do you make of it?' Shelby asked.

'There's no doubt. It's pukka. One hundred per cent pukka.'

'You have good reason to think so?'

'The best,' Barratt said quickly. 'The lad mentioned the White Knights. They're real, a secret Fascist organisation that play very close to their chest. They were formed about the time we locked up Mosley and include some of the top men in banking, insurance and City business in their ranks. They were all dedicated followers of Mosley in the Ridley Road days, but none of them was high enough up the ladder to be interned. Maybe we should have locked them all up but the estimation was that there were well over twenty thousand followers. Where could we have put them all?'

'Some remote isle in Scotland would have been as good a place as any,' Shelby remarked.

'Anyway, I know I can tell you in confidence that the League of White Knights are towards the top of our list of surveillance,' Barratt continued. 'I think they've just taken first place. It's very tricky though. They have allies everywhere. Get in at the top and the rest will fall like a house of cards.'

'Do you have any names?'

'Yes, but only from unreliable sources. Any attempt on our part to get hard evidence has ended in failure up until now. On the surface they're as pure as the driven snow.'

Shelby leaned back in his high-backed chair and brought his fingertips together. 'How are we going to run this one?' he asked.

'Firstly, I want you to keep the Stepney police out of this,' Barratt told him. 'This is going to be a very tight operation, but of course I'll keep you in the picture. Now as far as the Bermondsey police are concerned, I would be grateful if you could authorise their full co-operation with our people. Only the inspector and his subordinate named in this report are to be put in the picture, and if you agree I'll do that personally. Secondly, I'd appreciate your assurance that you will not act on this matter independently, at any stage, for obvious reasons.'

'Well, I'm fully behind you, old man,' Shelby replied.

'I'll be eternally grateful, Nigel.'

'Think nothing of it. That's what we're here for,' Shelby said magnanimously. 'We're talking about the nation's security here.'

'You're perfectly right,' Barratt replied. 'Remember the cock-up when we took Mosley in? There were far too many fingers in the pie.'

Shelby nodded. 'I see that the sun's coming up over the mast-head. Would you care for a little refreshment, Jock?' he asked. 'I take it you still have a distinct preference for my ten-year-old Scotch?'

'Aye, that I do,' Barratt answered with a deep chuckle.

Chapter Twenty-Six

The Quay Street totter hurried from the estate office hoping to catch Bel Fiddler before she went to the newspaper, but when he arrived at her house it was Charlie who opened the door. 'I've come ter see Bel,' Stymie said breathlessly.

Charlie was on the afternoon shift at the brewery that week and was enjoying an unusually quiet couple of hours with his feet up. 'She's at work,' he replied irritably.

'She's got a job then?' Stymie remarked.

'Yeah, about time,' Charlie growled. ''Er an' Chloe 'ave started at Pearce Duff's, though I dunno 'ow long that's gonna last. Them two 'ave 'ad more jobs than I've 'ad 'ot dinners. Anyway, is there a message?'

Stymie scratched his thinning hair and started to explain about his jaunt to the estate agent's. 'Yer'd better come in,' Charlie said reluctantly.

After the totter had made himself comfortable in the armchair and finished his story Charlie Fiddler felt a little more charitable towards him. 'Those bloody gels o' mine can't keep their nose out of ovver people's business,' he puffed.

'Bel was only tryin' to assist me,' Stymie said quickly. 'She was a big 'elp gettin' people round 'ere ter sign the petition.

Trouble is, it's backfired on us, or it will if she goes ter the papers.'

Charlie studied his visitor for a few moments. 'You an"er get on well, don't yer?' he remarked.

'Yeah, she's a nice gel,' Stymie replied. 'We're good friends, as it 'appens.'

'Yeah, I can see that, but what's yer plans?' Charlie asked.

'Plans?'

'Yeah, plans. I mean, are they honourable?' Charlie wanted to know. ''Cos I would 'ate ter fink yer just after a good time. Our Bel might be a bit flighty an' she might drive me ter distraction at times, but she's me daughter, all said an' done. I wouldn't want 'er 'urt.'

Stymie leaned forward in his chair and fiddled with his hands. 'We ain't goin' steady an' we ain't doin' anyfing wrong,' he assured him. 'Like I said, we're just good friends.'

'Well, that's all right then,' Charlie said. 'Yer know 'ow people talk. Nuffink misses their eyes round 'ere. Only the ovver day I was stopped by a certain person who saw a woman comin' out o' your place. Okay, you could say it was none of 'er business who comes an' goes, but knowin' that you an' our Bel are friends she felt obliged ter warn me, just in case you was playin' a dodgy game.'

Stymie smiled. 'That was Mrs Taylor. She was out when me an' Bel knocked ter get the petition signed so she called in ter sign it. She was in an' out in less than five minutes.'

Charlie breathed a sigh of relief. He had refrained from telling Bel about it and was glad now that he didn't have to incur her considerable wrath. 'As I told the woman, you wasn't the sort o' bloke who'd take anybody on,' he lied.

'Much obliged,' Stymie replied.

'So what we gonna do about your little problem?' Charlie asked.

The totter scratched his head once more. 'D'yer fink she'd go ter the paper office in 'er dinner 'our?'

'Nah, she wouldn't 'ave time. She might go straight from work though.'

Stymie nodded. 'I fink the best fing fer me is ter meet 'er comin' out o' work. Just in case.'

'Good idea,' Charlie said smiling.

'Well, fanks fer talkin' ter me,' Stymie said as he got up, realising there was no chance of Charlie Fiddler offering him a cup of tea.

'Fink nuffink of it,' Charlie replied. 'I'd offer yer a cuppa but I've gotta go out now.'

Stymie made for the door. 'Pearce Duff's yer said?'

'Yeah, that's right.'

'Well so long then.'

Charlie rubbed his hands together gleefully as he closed the front door. He had never wanted Bel to get tied up with the totter in the first place and now things might take a turn for the better. She wouldn't be too happy having Stymie waiting outside the factory for her with his horse and cart on her first day there.

At four o'clock that afternoon Detective Sergeant Ray Black called at number 6 Quay Street and displayed his warrant card. 'Mrs Bailey, you remember me?'

'Of course,' Nell replied quickly. 'What's wrong?'

'Nothing at all,' the detective said smiling. 'Is it possible for you to come to the station right away? There's someone there who wants to have a chat with you. It won't take long. I've got a car waiting round the corner.'

Nell nodded. 'I'll just get me coat,' she told him.

'I didn't want to pull up in front of the house,' the policeman explained as they drove along Jamaica Road. 'It might have set the neighbours off talking.'

'You could say that again,' Nell replied with a smile.

A few minutes later she was sitting comfortably in the inspector's office sipping a cup of tea.

'Mrs Bailey, I want you to meet Commander Barratt,' Malkin said as the tall grey-haired secret service chief came into the office.

Nell looked a little overawed but Barratt was quick to put her at ease. 'Carry on with your tea, Mrs Bailey,' he said as he pulled up a chair near to her. 'Now it would appear that your son Tommy has stumbled across a very serious business which could have dire consequences for this country if we don't act immediately. You will already know that someone is in danger of being killed by a hired assassin, and I can tell you now that the intended victim is a person of very great importance to our country, so we have been forced into using a little deception. You remember that when Tommy was asked his name he said it was Bob Franklin and he came from Stepney Green. His quick reaction has undoubtedly helped keep him out of immediate danger but if the men he got away from start making inquiries they might stumble on the truth.'

Nell nodded. 'It's been worryin' me sick,' she replied.

The commander took out a folded newspaper from his coat pocket. 'It's worried us too,' he said, 'but we've managed to do something about it. I'd like you to take a look at this piece in the early edition of the evening paper. Similar accounts will appear in the other papers and we have to hope our enemies see them too.'

Nell reached down for her handbag at her feet and took out her glasses.

'Boy Found Drowned

The body recovered from the Thames at Wapping Stairs late last night was confirmed as being that of Robert Franklin, fourteen, of Trapp's Lane, Stepney Green. The formal identification was made by his mother, who had reported him missing after he failed to return home on Saturday night.

Mrs Franklin was too distressed to talk to the press but a neighbour who did speak to us said that Robert was a loving son who was looking forward to starting work later this month.

The tragedy remains a mystery, but a spokesman from the river police did tell us that many youngsters play on the moored barges in the area and they are constantly having to be warned off. The spokesman went on to say that very few people would survive a fall into the river when the tides are running. The currents around Wapping and Stepney are powerful enough to overcome even the strongest of swimmers.'

When Nell finished reading the article she looked up at Barratt and shivered involuntarily. 'This could quite easily 'ave bin my Tommy,' she said. 'It was a miracle 'e wasn't drowned.'

Barratt nodded. 'It was providence, Mrs Bailey,' he answered quietly. 'If your son had been drowned we would never have known what this group of people intended, until it was too late. Now we must stop them at all costs and you and your whole family have a part to play.'

''Ow can we 'elp?' Nell asked him.

'Firstly you must instruct your son not to go anywhere near Stepney until this matter has been resolved,' Barratt impressed on her. 'Secondly we would ask you to warn your son about straying too far from the house. We don't want to turn him into a prisoner, but the less he moves about the better. This article should stop them looking for him, but it's better to err on the side of caution.'

Inspector Malkin leaned forward on his desk. 'As I said to you before, Mrs Bailey, we would also expect you and your family to treat this as confidential, even where your closest friends are concerned. We can't be too careful.'

Nell nodded her head vigorously. 'I understand,' she assured them. 'I just 'ope you catch 'em all very quickly. I won't rest till yer do.'

'I've instructed your local beat bobby to keep a special eye on Quay Street,' Malkin told her. 'PC Woodhouse has been warned to keep quiet and I'd prefer it if you avoided drawing him into any conversation regarding this matter. Someone might just overhear and spread the news.'

Nell nodded again in compliance. 'You can trust me,' she said smiling briefly.

Commander Barratt stood as Nell Bailey prepared to leave and shook her hand. 'I think we can trust you implicitly,' he remarked with a smile.

Detective Ray Black had been sitting there quietly at the back of the room and he opened the door for her. 'I'll run you home, Mrs Bailey,' he offered.

Suddenly she turned with a frightened look on her face. 'I've just thought o' somefing terrible,' she said quickly. 'S'posing' those men suspect the bit in the paper is ter put 'em off an' they go checkin' up wiv the neighbours.'

Barratt smiled reassuringly. 'We did think of that eventuality, Mrs Bailey,' he replied. 'Trapp's Lane was destroyed by a flying bomb two months ago and it's now just a desolate ruin. All the survivors were put into various rest centres and some have been rehoused. It would be very difficult for anyone to check. Hopefully it should do the trick.'

Nell left the police station and sat quietly during the short journey home. 'Fanks fer the ride. I've got me fingers crossed,' she said bravely.

Detective Black gave her a smile. 'Try not to worry too much, Mrs Bailey,' he said. 'We're all watching out for you and your family.'

At ten minutes to five Stymie Smith pulled his horse up outside the Pearce Duff's factory and lit a cigarette. The horse turned his head as if questioning Stymie's judgement and the totter chuckled. 'You ain't gettin' a nosebag just yet,' he said. 'Anyway we won't be long.'

At five o'clock he heard the factory hooter sound and a minute or two later the workers came streaming out. 'Oi, Bel,' he called out as he saw her pass by chatting to Chloe and another young woman.

'What you doin' 'ere?' she said looking surprised as she walked up to him.

'Tell me somefing,' he asked anxiously. ''Ave yer bin in touch wiv the newspaper yet?' Her sly grin confirmed his worst fears and he slumped in his seat. 'Oh my good Gawd!' he wailed. 'I knew it. I knew yer'd do it.'

'Well, that was what we agreed, wasn't it?' she asked in puzzlement.

'Yeah, but fings 'ave changed,' he told her. 'When I went ter give the petition in, the bloke there told me the owner's already agreed ter give me a year's extension. Now 'e won't after 'e reads what a nasty bastard 'e is.'

Chloe and the other girl had walked on but some of the factory girls were standing nearby, trying to catch the conversation, and Bel gave them a hard look as she climbed up on the seat next to Stymie. 'Come on, let's get out of 'ere,' she said quickly. 'I feel like a bloody puppet show.'

The totter flapped the reins and clicked his tongue and the horse set off with his usual enthusiasm.

'When did yer go an' see 'em?' he asked.

'I sent 'em a letter,' she replied. 'As a matter o' fact I sent it off this mornin'.'

'Bloody 'ell,' he groaned.

'I dunno,' Bel frowned. 'I can't seem ter do right fer doin' wrong. I was only tryin' ter 'elp.'

'Yeah, I know yer was,' Stymie told her, not wanting to seem ungrateful. 'I jus' gotta 'ope the estate office people an' the owner don't read the papers.'

'I dunno what yer worried about,' Bel remarked. 'They won't write nuffink till they interview yer. I just told 'em that you 'ad a good story for 'em an' they should get in touch.'

'Is that all yer said?'

'Well, I did say roughly what it was about. I 'ad to, ovver-wise they wouldn't bovver.'

Stymie looked troubled as he drove them home but Bel was smiling, and as they turned into Quay Street he caught her expression. 'It's nuffink ter laugh about,' he growled.

'Don't be so tetchy,' she told him. 'I was just finkin'.'

'What about?'

'When that reporter comes ter see yer you can tell 'im 'ow well the estate office an' the owner 'ave treated yer,' Bel replied. 'Play yer cards right an' yer might get two years' extension.'

Stymie immediately chirped up. 'Yeah, I never thought o' that,' he said grinning. 'Bel, you're a diamond.'

'Yer not so bad yerself.'

'Fancy comin' out fer a drink ternight?' he asked.

'Yeah, all right. Then back ter your place?'

'If yer like.'

'No, if you like.'

Stymie's face lit up. 'D'yer know somefing, Bel,' he said. 'I ain't collected sod all terday, but I got a feelin' this is gonna be a good week.'

Bel grinned. 'Like I just said, it will be, if yer play yer cards right.'

Chapter Twenty-Seven

On Monday night Ben Thorburn stepped out of a taxi by Trafalgar Square and bought the *Evening News* at a corner stand before walking to his club in St James's. It had been a tiring day, and after a meal and a couple of brandies he retired to the quiet reading room and carefully scanned through the paper. He soon found the article and breathed a huge sigh of relief. It was unfortunate that the boy should have been on the tug at the time, he thought, but fate had taken a hand and the plan to carry out the assassination remained secret.

Thorburn ordered another large brandy and reclined in his leather armchair to study the details of the new proposals which had been put to his company. It was peaceful in the large lofty lounge and only the muted snoring of an elderly member disturbed the silence. An ideal time to study the offer, he thought, fortified with his favourite tipple and a large cigar.

Thorburn attempted to settle down, but try as he might he could not concentrate on the figures. Something was niggling away at the back of his mind and it troubled him. He picked up the newspaper once more and read the article again. His sense of disquiet grew and suddenly he realised what it was. He checked his pocketwatch and saw that it was almost nine o'clock. There was time, he decided. 'George, will you ask reception to order me a cab, please, and let me know when it arrives?'

The attendant nodded dutifully and hurried off, leaving Thorburn with a nasty qualm of apprehension. Thirty minutes later he paid off the cab driver on the corner of Arbour Square and walked into the maze of East End backstreets. Stepney Green was where he had his London house and he knew Trapp's Lane. It was as he remembered it the last time he had chanced to pass by and he frowned thoughtfully as he walked through the bomb-ravaged turning. There was no sign of life, only piles of rubble on both sides of the road where once a row of neat terraced houses had stretched along opposite industrial buildings. He recalled reading about the row of houses in Trapp's Lane being hit by a high explosive during the Blitz and the street being finally destroyed by the flying bomb which had fallen on the surviving buildings.

Thorburn walked out of the eerie wasteland and found a nearby pub that had a cosy saloon bar. He ordered a beer, his mind racing as he watched the barman pull down on the pump. The Franklin boy was reported to have come from Trapp's Lane so he must have lived in the buildings, since the houses had been destroyed three years earlier.

'Do you ever get any of the industrial buildings' folk in here?' he asked as the frothing glass was placed in front of him.

The elderly barman shook his head. 'Not often,' he replied with the reluctance most of his ilk displayed when quizzed by strangers.

'The reason I asked is, a friend of mine used to live in the buildings and I've not clapped eyes on him for ages,' Thorburn said casually.

'What was 'is name?' the barman asked.

'Wilson. Fred Wilson.'

'Nah, that name don't ring a bell.'

Thorburn sipped the froth from his glass. 'I was reminded of him by a piece I read in the paper this evening.'

'Oh?'

'Yes, it was sad really. A young lad's body was fished from the Thames and it was reported that he lived in the buildings.'

'What was the name?'

'Franklin. Robert Franklin, fourteen.'

'Nah, I don't know anybody by that name,' the barman went on. 'Mind yer, not everyone in the buildin's used this boozer. Shame about the lad though.'

Thorburn nodded and took another draught of his beer. 'I'd like ter get in touch with my pal again, assuming he's still alive,' he said. 'I s'pose I'd be better off calling in at the nearest rest centre. That's where the survivors would have been taken, I'm sure.'

'If yer interested yer'll find it in Croft Street, two turnin's along. It used ter be the ole drill 'all.'

Thorburn finished his drink quickly, keen to get on with his inquiries and he thanked the barman for his help before setting off for Croft Street.

The rest centre had been re-opened after the onset of the flying bombs and the warden, a smart woman in her fifties, was very accommodating. 'Now let me see,' she said as she reached into her desk drawer and took out a large folder. 'The buildings were destroyed on the second of July and we took in most of the survivors, all we could cope with in fact. There's the list of names if you'd care to look at it.'

Thorburn could see no sign of the Franklin family and he passed the sheet of paper back with a brief smile. 'I'm afraid the name's not there,' he told her.

The woman smiled back sympathetically. 'There were some

who were sent to the rest centre in Dock Street and one or two families went to stay with relatives,' she said helpfully.

Thorburn made his way to Dock Street through the rising river mist and finally left the rest centre there feeling very worried indeed. Once again he had found no trace, and unless the Franklins were one of those families who had gone to live with relatives as the warden explained, the whole business would take on a new dimension.

Thorburn decided against going home to his house in Stepney Green, even though it was only a short walk away. He had already booked a room at his club and he needed another drink while he puzzled over the mounting problem. He hailed a cab and sat back in the darkness to ponder. The Franklin boy could have survived the river and gone to the police to report what he had overheard. They would have realised it was out of their league and contacted the secret services. MI5 would then have taken over and decided to fake the death of the boy, partly to protect him, and partly to create a false sense of security amongst the plotters.

The cab driver weaved his way through the quiet City streets and on to the more lively Strand, dotted with servicemen and women of many nationalities, speaking different languages but all united in one mammoth task, the destruction of the Nazis and a speedy end to the war. Thorburn saw the huge poster fixed on the base of Nelson's Column urging people to buy savings bonds, and then he saw the group of black African servicemen looking up at the statue of one of England's greatest, which smothered the feeling of patriotism which had threatened to surface within him as he climbed from the taxi. He was prepared to accept assistance and funds from any source to bring about the firm government he and the League of White Knights so fervently desired. Although the way might be harsh and radical, the end would justify the means.

It was late when Thorburn finally entered his club. It had been a worthwhile foray into the East End though, he felt. Unless he was very much mistaken the secret services were on to the assassination plot, and extreme caution was now called for. The Pedlar had gone to ground and could not be contacted but he would know how to gauge the situation, however it changed. With his past record he could be expected to succeed and the League of White Knights had to be ready to carry on with their fight. For that reason it was imperative that the Franklin boy be found and silenced before he could formally identify any of the League members. Should he be allowed to live, there was a very real chance of the League being broken, falling like a house of cards.

On Tuesday morning Stymie was up early, and with a new-found enthusiasm he set about hitching his horse to the cart and then filled a nosebag full of chaff from the sack, which he placed under his seat. Last night had been a very exciting experience, he recalled with a thrill of pleasure. Bel had daringly tempted him up to the bedroom and in the darkness she had taught him things he never could have imagined. They had stopped short of actually doing the act but, as she demonstrated, there was more than one way of achieving satisfaction. Going all the way was on the cards soon, if last night was anything to go by, and Stymie decided that whatever happened that day he must not forget to pay a visit to the chemist. It was going to awkward, especially if there was a woman behind the counter, but then he could always avoid the embarrassment by going to get his hair cut. The barber was always asking him if there was anything he wanted for the weekend and it would only be a question of pointing casually to the shelf where the rubber johnnies were stacked.

As he was about to set off a young woman looked in from the street. 'Are you Mr Smith the totter?' she asked him.

'I'm 'im,' he replied.

'I'm from the *South London Gazette*,' she said smiling as she walked into the yard. 'I understand you've been given short notice to quit.'

'Yeah, but it's all bin sorted out,' he told her.

'Oh, and how?' she asked.

'I got a year's extension.'

The reporter looked disappointed. 'I understood from the letter Miss Fiddler sent to the office that you were getting up a petition to put pressure on the owner to reconsider.'

'Yeah, that's right,' Stymie replied, scratching his head.

'And did you present the petition?'

'Nah, I didn't 'ave to.'

'But you let the estate office know of your intentions?'

'Nah, they was very nice, so I didn't tell 'em about the petition.'

The reporter realised that there was nothing to be gained in talking to him any further and she closed her notepad and put it in her handbag. 'Well, I don't think there's anything of news value here, Mr Smith. Thanks for talking to me anyway.'

'You're welcome,' he replied as he climbed up on to the cart. 'D'yer need a lift?'

'On that?' she replied contemptuously.

Stymie smiled proudly at the young woman. 'Let me tell yer somefing, luv,' he said slowly. 'Not so many years ago this was the way people travelled to an' fro, an' it's still better than yer cars, buses an' trams. Now the ole work'orse is a dyin' breed an' that goes fer us general dealers or totters as people like ter call us. We ain't seen as bein' right an' proper fer most places these days, so most of us end up underneath the arches as the song goes. You take a look round Rovverhithe an' Deptford, that's where yer'll find us.'

'Not you though, Mr Smith.'

'No, not me, not just yet, but my time'll come. One year, that's all I've got in Quay Street.'

Unwittingly Stymie had whetted the reporter's professional appetite and she saw a good story in taking up the plight of the general dealers in her paper. 'Would you mind if I called again this evening?' she asked.

Stymie thought quickly. Bel was coming over that evening. 'As long as it's before eight,' he told her. 'I gotta go out at eight.'

'Will seven o'clock suit?' she asked.

'That'll do fine,' he replied.

As the young reporter left the yard she was spotted by Iris Meadows who was sweeping her doorstep. 'Bloody 'ell, it's gettin' ter be like a bleedin' brothel in there,' she mumbled aloud.

Annie Francis was dusting her parlour and she picked up the library book that Johnny had left lying around. ''Ave you finished wiv this?' she asked him.

He nodded. 'Don't go an' 'ide it, Ma,' he said quickly. 'It's due fer returnin'.'

'Well, why don't yer go round the library an' 'and it in then,' she suggested.

'Josie was gonna do it,' he replied nonchalantly.

'Well, she won't now, will she?' Annie replied.

'She will if I ask 'er.'

'But yer don't see 'er any more.'

'She only lives across the street,' the young man said puffing.

'Yeah, an' it might just as well be Timbuktu as far as you're concerned,' Annie went on. 'You an' 'er were gettin' on so well, an' now look at yer. Yer messin' around wiv all those brassy gels who didn't give a monkey's when yer needed company. Only Josie Bailey 'ad any time fer yer, an' what did yer do?

Give 'er the elbow soon as yer got on yer feet. I tell yer somefing. That gel's werf ten o' that lot yer fart-arsin' around wiv.'

'I didn't like bein' dictated to,' Johnny said sharply. 'Just 'cos I was dancin' wiv anuvver gel. Anyway, it won't be long before she comes creepin' back, you just wait.'

'That I'd like ter see,' Annie remarked contemptuously as she threw the book down on the table in disgust. 'An' who's gonna change yer library book in the meantime?'

'Josie'll do it. I'm bound ter see 'er round the street.'

'If yer take my advice yer'll do it yerself,' Annie said gruffly, 'an' while yer at it yer could do worse than carryin' on down ter the labour exchange, now yer got the all-clear from the doctors.'

'I need a bit more time before I start back ter work,' he replied quickly. 'The quack did give me the all-clear, true, but 'e warned me about doin' too much too soon.'

'I don't fink there's any danger o' that,' Annie said, sighing in exasperation. Jack had been right all along. Their son was lazy and indolent, with no consideration for those closest to him. He'll learn though, she thought. One day he'll realise where he went wrong, when one of those brassy tarts gets her hooks into him.

Johnny Francis walked out into the backyard and stood looking up at the thin drifting clouds. It had been nice when Josie used to call and they'd sit for a while chatting about almost everything. It could have got serious, if he had let it happen. Josie was keen, he could tell, but he had been too wary of getting trapped in a situation before he was ready, and now that the bubble had burst he found himself wanting the one girl he knew deep down that he stood no chance with. But that was defeatist thinking. It was obvious that Josie was playing him along by dating Billy Emmerson. She'd come back running if he made the effort.

Annie Francis frowned as he came into the parlour wearing his coat. 'Where d'yer put the book, Ma?' he asked. 'I'm gonna change it meself, an' I might be some time. I'm takin' your advice. I'm goin' down the labour exchange.'

Annie was about to remark that wonders would never cease, but she bit her tongue and smiled instead. 'Good luck, son,' she told him.

Chapter Twenty-Eight

On Tuesday morning the German agent stepped out of the phone box in Tower Bridge Road and made his way back to work. His call to the pub in north-west London had satisfied his suspicion that the Pedlar had gone to ground. He could not be contacted now by anyone, and the agent understood his motives. The assassin would not want to risk his phone calls being overheard, or anyone finding out where he was hiding at this late stage. To all intents and purposes he had disappeared off the face of the earth, and the spy smiled to himself as he thought about it. The Pedlar had been very successful in all the killings he had carried out over the years but he would no doubt see this particular job of work as his biggest test. Nothing would be risked and nothing left to chance.

The day was warm and pleasant with a light refreshing breeze, and the noises of the bustling market blended with the constant rattle of trams and the roar of passing motor traffic. Laden horse carts trundled past down the street and the agent smiled cynically to himself. It had been a quiet few days with less activity than usual on the London war front. Only a few flying bombs had arrived overhead and the casualties had been light, but very soon it would all change. In a few days the new weapon would arrive unannounced, and with its sudden violence and higher death tolls it was going to cause a certain amount of panic; but expecting the people of London to scream out hysterically in surrender was ludicrous. The German cities were now under constant attack day and night by two airforces but the inhabitants were suffering the bombardment stoically, just as the British people had during the Blitz and were doing again now with the current flying bomb attacks.

As he walked casually towards his business premises in Jamaica Road the agent nodded and smiled to one or two of his fellow traders. Like them he was no doubt a familiar face who hardly warranted a second thought, but one day it would all come out, either after he had successfully disappeared from the Bermondsey scene or after his demise. Whichever, things were never going to be the same, and the local folk would tell the story about the spy who had once lived in their midst to their children, and their grandchildren.

Ben Thorburn's face was familiar in the Lighterman pub and no one took any notice that lunchtime when he stood at the bar talking to the elderly nightwatchman. 'Do you get much trouble from the kids round here?' he asked him.

'Nah, not really,' the old man replied as he sipped his beer. 'Sometimes I 'ave ter shout out at 'em when they come soddin' about near the jetty but it ain't very often.'

'I was reading in last night's paper about that poor lad who was fished out of the river,' Thorburn went on. 'Terrible thing. Local lad too.'

The old watchman nodded. 'Once they fall in the water there's not much 'ope,' he said with an air of experience. 'The tides an' the currents round this bend are very dicey. I've known a few tragedies in me time.'

The buxom woman sitting on a bar stool nearby drained her

glass and banged it down on the counter to get attention. 'Give us anuvver, Joey,' she said loudly.

'Are you sure?' the barman asked, aware that she was downing the gin and limes like water.

'Course I'm sure,' she slurred.

'I'm only lookin' after yer, Betsie,' the young man remarked smiling. 'Wouldn't wanna see you fall in the river an' drown.'

'Like that poor little sod in yesterday night's paper?' she replied. 'I read about it in the *Star*. Scared the life out o' me when I saw the headline about a boy bein' drowned. At first I thought it was Frank Bailey's boy. I was speakin' to 'im outside 'ere on Sunday night. Lookin' fer Frank 'e was. Nice little kid. I 'ad ter tell 'im 'is dad 'ad bin an' gorn.'

Ben Thorburn's ears pricked up and he looked along the bar at the brassy blonde. 'That's not Frank Bailey who works on the tugs, is it?' he asked amicably.

The woman turned and had some difficulty in focusing her eyes on him. 'Nah, yer gettin' mixed up wiv Frank Watson,' she told him. 'Frank Bailey comes from over the water in Bermondsey. That's where 'is family live. Frank an' 'is ole woman don't get on, yer see, an' 'e's gone on the turps ter drown 'is sorrows. Comes in 'ere quite a lot 'e does. Drinks wiv Nobby Swan. When 'e's really pissed out of 'is brains Swanny lets 'im kip on 'is boat. Nice bloke is Swanny.'

Thorburn put his hand into his pocket. 'Here I'll get that one,' he said to the barman as the blonde laid down a ten-shilling note on the counter, 'and the same again for us.'

''Ere's ter you,' the blonde said as she picked up the glass. 'I didn't catch yer name.'

'Thorburn. Ben Thorburn.'

'Well, 'ere's ter you, Ben, an' may the grass not grow under yer feet.'

Thorburn raised his glass. 'Did the lad find his father after all?' he asked.

'Gawd knows,' the blonde replied.

'Did he look on the boat I wonder?'

''E might 'a' done.'

'Did you tell him to try the boat?'

The woman's glassy gaze drifted sideways before it settled on the large distinguished figure once more. 'I didn't tell the boy nuffink o' the sort,' she said sharply. 'I didn't want 'im messin' about on the boat in case 'e fell in the water. I wouldn't 'ave fergiven meself if 'e 'ad.'

'Quite right too,' Thorburn agreed.

'Nice little face 'e 'ad. Angelic it was,' the blonde rambled on. 'I could 'ave cried when 'e asked me ter see if 'is dad was in 'ere. "Tell 'im Tommy's outside", he said.'

'And he came all this way to find his dad.'

'Yeah, it makes yer wanna cry.'

Thorburn had heard enough and as soon as he could he extricated himself from the company and walked quickly to the nearest phone box.

'Hello, is that Peter? Peter, this is Ben Thorburn. I want you to get in touch with Holman and Anderson immediately. Tell them I'll meet them in the usual place at seven. Oh and Peter, can you get Lennie to take a ride to Bermondsey. I want him to go through the voters lists. He's there with you? Put him on then, will you? Hello, Lennie. I want you to take a trip to Bermondsey. I'm looking for a family called Bailey. Head of household Frank Bailey. Yes, it's a fairly common name but the Bailey I'm interested in has a son named Tommy. No, I know the boy's name won't be on the voters lists but you might be able to do a follow-up. But Lennie, be discreet. I don't want the family to know they're being checked out. Can I rely on you? Good man. Give me a call as soon as you find out anything. Yes, that's right, I'll be at the office until seven.'

The Pedlar left the Rotherhithe Infirmary leaning heavily on his stick and smiling to himself. It hadn't been hard to pile on the agony and convince the overworked doctor that his knee was still very painful, and after studying the X-rays the consultant had prescribed a course of rehabilitation for what he said was muscle wastage due to a damaged cartilage. Going to the gymnasium every morning for exercises was an ideal state of affairs. It gave him the opportunity to become a regular face to the staff and at the same time to familiarise himself fully with the layout. All the entrances, exits and fire doors were becoming fixed in his mind, and furthermore he had a perfect means of carrying the rifle with him on the day. When he had practised using the broom handle it had been unnoticeable.

One thing puzzled the assassin as he made his way along the corridor that led to the new wing. The small curtain fixed to the wall had to be covering the commemorative plaque which was obviously going to be unveiled by the Prime Minister after he cut the tape to open the wing, but where would the tape be? Would it be placed there at the end of the corridor adjoining the old building, or at the main entrance in Jamaica Road? The latter would make Churchill an easier target and his security men would know this. It was more likely that they would arrange for the tape to be placed inside the corridor leading into the children's wing, thereby minimising the risk.

The Pedlar stood looking along the empty corridor deep in thought. Putting a bullet into the country's leader was not going to be practicable at whichever place was chosen to open the wing. Inside there would be too many people gathered around him to offer any sort of target, while at the front entrance he would be closed in by many more of the general public. The best chance would come when he was at his most vulnerable, getting out of the car. There would be just two or three seconds to take aim and fire, from a position which gave him the best chance of making good his escape.

'I say, yer can't go down there, mate.'

The Pedlar turned to see a porter standing behind him. 'No, I know,' he replied. 'I was just looking at what a nice job the builders have made.'

The porter nodded. 'It'll be nice ter see it opened again,' he said. 'I was on duty the night it got destroyed. Terrible night that was. Don't fink I'll ever ferget it.'

'That's understandable,' the assassin replied. 'Still the opening'll give you some satisfaction, I'm sure.'

'That it will.'

'I suppose they'll unveil some sort of plaque.'

The porter pointed to the drawn curtain. 'There it is,' he said.

'I thought it would be,' the Pedlar replied. 'I wonder who's going to do the honours?'

'They only screwed the plaque on yesterday,' the porter told him. 'I took a gander when it was all quiet last night.'

'I know I shouldn't ask, but it's not the King doing the ceremony, is it?' the Pedlar asked quietly.

The porter looked left and right then leaned closer conspiratorially. 'It's Winnie,' he whispered. ''Is name's on the plaque.'

'Not Winston Churchill!' the Pedlar remarked with appropriate surprise.

The porter nodded emphatically and put a finger to his lips. 'Don't breavve a word though,' he said with a nervous look on his thin face.

'When is it to be?' the Pedlar asked.

'Next Monday.'

'That'll be a day to remember.'

'They're takin' the visit very serious,' the porter went on. 'They're shuttin' the 'ospital gates on the day an' the forecourt's gotta be cleared ter make way fer the official cars.'

'That's understandable,' the Pedlar replied, 'but will I be able to get in? I have to go to the gym daily you see.'

'You'll be all right,' the porter told him. 'They'll let you patients in at the side gate.'

'There'll be a tape to cut at the main entrance as well, I expect,' the Pedlar remarked, 'and they have to be careful to keep the place clear in case some maniac tries to harm him. It's happened in other countries.'

The porter nodded again. 'I'll be glad when it's all over, ter tell yer the trufe,' he sighed. 'It makes a lot of extra work fer the likes of us.'

'I've no doubt,' the assassin replied. 'Still it'll all be over by the early evening, I expect.'

'I'm expectin' it ter be over by midday,' the hospital worker said quickly. ''E's an early bird is ole Churchill. Each time 'e's visited Bermondsey it's bin in the mornin'. In the afternoons 'e's naggin' away in Parliament.'

'Well, it's been nice talking to you,' the Pedlar said smiling as he started off.

The hospital worker watched him limp away down the corridor. Nice man, he thought. Shame about his leg.

On Tuesday evening Johnny Francis was standing on the corner of Quay Street talking to some other young men when he saw Josie coming along Jamaica Road. Making his excuses with a smug smile he fell into step beside her as she walked into the turning. 'Josie, I just wanna tell yer not ter worry about that library book o' mine,' he began. 'I changed it meself this afternoon.'

'I'd fergot all about it, ter tell yer the trufe,' she replied.

'It's all right, I couldn't expect you ter keep runnin' errands for me,' he told her with a disarming smile.

It was that smile of his that used to set her heart beating faster, but things were different now. 'It was no trouble,' she said quietly.

They had stopped outside her front door and the young man looked down at his shoes for a few moments. 'Look, I'm sorry the way fings turned out fer us,' he said. 'I've bin stupid. I'm never gonna ferget what yer did fer me when I needed 'elp.'

'I'm sorry the way fings turned out too,' Josie told him calmly. 'I thought we were gonna get serious wiv each ovver, but it wasn't ter be.'

'We still could, if we gave it anuvver try,' Johnny said earnestly.

'No, it's too late,' Josie answered quickly. 'I'm goin' steady wiv Billy Emmerson now an' I wouldn't drop 'im. I couldn't.'

'Me an' you could really make it tergevver,' he went on. 'I'd make sure yer'd never regret it.'

'I'm sorry, Johnny, but it's no good. I'd be ferever worryin' that you were two-timin' me.'

'All those ovver gels don't mean anyfing ter me, Josie. You're the one I want an' I can say it ter yer now.'

'Now's too late, Johnny.'

'Give me anuvver chance, Josie.'

'I can't.'

'Yes, you can,' the young man insisted. 'Billy Emmerson ain't the feller fer you. You want someone like me, someone who can bring out that passion inside yer.'

Josie's face became dark with anger. 'Now you listen ter me,' she said firmly. 'Me an' Billy 'ave got a good fing goin' an' you're the last one ter criticise a feller like Billy. Wiv 'im I can feel safe an' sure of meself. That's more than I could wiv you.'

Johnny Francis smiled at her, trying to appease her. 'Just fink about it,' he said. 'Just give me one chance ter show yer I've changed an' yer won't regret it, I promise.'

She turned away from him and pushed open her front door, then she turned back and looked him squarely in the eye. 'Give up, Johnny, an' stay friends,' she told him. 'Don't fink yer still in wiv a chance, 'cos you definitely ain't.'

Johnny Francis walked off down the street with anger festering inside him. Billy Emmerson had come between them with his little-boy-lost act and Josie had fallen for it. She'll soon learn, he fumed.

Stymie Smith was woken from a snooze by the knocking and he dragged himself down the stairs and opened the front door to see the reporter standing there.

'Good evening, Mr Smith, you remember me?'

He nodded blearily. 'You're from the *South London Gazette*.'

'Right first time,' she said winningly. 'I don't think I introduced myself properly this morning. I'm Maggie Phillips and I write a regular column for the paper.'

'You'd better come on up then,' Stymie yawned.

She made herself as comfortable as she could on the tatty settee which had rogue springs threatening to fly out at any minute. 'I'd be grateful if you could give me a brief outline of the plight of your general dealer friends at the arches in Pollock Street,' she began as she flipped open her notepad. 'I went to take a look there after I left you this morning and I have to say I was shocked by the state of the arches.'

'Fancy a cuppa?' Stymie asked, trying his best to pull himself together.

'That'll be nice,' she replied. 'I understand that Southern Railway are the landlords and they rent the arches out on a weekly basis.'

'Yeah, that's right,' Stymie told her as he lifted the simmering kettle off the gas-stove.

'I actually looked in a couple of the arches and saw that they were dripping with condensation,' Maggie Phillips went on. 'There was a lot of fungus too. It really was a nasty place.'

The totter nodded as he filled the teapot and stirred the leaves thoroughly. 'Mm, I feel sorry fer those lads at the Pollock Street arches,' he remarked. 'Some of 'em are good friends o' mine. I wouldn't put up wiv it. I'd be on ter the railway ter clean the bloody area up. I told 'em they should 'ave a nag about it. Yer get nuffink if yer don't try.'

'Can I quote you there?' the reporter asked him.

'Yeah, course yer can. I'd be there up the front 'avin' a dig meself if I 'ad more time. As I said they're good friends o' mine.'

Stymie poured the tea and the young woman frowned as she looked down at a reddish liquid in a chipped mug. 'So you think the general dealers there should get together and put pressure on the landlords?'

'Yeah, I do.'

'How would you go about it if you were organising things?'

'I'd stop payin' the rent an' picket the place till they did somefing about it.'

'Well, I'll try to get back to you, Mr Smith,' Maggie Phillips told him. 'In the meantime keep your eyes open for the Thursday edition of the *Gazette*.'

'Yeah, I will,' he replied.

The reporter left ten minutes before Bel Fiddler knocked, the comings and goings witnessed by the widow Meadows who was standing at her front door talking to Ginny Allen. ''Ave you ever done somefing an' then regretted it?' she asked.

'Plenty o' times,' Ginny replied.

'Well, I wish I'd never signed that poxy petition fer

that bloody totter,' Iris went on. ''E's givin' the street a bad name. That place of 'is is gettin' like a knockin' shop wiv all those women goin' in an' out. Gawd knows what's goin' on in there.'

'There's only one way ter find out,' Ginny said grinning. 'Me an' you go over there, knock at 'is door an' tell 'im we've come fer a piece o' the pie.'

'Up yer pipe,' Iris growled.

Chapter Twenty-Nine

Nell Bailey finished tidying up the parlour on Wednesday morning and glanced through the curtains to see Tommy talking to Dennis Taylor some way along the turning. Ever since the police had called she had had a dread feeling that her son would go missing. Try as she might, Nell could not get it out of her head, but she resisted the urge to keep him in the house all day long while the school holidays were still on. It wouldn't be fair on the lad and would only serve to make him as nervous as she was. The only restriction she put on him was that he stayed in the street.

Nell sighed uneasily and went into the scullery to put the kettle on. Polly Seagram would be making her usual morning call and it would be an excuse not to do any more work about the place. She was supposed to be taking it easy anyway.

At eleven o'clock Polly knocked. 'What yer got yer front door shut for?' she asked. 'It's a lovely day.'

Nell had an excuse ready. 'I did leave it open. Our Tommy must 'ave shut it be'ind 'im when 'e went out,' she told her.

'Shall I leave it open?' Polly asked.

'Nah, yer might as well shut it,' Nell replied. 'I've just done me passage an' I don't want all the dust blowin' in.'

Polly made herself comfortable. ''Ave you 'eard anyfing from Frank?' she inquired.

Nell shook her head grimly. 'Nah, I ain't seen nuffink of 'im since I come out the 'ospital.'

''E'll be callin' soon, mark my words,' Polly said encouragingly. ''E's just gettin' 'imself tergevver.'

Nell shrugged her shoulders. 'I dunno, it makes me wonder if 'e is makin' the effort. The last time 'e came in the 'ospital ter see me 'e stunk o' beer an' 'is eyes were all glassy.'

'It won't be easy fer 'im, that's fer sure,' Polly replied, 'but 'e'll do it. You'll see.'

Nell wished she could confide in her best friend about what had happened but she knew she mustn't. She wished too that Frank was there to take charge. He would know what to do and she'd feel much safer. As it was she just had to carry on and try to reassure her brood that everything was going to be all right.

''Ere, I gotta tell yer,' Polly grinned. 'I was talkin' ter Ginny Allen an' she told me Iris Meadows stopped 'er an' prattled on about the goin's-on at Stymie's.'

'Goin's-on?'

'Yeah, accordin' to Iris there's bin women goin' in an' out of 'is place nonstop.'

'That don't sound like Stymie,' Nell replied. 'I always reckoned 'im ter be a born bachelor, before Bel Fiddler came on the scene that is, though ter be honest I don't fink there's anyfing serious goin' on between those two. You know what Bel Fiddler's like. She gets in wiv everybody.'

Polly followed Nell out into the scullery. 'I see yer bin doin' a bit o' tidyin' up,' she remarked. 'You mind yer don't overdo it. I told yer I'd come in an' give yer a bit of 'elp. You've only gotta ask.'

'I can't sit around doin' nuffink,' Nell sighed. 'All this rest is drivin' me right round the twist.'

'Yeah, I know 'ow yer feel,' Polly replied. 'I was the same when I 'ad phlebitis. My Bernie wouldn't let me lift a cup.'

Nell made the tea and slipped a patchwork cosy over the enamel pot. 'I shouldn't be moanin' like this,' she said. 'Our Josie's bin a good 'un. The ovver two 'ave done their share as well. I've never known our Kathy ter do so much as lately.'

'They're good kids,' Polly remarked. 'Young Tommy's springin' up too.'

''E'll be startin' work soon,' Nell told her. 'It makes me feel old.'

Polly Seagram sat down at the small table and watched Nell pour the tea, and she was surprised when her friend suddenly stopped midway and hurried into the parlour. 'Anyfing wrong?' she asked when Nell came back.

'Nah, I thought I 'eard Tommy call out,' she said.

'Are you sure there's nuffink wrong?'

'Sure I'm sure.'

Polly picked up her tea and sipped it, pulling a face. 'Are you out o' sugar?' she asked.

Nell tutted. 'Sorry luv, it must be all this sittin' around. It's makin' me fergetful.'

'If there was somefing wrong yer would tell me, wouldn't yer?'

'Course I would.'

Nell wished she could tell her something, but she had promised not to speak a word about the situation she was in and she knew she couldn't make any exceptions, not even for her best friend. 'If there was anyfing wrong you'd be the first ter know,' she said.

Polly got on with her tea. Nell was missing Frank, that's

295

what it was, she told herself. It was natural that she didn't want to talk too much about it. ''Ere, I gotta tell yer . . .' she began in an effort to raise her spirits.

Nell tried to concentrate on what Polly was saying but all the time she had a terrible sense of foreboding that something dreadful was waiting to happen, and she felt like crying.

Tommy and Dennis were flipping through a stack of cigarette cards when the man walked into the street. The boys took little notice of him until he stopped to talk to the Brady brothers.

'I bet 'e's a 'tec,' Dennis remarked.

'Well, 'e can't be the schoolboard man,' Tommy said grinning.

They watched him walk out of the turning and then they ambled over to the two brothers. 'Who was that?' Dennis asked them.

''E said 'e was from the church,' Ken Brady replied. ''E said they was givin' a party soon an' 'e wanted names o' the kids in the street who might like ter go.'

'Cor!' Dennis exclaimed. 'Are you two goin'?'

'Yeah, but don't worry, we gave 'im your names as well,' Terry Brady piped up.

'When's it ter be?' Dennis asked.

'Two weeks' time.'

'I 'ope they give us presents.'

'Yeah, that'll be good.'

Tommy remained quiet. The man might really have been from the church, he thought, but he'd better let his mother know, after what she had told him about being extra careful, even in the street.

''Ere, Tommy, show 'em the knife I gave yer,' Dennis said.

'I ain't got it wiv me,' Tommy replied.

'It's no good leavin' it indoors,' Dennis remarked disapprovingly.

'I was usin' it last night an' I fergot ter put it back in me pocket,' Tommy said quickly, thinking how it had probably saved his life when he used it to stab the man on the boat. He was at a loss to remember what had happened to it after that, whether he had left it stuck in the man's arm or dropped it on the deck as he jumped into the water, but he felt very guilty for losing it.

'Go an' get it,' Dennis urged him.

'I can't,' he replied. 'Me mum said if I keep goin' in an' out I've gotta stop in.'

'We can't go in neivver,' Ken Brady said. 'Our muvver's gone out, but she give us our dinner money. We're goin' up the pie shop. Wanna come?'

'I can't,' Dennis told him.

'No, neivver can I,' Tommy added.

Less than a hundred yards away in Jamaica Road the visitor to the street was making an urgent phone call. 'Yes, I checked it out. The Bailey family live at number six, Quay Street. No, no problems. One of the boys in the turning pointed Tommy Bailey out to me. Yes, I'd recognise him again. Right then, I'll come straight back.'

The Quay Street totter sat slumped on the high seat of his cart as the horse plodded on through Long Lane. Normally the nag would raise no objections at the start of the day when he was harnessed up and shunted between the shafts, but this morning Stymie recalled the animal had acted up. He blew hard and resisted when he was pulled from his stall. The totter put it down to old age. After all he wasn't always in the pink of condition himself every morning. Horses no doubt felt the same, and Benny wasn't exactly a young horse.

Stymie steered a course that took him through the backstreets to Pollock Street, and as he pulled up at the arches he saw a few of his pals chatting together around a parked cart. 'Oi, Stymie, just the bloke,' one of them called out.

''Ow yer doing?' the totter asked pleasantly.

'Never mind 'ow we're doin'. What's all this about the newspapers?'

'Newspapers?'

'Don't play the innocent wiv us,' the Pollock Street totter went on. 'An' don't tell us you ain't bin talkin' ter the papers 'cos we know yer did.'

'It's no secret,' Stymie said quickly. 'I was just tellin' the reporter 'ow we're all made ter feel like we're not wanted round 'ere.'

'Yeah, we know that,' another totter chimed in. 'That reporter woman come round earlier this mornin' an' she told us what you said.'

'What I said?'

'Yeah, about goin' on a rent strike an' forcin' the railway ter clean the arches up. She said you was our spokesman an' you wanted ter get us all organised.'

'I never said no such fing,' Stymie told them indignantly.

'Well, eivver she's lyin' or you are,' the man retorted angrily. 'What gives you the right ter come pokin' yer big nose in our business?'

'I was only explainin' 'ow 'ard it is fer us at times,' Stymie said meekly.

'Do you realise if that prat writes up a piece about us we could be chucked out of 'ere termorrer. Then where we all gonna go, round your place till we find somefing?'

'She'll only write what yer told 'er,' Stymie said with spirit.

'Nah, she'll write what you told 'er,' the angry totter replied. 'As fer us, we ain't plannin' no rent strike an' we told 'er so.'

''Ave yer thought o' gettin' a petition up?' Stymie asked.

'Do us a favour,' the totter said in disgust. 'Who the poxy 'ell would sign a petition ter keep us 'ere? Most o' the people on this manor want us out of it. Some of 'em even fink we're gyppos.'

'Well, I'm sorry yer feel that way about it,' Stymie said quickly. 'I was only tryin' to 'elp me ole pals.'

'The best way you can 'elp is ter stay clear of us, an' keep yer bloody mouth shut in the future.'

'Well, if that's the way yer feel, sod the lot o' yer.'

'An' sod you too, you ugly-lookin' git,' the totter shouted out as Stymie drove off.

The sun was shining, the birds were singing in the trees and a light breeze wafted through the backstreets, but as far as the Quay Street totter was concerned there might just as well have been hailstones raining down as he sat slumped dejectedly on his cart. 'That's what comes o' tryin' ter be friendly,' he moaned to his horse. 'You must 'ave known somefing I didn't this mornin'. I wish I'd stayed in bed.'

A woman came out of her house and waved to him as he turned into Weston Street. 'I got an ole wringer,' she called out. ''Ow much will yer give me fer it?'

Stymie pulled up and got down from the cart. 'I'd need ter take a look at it,' he told her.

The woman led the way through a long passage into the backyard. 'There it is,' she said.

Stymie stared at the wrecked wringer in disbelief. 'I wouldn't even take that away fer nuffink,' he snorted. 'Just look at it.'

'What's the matter wiv it?'

'What's the matter wiv it? The bloody fing's rusted to 'ell an' one o' the cogs is missin'. The rollers are split beyond repair an' what's more the 'andle's cracked.'

'Well, I wouldn't wanna get rid of it if it was any good, now would I?' the woman said indignantly.

Stymie puffed loudly. 'That contraption ain't no good ter me as scrap. Old iron don't bring much these days,' he explained.

'The only way it's werf anyfing is if I can repair it, but tryin' ter repair that bloody ole fing'd be like tryin' ter tart up the *Lusitania*.'

'*Lusitania*? What's that?'

'The liner that was sunk by the Germans in 1915,' Stymie replied sardonically.

'Sorry to 'ave bovvered yer,' the woman scowled at him. 'I was finkin' o' givin' yer a quid ter take it off me 'ands before one o' me kids 'as an accident wiv it, but I wouldn't dream of it now, yer miserable ole git.'

Stymie did not like being thought of as miserable, and more than that he did not like being referred to as old, but he realised his confrontation with the other totters had put him in a vile mood and he deserved the slur. He took a deep breath and smiled briefly. 'You're right, luv,' he said in his most endearing way. 'If I was spoken to like that by anybody I wouldn't wanna lift a finger to 'elp. As it 'appens I've got a bit o' trouble an' I took it out on you. Will you accept my sincere apologies?'

The woman looked a little chastened. 'I'm sorry to 'ear you got troubles, but it ain't my fault,' she replied.

'Course it's not.'

'We've all got troubles, luv,' the woman went on, 'but it's no good takin' it out on ovver people.'

'You couldn't be more right.'

'Look, I'll give yer a quid if yer take the bloody fing away,' she offered.

'After the way I've bin wiv yer?' Stymie queried.

'We all 'ave bad days now an' then,' she said smiling. 'You get it out an' I'll put the kettle on. A good strong cuppa might make yer feel better.'

'You're a diamond, luv,' Stymie told her with a big smile.

'I wish my ole man thought so,' she replied.

★

When Tommy told his mother about the man in the street she grabbed him tightly. 'Yer mustn't talk ter strangers,' she almost screamed.

'But I never, Mum,' he said quickly. 'Nor did Dennis. It was the Brady bruvvers who spoke to 'im. It was them who gave 'im our names.'

Nell took a deep breath in an effort to control her nerves. 'We'll 'ave ter report this ter the police, an' I want you ter stay in the 'ouse fer the time bein'. D'you understand?'

'Aw, Mum,' Tommy groaned.

'Never mind about "aw Mum". It's yer safety we're talkin' about. I don't fink you realise the seriousness of all this.'

Tommy slumped down in the armchair. 'It could 'a' bin real,' he remarked.

'We don't know, do we?'

'We could do, if we found out whevver any o' the churches round 'ere was finkin' o' gettin' up a party,' he suggested.

Nell saw the sense in her son's thinking. 'I'll 'ave a word wiv Josie when she gets 'ome,' she said nodding. 'An' if I don't see the bobby in the street by the time she gets in I'm gonna go down Dock'ead police station.'

At four o'clock PC Woodhouse strolled into Quay Street for the umpteenth time that day on his special patrol and was immediately accosted by Nell Bailey, who had been watching out for him from her parlour window. When she told him what had happened his face grew dark. 'I don't like the sound of it,' he told her. 'I'm due back at the station in 'alf an hour. I'll report it then. In the meantime keep the lad in the 'ouse an' yer front door shut. I'll make a few inquiries at the Catholic church in Dock'ead on me way back ter the station an' I'll look in at the Methodist church just up the road. I'll pop in on me way 'ome ter let yer know the outcome. An' try ter stay calm. This might be genuine.'

When Josie came home at ten minutes past five Nell was waiting, and after she had told her what was going on the young woman took the initiative. 'All right, the bobby's callin' in at the Catholic church an' the Methodist one in Jamaica Road, but there's anuvver one nearby, don't ferget, the Anglican church in St James's Road. Put me tea in the oven, Mum, I'll go there right away.'

As Josie left the house Johnny Francis was coming into the turning from the River Lane end, and when he spotted her he hurried up. She heard his footsteps behind her as she turned into Jamaica Road and she looked over her shoulder.

'Josie, where are you off to?' he asked. 'I wanna talk.'

'Not now, Johnny,' she said irritably, 'I'm goin' somewhere.'

'Yeah, I can see that,' he said smiling. 'I won't delay yer. Just let me walk wiv yer fer a few minutes.'

Josie did not want to lose any time arguing with him and she shrugged her shoulders as he fell into step beside her. 'As a matter o' fact I'm goin' ter the Anglican church in St James's Road,' she told him.

They reached the traffic island and hurried across the wide, busy thoroughfare and the young man gave her a puzzled look. 'Why the Anglican church? You don't go ter that church.'

Josie knew that she had to satisfy his curiosity or be plagued with questions. 'There was a man in the street this afternoon talkin' ter the kids. 'E said 'e was takin' names fer a party the church was givin' but it seemed suspicious. We told the policeman an' 'e's checkin' the Dock'ead churches so I'm doin' this one.'

Johnny Francis glanced at her. 'I got a job by the way. I start Monday.'

'I'm pleased for yer,' Josie replied. 'What will yer be doin'?'

'It's just a ware'ouse job in Tooley Street, but it's a start,' he remarked. 'It's only light work.'

They were walking under the wide railway bridge in St James's Road and a train rumbled overhead, making conversation difficult. 'Look, I'm sorry if I offended yer over Billy, but I meant what I said about bein' serious about yer.' Josie did not catch his words and remained silent. 'I mean it,' he said sharply, taking her by the arm as they came out of the long arch.

Josie pulled away. 'Leave it,' she said angrily.

He shrugged and followed her as she turned into the church gardens. 'I'll wait 'ere for yer,' he said, taking a packet of cigarettes from his coat pocket.

A few minutes later the young woman emerged from the church and Johnny got up and stubbed out his cigarette under his foot. 'What they say?' he asked.

Josie shook her head, trying to hide the panic she felt inside. 'They're not givin' a party,' she told him.

He stepped up close and took her by the shoulders as they stood in the deserted gardens. 'Did you 'ear what I said, Josie? I am tryin' ter let yer see I'm serious about yer.'

'Johnny, yer wastin' yer time,' she answered quickly, her hands coming up against his muscular chest.

He resisted her efforts to break free, pulling her tightly to him. 'I need yer, Josie,' he said in a husky voice.

He forced his lips on hers and she felt his strong arms round her protesting body and the pressure against her hips. 'Stop it,' she gasped as she drew her head back. 'Johnny, you're 'urtin' me.'

'So there is some fire in there after all,' he said breathlessly, his face contorted in a lopsided grin. 'You need me, Josie. You need a man, not a mouse. Come on, I'll show yer what it's all about.'

Suddenly she felt frightened as he pulled her towards the high foliage at the side of the church. His strength was overpowering and though she tried to pull away he half carried her on to the grass and stumbled into the thick laurel bushes. Josie fell on to her back and he quickly reached out and pinned her by her wrists, his lecherous smile striking sheer terror into her. He had gone berserk and was going to rape her. She attempted to turn on to her side but he was leaning heavily down on her and trying to push his knee between her legs. 'No, Johnny! Please!' she gasped. 'Don't!'

He pulled her wrists up over her head and crossed her arms, pinioning her with one hand as he reached down and slid her cotton dress up over her thighs. She felt his hot hand touching her between her legs and his heavy breath on her flushed cheeks. 'No, please!' she cried. He tried to pull her knickers down but the material split, and with a supreme effort she managed to get one hand free. The blow on the side of his face was hard and it enraged him. His lips found her open mouth and he kissed her savagely until she thought she was going to faint. He was rubbing against her now, and she hit him again. This time her clenched fist cracked against the bridge of his nose and his head jerked backwards. Turning quickly on to her side she brought her legs up and savagely kicked out at him. He rolled away from her and dragged himself up on to his feet. 'You little tease,' he sneered as he felt his nose.

Josie staggered to her feet, adjusting her dress and short coat with trembling hands. 'I never gave you any encouragement, you bastard,' she said in a tearful rage as they both stepped back on to the gravel path.

'Go back ter that dozy git,' Johnny snarled. ''E's welcome ter yer.'

Josie felt herself shaking violently as she watched him slouch off, and for a time she sat on a bench in the gardens while she tried to pull herself together. She had come so close to being raped and she dreaded the thought of having to see him again.

It was inevitable though. They lived in the same small street and she could hardly avoid bumping into him at some time or other.

An old man came into the gardens walking a dog and Josie got up and made her way out into the street. She had to put the ordeal out of her mind. There were other, more important, things to deal with and she had to be strong.

When she arrived home Josie's worst fears were realised. PC Woodhouse had called in as promised and told Nell that neither of the other churches had any parties planned. The most likely conclusion had to be faced: what had the stranger been doing in Quay Street if not to find out in which house the Baileys lived.

Chapter Thirty

Stymie Smith got out of bed early on Thursday morning and hurriedly got himself ready for work. Today was going to be a bumper day, he told himself as he munched on a slice of burnt toast and washed it down with tea. The streets around Long Lane were likely to yield a few bits and pieces and with the buildings in Crispin Street getting ready for the demolition men the departing tenants would no doubt have a few things to get rid of.

The realisation that the *South London Gazette* was coming out today worried him but he tried to put it to the back of his mind. It was all a storm in a teacup. The totters at Pollock Street would surely see that he was only trying to be helpful in shouting their corner.

'Come on, you ole flea-bag,' Stymie growled as he tried to slip the halter over the horse's head. 'Come on, don't balls me about, we got work ter do. Now come on, keep still. Get off me foot, yer dopey lump o' cat's meat!'

With some persuasion, some pushing and pulling and much cursing Stymie managed to get the harness on the animal and manoeuvre him between the shafts of the cart. 'What's the matter wiv yer this mornin'?' he growled. 'Yer've 'ad yer oats an' I've given yer stall a good muckout. Yer never satisfied lately.'

The horse turned his head and looked at the totter with large doleful eyes, and Stymie shook his head as he climbed up on to the cart and clicked his tongue. Benny did not attempt to move and he needed a sharp flick of the reins to remind him that there was work to do.

At the first paper shop in Jamaica Road the totter bought a *Gazette* and immediately saw the picture of the Pollock Street arches on the front page. Above it the caption read: 'Pollock Street's Totters Fight With Southern Railway'. The article beneath described in lurid detail the decrepit state of the lock-ups and said that the general dealers who rented the premises were up in arms over the lack of maintenance. It went on to name Seth Smith as the totters' spokesman, who had voiced the opinion that the men there should do something radical to alleviate their plight.

Stymie threw the newspaper into the back of the cart in disgust. 'That's put the cat amongst the pigeons,' he told his disinterested horse.

Still feeling troubled by the article, Stymie decided to go along to Pollock Street and try to put things right, and when he arrived the men were waiting. ''Ere 'e comes,' one shouted out.

'Go on, piss orf. You ain't welcome 'ere, yer mouthy git,' another called out.

Stymie got down from his cart and faced the angry men. 'Look, I'm very sorry but I only wanted ter support yers,' he told them. 'Anyway the prat misquoted me. I never said all that.'

'You dropped us right in it,' the first man said scornfully. 'The railway people are comin' round 'ere terday an' their tails are up, I can tell yer. It'll be your fault if they chuck us all out.'

'They won't do that,' Stymie said encouragingly.

''Ow the bloody 'ell d'you know what they'll do or won't do? Go on – piss orf.'

Stymie shook his head sadly and climbed back on to his cart. 'All I can say is, if none of yer ain't got the guts ter stand up to 'em then yer deserve ter be chucked out.'

The second totter stepped forward and gave Stymie's horse a hard slap on the rump, shouting loudly as he did so.

The nag was not used to that sort of treatment and he set off at a fast trot, almost unseating Stymie who had to fight with the reins. He finally brought the animal under control but he still seemed unsettled and it required all the totter's expert skill to keep him to a normal gait.

By teatime Stymie was feeling less upset. The jaunt to Long Lane had proved to be profitable, and with his cart well laden he sat back and let his tired horse take him home. Benny too seemed to have all but shaken off the morning's tribulation, and now and then when he appeared to miss his step and break into a trot Stymie was soon able to calm him with a quick jerk on the reins.

Tommy Bailey had been reluctant to go out that day, having heard what was said when Josie returned from the church the previous evening, and Nell allowed him to take Dennis up to his room where they sat going through Tommy's large collection of comics and cigarette cards.

Nell checked the potatoes simmering on the gas-stove and stuck a fork in the shoulder of lamb in the hot oven, then called out, 'Tommy, yer friend'll 'ave ter go now, it's nearly teatime.'

She stood at the front door as Dennis crossed the street and saw Josie turn the corner. Her daughter looked pale, she thought, and she had been a little subdued when she got back last night. This whole business had obviously got to her. It had got to them all. Kathy had been tearful and reluctant to go to work that morning. They would have to be reassured, Nell told herself. Kathy would be in soon, and after the meal she would sit down and try to talk things over calmly and sensibly.

'Are you all right, luv? You look a bit peaky,' Nell remarked as Josie reached her.

'Yeah, it's bin very busy terday,' she replied. 'The phones 'ave not stopped ringin' an' I've got a bangin' 'eadache.'

'Never mind, luv, go in an' sit down,' Nell told her kindly. 'I'll get yer a nice cuppa while we're waitin' fer Kathy ter get 'ome.'

As they were about to go in the house a van drove into the turning, but with her mind preoccupied Nell did not pay it any attention. On any other day she would have wondered what a laundry van was doing coming into the street at that time of day. Normally deliveries and collections were made during the morning.

Josie called up the stairs and Tommy came bounding down. 'I bin goin' frew me comics wiv Dennis,' he told her.

Josie ruffled his hair. ''Ave yer been out terday?' she asked.

Tommy shook his head. 'Mum reckoned it wasn't a good idea, but she let Dennis come in.'

'It's better fer the time bein',' she replied, running a hand over her forehead. 'Once the police get all this sorted out we'll know where we stand. It don't do ter take chances in the meantime.'

'Yeah, but when d'yer fink it'll be okay fer me ter play out in the street again?' Tommy asked.

Josie shut her eyes tightly for a few moments against the throbbing inside her head. 'I really don't know, Tommy,' she sighed tiredly.

The knock on the front door sounded loudly just as Nell was taking the cooked shoulder of lamb out of the oven. 'Answer it, Josie, I got me 'ands full,' she called out. 'That gel of ours never takes 'er key wiv 'er.'

'I'll get it,' Tommy said.

As he reached the passage Josie caught him by the arm. 'I'll go,' she told him.

When she opened the front door there was a man standing on the step with a bag of washing held up in front of him and behind him stood the laundry van, its engine still running. 'Wrong 'ouse,' she said, going suddenly cold with terror as he lowered the bag and she saw the dark handkerchief over his face. Before she could slam the door he pushed his way inside, sending her sprawling, and grabbed Tommy. She tried to stop him by grabbing at his leg but he shoved her away and loped out of the house dragging Tommy with him in a neck lock. Nell screamed out in panic, dropping the baking tin as she dashed from the scullery. Quick as she was, the men were quicker, and as she and Josie reached the door Tommy was being bundled into the back of the van which then roared off into Jamaica Road, almost dragging Nell under the wheels as she made a grab for the nearside door handle.

It was over in seconds and Nell staggered back on to the kerb and raised her eyes to the sky as a scream of terror burst out of her. Josie was shaking violently as she held on to her mother and immediately the street was alive with people. Polly Seagram was the first to get to her. 'Nell! Nell! Whatever is it?!' she shouted at her.

'They've took Tommy!' the anguished woman cried out.

Bel and Chloe Fiddler came running. 'We saw 'em. It was that laundry van,' they said together.

'They forced their way in,' Nell gasped as she leant against the wall for support.

'Who? Why?' Polly asked, trying to make some sense out of what had happened.

'I saw the van,' Ginny Allen said as she came running over. 'It pulled in the street an' turned round at the end. I wondered what it was doin' 'ere.'

'Get the police! Now!' Nell shouted hysterically.

Bernie Seagram had followed his wife out of the house at the first scream and he ran along to the nearest phone box. Nell was being restrained by Josie and the Fiddler girls as she tried to set off after the van. 'Yer can't do anyfing, gel, leave it ter the police,' Ginny urged her.

'Get 'er inside,' Polly said quickly.

More people were arriving and they stood in a shocked group as they learned of the kidnapping, while inside the Baileys' home Polly took charge. 'Get 'er in that chair. Bel, put the kettle on. Chloe, fetch that cushion over. No, Josie, you sit down wiv yer mum.'

Kathy Bailey turned into Quay Street white-faced from the accident she had just witnessed in Jamaica Road and when she saw the crowd outside her house she thought she was going to faint. 'What's wrong?' she gasped.

'Someone's took Tommy,' Ginny told her.

'Took 'im! What d'yer mean took 'im?' Kathy's voice broke and she dashed indoors.

'I was in the scullery doin' the tea,' Nell blurted out breathlessly as she dabbed at her eyes. 'There was a knock an' these men forced their way in, pushed Josie over an' grabbed Tommy. They forced 'im inter the back o' the laundry van an' drove off. I tried ter stop 'em but they were too quick. I couldn't do anyfing. Oh my God, what's gonna 'appen to 'im?'

Kathy broke down in tears and Polly put her arms around her. 'Never mind, luv, the police'll soon get 'im back.'

Chloe had her arm around Josie who was shaking with sobs. 'Where's that tea, Bel?' she shouted out.

'I saw the van drive out the turnin',' Kathy cried. 'It tore

311

off an' smashed right inter Stymie Smith's 'orse. I never realised our Tommy was inside. 'Ow could I?'

'Course yer couldn't,' Polly said quietly as she patted the distraught young woman's back. 'Yer couldn't 'ave done anyfing anyway.'

PC Woodhouse came hurrying into the parlour. 'The all-car call's gone out,' he told Nell. 'Every police car fer miles around'll be on the look-out. They won't get far. Are yer feelin' up ter givin' me a statement, luv?'

Stymie hummed a tune as he sat slumped on the cart. He could see the turning up ahead and was looking forward to putting his feet up for a while after such an eventful day. The horse plodded on, holding his head low, the way he invariably did when he was feeling ready for the stall.

''Ad a good day then?' the paper seller shouted out as Stymie drove by.

Distracted for a moment or two the totter nodded and smiled at him and when he saw the van accelerating towards him out of the turning he yanked desperately at the reins but it was too late. The vehicle swung across his path and smacked into the horse with a loud thud before roaring off. Sparks flew from the hooves scraping against the flint cobblestones as the animal crumpled in a heap. He lay there in the roadway shuddering and Stymie knew instantly that he had been dealt a mortal blow. People came running and stood looking helplessly as the totter jumped down from his seat and knelt down beside the stricken creature. 'It's all right, Benny. You'll be all right,' he said hoarsely as he stared in horror at the broken leg and severely torn flank. Tears fell as he tried to cradle the horse's head on his lap. 'I'll need a vet,' he said to the man who had knelt down beside him.

'I'll phone the police, guv,' he replied kindly with a sympathetic look. 'They'll fetch the vet.'

''E was a bloody maniac comin' out o' the turnin' like that,' Stymie growled. 'I'll kill the bastard if I get me 'ands on 'im.'

'I saw exactly what happened,' the man said as he got up. 'I'll give the police a statement. You never had a chance.'

'Nor did poor Benny,' Stymie mumbled as the man went off to use the phone.

The crowd stood silently watching as the horse lay shaking, and Stymie gently rubbed his hand down his neck. 'There, there, lay still, me ole mate. Don't try ter move. That's right, take it easy, we'll soon 'ave you out o' yer pain.'

The watchers saw the tears drop on to the animal's head as the distraught totter bent over him. 'They'll 'ave ter shoot him,' one remarked.

Stymie lifted his head, unable to focus on the speaker through his brimming eyes. 'Yeah, they'll 'ave ter shoot him,' he gulped. 'What a way ter go. 'E didn't ask fer much, only a nosebag o' chaff an' a few sugar lumps now an' then. That ain't much to ask for, is it?' he said as he let his head drop on to the animal's twitching neck.

The police van pulled up followed by a high-sided lorry and the police driver got out and laid a hand on Stymie's shoulder. 'Come on, ole son. It's not nice we know, but it's gotta be done.'

Stymie gripped Benny tightly round his neck. 'I can't let yer,' he sobbed.

'Come on, lad, pull yerself tergevver,' the policeman said quietly. 'Yer wouldn't want the animal sufferin' unnecessarily.'

As the policeman led Stymie away two men climbed down from the lorry carrying a folded screen which they placed around the dying creature. A few seconds later a shot rang out and the vet emerged with a small canvas bag tucked under his arm. The lorry then drove into an adjacent turning and reversed out towards the dead horse. The men lowered the ramp and capably they secured the animal's hooves to heavy chains and winched it up on to the lorry.

'Where d'yer live, mate?' the policeman asked as he stood by the totter's side.

'In there, Quay Street,' Stymie told him, pointing. 'I was almost 'ome, till that maniac tore out o' the turnin'.'

'Yeah, we're lookin' fer that van,' the policeman remarked. 'It's bin involved in a kidnappin'.'

'When yer catch 'im just let me 'ave five minutes wiv 'im,' Stymie growled through clenched teeth.

'We'd better get yer cart sorted out,' the officer replied. 'We can't leave it there. We'll get a tow rope on it an' pull it in the turnin'.'

It took less than fifteen minutes from the first all-cars call to find the laundry van. It had been left on a cleared bombsite in Rotherhithe. Beside it the police found the bound and gagged driver. He was in a state of shock and unable to help them very much. All he could remember was a sudden whack on the head as he was throwing a bundle of washing into the rear of his van. He had woken up in complete darkness and found he could not move a muscle, and after a seeming eternity he was lifted out of what he guessed to be a car boot and thrown roughly down by the side of his vehicle. His attackers then carried someone who was bound hand and foot from the van and into the car which roared off immediately. 'I couldn't do anyfing to 'elp,' the driver said, 'so I just stayed quiet, like I was still unconscious.'

'Which was a good move on your part,' the detective told him. 'If they'd not thought you were still out cold they might well have put a bullet in your head. Dead men can't talk.'

★

Commander Jock Barratt heard about the kidnapping at the same time as the police call went out and he summoned his small team together at the most convenient of venues, the Dockhead police station. Chief Inspector Malkin was present as well as his assistant Detective Sergeant Black and the local beat bobby, PC Woodhouse.

'You have all been briefed and know the seriousness of this kidnapping business, gentlemen,' Barratt frowned. 'I'm afraid that our ploy to protect the boy didn't work, but we had to give it a try. The latest news is that the laundry van was found a few minutes ago on a Rotherhithe bombsite with the driver beside it bound and gagged. He'd been stowed in the boot of the car which the kidnappers switched to.'

A phone at Barratt's elbow rang and he picked it up quickly. His face grew dark as he listened to the caller then he put the receiver down with a sigh. 'That was Traffic Section. Apparently the car had been stolen from a lock-up garage in Streatham,' he informed the gathering. 'It was found in Greenwich Park. They've made another switch eastwards, which could mean anything. There's the Blackwall Tunnel nearby as well as the main routes to Kent and the south coast. We need a miracle, gentlemen,' he said heavily. 'If they're using another stolen car we might hit lucky, but if the switch was to a legally-owned car then our job is going to be all that much harder. We have to pray that tonight's police broadcast will jog someone's memory. Any scrap of information would be a help.'

Inspector Malkin raised his hand for attention. 'It's pretty obvious that someone was watching the house,' he said. 'It's only the third one in Quay Street and easily seen from a vantage point in Jamaica Road. They must have known that the boy was at home, and who would question a laundry van in the turning?'

Commander Barratt looked around slowly at the group. 'Gentlemen, we are dealing with desperate and clever people here,' he said in a measured voice, 'and we've got to match them. From now on forget everything you're working on except this case. I want two hundred per cent from all of you.' Then he turned to PC Woodhouse. 'Constable, would you call in again at the Baileys' for a few minutes. Try to do what you can to reassure the poor woman that we're devoting all our energy to solving this business speedily and safely.' He looked towards Malkin once more. 'James, we'll need to bring the Stepney police in now. You and I'll go over there and brief them personally as soon as we leave here. Mackinnon, I'll want to take another look at that report you submitted on the Lighterman public house. We're now obliged to show our hand and we've got to make sure it pays off. We'll need to locate and talk to the boy's father, and that woman the boy said accosted him outside the pub, and any other soul who might be of some assistance, such as the nightwatchman in charge of those tugs. He must know something he hasn't told us. I'll want the landlord, the barman and other staff made available for questioning too. The lack of substance in the report worries me, and in saying that I'm in no way blaming you, Mack. It just seems to me there's a wall of silence between us and them. We'll be obliged to put the screws on, and if we spell out the penalties for harbouring and abetting kidnappers it might loosen a few tongues. I'll go over your report again on the way to Stepney. Right then, let's get going.'

Chapter Thirty-One

The inevitable air-raid siren and the throaty roar as a flying bomb flew overhead seemed suddenly almost unimportant to the people of Quay Street. Fate had dealt a severe blow to one of their own and they felt inextricably involved as both friends and neighbours.

'Now you understand why I couldn't say anyfing before,' Nell tearfully explained to her best friend Polly Seagram. 'It doesn't matter now. We've just gotta wait an' 'ope an' pray they find our Tommy quickly. That poor little sod'll be terrified. They wouldn't 'urt a little boy, would they, Polly?'

'Course they won't,' Polly said patting her friend's back gently.

'Tommy saw their faces though,' Nell went on fearfully. 'Those sort o' people stop at nuffink.'

Polly took Nell's hot hands in hers and looked into her frightened eyes. 'Now, you listen ter me,' she said quietly. 'From what yer just told me those people are plottin' ter kill someone important, an' while they're 'oldin' your Tommy they know that they can't be identified. Once they've done what they intend ter do they'll set 'im free an' they'll be out the country.'

'You're assumin' a lot,' Nell replied.

'Believe me, luv,' Polly said calmly. 'Nuffink bad's gonna 'appen ter young Tommy. I know. I get a feelin' about fings at times, as you well know. Trust me an' keep believin'. Tommy's gonna be back 'ome before long, you mark my words.'

Josie had been listening quietly, her arm around her mother's heaving shoulders. 'I'll 'ave ter go over ter Stepney an' tell Dad,' she said. ''E's gotta know.'

'You go on, luv,' Polly told her. 'Yer mum'll be all right. I won't leave 'er till yer get back.'

Nell reached out and grabbed Josie's arm. 'No, don't go over there ternight,' she said anxiously. 'It'll be dark before yer get back an' I don't want you out in the dark. There'll be time enough ter tell yer farvver termorrer.'

Josie sat back down on the arm of her mother's easy chair. 'All right, Mum, I'll wait till termorrer. I won't be goin' in ter work anyway. I just wish Billy was 'ere. 'E could 'ave taken me over there.'

'What time will 'e get 'ome?' Nell asked.

'It'll be very late,' Josie replied. 'They're rewirin' a big manor 'ouse down in Kent an' they're workin' overtime on it.'

'Don't worry, it's best left till termorrer ter tell yer farvver anyway,' Nell said as she wiped her eyes. 'At least then yer might be able ter make 'im understand what's 'appened.'

The totters of Pollock Street were gathered together in one of the arches and their elder spokesman, Danny Gillett, was addressing them. 'Okay, so Stymie took quite a bit on 'is shoulders in blabbin' 'is mouth off to the newspaper an' it could 'ave worked against us, but it didn't,' he was saying. 'The geezer from the Southern Railway was pretty sympathetic, considerin' everyfing that 'ad bin said, an' that idea of 'is ter put up some corrugated sheets under the arches'll certainly 'elp. We ain't bein' chucked out so I fink we should bury the 'atchet an' take stock ter see what we can do to 'elp one of our own when 'e needs it.'

'I'm all fer that,' Jack Dunkley remarked. 'I was on the ovver side o' the road an' I saw the accident 'appen. I got off the cart an' went over. Stymie didn't see me but I stood there watchin'. The poor sod was beside 'imself the same as we'd be if it 'appened to any of us. Stymie loved that ole nag.'

'Was the cart damaged?' Fred Catlin asked.

'Not a mark on it,' Dunkley told him.

Danny Gillett held his hand up for order. 'Right, lads, what can we do to 'elp the poor bugger?'

'We could 'ave a whip round 'an see if ole Tubby Carmody'll sell us 'is 'orse,' Jack Dunkley suggested. 'Tubby said 'e was callin' it a day, what wiv 'is age an' 'is bad back.'

'I 'eard 'e's already promised Scratcher Morris the 'orse-an'-cart,' Catlin replied.

'Not that lousy no-good bastard,' Dunkley growled. 'Scratcher ain't one of us. Never gives us the time o' day, an' if 'e thought there was somefing goin' 'e'd go out of 'is way ter make sure none of us got a look-in.'

Fred Catlin turned to a tall lean totter who was chewing on a wad of tobacco. ''Ere, Percy, you know Tubby better than any of us. Is there a chance you could sound 'im out? If yer tell 'im about what's 'appened ter Stymie 'e might come good.'

Percy Cadman spat out a stream of tobacco juice in the direction of the arches' cat, who appeared to be taking an interest in what was going on. 'Yeah, I'll give 'im a try,' he said nonchalantly. 'I'll pop round an' see 'im this evenin'.'

Ben Thorburn had called an emergency meeting at his Stepney house on Thursday evening and Holman and Anderson sat grim-faced as they listened.

'We've got the boy and he's in a safe place,' he told

them. 'We'll just have to wait now for the cadre to make a decision.'

'I don't like it,' Holman declared. 'We're digging our own graves if you ask me.'

'What else could we do?' Thorburn said turning on him. 'If the boy was able to identify us we'd all swing for treason.'

'Granted, if we were picked up and put on an identification parade,' Holman replied. 'But none of us are known to the police or MI5. To all intents and purposes we're respectable businessmen. Why should they pick us up?'

'You forget the night in the Lighterman when I spoke to the landlord about hiring a room and he had a word with the tug nightwatchman,' Thorburn reminded him.

'Christ!' Anderson exclaimed. 'He knows you, knows your name. What if he talks?'

'It's all right for the moment,' Thorburn said calmly. 'I've already primed him. I told him that the CID would be making inquiries about one of the tugs being used for a meeting and they were under the misapprehension that the men taking part might be foreign agents, after someone with a grudge had lied to the police about overhearing them. I warned him of the consequences, for him as well as me, if the police linked me with the meeting that night, considering that it was he who organised it through the nightwatchman. I frightened him. He was scared stiff of being implicated and he told me that as far as he's concerned he knows nothing about a meeting.'

'What about the nightwatchman?' Holman cut in. 'Have you talked to him?'

Thorburn's face creased into a strange smile. 'I don't think the police will get anyfing out of the watchman,' he replied.

Holman and Anderson both looked intently at their host.

'What makes you so sure?' Holman asked.

'Look, let's not waste time going into details about him,'

Thorburn replied. 'Just accept that the nightwatchman's of no danger to us.'

Anderson remained impassive, believing that the end fully justified the means, but Holman was feeling sick to his stomach. Kidnapping and murder, on top of treason, was more than he could tolerate and he felt he had to protest. 'Look, we have to decide here and now what we actually do with the boy,' he said firmly. 'We can't just kill him under orders.'

'What other choice is there?' Thorburn put it to him. 'After the assassination takes place the police and the secret service will be pulling in anyone on their lists who they feel might have been implicated. How can we be totally sure that some, or indeed all of us, are not on those lists? Each of us was active on the Mosley marches in our younger days and some of us have had our names taken by the police. I certainly have. All right, I can plead, as we all could, that that was when we were young and ignorant, and we've long since renounced any ties with the Fascists, but you have to remember that I live here in Stepney, very near to Stepney Reach where the meeting took place. The authorities might put me up on an ID parade just to eliminate me. For that reason alone the boy has to be silenced.'

Anderson looked at each of the others in turn. 'We have to accept another possibility, that our organisation might be known to the authorities despite all our efforts to the contrary,' he said, 'and even though we can plead that it's nothing more than an old boys' club, the members' names would tie up with old lists of Mosley supporters. Circumstantial, yes, but not if the boy's allowed to pick any of us out. We'd be investigated and implicated.'

'There is an alternative,' Holman said, desperately trying to elicit a change of heart. 'We could release the boy after the assassination, with a warning that if he was asked to go on an ID parade he must not pick any of us out, on pain of being taken again and killed for sure. We could even tell him it applied to his family too. I'm sure he'd never dare to defy us then.'

'But we couldn't be sure,' Thorburn answered quickly. 'Once the secret service people got to him they'd give all sorts of promises to make him go along with their plans.'

Holman slumped down in his seat, knowing he had been defeated. They were getting in deeper by the hour and as far as he could see, at the end of it all, there would be nothing but a stout rope and a long drop for them all. The boy was going to die and there was nothing he could do about it.

While the Stepney police were engaged in a thorough search of the area in an attempt to find Tommy Bailey, a purposely low-key investigation began in a back room at the Lighterman public house, where the interviewees were simply told that they might be able to throw some light on the kidnapping of a young boy who had been in the area. The landlord of the establishment, Patrick Brierley, was the first to be questioned and said that as far as he was concerned there were no strange faces in the pub on the night in question. Pushed further he told Commander Barratt that his pub was a place which seemed to draw all sorts of customers who were interested for one reason or another in visiting the seedy dock area, but on that particular night it had been rather quiet. He was able to give the name of the woman who had spoken to Tommy Bailey outside the pub, and later she was brought in. She was clearly under the influence of drink but nevertheless seemed to have a clear recall. She had not seen any strange faces around that night, she maintained; she had talked to the boy and told him that his father was not in the pub, but she had not seen him go on the tug. 'Yes, I am a friend o' the lad's farvver,' she admitted, 'but there's nuffink in it. We're just good friends.'

'Do you know where the lad's father lives?' Commander Barratt asked her.

'No, I don't.'

He pressed her a little more and she told him that she knew the nightwatchman in charge of the tugs and to her knowledge he was honest and trustworthy.

During a short break in the proceedings Barratt discussed the progress with Inspector Malkin and Inspector Frank Roberts of the Stepney police and secret agent Joe Mackinnon. 'There's nothing of substance yet,' he told them, 'but we just have to press on. I'd quite like to ask that nightwatchman a few questions. He might give us the breakthrough we need. After all, he was in charge of the tugs. He would know if anyone went aboard one of them that night, even though he told you it was against company rules.'

Joe Mackinnon thought otherwise. He had made an initial foray to the East End pub to glean as much information as he could without revealing his identity, and during the evening he had managed to get into conversation with the nightwatchman. The old man had told him that he was allowed to use the pub while he was on duty as long as he checked now and then to make sure it was all quiet at the moorings. Mackinnon had asked him casually whether or not he ever let anyone look over the tugs and he replied emphatically that it was against the rules. The fact that the old man had sat in the pub for over two and a half hours without checking on the tugs made the agent feel that the watchman was unreliable and probably ignorant of what had gone on. Taking a more positive view though, if he was hiding something he might just decide to be a little more helpful when reminded that this was a serious business and aiding and abetting a crime of kidnapping carried a very heavy sentence.

'The landlord said he'll send the nightwatchman in as soon

as he arrives but it's getting late,' Malkin remarked. 'If he intended coming in at all he should be here by now.'

'And there's no answer at his flat. I think we'd better get the constable to check the moorings again,' Barratt replied.

The landlord looked into the room and said that a certain Albert Swan had just come in and might be of assistance in locating the boy's father.

'Yeah, me an' Frank Bailey go back a long way,' the old man told the commander once he had made himself comfortable, leaning back in the chair and crossing his legs.

'Can you give us his address?'

'Nah, 'cos 'e don't live there any more.'

'Do you know where he's currently living?'

'As a matter o' fact yer'll most likely find 'im at Don Brady's cooperage in Bell Street. Frank does a bit o' part-time work there an' I understand Don's fixed 'im up wiv a camp-bed on the premises.'

A policeman was immediately sent to Bell Street and while they waited for news of Frank Bailey they learned that the old nightwatchman had been located. His body was discovered in the cellar of a bomb-ruined house by an inquisitive dog who stood barking over the hole. The old man's head was caved in and it posed yet one more problem for Commander Barratt and his team. Had the night-watchman fallen into the cellar whilst drunk, or had he been deliberately killed?

The delegation to Quay Street late on Thursday evening looked somewhat shamefaced as they entered the little turning, and seeing that the yard was locked they knocked on Stymie's front door.

'Sorry ter disturb yer at this time o' night, Stymie,' Danny Gillett said. 'We 'eard what 'appened an' we've come to offer our condolences. Jack Dunkley 'ere saw the accident 'appen as 'e was passin' by. We may 'ave 'ad our differences but we're all totters tergevver, so me an' the lads decided it was time to offer some 'elp instead o' hard words.'

Stymie lowered his head for a few moments feeling overcome by their gesture. Bel was standing behind him and she put her hand on his shoulder. 'That's nice of 'em, Stymie,' she said.

He raised his head and gave the spokesman a weak smile. 'Yeah, I appreciate it,' he replied.

'The lads 'ave 'ad a bit of a whip-round, Stymie, an' they've managed ter raise enough dosh ter get yer anuvver 'orse,' Danny told him. 'As a matter o' fact it's Tubby Carmody's, but Tubby's gonna call it a day 'cos 'is back ain't none too clever, so we persuaded 'im ter let us 'ave it. It was Percy Cadman's doin' actually. 'E told 'im about what'd 'appened an' persuaded 'im ter sell it to us at cut price.'

Stymie looked shocked. 'I dunno what ter say,' he fumbled.

'Try sayin' fanks, lads,' Bel prompted him.

'Yeah fanks, lads. I'm just up to 'ere,' he said holding a hand up to his throat. 'It's really bloody nice of yer.'

Danny smiled and looked around at the assembled company. 'I fink this calls fer a drink, lads,' he said. 'We got a bit o' time before the pubs close. Yer welcome ter join us if yer want to, Stymie.'

The Quay Street totter shook his head. 'I don't fink it'd be proper, not ternight, not so soon after Benny's . . .'

Bel's hand tightened on his shoulder as he lowered his head again with grief. 'Fanks fer everyfing, lads,' she told them.

Stymie suddenly straightened up, a hard look glinting in his grey eyes. 'Before yer go, lads, I gotta tell yer somefing you should know,' he began. 'The van that knocked Benny down 'ad a kid locked up inside it. Yeah, that's right. Young Tommy Bailey who lives at the ovver end o' the street was kidnapped this evenin'. 'E's only firteen.'

'Look, why don't yer come in fer a cuppa an' we can put yer in the picture,' Bel suggested.

When the whole, extraordinary story had been told the totters had some practical ideas of their own. 'Look, we've got connections the ovver side o' the water an' us totters get ter know fings ovvers don't,' Danny Gillett said between sips of his tea. 'We can suss fings that don't seem kosher too. It comes wiv scrapin' an' scroungin' a livin'. We can spend a couple o' days scourin' the Stepney area, providin' we let the Stepney boys know in advance, in case they fink we're musclin' in on them.'

'They'd 'elp too,' Fred Catlin added. 'They're a good crowd, from what I remember of 'em at that 'orse-an'-cart show we all went to.'

'I'm out first fing termorrer,' Stymie told them with a face like thunder. 'I wanna get my 'ands on the bastard who killed Benny an' when I do . . .'

'Take it easy, luv, the boys know 'ow yer must feel,' Bel said quietly.

'Talkin' about goin' over Stepney, you ain't finkin' o' leggin' it round the area are yer?' Danny Gillett queried.

'Well, I ain't got a bike,' Stymie said in a weak attempt at humour.

'If yer can wait till after we collect Tubby's 'orse yer'll be able ter use the cart,' Danny told him. 'All bein' well we should 'ave it round 'ere about ten o'clock.'

'Well, that's very nice of yer, I 'ave ter say,' Stymie remarked with emotion creeping into his gruff voice.

It was dark as the Pollock Street delegation made their way home, and the lights burned on into the long night at number 6. Nell Bailey had been persuaded to try and get a few hours' sleep but Josie had decided to stay up in case someone called with news. She sat next to Billy on the settee, her head resting on his shoulder. Kathy had insisted on staying up too but she had finally fallen asleep in the armchair. Polly Seagram had stayed until after midnight when she was finally persuaded to go home and get some rest herself. The neighbours had been calling all evening to offer their support and help, and Wilco Johnson had vowed to go over the water himself to find his old drinking partner. Now, in the dead of night, with only an occasional tug whistle and the muted sound of a train to be heard, Josie found some comfort in Billy's arms as the questions rushed through her tortured mind. Was Tommy still alive? Had they harmed him? How was it all going to end?

Chapter Thirty-Two

Frank Bailey had been in a drunken sleep when the policeman arrived late at night and Don Brady had to be woken up for the constable to gain entry to the cooperage. Their attempts to rouse the inebriate failed and it was the next morning when Frank finally learned about his son's abduction.

'It's all my fault,' he groaned as he sat on the edge of the camp bed with his head in his hands. 'The lad came lookin' fer me an' now I don't even know if 'e's still alive.'

'Get the rest o' that coffee down yer,' Don Brady told him crossly. 'Yer gotta pull yerself tergevver.'

Commander Barratt had been up most of the night and he was feeling very uncharitable as he stood over the drunk. 'Yes, it was partly your fault,' he said in a measured tone of voice, 'but it's happened, and there's nothing you can do to turn back the clock. What you can do is get your sozzled head under a cold tap and then take a shave, and get something inside you, man – food I mean – before you go home to your family.'

Frank looked up at the operative from MI5. 'I couldn't face Nell, nor the gels,' he groaned. 'I just couldn't.'

Don Brady had heard enough. 'Now you listen 'ere, you scruffy, drunken bastard,' he raged. 'Everybody's fed up wiv panderin' ter you. I am, fer one. I gave yer chance after chance an' yer let me down. Yer told me you was finally off the booze, an' like an idiot I believed yer. Is this what yer call bein' off the booze?' The cooper picked up the empty whisky bottle by the foot of the bed and threw it hard against the far wall, and Frank winced as it shattered. 'Now you do as the man said, an' then get yerself over ter yer family, or I swear ter God yer'll 'ave me ter deal wiv, Frank.'

Jock Barratt smiled appreciatively at the cooper's tirade, then he looked down again at the drunk. 'I'll be going back to Bermondsey myself this morning,' he told him. 'I'll be back in an hour and if you're ready I'll drop you off. So you'd better get moving, don't you think?'

Tommy Bailey had endured his terrifying ordeal with his heart thumping against his ribcage, but he had been determined not to let the two men who sat with him inside the laundry van see him cry. 'Big lads don't cry,' his father had often told him.

Now, as he sat on an upturned wooden crate in a damp airless room that had once served as an office, Tommy took stock. The initial journey, during which he was bound hand and foot, had not taken long, and then he had been carried from the van and thrown into the roasting hot boot of a car. He had struggled to breathe properly until he was unceremoniously dragged out and then dumped into the boot of another car. It had been less hot, with a draught coming from somewhere underneath him and he had lain there trying to stay calm. The journey had ended in a factory or warehouse yard and he had been bundled up some stairs and into the room where the bindings were removed. He was ordered to stay quiet or else, and the young lad did as he was told, frightened by the cold, menacing look in the man's eyes as he left, turning a grating key in the lock. What were they going to do to him, Tommy wondered? Trying hard not to panic, the young lad looked around the room and noticed another door, hanging from only one hinge, and he found that it led to an evil-smelling toilet. He wanted to cry, but he clenched his teeth until his jaw hurt. He knew he had to be grown-up and not provoke his captors into harming him. The police would be looking for him, and his dad would be searching too, once he found out what had happened. They'd find him soon.

Tommy looked up disconsolately at the one high window which had been crudely boarded up and still allowed some daylight in. Over his head a bare electric light bulb hung from the ceiling by a frayed flex, and he tried the wall switch with no response. He began to feel tired and hungry and his mouth had become very dry, and it seemed like hours before he heard the key in the lock once more. His cold-eyed gaoler brought him a glass of milk and a cheese sandwich which he bit into gratefully, but when he asked where he was the man grew angry. 'Shut yer noise up an' eat yer grub,' he was ordered. 'It could be some time before yer get anyfing else.'

Later the man brought him a pallet filled with straw and a blanket and he was told to get to sleep. The room was becoming dark as the sun descended and Tommy tried to settle down, hoping this was all just a bad dream and he would wake up in his own little room, but the mattress was uncomfortable and he twisted and turned, becoming more frightened as he wondered whether he was going to die. They had kidnapped him for a purpose after all. They knew he could identify the men who had been on the tug and they would obviously hold on to him until they had carried out their plan to kill the important person. But what then? They would have to kill him to be sure he wouldn't talk, and if that was what they were going to do, why wait? They could have thrown him in the river while he was still tied up. Perhaps they had poisoned the milk or the sandwich.

Sheer terror made his heart hammer and his breath come in gasps, and Tommy fought back tears as he lay curled up in a corner of the damp room. A tug whistle sounded in the distance and for a moment he took heart. The warehouse could not be that far from the river and his dad would not be too far away either. He would find him and take him home and the police would arrest the kidnappers. It would all end up like it always did in the *Adventure* and the *Wizard*.

Sir Barry Freeman arrived in London early on Friday morning and met with Anderson for breakfast at the Savoy Grill. He looked very serious as he lit his first cigarette of the day, much too early for his liking, but something he had become prone to do during the last few days. Anderson too looked worried as he greeted the League's chairman.

'We had some difficulty with Holman,' he reported. 'He was totally against killing the boy and Thorburn and I had to spell it out to him that there was no alternative.'

'There is no other solution,' Freeman replied as he looked down at the glowing cigarette held between his podgy fingers. 'The cadre agreed last night.'

Anderson looked relieved. 'I was hoping for a speedy decision,' he said quietly. 'The sooner this business is over the better.'

Freeman nodded and drew deeply on his cigarette. 'We still have some time on our side though,' he remarked. 'The warehouse in Downtown Rotherhithe was a good choice, if I may say so. It's been derelict since the start of the Blitz and there are several escape routes from the property should they be needed. My information is that the Stepney police are working with secret service agents in scouring the Stepney and Wapping waterfront and there are a lot of disused properties to be checked out. Once they've finished they'll realise the Greenwich change-over was a ploy to make them think the kidnap route was through the Blackwall Tunnel to Stepney.'

Anderson sipped his coffee. 'They could be forgiven for thinking so,' he replied. 'Since we knew the area well enough to hold a meeting at Stepney Reach, they would have assumed that we'd know where to hide the boy.'

Freeman stubbed out his cigarette and poured himself some more coffee from a silver pot. 'Nevertheless, I under-stand that the Bermondsey police are already searching the Rotherhithe area, knowing that Downtown Rotherhithe is full of derelict warehouses and wharves, and considering that the kidnappers had very little time before the general call went out to the police patrol cars. I think we should get this busi-ness over immediately. How do you feel about it, Victor? Are you up to it?'

Anderson nodded and the leader drew out an envelope from his coat pocket. 'This'll take care of the men. There's a bonus added. They did a very efficient job, and bearing in mind they both have police records a mile long we'll have no worries about either of them blabbing.'

'This evening there's a high tide,' Anderson informed him. 'It'll be done then.'

'I want Thorburn and Holman to be present,' Freeman said, stirring his coffee. 'Thorburn would expect to be there in any case, but Holman might try to cry off. I have to say that he's become a source of worry for the cadre. He must be made to feel he's involved up to his neck, and maybe then we can all breathe a little easier.'

Anderson sat back in his chair with an amused look on his face. 'It's just occurred to me,' he said quietly. 'Today is the eighth of September.'

'I hadn't forgotten,' Freeman replied with a smile. 'Yes, the new weapon. Actually it'll be interesting to see what the public's reaction will be, considering the politicians' promises of late that the flying bomb menace will soon be over now that the sites in Europe are being overrun.'

With breakfast over, Sir Barry Freeman left the Savoy Grill in a taxi, and as he made his way to his offices in the City he sought to put the League's immediate business out of his mind. It had to be done, he told himself. One life against the lives of many. One small life cut short to ensure the continuity of the League and their hopes of achieving a brave new Britain, which would lead the world once more and overcome the Jewish conspiracy and the growing threat of Communism.

The poster looked down at him as he climbed from the cab. The thick-set figure was wearing a Homburg and clasping a thick cigar in one hand, with two fingers of the other hand held up in a V sign. Freeman did not give it more than a cursory glance. He was still trying to put the League's immediate business out of his mind.

Josie had tried to persuade Kathy to go to work but she had only succeeded in reducing her younger sister to tears. ''Ow can I go ter work wiv our Tommy on me mind?' she sobbed. 'I wanna be 'ere in case there's any news. Mum needs me anyway.'

'All right,' Josie said softly. 'You look out fer Mum. I've gotta get over ter Stepney.'

Billy Emmerson had managed to catch a few hours' sleep and was now back and looking determined to get started.

'Are yer sure it's all right you not goin' ter work this mornin'?' Josie asked him.

Billy smiled. 'I'm goin' in the army next week,' he said with a chuckle. 'What can they do? Anyway they've already got me notice.'

Josie looked up at the clock. 'We'd better make a move,' she remarked.

There was a knock at the door and Nell looked up quickly with fear etched on her face. 'Please God it's not bad news,' she muttered shakily.

Josie's heart was pounding as she hurried out of the parlour and when she saw her father standing on the doorstep she gave out a strangled cry and fell into his open arms.

'The police told me about Tommy,' he said as he came into the house.

Nell had heard his voice and was out of her chair, her arms held out to him. 'You gotta get our Tommy back, Frank,' she sobbed as she went to him. 'I don't care about yer drinkin'. I don't care, just as long as yer stay 'ere wiv us. I was wrong ter turn you out. I know it now. I was more concerned about the neighbours than you. Josie knew I was wrong an' she told me lots o' times, but I wouldn't listen. I've bin such a selfish cow. I never thought about you an' what was 'appenin' to yer. I chucked you out when yer needed me an' I'm so sorry.'

Frank had buried his face in Nell's hair and he patted her back tenderly, glad that she could not see the tears welling up in his eyes. 'I'll get Tommy back some'ow,' he said firmly. 'An' yer don't 'ave ter worry about the drinkin'. I stopped fer sure now, an' may the good Lord strike off me arm if it lifts anuvver drink.'

'You gotta get our boy back, Frank,' Nell implored him as he held her closely in his arms.

'I'm gonna go look fer 'im straight away,' he told her. 'They couldn't 'ave gone very far. The police are searchin' all along the riverside ware'ouses an' wharves in Wappin' an' Stepney' an' I'm gonna try all the places on this side o' the water.'

Josie handed her father a mug of steaming tea. 'Yer better get this down yer first,' she remarked.

Polly Seagram was not one to stand on ceremony, and seeing that the Baileys' front door was open she strolled straight into the house. 'Mornin', luv,' she said brightly, and when she spotted Frank her face lit up. 'Nice ter see yer, Frank,' she told him.

Nell smiled at her through brimming tears. 'There's some tea in the pot, luv.'

Stymie Smith was overjoyed when he saw the lively grey pony. 'I dunno what ter say,' he whistled.

'You ain't gotta say anyfing,' Danny Gillett replied as he untied the rope which tethered the animal to the back of his cart. ''E's a good trotter. 'E certainly kept up wiv my ole beauty.'

'I'm just at a loss fer words,' Stymie said shaking his head. 'I'm gonna go lookin' fer Tommy Bailey right away an' I just 'ope I can find those bastards who took 'im. I'll swing fer 'em.'

'We're wiv yer,' Danny told him.

Stymie rubbed at his stubbled chin. 'I was finkin' about your offer,' he said. 'My gelfriend told me that accordin' ter the boy's muvver the police are scourin' the riverside over the water. If you can get the East End totters ter give 'em some 'elp we can start lookin' over this side. All right, I know it's like lookin' fer a needle in an 'aystack but we 'ave ter try. Bel, that's me gelfriend, she finks they could 'ave took the boy Downtown. It's werf a try, bearin' in mind the amount o' derelict ware'ouses there are in that area.'

'Sounds a good idea,' Danny replied. Then he turned to Fred Catlin. 'If I drop you off at the arch fer yer 'orse-an'-cart, can yer get over the water an' prime the lads up?' he asked.

'Sure fing,' Fred said nodding sternly.

'Right then, let's get started,' Stymie urged them. 'By the way, I wanna call at the Baileys' on the way out ter let the boy's muvver know what we're doin'.'

A few minutes later Danny Gillett drove his horse-and-cart out into Jamaica Road with Fred Catlin sitting by his side. Following close behind was Stymie, with Frank Bailey holding on to the seat rail tightly as the grey pony pulled the cart out into the morning traffic at a steady trot.

Chapter Thirty-Three

Everyone in Quay Street now knew the reason for Tommy Bailey's abduction and in their various ways they all attempted to aid and support the stricken family. Polly Seagram had become a fixture at number 6 and Ellie Woodley, Nell's other next-door neighbour, had insisted on taking over her ironing, which had begun to pile up. Wilco Johnson had called to say very dramatically that he was making his own inquiries over the water, and Nell accepted the gesture with forbearance. The man had been a drinking partner of Frank's and was still hardly ever sober, but a little help, however ludicrous it sounded coming from Wilco, was better than a lot of pity and she thanked him kindly.

Bel and Chloe Fiddler had both looked in on their way to work and then Sandra, the youngest of the three, called to ask if Kathy might like to come over that evening for a chat.

'What's the matter wiv 'er?' Kathy sneered angrily. 'There's our Tommy bin taken an' she wants me ter go over fer a chat. That's just like the Fiddlers. Silly as a box o' lights.'

Nell was trying to stay calm, constantly telling herself that everything was being done to find the lad. 'Don't be like that, Kathy,' she said quietly. 'The gel knows just 'ow yer must be feelin' an' that's why she asked yer over ternight. There's little any of 'em can do but they're all tryin' as best they can. Bel Fiddler was a big 'elp ter me last night, an' so was Chloe. Don't make 'em out ter be stupid.'

Kathy realised that she was being a little hasty and she nodded. 'Yeah I know, Mum,' she sighed. 'Sandra's nice really. She's funny, an' she was showin' me 'er dance band records the last time I was over there.'

Ginny Allen and Eileen Taylor called briefly to see how things were and later Nell was surprised to see Iris Meadows at the front door.

'Can yer spare me five minutes?' the widow asked hesitantly.

'What is it, Iris?'

'I know it must be a terrible time for yer, but I just 'ad ter come,' the old lady said as she was shown into the parlour.

Nell waved her into the armchair. 'It's all right, Iris,' she reassured her. 'I've 'ad plenty o' callers already this mornin' an' I don't mind one little bit. It's nice ter know people care.'

The widow placed her large handbag on her lap and rested her hands on it, fixing Nell with her rheumy eyes. 'Your Tommy's gonna be all right,' she announced. 'Very soon they'll find 'im safe an' sound.'

'I 'ope an' pray you're right,' Nell said fighting back tears. 'Would yer like a cuppa? The teapot's never bin empty since yesterday.'

'That'll be nice,' Iris replied. 'Not too strong an' just 'alf a spoon o' sugar.'

Nell was soon back with the tea and the widow sipped hers appreciatively. 'Just right,' she remarked.

Nell smiled, suddenly realising that it was the first time the old lady had been inside her house. Iris Meadows on the other hand seemed relaxed, as though she were a frequent visitor. 'Is yer tea all right?' Nell asked, at a loss for something to say.

'Very nice, fanks,' Iris told her.

'My Frank's back, by the way.'

'Yes, I know.'

''E's gone out lookin' fer our Tommy with Stymie.'

'Yes, I know. I saw 'em leave tergevver.'

'I almost fergot. Would yer like a biscuit wiv yer tea?'

Iris shook her head and drained the cup, and as soon as Nell took it from her the old lady clasped her handbag tightly. 'I don't know if yer believe in messages from up there,' she said suddenly, flicking her eyes towards the ceiling, 'but I do, an' I can tell yer now that I've 'ad a message about your Tommy. 'E's safe an' well an' 'e'll be back 'ome before very much longer.'

'Christ, I 'ope you're right,' Nell said with a huge sigh.

'Like I say, I do 'ave the gift,' Iris went on. 'Six years ago my little gran'daughter Lucy was very ill an' my Peggy feared fer 'er life, it was that bad. The little mite was on the open order fer two days. Anyway I 'ad this visitation. Some might call it a dream but I know it wasn't. I could see little Lucy sittin' up in 'er cot at the 'ospital an' she was smilin' at the nurse. I could see 'er clear as day. She was wearin' a little pink nightdress wiv flowers on it an' she 'ad 'er 'air in plaits, somefing she would never allow 'er muvver ter do. The next mornin' when Peggy got back from 'er visit she told me that Lucy 'ad turned the corner an' she was shocked when I told 'er I already knew. She started laughin' at first, but when I described the nightdress she soon 'ad the smile wiped off 'er face. '"Ow could yer possibly know?" she asked me. "'Cos I saw it in the visitation," I told 'er. She was still sceptical but the second time it 'appened she 'ad ter believe it. It was the year the war broke out. Early summer it was. Anyway, Peggy's ole man Charlie was startin' a new job at the gasworks in New Cross an' two nights before I'd 'ad anuvver visitation. I saw the flames goin' up inter the sky an' men bein' dragged out o' the burnin' buildin'. It was a terrible sight. So I told our Peggy ter do 'er best ter make Charlie give the job a miss, but 'e wouldn't listen. Pig-'eaded as they come, 'e is.'

Nell waited while Iris fiddled with her handbag straps. 'Go on,' she said impatiently.

'Well, Charlie went ter work there after all an' the next week the bloody gasworks blew up. Charlie was one o' the lucky ones. 'E got out wiv a few minor burns to 'is 'ands but six o' the men got killed an' ovvers were badly burned.'

'What did yer see that makes yer fink our Tommy'll be all right?' Nell asked anxiously.

'I saw your boy standin' outside a big buildin',' Iris told her. 'It must 'ave bin a wharf, 'cos they were lookin' down at the body of a man as it floated away down the river. I could see your Frank too an' 'e 'ad 'is arm round the boy. Then Stymie the totter came up on 'is 'orse-an'-cart an' Tommy an' Frank got on the back. So yer see why I'm tellin' yer not ter worry. It was a message fer you what's come frew me.'

Nell found herself strangely uplifted as she went to fetch some more tea, and when the old lady finally left she busied herself about the place, something she had not been able to do since Tommy had been taken.

Iris Meadows walked slowly back to her house with a satisfied smile on her gaunt face. People who were desperate would cling to anything, she thought, however far-fetched or unlikely. But if it helped them get through bad times it was justified. Her story was only untrue in parts anyway. Little Lucy had been very ill and Charlie had been caught up in an explosion at the gasworks, but as for the visitations, they were only the invention of an old woman who thankfully was still blessed with a fertile imagination. Her words of comfort for Nell Bailey might serve to ease her pain for a while, but in reality there was only one prayer for those who waited, and Iris Meadows vowed that she would do a bit of praying herself on that bright sunny morning.

Josie and Billy Emmerson drove over to Stepney on Billy's trusty motorcycle and went immediately to Stepney Green police station. Frank had told them about being brought to Bermondsey in Commander Barratt's car, mentioning that the man was going back to Stepney after he had checked on the progress of the Bermondsey police hunt.

'We'll wait then,' Josie told the desk sergeant when he informed her that the chief had not returned yet.

Billy led her over to a bench. 'I'm sure they're doin' all they can,' he said quietly.

'Yeah, I know, but we've still gotta try,' Josie replied. 'It's better than just sittin' about waitin' fer news.'

Billy took her hand in his. 'We'll find 'im, Josie. We'll find 'im.'

She gave him a warm smile. 'I dunno 'ow I could 'ave coped wivout you,' she remarked with a warm glow in her large hazel eyes. 'You're always there fer me.'

'I want ter be,' he said smiling, his eyes fixed on hers. 'Maybe this isn't the time, or the place, but right now I know more than ever before that I'm in love wiv yer, Josie.'

'I love you too, Billy,' she said softly.

He leaned forward on the bench, still holding her hand. 'I fink I've loved yer fer ever, from the time I first saw yer. You were cuddlin' a mangy cat, an' it 'ad a string tied to its tail.'

'Yeah, I remember,' Josie said with a grin. 'Some boys 'ad tied a tin can to its tail an' it was goin' mad. I got a few scratches before it realised I was just tryin' ter get the string off its tail.'

'You must 'ave bin all of twelve,' he said chuckling.

Commander Barratt came hurrying into the station and when the desk sergeant whispered something into his ear he beckoned the two young people to follow him. 'We're covering every likely hiding place,' he explained when they were inside his office. 'If we've not found Tommy soon we'll be transferring the main search south of the river. I know how you must feel, but I can only say again that we're doing everything possible to find him.'

'We wanna 'elp,' Billy told him.

'It's better if you leave it to us,' the commander replied kindly. 'The people we're dealing with are very dangerous and they'd stop at nothing to avoid being caught. My men are trained for such emergencies. Please believe me, we won't fail you.'

'Do you know who it is these men are plannin' to assassinate?' Josie asked.

Barratt smiled briefly. 'I do, my dear, but I can't tell you who it is, not until we have the conspirators safely under lock and key. I promise you that you'll know the full story then.'

Josie and Billy left the police station feeling totally helpless.

'The man was right, I suppose,' Billy puffed.

Josie nodded reluctantly. 'Take me back 'ome, Billy.'

The three League associates climbed out of the taxi some distance from Watson's Wharf and made their way along the cobbled street which led to what had come to be known as Downtown, a man-made island left since the wharves were built and waterways were hollowed out of a loop of riverside land in Rotherhithe.

'It'll be high tide in less than an hour,' Anderson told his colleagues. 'We'll do it then.'

'How?' Thorburn asked.

'A bullet in the back of the head.'

Holman felt cold fingers clutching at his insides. This was madness, he thought. Sheer madness, and evil.

'At least it'll be quick,' Thorburn remarked.

'And certain,' Anderson replied. 'The little brat survived the river once so we have to be sure he's dead when he goes into the water this time.'

They reached the wharf and with Anderson leading the way they made their way to the rear, where he knocked three times on the door with his clenched fist. The heavyjowled man who opened it looked relieved. 'We were beginnin' ter wonder where yer'd got to,' he said gruffly.

'Is the boy still locked in the room?' Anderson asked him.

The man nodded. 'Safe an' sound.'

'You can leave now,' Anderson told him peremptorily. 'If you'll just get your partner.'

The two captors hurried off gratefully, both the richer, and neither wanting to dwell too much on the impending fate of the small boy they had been guarding.

Anderson led the way up the dusty stairs to the first floor and into a room that was empty except for two large padded chairs and a bare table with some used mugs and a nearly empty bottle of milk. He took out the key one of the men had handed to him and then turned to his colleagues. 'I'd better go and check on the boy,' he remarked.

Tommy had heard movements and was listening with his ear to the door as the key was inserted. He moved back quickly, and as he saw Anderson his heart began to pound. It was the man he had stabbed on the tug and he saw the hostile look on his face.

'I hope you've been fed and watered,' Anderson said as he locked the door behind him.

Tommy nodded and his captor eyed him up and down slowly. 'What's the matter? Has the cat got your tongue, boy?'

343

'No,' Tommy told him quickly.

'You remember me?'

'Yes.'

'And I remember you — the little guttersnipe with the trusty blade.'

'I was scared you was gonna kill me,' Tommy managed.

'Kill you? How stupid of you to think we'd kill a boy, just because he'd overheard us talking. You did overhear us, didn't you, Tommy?'

'I couldn't 'ear much.'

'But you heard enough to feel that the police should be told.'

'I didn't, but me mum said it was best ter tell 'em.'

'So you told the police everything you'd heard.'

'Yeah, but it wasn't much.'

'If you expect me to let you go you must tell me everything you told the police,' Anderson said quietly.

'I just told 'em I 'eard a man say that someone was gonna be assassinated an' I thought you were German spies.'

'German spies?' Anderson said smiling. 'How silly. And what gave you that idea?'

Tommy remained silent and his captor sat down on the crate and looked him up and down. 'We're going to let you go,' he declared, 'but you must promise me that you'll never talk to the police again. If they approach you you must tell them that you were lying in order to avoid getting a spanking for being where you shouldn't have been. Is that clear?'

Tommy nodded, his spirits lifting. 'I won't breavve a word,' he said enthusiastically.

'Right then,' Anderson said as he stood up. 'We're going to have to wait about an hour until the traffic dies down, so make yourself comfortable for a while.'

★

The searchers had spent all morning going through the derelict factories, warehouses and wharves of Downtown Rotherhithe which had been all but destroyed during the first bombing raid on London. Tired and dispirited, they broke off the search and made their way back to the nearest working-men's cafe to get something to eat and drink.

It was while they were gobbling down eggs, bacon and beans that they heard the muffled explosion and Danny Gillett frowned. 'That couldn't 'ave bin a flyin' bomb,' he remarked. 'There's bin no air-raid warnin'.

'It could 'ave bin one o' those unexploded bombs,' Stymie suggested.

As they left the cafe another explosion sounded, much louder this time, and the men looked at one another in puzzlement.

'Gawd knows what that is,' Jack Dunkley said.

'Could 'ave bin a gasworks gone up,' Danny replied. 'Remember the one that went up in Deptford?'

'Nah, that was in Sydenham,' Stymie told him.

There was no time for any more conjecture as the hunt began once more. It went on well into the afternoon and was joined by Fred Catlin, who had been successful in getting the Stepney totters involved in the search north of the river. The men realised that they would soon have no more places to check and Frank Bailey's heart felt as heavy as lead. Time was running out fast, if they were not too late already, and the pain in his stomach was getting worse after the food and hot tea he had reluctantly consumed.

It was well after five o'clock when Fred Catlin spotted it, and he strolled back to his cart looking as unconcerned as he could. The others had to know and there was no time to lose, he thought as he flicked the reins and got the horse moving. Some way along Rotherhithe Street Jack Dunkley was pretending to be interested in some discarded drums in a derelict warehouse yard but his eyes were elsewhere, darting to and fro as he appraised the buildings.

'Jack, I got a suss!' Fred called out as he drove up. 'Where's Danny an' Stymie?'

'They're workin' furvver down,' he was told.

Fred climbed down from his cart. 'I was checkin' over Watson's Wharf an' it 'it me right in the eye,' he said excitedly.

'What yer talkin' about?' Jack puffed.

'When we look around these places what do we see?' Fred asked quickly.

'This sort o' fing,' Jack replied.

'What about the padlocks?'

'Padlocks?'

'Yeah, the padlocks on the doors.'

'Well, they're all rusted fer a start,' Jack remarked.

'I've just drove in the yard belongin' ter Watson's Wharf an' there's a new padlock on the door,' Fred grinned triumphantly, 'which tells me that someone's bin in there recently.'

'Let's get the ovvers,' Jack said quickly.

They drove off at a fast trot, and some considerable way down Rotherhithe Street they spotted the parked cart with the horse nuzzling into a nosebag, before they saw Stymie Smith and Frank Bailey coming out of an alleyway that skirted a bombed-out warehouse.

'This could be it, but we've gotta be very careful,' Frank said as soon as Fred Catlin told them of his discovery. 'There's sure ter be anuvver way in but we've gotta make sure we use the element o' surprise, ovverwise it could make it bad fer my Tommy.'

The two carts clattered over the cobbles and suddenly Frank held his hand to his stomach and visibly winced.

'What's wrong?' Stymie asked him.

'Nuffink,' he said edgily.

With some way still to go they saw Danny Gillet coming towards them, and after getting a quick briefing he suggested that they all climb up on his cart. When they arrived at Watson's Wharf the five made their way gingerly over the rubble and old iron lying around in the yard and saw the new padlock that was attached to a wide wooden door. Danny signalled them to go round the back.

'I dunno if we're doin' this right,' Jack Dunkley remarked. 'If Tommy's inside we gotta let 'im know we're 'ere.'

'Yeah, an' alert the kidnappers,' Danny growled.

'If they know we're on to 'em they might just scoot off,' Jack replied positively.

Fred Catlin grabbed Danny by the arm. 'The way I see it, if there's anyone inside they'll be watchin' out, an' if that's the case we've bin spotted already.'

'What should we do, Frank?' Danny asked.

'Fred's right,' he replied. 'Let's check the back first then we'll shout out Tommy's name. At least it'll give the kid some 'ope, if 'e's still alive.'

'I've brought a megaphone wiv me, in case it's needed,' Jack whispered as they made their way stealthily along the side of the building. 'It's bin stuck in me yard fer ages an' I never got round ter gettin' shot of it.'

Suddenly they heard a sharp report which sent a cloud of pigeons flying.

'What was that?' Frank croaked.

'It sounded like a gun goin' off,' Fred replied.

'Fetch us that megaphone, Jack,' Frank hissed as the pain across his middle caught him again.

'Are you sure you're all right?' Danny asked anxiously.

'Don't worry about me,' Frank told him. 'Let's find my Tommy!'

Jack Dunkley came scurrying back clasping the rusted

megaphone and, after they had checked the one other door to the rear of the warehouse and found it securely locked from the inside, Frank Bailey stood upright and took a few deep breaths. Then praying he was doing the right thing he bawled out his son's name as loud as he could through the metal cone.

Chapter Thirty-Four

Victor Anderson walked over to the window and looked down into the muddy, fast-flowing River Thames. It had reached high tide and was starting to turn. 'It's time,' he said quietly.

Thorburn glanced quickly at Sidney Holman and saw the revulsion written all over his face. He too felt some qualms, but he was not going to pull the trigger, Anderson was. The man had to be a cool, callous bastard, he thought. No emotion, no nerves. He would be an ideal candidate to succeed when Sir Barry Freeman decided to call it a day. Anderson would pick his own men, men he could trust implicitly, and there would be a place for him, providing he was able to hide his true feelings and show his support for what had to be done.

Holman looked horrified as Anderson took out a service revolver and flicked the chamber. He wouldn't be able to face it. He could not stand by and watch a young boy being summarily executed with a bullet which would most likely tear the top of his head off. 'We can't kill him,' he said suddenly. 'It's not right. It's evil.'

'We've been through all this before,' Anderson answered testily. 'He has to be dispatched. There's no other solution if we're to survive. He could send us all to the gallows.'

Thorburn nodded. 'It's not pleasant but it's absolutely necessary, and you'll come to look on it in that way in time, Holman.'

'Never. Not as long as I live.'

'Which could be a very limited time indeed if we don't do what we came here to do,' Anderson growled.

'I can't face it. It's cold-blooded and senseless,' Holman said with outrage in his voice as he rounded on the taller man.

'You'll come with us, like it or not,' Anderson replied, pointing the loaded revolver towards the dissenter. 'We're all in this together. If one of us goes down for this then we all go. If you're present then you're an accessary, before, during and after the fact, which ensures that none of us will ever dare breathe a word of what took place today.'

Thorburn led the way out of the room with Anderson bringing up the rear, his revolver aimed at Holman's back. They walked down the long dark passageway and Anderson slipped the revolver down inside his wide leather belt. Tommy looked frightened when he saw the three men standing there in the opening. 'Can I go now?' he asked.

'Yes, but there's something we need to go over first, young man,' Anderson told him. 'Let's go upstairs.'

Thorburn had his arm around Tommy's shoulder as they climbed up to the second floor level and they all followed Anderson into a large chamber with iron uprights supporting the ceiling.

'I want to show you something,' Anderson told the boy as he walked over and pulled back the double doors overlooking the river. 'This was where they used to do the loading and unloading. And this rope by the side here controlled the crane. Hold on to it in case you fall.'

Thorburn gave Tommy a little nudge and Holman took a pace backwards, feeling as though he was going to be sick as he watched the obscene scene being played out. He saw

Anderson nod urgently to Thorburn who stood to one side out of the way.

'Point out to the boy where Galleons Reach is, Ben,' Anderson told him. 'That was once the part of the river where they hung the pirates.'

Tommy turned to Anderson momentarily, but it was enough for Holman. He had seen the wonderment in the lad's wide blue eyes, the innocence of a child and the bright trust in his gaze.

'There we are, can you see?' Thorburn said, moving sideways out of the line of fire.

Anderson took out his revolver and raised it as Tommy looked in the direction Thorburn was pointing. His finger closed over the sensitive trigger and he steadied his arm at the elbow with his free hand.

Suddenly Holman moved, knocking past Anderson to spoil his aim and placing himself between the victim and his would-be killer. 'Tommy, move away from that rope! Stand closer to me. Quickly now!' he barked. Thorburn tried to grab Tommy but the boy was too quick. 'Put that gun down, Anderson. It's all over. There'll be no killing.'

'Don't be stupid, man,' Anderson snarled. 'Move aside or I'll put a bullet through you too.'

'I told you there'll be no killing,' Holman replied quickly, backing away towards the doorway as he shielded Tommy with his broad frame.

'You're not thinking clearly, Sidney. This is the way it has to be,' the taller man said, still pointing the gun. 'Don't make me kill you. It'd be a tragedy for it to end this way. Now stand aside.'

Holman reached his hand round behind him and squeezed the boy's arm as a signal. 'Run, Tommy!' he shouted, manoeuvring himself between the door and the weapon. Anderson moved quickly to one side and as he fired Holman dived to cover the boy. The bullet caught him squarely in his chest and he staggered back with a surprised look on his face before sinking down on his knees. A line of blood began to trickle from his mouth and he tried to say something as he keeled over on to his side. Thorburn was rooted to the spot, but Anderson walked over slowly with the smoking revolver held down at his side. 'Don't worry about the boy, he can't get out,' he said, bending over the dying man. 'Why did you make me do it, Sidney?' he said in a low voice.

'I . . . I . . . knew I couldn't . . . let this happen. The bullet finished me . . . but it . . . it finished you too, Victor.'

Anderson stared at him in the heavy stillness, then he looked up at Thorburn. 'He's dead,' he said quietly.

A loud booming sound filled the large gallery. 'Tommy! Tommy!'

'What the . . .! Quick, get the boy,' Anderson shouted. 'They're on to us.'

'What can we do?' Thorburn asked, his face ashen.

'We'll use the brat as a shield, what other choice have we?' the leader growled.

At the sound of breaking glass below the two men ran down the stairs to the first level. 'It's no good, Tommy, you can't get away. The doors are all locked,' Thorburn called out.

Tommy had heard his father calling him and managed to throw a small chunk of concrete through a high window in the large storage room. He heard the hurried footsteps on the stairs and turned to see the two men coming towards him. He saw the wild look in the eyes of the man carrying the revolver and thought that this must be the end.

Down in the rubble-strewn yard the totters had heard the sound of breaking glass and the thud as the chunk of concrete hit the yard.

'Come on, this way,' Frank shouted to them.

Below the broken window there was a locked door and Frank put his shoulder to it, but in vain. It was solid. 'This is the only other way in,' he shouted as the rest came running.

'We'll never break that down,' Stymie groaned. 'Wait a minute. I got an idea.'

The totters followed on after him and watched as their Quay Street friend took a coil of thick rope from his cart. 'Quick! Get that nag out the shafts,' he ordered. 'You too, Danny. Bring yer 'orse up.'

Stymie's plan very soon became obvious as they watched him slip the rope through the hasp of the padlock which was fixed to the main door. He then tied the other end of the rope tightly to the harness of both the animals, and as he brought them forward to take up the strain Stymie said a very short prayer. 'Gerrupp!' he shouted, giving his grey a sharp slap on its flank.

The two animals reared up and dashed forward against the rope, and Stymie smiled as the whole fitting was suddenly torn away from the door. Danny Gillett steadied the excited horses with a few calming words while the other totters ran to the door and pulled it open. Frank reached the first level in front of the rest and rocked back on his heels as he saw his son being held around the neck with a gun pressed to his temple. 'There's no way out,' Frank barked at the tall man, one eye on the other man who had moved to the side.

'Tell your friends to move away from the door or I swear I'll kill the boy this instant,' Anderson growled.

Frank stood his ground. 'Let the boy go,' he said calmly. 'Yer only gonna make it 'arder on yerself.'

Thorburn's nerve had gone and as he dashed for the door he was grabbed by Stymie, who quickly wrestled him to the ground. Jack Dunkley grabbed Thorburn's arms and brought them round behind his back. 'Get some rope from me cart, Fred!' he said breathlessly.

''Ere, use me belt,' Fred told him as he quickly unfastened the buckle.

Anderson moved forward. 'There's five more bullets in this gun,' he hissed. 'The boy gets the first one, then the next one is for you,' he told Frank grimly. 'Does anyone else want to volunteer for one? Now move aside.'

The wild, desperate look in Anderson's eyes was enough to make the totters step to one side and they were forced to watch helplessly as the killer moved sideways to the doorway still holding Tommy around the neck. As he started off slowly down the stairs his eyes never left the totters above him and he did not see Danny Gillett creeping up the stairs towards him. As the totter went for him Tommy slipped out of Anderson's grasp and ran to his father. Danny had grabbed the man's gun wrist and was grappling dangerously with him, until Stymie loped down the wide stone steps and quickly disabled Anderson with a hefty punch in the head. The dazed killer slid down along the damp wall, and as he tried to find his feet Stymie pole-axed him with a massive wallop. 'That's fer Benny,' he growled.

Tommy was shaking but unharmed, and beginning to feel embarrassed at the attention he was getting. 'Don't, Dad,' he pleaded as Frank held him close. 'They'll fink I'm a kid.'

The totters ruffled the lad's hair and slapped each other on the back as they savoured their triumph.

Along through Rotherhithe they travelled, with Danny Gillett leading the way on his cart and Tommy and his father standing proudly behind his seat. Stymie followed next, looking thoroughly pleased with himself as he held the reins loosely and gave the grey pony its head, its mane flowing in the breeze. On the back of the cart there were two figures, bound head and foot with enough rope to ring off half of the riverside borough. The Quay Street totter had been accorded the privilege of actually bringing in the two miserable-looking plotters. Behind him came Fred Catlin, and bringing up the rear was Jack Dunkley, who could not resist the occasional call through his megaphone. 'Any old iron. Ole lumber.'

The police station at Dockhead had never witnessed such a scene and Commander Jock Barratt called for more glasses as the totters crammed into his small office. While Detective Sergeant Ray Black poured the drinks the secret service operative pulled Frank Bailey to one side. 'I've got some real old-fashioned lemonade in the cabinet,' he said with a serious look, 'if that's all right with you?'

'Me stomach's bin turnin' somersaults all day,' Frank said smiling. 'That'll do fine.'

It was a very tired but happy young man who walked into Quay Street with his father by his side. Everyone had already heard the news from PC Woodhouse, who had cycled from the police station earlier.

'I've never seen anyfing like it,' Charlie Fiddler chuckled as he stood at his front door.

'There'll be a glorious piss-up in the pub ternight, that's fer sure,' Chloe remarked.

'Do you 'ave ter be so crude?' Sandra asked with a haughty look.

'I can't believe it,' Bel said excitedly. 'My Stymie bringin' those kidnappers in. It's sure ter make the newspapers. I just 'ope 'e don't go over the top when the reporters come round.'

Iris Meadows stood at her doorstep talking to Eileen Taylor. 'As a matter o' fact I wasn't a bit surprised when the bobby came ter tell us. Yer see I get visitations.'

'Visitations?'

'Umm.'

'What are they?'

'Sort of presentiments.'

'I'm still none the wiser.'

'I don't really like talkin' about it,' the widow went on, enjoying every second of it. 'It's sort o' personal, but I can sometimes tell the future an' what it 'olds.'

''Ow d'yer do it? D'yer look at tea leaves in the cup?' Eileen asked.

'Tea leaves me arse,' Iris said. 'This is more yer medium stuff. I get messages.'

'You don't go in one o' them trances, do yer?'

'Course not. I get visitations like I just said.'

'It's all double Dutch ter me,' Eileen told her.

'You go an' 'ave a chat wiv Nell Bailey when the fuss 'as died down,' Iris said, smiling slyly. 'She'll put yer in the picture.'

Wilco Johnson came into the turning looking slightly the worse for wear. 'We got them, dear,' he announced to the widow.

'We?'

'Yes, it was a combined effort from all concerned.'

'Well, I'm pleased to 'ear it,' the old lady said with a sceptical look.

Wilco let himself into his house, not wishing to elaborate on just what his contribution had been. It was with the best intentions that he had strolled into the church gardens in Rotherhithe to make inquiries when he saw the two tramps sitting there. They were unable to give him any information on the whereabouts of Tommy Bailey, but they did give him a few swigs from their bottles of cider which had been liberally laced with methylated spirits. Primed and raring to go, the Quay Street drunk then went to the nearest pub to get the taste out of his mouth and there he stayed till closing time. A nap in the park followed, then home he went to rest up for a while. Making official inquiries could be a very tiring business, he told himself.

Chapter Thirty-Five

The sun had long since disappeared behind the rooftops as the Bailey family sat down to a late meal. Nell was wearing her best skirt and blouse and Josie had put on her new summer dress, having done Kathy's hair up in light curls. Billy Emmerson had joined them, and as he looked round the table the happiness and relief on their faces was quite something to see.

Frank tapped his plate and cleared his throat. 'I just wanna say that this 'as bin a day I'll never ferget,' he declared solemnly, 'an' ternight, sittin' round this table wiv those I love dearly, is somefing I'll keep close ter me ferever. After all, not everyone's blessed wiv a lovin' family like yous. A lovin' family's all about sharin', givin' of yerself an' bein' willin' ter make allowances. It's all about fergivin' too, an' knowin' deep down inside that it's what yer want out o' life, what yer really want. So I won't go on any more ovver than ter say, Gawd bless this 'ouse an' Gawd bless 'appy families.'

Nell smiled at him and her hand crept across the table to rest on his. 'We've bin married a lot o' years, Frank, an' that's the first speech I've ever 'eard you make,' she told him.

'It wasn't before time then,' he said quietly, his other hand coming up to cover hers.

Josie gripped Billy's hand under the table and she looked lovingly into his deep grey eyes. Kathy touched her curls with her cupped hand and looked from one to another, feeling warm and safe inside. 'It's lovely, all of us sittin' down tergevver,' she remarked.

Tommy was busy scraping his plate. 'That was 'andsome, Mum,' he said with a bright-eyed grin.

Nell had the last word. 'I've not been slavin' over an 'ot stove fer hours on end to 'ave the rest o' the food wasted,' she told them sternly. 'Now who's fer apple pie an' custard?'

After the jamboree atmosphere of the last few hours, Dockhead police station had finally settled down to something approaching normality, and in the control room a deadly seriousness had returned.

'We struck lucky today,' Commander Barratt said as he leaned back in his leather-bound chair. 'Tommy Bailey's back with his family, thanks to the totters, but it could have gone bad on us. As we all know the final curtain's still a long way from dropping. Somewhere out there is a paid killer. Someone who's thwarted all our efforts and those of police forces throughout the country. He's also confounded the Americans. The F.B.I. were hoping to pick him up, but somehow he managed to flee the States under their noses and go to ground over here. It's the way he works. No one can contact him and he has this knack of getting in where castor oil can't. Make no mistake, men. We're facing a very intelligent and ruthless operator.'

Inspector Malkin nodded in agreement. 'Have we any more leads on who the target is?' he asked.

Commander Barratt shook his head, feeling bad about the deception. He was under orders from the very top and he knew that the whole success of the counter-plan rested on total secrecy. Even his closest colleagues at MI5 had been left in the dark. As it stood the police forces and secret agents were up against a killer with no face, a victim who could not be named, and a powerful and secret organisation which had become the assassin's paymaster. It was sheer madness, but as the saying went, sanity was only madness put to good use.

The Pedlar attended the orthopaedic clinic at the same time as usual and did his specified exercises, then he walked slowly through the hospital corridors leaning heavily on his walking stick. The whole place had become very familiar and he had made mental notes of the general layout of the buildings and the large forecourt, as well as estimating the distances and angles involved. He had gathered quite a bit of valuable information from various sources. The friendly porter who he often bumped into as if by chance was a mine of information, and the Pedlar now knew that the hospital would be thoroughly checked over early next Monday morning, the actual day of the opening ceremony. He had also confirmed that the out-patients would be asked to use the side gate that morning as the main gates would be closed to traffic, and he anticipated that there would be a police presence at the gate to check the patients' appointment cards. The authorities were intent on leaving nothing to chance, but in every plan there was a weak spot, and this particular national security operation was no exception.

He had discovered it over a week ago when he managed to slip unnoticed on to the fire-escape stairs and then on to the roof of the new wing, but it had taken a few days before he had had the opportunity to do a trial run. No one had queried his presence when, dressed in a smart suit and carrying folded papers under his arm, he had examined the boiler room, pipe runs and ventilation ducts in the basement.

The Pedlar left the hospital feeling happy with his progress so far. He had established that the Prime Minister's official car would drive through the gates of the infirmary into the empty forecourt and he would be led through the main entrance to the corridor joining the hospital with the children's wing. The porter had told him confidentially that there would be a ribbon placed outside the main entrance of the new wing, but it was just a ploy. Churchill was going to cut the other ribbon, inside the hospital and in comparative safety. The porter had gone on to say that at the staff meeting he had attended they were not told the reason for this, but he knew the decision had been taken due to the fact that there were too many buildings facing the main entrance where a marksman could hide. The Pedlar smiled to himself as he recalled the chat. He had complimented the hospital worker on his astuteness and had gone on to remark that he would have made a good detective. The flattery served to elicit another little piece of information from the man. He had said that the flat roof of the new wing would be sealed off and patrolled by a security man.

'You mean the officer'll stay up there during the visit?' he had asked the porter.

'Yes, that's right. The fire-escape stairs are gonna be guarded too. Me an' a copper are gonna be at the bottom in the corridor, so I'll get a pretty good view o' the ceremony.'

'Well, I'll be attending the clinic as usual on Monday morning,' the Pedlar told him. 'I bet you'll see more of the ceremony than I will though.'

Sir Barry Freeman was beside himself as he waited by the phone at his country home. It was after ten o'clock at night and still there had been no call. Something must have gone terribly wrong, he thought. The news broadcast had failed to mention anything remotely connected to the immediate business of the day and it was now left for him to make contact with the German agent to find out what, if anything, he had heard. There was a standard method of contact which was strictly adhered to, utilising public callboxes which were varied for extra security. Freeman went to a small plaque on his study wall and moved it aside to access his safe. With trembling hands he spun the dial and pulled the door open. The little black book he removed gave him the information he needed. Tomorrow was the ninth and beside the figure nine there was the letter B.

Freeman replaced the book and closed the safe, then quickly went over to his large oak desk and seated himself in his high-backed chair. The phone book in the drawer was full of numbers under B but the one which he wanted was at the very top of the page, and the numerals had to be read from right to left. A simple dodge, but one that could well confuse any trespasser. Freeman jotted the number down on a scrap of paper and slipped it into his waistcoat pocket. The call could be made safely from a public phone-box in Cambridge. Now he had to ascertain the correct time of day when the agent would be waiting by the appropriate phone-box.

Freeman poured himself a large scotch and added a liberal amount of soda water. It was late for the cryptic call he had to make but the agent would know that it betokened some emergency, he told himself as he picked up the receiver. 'Hello operator, I want to make a call to Bermondsey 1552. Hello, Patricia? Daddy on the line. Sorry it's so late but Mummy was worried she hasn't heard from you. Do pay us a visit as soon as you can.'

The voice at the other end was short and to the point. 'You've got the wrong number.'

The actual wording chosen gave him the time. The first letter of the sentence was Y. In his phone book the last number on the page listing names beginning with the letter Y was BMA 5401.

Again reading from right to left it told Freeman that the agent would be at the designated phone-box at 10.45am.

The League chairman downed his drink and poured another. It was going to be a long night, he realised.

Marcus Liversage sat waiting for his old college friend to come home to the Albany flat they were sharing, and as the time slipped away he became more and more concerned. His instructions had been as clear as they could have been, and he had even been made to repeat them to make doubly certain.

Marcus was a simple soul, at least that was how he was prone to describe himself. An academic with a mastery of four languages including Arabic and an interest in Egyptology which had involved him in an in-depth study of hieroglyphics, nevertheless Marcus considered himself to be a man who enjoyed the simple things in life.

At eight o'clock he was getting very worried, and at ten o'clock he repeated to himself the instructions Sidney Holman had given him. It appeared that the time had come to do what was required of him, he decided with a poignant feeling of sadness.

The neatly sealed package was taken personally by Marcus to Scotland Yard, and while he waited to be seen the young man applied himself to *The Times* crossword. Finally the desk sergeant called him over. 'The commissioner can't be traced tonight, I'm afraid, but the package will be on his desk first thing tomorrow morning.'

'I'll need your signature,' Marcus told him.

The sergeant signed a slip and passed it over.

'I don't want to be an utter bore, but you are aware that the contents are marked "Private and Confidential"?' Marcus queried.

'Yes, sir, I am aware of that,' the sergeant said with a trace of sarcasm in his voice.

'Well, shouldn't you have made an acknowledgement to that effect on the receipt you gave me?'

Without answering him the sergeant held out his hand and Marcus placed the slip of paper in his palm, giving him an exceptionally sweet smile.

The scholar made his way back to the Albany rooms knowing that something terrible must have happened to his old college chum. As to the contents of the package, he had no idea what they were, nor did he care to know. He had no intimation that early next morning the Commissioner of the Metropolitan Police was going to get a big surprise. Along with a full report on the recent activities and treasonable acts of the League of White Knights was the letter which Holman had found at Charles Pelham's farmhouse in Hertfordshire, the last testament of a murdered man.

It was late when Josie Bailey and Billy Emmerson walked hand in hand along the deserted River Lane. High wharves and warehouses cast long moon shadows, and the sweet smell of spices blended with the strong aroma of brewer's grain. It was a magical night for Josie, its special spell tinged with the sadness of knowing that in a few days Billy was going off to war.

'I'll be glad ter get goin', ter be honest,' he told her. Her frosty look stopped him in his tracks. 'I didn't mean it like that,' he corrected himself quickly. 'I'm gonna miss yer like mad, Josie, but the waitin's awful, not knowin' what to expect.'

'I understand,' she said smiling. 'Wiv a bit o' luck the war'll be over before yer finish yer trainin'. I 'ope so anyway. I don't wanna be worryin' about you gettin' wounded, wakin' up every mornin' wonderin' where you are, whether yer still alive.'

He pulled gently on her arm and turned her to him and she moved closer, anticipating the kiss. His lips were warm and sent a shiver down her spine.

'You remember when we talked about not gettin' serious an' all that while the war was on?' she reminded him. 'Well, I want us ter be serious, very serious. I wanna know that all the time you're away yer'll be finkin' of me, just like I'll be finkin' o' you.'

He kissed her again, this time with unbridled passion and it made her shudder with anticipation. She could feel his urgency, his trembling desire and at that moment she desperately wanted him to make love to her. She ran her hands down his sides and down his thighs, pulling him even more tightly to her and he broke away and gasped. 'God! I want you, Josie! I want yer like mad!'

She took his hand and urged him into the deep dark doorway of the spice warehouse. 'I wanna do it, Billy,' she said breathlessly.

He kissed her again, his hands pulling her summer dress up around her thighs. She slid her knickers down as he fumbled with his buttons and she gasped at the feel of him. 'Go careful,' she murmured in a croaky voice. 'I'm a virgin, Billy.'

He touched her between her legs and immediately knew that she was more than ready for him. He moved into her, very gently at first, and she gasped with excitement, stiffening momentarily and then urging him to fill her deeply, closing herself around him and pulling him tightly inside. There was no need for either of them to work for the explosion of love, it happened there and then, overwhelming them both. 'I love you, Josie,' he panted.

'I love you too, Billy,' she said in a voice she hardly recognised.

They moved apart and Josie quickly adjusted her clothes as the sound of footsteps on the cobbles grew nearer. Billy did likewise and slipped his arm around her waist as they stood back in the shadows. They heard a tuneless whistling and saw the beam of light played into the doorways as the policeman drew near.

Billy shuffled his feet and Josie gave a little cough, and the beam from the torch momentarily lit up their faces.

'Time fer bed, folks,' the officer said as he plodded by.

They stepped out of the darkness and walked through the shadowy lane to Quay Street, their footsteps echoing on the mist-dampened cobblestones.

'When we're old an' we talk about ternight it'll sound very romantic,' he remarked.

'It was, an' I'll tell our kids it was,' Josie said smiling as she squeezed his arm. 'I'll tell 'em about the smell o' spice an' the moon shinin' down on us, an' you goin' off ter war, an' me losin' my virginity in a dark doorway, standin' on the cobbles.'

'You wouldn't tell 'em. You couldn't!'

'I might at that,' she said as they drew close for a goodnight kiss.

Chapter Thirty-Six

When Sir Barry Freeman stepped into the phone-box outside King's College on Saturday morning he learned the truth. Anderson and Thorburn were in custody, assisting the police with their inquiries, and Sidney Holman was dead. The boy had been reunited with his family and the whole episode had been subject to a police blackout. A shudder of mortal fear shook Freeman to the core and he rubbed a hand over his sweating forehead. 'If I'm to salvage anything from this, he has to be stopped.'

'It's too late,' the German agent said, and Freeman could not see his smile. 'The Pedlar's beyond reach now and the next we'll hear is that Churchill is dead.'

'Oh my God!' Freeman groaned. 'Surely you can find him. I'll make it worth your while. Name your price. He has to be stopped.'

The agent thought for a few moments. 'There may possibly be a way, but it'll be very expensive. It'll mean putting my life on the line.'

'Name it. Anything.'

'I'll require the same amount as you paid the Pedlar.'

'Done.'

'I'll arrange to meet with you after things have been taken care of,' the agent told him. 'You'd better wish me luck. I think I'm going to need it.'

During Sunday one or two more explosions were heard and the information given out on news broadcasts that yet another gas main had blown up was quickly being treated with the contempt it deserved. The general feeling was that if that was the case, then they must be flying gas mains.

On Monday morning the Government were forced to admit that another German secret weapon, a supersonic rocket, was being used on London. People were told not to panic and to expect a speedy end to the ordeal as the Allies overran the launching sites.

The widow Meadows summed it up on behalf of the Quay Street folk. 'Panic? 'Ow the bloody 'ell can we be expected ter panic when we can't 'ear the bastards comin',' she remarked to Ginny Allen and Freda Baines. 'I mean ter say, can you imagine us lot walkin' along the Jamaica Road an' me sayin' ter you, "Come on, gels, let's panic, just in case one comes over." Flyin' gas mains, me arse. An' now it's "don't panic". What do they take us for?'

'I'm sure I don't know,' Ginny replied sighing.

'Well, if you don't know I'm sure I don't,' Freda said.

That Monday morning the Pedlar rose early and left his lodgings at Blackheath, taking a steady walk through Greenwich Park to catch a tram to Rotherhithe. He walked stiff-legged, leaning heavily on his walking stick, and the high-powered rifle strapped to his leg remained perfectly concealed. As he stepped from the tram outside the infirmary he could see the policeman standing by the side gate and he walked up with a smile. 'Anything wrong, officer?' he asked casually.

'Are you a patient, sir?'

'Yes, there's my appointment card.'

'Righto. 'Way you go.'

The Pedlar checked his wristwatch. It was just nine fifteen. He turned left along the corridor, away from the information signs and quickly slipped through a side door. The stairs led down into the basement and he followed the line of dusty pipes fixed to the wall, aware of the heat from the boilers. Someone was working inside a laundry store room but he crept past without being seen. He reached the new section of piping and looked up, mindful that the next step was the crucial one: a climb up the iron rungs which were fixed to the wall of a bricked vent shaft. Taking a deep breath he unstrapped the rifle from his leg and began the ascent, finding it was tricky to negotiate the rungs while holding the weapon. Above him was the circular vent, a wide corrugated cylinder ending in a mushroom-shaped top with slits open to the air, bolted to the roof between the two fire-escape stairs.

The Pedlar had made the climb before and knew that the lid of the vent could be removed from the inside by releasing two large spring clips, and as he reached the top he peered through the metal slits and saw the figure of a uniformed policeman leaning over the chest-high wall. Silently he climbed out and replaced the lid, then gingerly laying down the rifle he slid his hand into his coat pocket and took out a small handgun. The policeman turned suddenly while the Pedlar was still a few steps away, but before he could react there was a dull thud from the silencer and a bullet hit him between the eyes.

The Pedlar squatted down with his back against the wall to catch his breath after propping the body up with a length of wood he had found nearby, pulling the helmet down to shadow the broken face. To all intents and purposes the policeman was in place and eyeing the scene below. The assassin could see that the fire doors had been wedged with pieces of stout wood to prevent anyone opening them from the inside and he smiled to himself. The vent must have been checked by the officer, but obviously not from the inside, and he would not have known that the cowling lid could be removed. It had cost him his life, but the Pedlar was unmoved by another incidental kill. He had come for the big prize, and if all went well he would fire from a concealed position behind the dead man and make his escape the way he had come while his pursuers were still trying to break their way through the jammed fire doors.

Commander Barratt had been co-ordinating the security, as well as the search for the assassin, and after he had been assured that all areas had been checked and sealed he made his report on a special phone line. He had barely put the receiver down when one of his men rushed into the office he was using at the infirmary. 'There's something wrong, sir,' he said anxiously. 'The policeman on the roof of the new wing is not responding to our signal.'

Barratt picked up his powerful binoculars and rushed out into the forecourt. 'Jesus Christ!' he muttered in a shocked voice. 'The man's dead. He's been propped up by the look of it. Follow me, Kinsella.'

The two dashed up to the top landing of the infirmary and snatched a ladder from its bracket on the wall to gain access to the loft. When they finally stepped out through the small window on to the tiles they were able to look down on the flat roof of the children's wing. 'The doors are sealed,' Barratt said quickly. 'I can't see anybody. He must be down behind the wall. The vent! My God! That's the way he must have got up there.'

'I'm on my way,' Kinsella replied.

★

The Pedlar lay on his stomach with the rifle by his side as he peered down over the forecourt through a drainpipe outlet. He could see the gates clearly but the shot would be a steep-angled one and had to be taken from a standing position. He must wait until the last second before taking aim.

The clatter made him reach for his rifle but the warning shout froze his marrow. 'I wouldn't try it, O'Grady.'

The Pedlar found himself staring at the muzzle of a service revolver and his hand moved away from his weapon. 'You know me?' he said incredulously.

'I know you, Gavin O'Grady and I've been waiting for this moment for a long time, too long in fact.'

'Who are you? Police? MI5?'

'You can take your pick,' Mick Kinsella told him. 'I've used a few aliases in the time I've spent hunting you. Try Danny Kelly, the guy who made the initial request for your services. That's right, the contact.'

The Pedlar looked shaken. 'I don't understand,' he said.

'No, I don't suppose you do,' Kinsella replied smiling as he walked closer to the prone assassin. 'You could try George Stephens, watchmaker, too. Or Michael Kinsella. Mick to my friends, and my uncle Joe Burke the loyalist leader, before you blew a hole in him on his doorstep. One of his brothers shoved me into the cupboard under the stairs at the first shot, before you killed him and the others. Yes, that's right, I was there, and I saw your ugly face after you pulled your mask off and walked out of the house as though nothing had happened.'

The Pedlar had gone white. 'But you're working for the other side,' he said breathlessly. 'You're a Nazi agent.'

Kinsella grinned and narrowed his eyes. 'Well, the Nazis certainly think so. An accident of birth, mein Herr. My mother was Swiss and I grew up speaking fluent German. When the war started, I was accepted as a disgruntled Irishman and in no time at all I was being trained in espionage by the spymasters of the Third Reich. With the British secret service's approval, of course. The thing that really bothers me, though, and perhaps you can relay this to our maker when I execute you in a minute or two, is the fact that the poor bastards in Croydon are suffering and dying because I had to lie to the Germans about the flying bomb strikes. The generals think they're landing in the centre of London but I had to make sure that they were targeted short. Take my guilt with you, O'Grady, and maybe the good Lord'll take a few seconds off the endless centuries that you'll be burning in hell.'

The sound of motorcycle engines reached the roof and Mick saw the gates opening as the police outriders drove into the forecourt. 'Get up, O'Grady,' he ordered, needing an excuse to put a bullet through him. Suddenly the assassin rolled over and gripped Kinsella by his legs in desperation, upending him before he could shoot, and as he tried to struggle to his feet O'Grady clubbed him into oblivion with the butt of his rifle. He reached into his pocket for his handgun to finish him off but he heard the car's tyres on the gravel and half fell against the wall, propping his rifle against the side of the dead policeman and sighting the rear of the car through the telescopic lens. He knew from studying newspaper photos and from Movitone News pictures that, due to his bulk, Churchill found it easier to step out backwards from his car, and there he was, getting up from his seat as a security man opened the door. As the broad back presented itself in the sights for a brief moment O'Grady pulled the trigger. The shot was true, and the victim fell forward into the car.

At that moment pandemomium erupted. The watching medical staff ran forward to help the stricken man and nurses and cleaning staff started screaming. People were fleeing in panic but the assassin had no time to watch. He pulled the handgun from his pocket as he turned from the wall. A quick bullet to finish Kinsella and then back down the vent. It would be tricky but he would make it somehow, by the bullet or by guile. After all, he was still the crippled patient.

Mick Kinsella's head was swimming with coloured lights but he had recovered enough to know that O'Grady was about to kill him. As the assassin stepped between his splayed legs and pointed the gun he rolled quickly on to his side and knocked him off his feet. They grabbed at each other in a deadly scrum, clawing, biting and gouging as they slammed back and forth. Slowly Kinsella's superior strength began to tell, and with a sharply delivered blow to the stomach he bundled O'Grady up against the wall. The assassin was bent backwards over the drop but he flailed and lashed like a tiger till his energy failed him, then with all the power he could muster Mick Kinsella lifted the killer off his feet and tipped him over the top of the wall. He bent double, gasping for breath, still seeing those cold killer eyes staring at him, and it was nearly a minute before he managed to straighten up painfully and look down into the courtyard. Someone had thrown a blanket over O'Grady's body, then with a terrible sinking feeling Kinsella saw the stretcher being wheeled quickly from the car. He had been too late. The Pedlar had succeeded for the last time.

When he kicked the wood away from a fire-escape door and walked down, Barratt and some of his men were waiting. 'They wanted to come up, Mick, but I thought it better you had your time with him,' he said.

Kinsella nodded dejectedly and met Barratt's eyes. 'I'm sorry I was too late. Is the Prime Minister dead?'

Barratt smiled. 'He was very much alive a few minutes ago. Oh and he'd like to meet you.'

'The man in the car?' Kinsella queried.

'A decoy, and a very brave man I might add,' Barratt told

him. 'We use him a lot to impersonate Churchill, but this was the hardest job he has undertaken to date. His words.'

'He was hit though?' Kinsella remarked.

'Between the shoulder blades, but fortunately he was wearing the latest armoured vest and coat, as well as a steel-lined Homburg,' Barratt informed him. 'It all weighs a ton, as I know, from helping him on with it. It saved his life, but the force of the bullet still gave him one almighty shove in the back. He's moaning about having to be checked over, but that's the measure of the man for you. Anyway, can't stop here chattering all day. There's a hospital to be opened and the old man's getting more impatient by the minute. Mind you, I suppose it's understandable really. He's been here since six o'clock this morning. Sitting in matron's office, I might add.'

Epilogue

When the police called at Sir Barry Freeman's country home with a warrant for his arrest they found him slumped over his large desk, a used revolver still clasped in his lifeless hand. Down below in the wine cellar the flames were taking hold, and by the time the smoke had filtered up to the ground level it was too late. The police were unable to stop the place burning down and they assumed correctly that Freeman had taken most of the incriminating evidence with him.

Anderson and Thorburn were later charged with child abduction, attempted murder and the manslaughter of Holman and both received life sentences. Anderson refused to co-operate with the police but Thorburn told all, and his sentence was reduced on appeal to ten years. The League of White Knights was no more, but its passing was still mourned by a shuffling, bowed Victor Anderson who finally obtained his release from prison fifteen years later through health reasons.

Thorburn was not so lucky. He was found hanging in his cell two days after he had given evidence before a special Government committee. The coroner's verdict was, 'Murder by person or persons unknown.'

★

British secret agent Mick Kinsella, alias George Stephens the watchmender, had one more task to complete before he resigned his post. He and a colleague took the first available clipper to Lisbon, where they relaxed for a few days while extradition papers were speedily processed. Their quarry, Ralph Hennessey, took his last flight without the diplomatic bag, handcuffed instead to the two special agents.

In the heart of the battered and crumbling Third Reich General Von Mannheim poured the last of his brandy and sat sipping it thoughtfully. In front of him was the last decoded message he would receive from London. It read: 'Assassination bungled. Victim was a publican shot and slightly wounded in mistake for Winston Churchill, who presided over the Cabinet this morning as usual. The new rocket weapon has so far had a minimal effect on morale. Londoners have named it the "Flying gas main". The League of White Knights now disbanded. Leader found shot dead and many arrests taking place. Tommy Dorsey and Harry James records on sale soon. Regards to Adolf. Message ended.'

Mannheim could not even raise a smile at the absurdity of it all. That day he had learned that his wife Lotte had been amongst those killed when her psychiatric clinic received a direct hit during an air raid.

'Lindsdorf, will you take this communique to the bunker please,' he said when the junior officer answered his call. 'I'm sure our Fuehrer will be interested in the contents. Oh and Lindsdorf. Tell my driver to be ready in ten minutes, will you. I'm afraid you and Hoess will have to hold the fort until I return.'

'Certainly, General,' the junior officer replied with a click of his heels. 'And when might we expect you back?'

'That's an interesting question,' Mannheim replied, and under his breath he muttered, 'Never would be too soon.'

★

In Quay Street life was slowly getting back to normal. The Baileys were granted the privilege of meeting Winston Churchill in person and Commander Jock Barratt escorted them to the House of Commons. Tommy's chest puffed out when the Prime Minister shook his hand and told him that he had been very courageous, and that he and his family had played a big part in foiling a dastardly Nazi plot.

As they were leaving the Prime Minister whispered to the Baileys that it was he who had masterminded the whole scheme to bring down the League of White Knights and end the reign of the notorious assassin, Gavin O'Grady.

'Take it with a pinch of salt,' Barratt told them later. 'The truth is, I had to twist his arm to agree to my plan.'

During that autumn of '44 Bel Fiddler married Stymie Smith at the local church and Chloe soon followed suit after a whirlwind romance with a Czech airforce pilot. Their younger sister Sandra preferred to bide her time, though she had had her eye on the office manager for some time. Charlie Fiddler was hoping that she would hurry up and make her feelings plain, for he had formed an attachment with a buxom barmaid at the Crown.

Wedding bells were threatening to ring everywhere. After his basic training Billy Emmerson was given seven days' embarkation leave, during which time he proposed to Josie Bailey and said goodbye to his trusty old motorcycle. Kathy Bailey was looking forward to being chief bridesmaid, and she got her wish the following year when Billy came marching home again.

Ralph Hennessey did not live to witness the defeat of Germany. In February '45 he was sentenced to death for treason and executed three weeks later in Wandsworth prison.

Have you read every novel by
Harry Bowling, the 'King of Cockney sagas'?

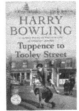

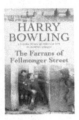

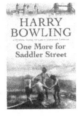

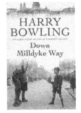

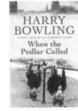

headline